D1485140

SWEET KISS

"Would you kiss me? Again?" Anthony asked. "As you did yesterday?"

"If I said no?"

"Then I'd have to accept that, wouldn't I?"

"You shouldn't be here."

"You've said that," he said. "You're not usually so lacking in conversation, my sweet." There was a smile in his voice that drew her eyes to his face. "You are very beautiful, you know." She shook her head. "Lovely, enticing, intriguing, tempting . . ."

"You are . . . rather tempting yourself."

"Not lovely, enticing, or intriguing?"

Again she heard the smile. "Oh, perhaps not *lovely.*"

"If you won't kiss me, may I kiss you?"

"Why do you find me, in all my oddity, attractive, when no one else has ever done so?"

"Perhaps I'm as odd as you."

Stephanie smiled and, giving into the yearning she always felt in his presence, pulled Anthony down, found his mouth, and remembering how he'd kissed her that first time, brushed his lips with her own . . .

Books by Jeanne Savery

THE WIDOW AND THE RAKE
A REFORMED RAKE
A CHRISTMAS TREASURE
A LADY'S DECEPTION
CUPID'S CHALLENGE
LADY STEPHANIE

Published by Zebra Books

Lady Stephanie

Jeanne Savery

ZEBRA BOOKS
KENSINGTON PUBLISHING CORP.

ZEBRA BOOKS are published by

Kensington Publishing Corp.
850 Third Avenue
New York, NY 10022

Copyright © 1996 by Jeanne Savery Casstevens

All rights reserved. No part of this book may be reproduced
in any form or by any means without the prior written consent
of the Publisher, excepting brief quotes used in reviews.

If you purchased this book without a cover you should be
aware that this book is stolen property. It was reported as "un-
sold and destroyed" to the Publisher and neither the Author
nor the Publisher has received any payment for this "stripped
book."

Zebra and the Z logo Reg. U.S. Pat. & TM Off.

First Printing: June, 1996
10 9 8 7 6 5 4 3 2 1

Printed in the United States of America

To Andi Bennett-Banks whose expertise with the Tarot made several scenes possible . . .

. . . and to Terey who kept me sane . . .
. . . and Joan and Joyce who kept me honest . . .
. . . and John and Esther who said I could do it . . .

Thank you each and everyone.

One

With growing anger, a slim, youthful figure watched the pair lying in the low-growing wild thyme in the sheltered glade. He was a dark-haired stranger and she a girl from the estate. The couple's behavior grew more heated, and the watcher's temper did as well.

"Go home, Mary."

The giggling sixteen-year-old daughter of Lemiston Priory's most respected tenant farmer turned her head. One look and the blood drained from her face. She squirmed, trying to get from under the tall, magnificent looking, but well-rumpled man lying half across her.

"Get along, boy," responded the stranger, controlling the chit easily. "This is no business of yours."

"Get up and away from her or I'll part your hair!"

Mary squeaked, her struggles increasing. With obvious reluctance the man rolled away. Mildly vexed, he watched the plump armful skitter off on all fours even as she attempted to scramble to her feet.

The stranger finally turned toward a gun trained directly on his head. "Now, lad, why'd you have to spoil sport?" he asked politely. "She's yours, perhaps?"

Lady Stephanie Morris, spoil-sport, held the gun steady, hoping her hat wouldn't come off and reveal the braid coiled out of sight.

"If she is," continued the stranger, "I apologize, but she's willing enough and she didn't say she's in anyone's keeping . . ."

Lady Stephanie admitted a grudging admiration for the cool head that allowed the man to sit relaxed, one leg drawn up, his hands loosely clasped around his knee, but it would never do to admit it. Instead she adopted a sneering tone and said, "It would never occur to you, of course, that she's an innocent and should be protected from the likes of you?"

"Innocent?" Laughing, the man threw back his head. Overlong hair, mussed by Mary's hands, slid down over his collar, drawing Stephanie's attention to its crackling good health. "That fine little madam hasn't a *great* deal of practice," he said, "but I'd be exceedingly surprised to discover she'd none." His eyes narrowed. "Put the gun down, boy. We wouldn't want an accident, would we?"

Stephanie ignored the mildly spoken order. "You've a fine mount there." She pointed with her chin. "Get on him and off Priory land."

"Ah! Then this *is* Lemiston Priory."

One of Lady Stephanie's brows arched, querying the satisfaction she heard in that.

A trifle apologetically, the stranger explained. "I wasn't certain exactly where I'd got to, and the land's in far better heart than I was led to expect."

Who the devil would have told lies about the Priory's condition? The insult to her home added fuel to Stephanie's outrage which simmered, roused by unexpected and unwanted tendrils of desire. "Leave! We want none of your sort here, despoiling the beauty and peace and causing trouble where there is none."

A slashing grin revealed white teeth in unfashionably dark skin. "Fine sounding words, boy, but it won't do. I've a standing invitation to the Priory and permission to use it when and as I will for so long as it remains Lemiston ground. So . . ." His eyes twinkled and a quirk to his mouth deepened the dip, not quite a dimple, to one side of it. "What do you say to that?"

For a moment Stephanie could say nothing for the strange prickles running just under her skin. She gritted her teeth, forcing control by feeding her anger.

"I'd say you're a born liar, but if, by chance, it's the truth, then take proof of it to Sir Francis at Warring Heights. And if you lie," Stephanie recognized the braggadocio creeping into her words, but couldn't stop it, "you're likely to discover you've *rights* to nothing but a six foot long patch of earth in the Lemiston Church grounds—as has any trespasser!"

"Don't think the marquess would approve of your sense of hospitality, boy," drawled the stranger. "Come to that, what right have *you* to forbid anyone anything?"

Lady Stephanie relaxed an increment as she realized he'd not yet guessed he dealt with a woman and, if not yet then very likely not at all. "The Marquess of Lemiston is *reputed* to be my father," she said in a tone as cold as any the marquess himself ever used. "If you've word of him, then take it with that invitation you spoke of to Sir Francis." Bitterness filled her at thoughts of the father she'd never known, and she added, "Whatever you decide to do, I hope I never again set eyes on you."

Lazily, gracefully, the stranger rose to his feet. "His son, hmm?" The Honorable Anthony Ryder eyed the boy closely. "You've the look of him. Those brows, particularly. A little on the scrawny side, though. More so than I'd have expected of a boy Chris had a hand in breeding."

"You're no gentleman!"

Straight dark brows rose on Anthony Ryder's broad forehead before they settled into a scowl and his mouth into a thin line. He slipped into a loose limbed but dangerous looking pose, legs slightly apart, arms akimbo, crop at an angle. "Boy, you irritate me."

"I irritate *you?* You've done nothing but insult me and mine since I found you here, randy and raking among the Priory

children." Stephanie, going beyond angry to livid, raised her pistol. "I'll not put up with it."

Again Anthony laughed, but this time there was a hint of deep-throated danger to it. "Children, is it? You think to call that ripe bit a *child*? Boy, someone should teach you a lesson."

A quick dip of a knee and a second pistol appeared in Stephanie's left hand. "Don't move."

"You haven't the nerve."

"I'll slice the top half-inch off your ear."

The man's brows rose again, angled the other way this time, into a questioning expression. "Can he do it?" he muttered. "Or is that empty air?"

"Twist your crop straight out to the side." Stephanie forced a sneer. "If you've the nerve."

The man did so instantly. Then came a moment's hesitation before he raised his arm, holding the whip farther from his body. "I've nerve, but not for the untested. And I don't trust mouthy cock-o-the-walks for anything more than over many bragging words and—"

Silenced by the gunshot and the twitch he felt at the end of his arm, he jerked around and stared to where the tip of his crop had been sheared away. "Dammit to hell! That was my favorite!"

Stephanie had some difficulty restraining a laugh.

When he turned back to her, she said, "As you see, I've a second gun and I say again I can take the top off your ear. What's more, you've insulted me once again, so perhaps I'm no longer in the mood to let you mount and leave. Perhaps . . ." Stephanie raised the remaining pistol and aimed it.

He straightened.

She smiled, a slow humorless smile which tipped only one side of her mouth and nodded. "Very good. That was no idle threat yet you face me with no cringing. You can't, therefore, be a complete coward."

He bowed a mocking bow.

"Sir Francis may be found some miles south and east of

here," she continued. "At the bottom of the lane is the coast road to Warring Heights. Follow it to where a stone fence has an iron gate open to the world. You'll find Sir Francis far more hospitable than I, stranger. More than that," added Stephanie, the bitterness back, "you'll find a man who welcomes you for the news you'll have of the long absent Lord Lemiston."

Anthony strolled to where his gelding grazed. He looped the reins over his arm and put a foot in the stirrup, but before he mounted, he glanced back. "You're an insolent pup, boy, and too idealistic for words, but if that sample of your skill was no fluke, you may be as good a shot as your father. And, believe me, that says a great deal." He mounted and, bending to avoid a low branch, rode from the clearing into the lane.

As he disappeared between the hedges Mary reappeared. Stephanie had bent to return her guns to the holsters built into the side of her boots. When she straightened, she wasn't the least surprised to see the girl. "Well, Mary? Explain yourself." She scowled. "If you *can.*"

"Offered me a golden boy, Lady Steph," said the girl with a touch of insolence. "Would've been a fine thing, that." There was a wistfulness in the way her eyes turned toward the lane. The stranger, fortunately, was gone beyond hearing. "A fine man, that one. Wouldn't a minded a tumble. Not at all."

"You're a fool, Mary. Your Timothy wouldn't thank you if a stranger put a pudding in your pan, would he?"

"For a whole golden boy?" Mary frowned, thinking. "Well, maybe not. But maybe I could've gotten two."

Stephanie pulled off her hat and let her braid unwind until the end brushed against the tops of her hips. "I'd better have a word with your father, Mary. For some reason," she said wryly, a sardonic eye going to the crushed herbs where the couple had lain, "I'm forced to conclude it's high time you and he met with the priest and settled things."

Mary pouted. "Won't. Not til Tim finishes his apprentice-ship with old Mr. Harry. Won't marry him 'til he can support me proper-like."

"I see." Stephanie's lips compressed. "In the meantime you want the benefits of the marriage bed without the responsibilities of house and home."

Mary shuffled her heavy-soled shoes in the thyme and the newly crushed leaves released more of their heady scent into the air. The girl peered sideways at Stephanie through hair she'd not tied back out of the way after the stranger's hands had loosened it. "You don't know how it is. How one sometimes needs—?"

Occasionally, Stephanie had, herself, wondered about those needs. "You are correct, Mary," she interrupted the girl, "that I've no notion. At least, I *do,* but only in *theory!*"

"Then—" Again the insolence was there for any ear. "—don't go giving orders where you don't know how bad it'd be to obey." The girl tossed her curls and gave Stephanie a pert look.

Stephanie's scowl deepened. "Mary, you are the most disrespectful chit on Priory property. It is truly unfortunate your father's last child was both female and lovely. Your beauty led to spoiling and that's ruined your character. But you'd best be careful, girl. Your fine looks brought the most eligible possible suitor to your door, but if you don't watch yourself, you'll lose him. You believe Tim so enamored he'd forgive you anything, but I'd guess he's more likely to *beat* you if he discovers you've been dallying with a stranger. It's worse that you expected to be paid for it." Again Stephanie scowled. "Mary, don't you see? That makes you nothing but a common whore."

"You can't say, my lady," said the girl, sassy as ever, "that I'm no better than a *common* whore. Not when he offered me a whole guinea." Mary flounced around and pushed through the bushes, disappearing in the direction of her father's flock—which, by now, was likely much in need of attention.

A faint hint of thyme wafted around Stephanie just as the sound of a snapping twig reached her ears. Before she could react arms came around from behind and pulled her against a hard chest. Stronger, more pungent, the scent of thyme teased her nostrils, assuring her of her accoster's identity. Stephanie bit her lip, but, except for that first surprised instant, didn't react. If the stranger could stand before her pistol and not flinch, she wouldn't give him the satisfaction of knowing how badly this situation frightened her.

"Now that you haven't a popper with which to threaten me, what will you do, my fine feathered bantam?"

"What *can* I do? You are far stronger than I and have the advantage."

"Well said. Now you've admitted that, admit the rest. You are no bantam, but a pullet."

"But not game!"

"Unlike the bird I lost?" Stephanie felt as well as heard the chuckle her words roused. "No, not a game pullet, but full of pluck, are you not?" His tone took on a threatening note. "You stole my game, pullet."

"I told you, she's none of yours."

"I didn't then and do not now agree, so—" His voice dropped to a soft menacing thread of sound. "—I deserve something in recompense, do I not?"

The stranger turned Stephanie so swiftly she'd no time to take advantage of the single instant she was no longer close to him. One arm pulled her against his long male body, nearer than she'd ever before been to one. His other hand rested on her throat. Much to her regret, she could feel a pulse pounding against the tips of his fingers, very likely revealing to him the extent of her fear.

Then, slowly, the hand slid higher, resting for a moment under her chin before, gently, he raised her face.

Rigidly motionless in his embrace, she stared up at him, studied him. Now that she could see them properly, she discovered the man's dark eyes were ringed with fatigue. They were deep-set, a straight blade of a nose between. Below, firm lips looked as though they knew how to smile but rarely did. He stared down at her, as absorbed as she was, and, hazily, Stephanie wondered what he saw beyond gray-blue eyes and mahogany brown hair. But the moment of mutual curiosity passed and, hypnotically holding her gaze, his head bent.

His lips brushed hers, brushed again.

Stephanie had expected crude pressure, pain perhaps. Certainly not the feather-soft touches which came again and again across her lips, her cheeks, her forehead, and down the side of her neck. She'd anticipated nothing that would affect her either physically or emotionally—except to hurt and anger her—and certainly she'd not guessed at anything approaching the tremors of sensation traveling in waves which rose slowly from her toes sweeping up her inner thighs, up her spine.

Nor had she had the least premonition she'd long for his lips to close over hers, that she'd feel a need to request, to *beg* if necessary, that he teach her more of what it meant to be loved, to be wanted, to find the satisfaction his long lean body promised . . .

Then his mouth did meet with hers, firmed, slanted one way, the other, his nose gently brushing hers when he turned. The very tip of his tongue slid into the sensitive area at one corner, slid across to the other. Stephanie felt her blood pound, couldn't seem to get quite enough breath. She opened her mouth for a deep draught . . .

. . . and found his tongue there instead.

The invasion was too startling and, thoughtlessly reacting, she bit down. Hard. Half a moment later she looked up from the ground where she'd been flung and, one part of her mind searched her memory, wondering if she'd ever seen a more angry set of features, while the other scrambled for words to soothe that anger, felt a panicky need to pacify him.

"How dare you?" he demanded.

His question brought her back to her senses and, bracing herself on both hands, Lady Stephanie glared up at him. "How dare *you?*"

The shock of the fall cleared her head of unforeseen and unwanted desire—however novel and intriguing the sensations might be. She scrambled to her feet and faced him, drawing herself up to her full height which was usually enough to give her an advantage.

"Is it your practice," she asked, her tone icy, "to treat the daughter of your host as Haymarket ware?"

"You weren't objecting," he accused.

"No."

Stephanie relaxed slightly and looked down at the herbs from which the scent of thyme, crushed by her fall, rose in intoxicatingly pungent waves. At one level, she was aware the aroma would, ever more, be associated in her mind with this man. At another, Stephanie studied her reaction, analyzing her thoughts and feelings.

"I didn't, did I?" she muttered. "I wonder why . . ." After a moment Stephanie glanced up, met his frown squarely. "I've never been kissed," she admitted. And then, honest to a fault, added, "at least, not like *that*. Not so that I liked it . . ." The faintest of frowns creased her wide brow. "I think I must have been curious." Her gaze slid away to once again rest on the aromatic plants at her feet. "It was very nice until . . ."

She glanced up when he chuckled, much surprised to discover his temper had dissipated and that, when he grinned in that sardonic way the crease beside his mouth became a deep dimple.

"Why do you laugh at me?" she asked, very nearly stamping her foot in irritation, a feminine and out-of-character reaction.

"You continually surprise me with comments which don't fit the mold."

"I haven't a notion what you mean."

He eyed her skin-tight britches, the neatly fitting coat she wore over the firm material of a stiffly lined vest which, in turn, covered a soft linen shirt open at the throat. "Who has let you run wild? Who taught you to shoot? Where are your petticoats? Do you think I'd have trusted you to shoot at my whip if I'd the least suspicion you were female? How could you have accosted a stranger as you did me, someone who might be dangerous to you?"

The questions were shot at her so fast Stephanie couldn't decide which to answer.

"And beyond that," outrage colored his voice, "what business do you, *born* a lady at least, have being curious about kisses?"

She relaxed, a low chuckle purring in her throat. "Now that last's a ridiculous question, is it not?"

"Is it?" He eyed her. "Why?"

"Weren't you curious?" She stared back, studying his healthy, fully mature, exceedingly male body. One brow arched. "Maybe fifteen years ago?"

"How'd you guess so accurately?" The stranger's well-balanced weight shifted more onto one foot as his anger faded in growing curiosity. When her arched brow quirked he admitted, a trifle ruefully, "Most think me older. My life has been rather rough and tumble of recent years, aging me."

He said that with something approaching an apology and Stephanie frowned. "I don't understand."

"No, and no reason why you should. But, since it's likely we'll make our home together for a time, we'd best come to an understanding. I apologize for treating my friend's daughter like Haymarket ware," he said, his features sober, but that twinkle back in his eyes.

Stephanie decided it a tongue-in-cheek apology at best and ignored it for the threat before it. "You'll not make your home at the Priory," she retorted. She straightened, her spine the same firm rod with which she'd met him in their initial confrontation. "I'm mistress here and I'll not have you."

Eyes narrowed, his head rearing back, the stranger stared down that blade of a nose—a pose and expression that teased Stephanie's memory, had her frowning, curious about the origins of the man and who he might be.

"Wrong," he said, interrupting her mental search. "I'll join you at the Priory soon enough. Very likely this evening. If I must see your Sir Francis first, I'll do so, but don't make yourself comfortable believing I'll not live under the Priory roof."

"You'll find out."

"Will I? We'll see." He turned away, turned back, his volatile emotions again swinging, this time to the teasing. "Just so you'll know from whom you've received your first real kiss, pullet, the name is Anthony Ryder."

"Ah! Now I see why you're so cocky!" *It certainly explained why he'd looked familiar when he'd tilted his head in just that way,* she thought. "You, Lord Huntersham, are in great measure the image of your father—" Now why, she wondered, did she feel like doing a little teasing in return? "—the old lord to the life!" Was this what they called flirting? "So, the blacksheep earl has come home, has he?"

Anthony had taken a step toward the lane, but, at her words, he stopped, stilled to immobility, and finally swung around. "The *what?* What did you call me?"

"The lost earl, my Lord Blacksheep." She bowed satirically. When she straightened, she discovered he was staring at her, uncomprehending. The impulse to tease faded. *"You."* He only looked more confused. "Everyone has talked about nothing but the search for you the whole of this past spring. For weeks now. That's what they call you . . ."

His only reaction was a deepening frown.

". . . the blacksheep earl."

Huntersham's expression of disbelief didn't change. Did that mean the man didn't know? That that *wasn't* the reason he'd returned to England? More gently, Lady Stephanie added, "The Ryders have had nothing but ill luck going on for a year now." She saw her words sink in, root themselves, and, finally, acceptance of the news. "You didn't know."

"No. I didn't know." After a long moment his stiff neck and shoulders relaxed a trifle. "My father?" he asked very quietly.

"He was thrown during the cubbing last fall. If it's any consolation, he died instantly of a broken neck."

"But I'd three brothers before me!"

She shook her head, compassion filling her.

"My brothers?" he asked, nearly whispering.

"I'm sorry." Stephanie's mouth twisted in a travesty of the quirky half-smile so characteristic of her. "Not that there isn't a bright side. However terrible the news is for you, it saves me your unwanted presence, does it not? That is, it does if you are truly Anthony Ryder and can prove it."

His brows arched, in silent query.

"You'll not live at the Priory," she explained. "Not when you're so badly needed up the coast at Hunter's Cove. Black-sheep that you are reputed to be, you can't possibly be as bad for the estate as the cousin who insists he's the earl, even though it's common knowledge the search for you has yet to be given up . . ."

Stephanie's voice trailed off as she realized her words might be interpreted by a stranger as rather taunting. She hadn't meant them that way and was relieved the new earl appeared, at some point, to have stopped listening to her.

Anthony Ryder, realization suddenly hitting hard, had reached for support, the bole of a nearby copper beech. "My father . . . my brothers . . ." he muttered before drawing in a deep breath. Once again he met her eyes squarely, but his skin, under the deep tan acquired in eastern climes, had grayed slightly.

"I must know what happened," he said.

The compassion she'd felt earlier deepened into something stronger as Stephanie realized the stranger was truly shocked. There was a warmer, more friendly glow in her eyes, a softer note in her voice, when she obeyed. "Your eldest brother died of an influenza a year or so before your father's death. I've heard it might not have been his death if he'd only taken care of himself, but he did not."

The deep sunken eyes seemed darker than ever, but he nodded and said, "That sounds very much like the James I remember."

"At his death, your next brother, who held a living up north somewhere, was ordered by your father to come home. It is said that the vicar refused to come until he was properly replaced and, while awaiting his successor, put himself in the way of Luddites, one of whom took overly strong exception to his interference. It is said the rebel only meant to knock him out of the way, but your brother hit his head, breaking his skull."

Anthony sighed. "Matthew always was an interfering sort of sapskull."

"The third, who inherited, drowned earlier this spring in a freak accident off the coast to the west of here. One of those sudden wild Cornish storms pushed him onto the rocks at Lizard Point."

"So . . ." He was silent for a long moment, staring at nothing. "All dead. *All* . . ."

Stephanie resisted a desire to touch him, to hold him until his pain faded. Her voice roughened. "I've been too blunt. You said you needed to know, but I should have tried to prepare you. Now however, you do know, and if you've any sense you'll ride hell for leather for London and prove your claim. The sooner you kick the current and exceedingly unwelcome resident from your home at Hunter's Cove, the better it'll be for everyone. Except," she added, thoughtfully, "for his counterfeit lordship, the worm. But nobody will care for his feelings."

Especially me, she thought. Stephanie had already had one too many run-ins with the thick-skinned would-be earl who refused to believe she found him something worse than detestable. Disgusting, perhaps? Stupid would-be suitor. Not that she wanted *any* suitor for her hand, of course.

Anthony swallowed hard. Lady Stephanie watched the effort it took to pull himself together and put aside his grief.

"My cousin, you said."

"Oakfield."

"Impossible." A hint of his earlier insouciance returned, although there was a falseness to it now. "If you refer, as I presume you must, to my unfondly remembered playmate, dear old James Cuthbert Oakfield?"

Stephanie nodded, making a moue of distaste at the thought of Oakfield's last insinuating visit to the Priory—a visit he'd not repeat if he knew what was good for him! Unfortunately, Oakfield seemed unable to comprehend what was good for him and appeared to be incapable of taking a no for a no.

"How the devil can he think himself heir when his birth is through an illegitimate line?" muttered Lord Anthony. He sighed. "Not that *he'd* ever admit that aspect of his grandfather's birth! Besides, he always was something of an idiot." His lips compressed into a hard line. "What do I do now?" he muttered after a long moment's thought. "I've responsibilities to your . . . but, now this new . . ." He compressed his lips, staring into the distance. "Bloody hell."

"Another mark against you," teased Stephanie, relaxing further as he grew more tense. "After discovering my gender, my lord, you've no business swearing in my presence."

He cast her a sardonic glance. "Where did you say Sir Francis lived?"

"At Warring Heights," she responded with sweet politeness. "It's directly on your way to Hunter's Cove."

"He's been your guardian all the years your father's been gone?" asked Anthony, ignoring the hint for him to ride on.

"Practically from the moment of my birth. I'm told my sire walked out very nearly at the instant he was informed of my existence." When Anthony looked startled, Stephanie nodded. "You are surprised I've never met Lord Lemiston. I assure you I've not missed him. Thanks to Sir Francis, who was a more than adequate substitute."

"How can you say so?" Anthony eyed her britches thoroughly before raising his eyes to her now heated face. "When your Sir Francis and I meet we must have a few words about your upbringing. I don't doubt he'll welcome the advice someone should have been kind enough to give him long ago."

Stephanie pushed aside the momentary embarrassment his

sardonic ogling had induced. "That he beat me more often?" she asked. "Or should have done, when he still had the right, back before I came of age?" Stephanie, her eyes twinkling, chuckled. "He's heard it many times. You'll be pleased to discover the neighborhood tabbies agree with you. Once you're settled in at the Cove, you may hold an afternoon entertainment and enjoy a proper coze over the tea cups. You can tell your own story about how terrible I am." She grinned broadly. "They'll be pleased at your bit of gossip. It's been months now since I last provided a tidbit on which they could chew!" She backed toward the woods. "Goodbye, my lord. My sympathy on the loss of your family, but good luck with your inheritance!"

After a long hard look, he said, "You'll wait."

Stephanie stopped. "What the devil do you mean by that?"

"I'll have time for you eventually, and when I do I'll be back."

It sounded to Stephanie's ears very much like a threat.

Anthony Ryder, Lord Huntersham, whistled. He gave Stephanie one more dark-eyed glance as he waited for the gelding he'd left out of sight when he'd returned. The animal trotted up the lane, holding his head to one side so the reins wouldn't get underfoot. When it reached Anthony, the man mounted and, with only a nod to the straight-backed wide-eyed figure watching him go, he turned the beast and, once again, trotted off between the hedges toward the coast road.

In Stephanie's mind the whistle echoed and, again in her mind, she saw his gelding approach. It was a trick Lord Lemiston was in the habit of teaching his horses. Or so Sir Francis said when he taught her to train her own young stock in just that particular manner!

"Damn and blast. It's true, then!" muttered Stephanie. "The Ryder blacksheep knows my father!"

Two

Early May—London

Christopher Morris, Marquess of Lemiston, blinked when he left behind the bright sun shining down on St. Martin's Lane. As he moved into the dim interior of Old Slaughter's Coffee House, he wondered why he'd chosen the place for his rendezvous with Anthony Ryder. It was convenient, of course, but it wasn't the cleanest place in London. It truly had little to recommend it—except, perhaps, that they were unlikely to run into any acquaintances!

His eyes adjusting, his lordship glanced around and, finally, located Anthony. His quarry was seated in a corner, his body slouched against the wall and his hat pulled over his eyes.

Christopher edged through the mass of humanity until he stood near the table on which rested a large sticky, nearly empty, mug. Chris studied his young friend, wryly amused.

Dead tired? Or dead drunk? If the rings decorating the table surface were an indication, the answer was drunk. Only once before had he seen Anthony in this condition. They'd believed they'd lost the first shipment in which Anthony had sunk funds—every last bit of his small fortune!

Chris looked for a pot-boy and motioned the lad nearer. "Does your master have a recipe for a composer," he asked quietly. He ordered the concoction which was guaranteed to sober the drunkest man. As the boy started to run off, Chris caught him back, holding him by one ear. "After you've asked for the nostrum, boy, bring us a big pot of strong black coffee. And we'll need only one cup."

He seated himself, waiting for his order to be set before him. "Take away that disgusting mug," he ordered when it was. The pot-boy obliged with a cheeky grin, scampering off at the call of another patron.

"Anthony," said Chris loudly. When Huntersham opened one eye and looked blearily across the table, Lemiston added, "Was this entirely necessary? Just when we're set to finish some rather important business?"

Anthony didn't respond except to close his eye.

"One would think you'd lost your best friend, but since I'm here, it can't be that." He grinned when Anthony grimaced. "You, my fine gentleman, are drunk as a lord!"

Eyes snapping opened, a gurgle of wry laughter escaped. "Drunk as a lord, the man says! Drunk as a lord!" Sottish mirth turned to belligerence. "Well, why should I not?" The belligerence faded into the easy-flowing tears of the drunken. "Not my best friend. Worse."

"There is nothing worse. . . . Or—" Lemiston's brows slashed into the vee shape typical of the Morris breed. "—this time you've truly lost a fortune?" The frown lightened to a more quizzical look. "Now, how could you manage such a thing," he asked thoughtfully, "when it's my understanding you've only just arrived in London?"

"Didn't."

"Didn't just arrive?"

Anthony waved a hand. "Besides, don't need a fortune. Not anymore." He fell back into his corner, pulling the hat back over his eyes.

Sighing, Christopher pushed the glass with its unlikely, but guaranteed effective, contents across the table. "Drink," he ordered.

Sighing even more loudly, in the overly dramatic fashion of the inebriated, Anthony straightened and obeyed. With a grimace he set the glass down and then frowned at the full cup of coffee which took its place. The cup, when emptied, was re-filled, and he drank that, too. Then, slowly, he finished the pot. Pushing aside the cup, he closed his eyes and leaned against the wall.

Christopher, Lord Lemiston, waited patiently for his friend's rather amazing constitution to return to something approaching normal and was finally rewarded when Anthony opened his eyes and looked across the table.

"Feeling better?" asked Chris sympathetically.

Anthony pushed himself away from the wall into a more or less upright position and ran both sets of opened fingers through his hair. He grimaced. "Not much."

"Want to talk about it?"

Anthony shrugged.

"Come, Ryder! You needn't play the fool when I know you are *not*."

Silence.

"Or should I go away and let you become blind drunk all over again?"

"Drunk as a lord," Thoughtfully, Anthony repeated Lemiston's earlier phrase. "And you call me Ryder. You, my lord, require an introduction." He struggled to his feet. "I'll have you know you aren't talking to the honorable Anthony Ryder, but to Lord Huntersham. I'm an earl now." He attempted a bow but, still unsteady on his feet, wobbled and, to save himself, sat down. Hard.

For a moment Chris was perfectly still. "This is your way of mourning, then? You managed, somehow, to maintain a rather odd affection for your family, given their scurvy treatment of you, did you not? Well, I'm sorry for you, even if I don't understand. But, I also see what you meant when you claimed you no longer need the fortune you earned—even if you *haven't* lost it as I posited. So . . . you've inherited Hunter's Cove."

When Chris eyed him, eyes narrowed to thoughtful slits,

Anthony leaned his head against the wall and once again closed his eyes.

"So . . ." said the marquess again, "where does that leave *us?*"

"I don't know," admitted Anthony. "What I do know is that you must think again about what we planned. Chris," he urged, his eyes snapping open, "you *can't* have thought it through."

"I have," said Christopher grimly. "I want rid of everything that ties me to England. You know that. We've discussed the fact that my life is now tied to Australia's future."

"But you've forgotten you've children here. I'd forgotten about your first marriage, but I don't see how you did so, and I think—"

A muscle jumped in Lemiston's jaw and he interrupted. "I assure you, *I did not.*"

Anthony frowned. "Years ago you told me you'd never return."

"And even at that early date in our acquaintance I'd been gone from England more years than it's been since you were exiled by your father. I'd not be back *now* if it weren't for wanting the money for investment in the Antipodes. My home, I tell you, is there."

"But your children," insisted Anthony. "Twins, if I remember rightly . . ."

Lemiston's hand made a chopping movement. "I won't discuss them! I don't want to know anything about them!"

"Mistake," persisted Anthony. "I met one. She's not in the common way, I admit, but she's *uncommonly* rather special. Chris, you really shouldn't sell the Priory."

A cold look crossed Lemiston's face. "Does that mean you refuse to buy?"

"I don't know." Anthony bit the side of his lip. "We shook on the deal." He shrugged. "There was a commitment—"

"Damn right there's a commitment!"

"But—" began Anthony.

"But you've inherited Hunter's Cove and have no need of

the Priory now your father's no longer here to impress." Chris grimaced. "Blast. I'll have to advertise and find another buyer."

"You still mean to sell?" asked Anthony cautiously. "Even though it *should* be left to your children?"

"Damned right I mean to sell." When Anthony stared at him, his lordship continued in a defensively belligerent tone. "It isn't entailed. I've every right to sell!"

Into Anthony's mind came a vivid memory of a slim figure with a pistol. Another of that same slim body held against his own. He fingered the sprig of herb in his pocket. Raising fingers to his nose, he sniffed, experiencing again the pungent scent of thyme. What would happen to Lady Stephanie if her father sold the Priory? Where would she go? What would she do?

Christopher pushed back from the table, but continued sitting, his hands clasping the edge and thinking outloud. "I must advertise. I'd best set my solicitor to the work immediately. Blast!" He scowled. "I'd thought to leave England within the month. Six weeks at most. Now there is no telling how long it'll take! I wish your father had had the grace to await your return before sticking his spoon in the wall!"

Chris was still threatening to sell? Anthony pressed his fingers against the ridge of his nose and inhaled the tang of thyme. Something resembling panic filled his soul. He looked up. "I'll buy. I didn't say I'd not buy!" He reached across the table. "Chris!"

Chris, who was in the process of rising to his feet, dropped back into his chair. "What?"

With more determination, Anthony repeated, "I'll buy." He was convinced it was the right thing to do, although, his mind somewhat the worse for drink, he couldn't, for the life of him, think why.

After a moment Christopher asked that very question. "Why?"

Anthony's head had cleared, but he wasn't yet completely

sober. "Why not?" he responded inadequately, but with something resembling his usual insouciance.

Another long moment of silence and Chris nodded. "Indeed. Why not? The fact is, you've just inherited a neat little property considerably nearer Brighton than the Priory lies. Brighton, where one would think a young man might find entertainment. You, however, have decided you want a *second* estate?"

"The Priory's larger. And, despite your fears, it's in far better condition than the Cove. M'father wasn't interested in modern improvements, especially if they interfered with his hunting. My brother, who held the title only a few months, appears to have been interested in nothing more helpful than gambling everything away as fast as he could. It may take years to bring the Cove to what it should be, even with modern methods."

"You've never expressed any interest in farming procedures—either modern or from a century ago!" said Christopher, suspicion in every word.

"Have I not?" Anthony remembered the excellent condition of the Priory. "Perhaps not. But then, I've never before met someone who knows anything about them." Someone surely did, or the estate would not be so well managed!

"That you've met someone rings true." Chris eyed Anthony. "Still . . . you're lying. Why?"

"Why would I lie?"

"How the devil should I know? But you are."

Anthony grinned. "Maybe I think my consequence would be enhanced if I owned *two* rather than only one fair to middling estate?"

"Maybe you're full of it!"

Anthony's grin widened. "Maybe I am." He relaxed and rubbed his face briskly. From behind his hands he asked, "Is it today we're to see your solicitor and sign the deeds?"

"It *was*."

"Well?"

Chris frowned. "I don't understand why you're doing this . . ."

"Is it necessary you understand?" asked Anthony, gently.

They eyed each other.

"I don't like it."

Anthony settled back and shrugged as if it made no difference to him one way or the other. "Well, then if you want to renege—"

"Dammit, I never renege!" Lemiston's baleful look didn't affect Anthony at all. "We've an agreement," he added.

"So we do! Shall we go?" Anthony pushed the table a little away and rose to his feet. He looked to where Chris still sat, an expression of confusion drawing together the oddly veed brows. He smiled, falsely benign, and waited.

"All right. I don't understand what you're up to, and I never like what I don't understand. But you're my friend, Anthony, and we do have an agreement." He too rose. "So be it."

It took less than an hour to make Anthony Ryder, Lord Huntersham, the new owner of Lemiston Priory. His other business, that of legitimizing his claim to the earldom, took far longer. It was a good ten days before he sent around a note to Chris's hotel saying he'd be leaving London early the following morning.

Chris's instant response was to tender what amounted to an order, even if it were in the form of a polite invitation, that Anthony was to appear at a certain soiree that evening. Curious, the new earl went.

In the first few moments after his arrival, Lemiston introduced Huntersham to Sir Francis. Lady Stephanie's erstwhile guardian had come to London some weeks earlier and had, therefore, been gone from Warring Heights when Anthony stopped there after meeting Lady Stephanie. Lemiston proceeded to abandon the pair, but not before he made the further demand that he have a few words with Anthony before he left London. In private.

Sir Francis, learning in Lemiston's brief introduction that Huntersham would be going to the Priory, although *not* that the new peer was now its owner, offered to write a letter to his ward and her chaperon recommending Anthony to them.

Anthony, on whom it hadn't been lost that Lemiston was up to something, was pleased to accept. He was *not* so pleased to discover, much later that evening, that Chris had invited guests to the Priory, using it as if it were still his own, *and* that he wished Anthony to allow him to play host there during the house-party. All Anthony had to do to, according to Chris, was forbear announcing his ownership of the estate until the party broke up, at which point Chris would leave England forever.

When Anthony learned the names of some of the guests, he was even less happy with the situation, but Chris had done so much for him over the years, he didn't see how he could do other than allow Chris to indulge this particular whim. Still, he was concerned. The couples Chris had invited were unexceptional. It was the unmarried men who were wild to a fault— at least those who were old enough for Anthony to remember a bit about from before he'd been forced into exile.

Prickles of uneasiness skittered up and down Anthony's spine. Why, he wondered, *that* particular group of men? He couldn't fathom it, but knew he'd find out eventually. Unfortunately, that would be when Chris was ready to explain, and not one instant before!

The next morning, though later than he'd intended thanks to the late hour he'd found his bed, Anthony rode Sahib out of London on the Brighton road. He'd follow it as far as Crawley where he turn off to Horsham and then south to the coast. His first stop, of necessity, would be Hunter's Cove, where he'd announce his existence as earl and current owner and take the time to set in motion the plans his solicitor had urged on him. When he'd finished there, he could ride west to the Priory.

Anthony was somewhat astonished to discover with what enthusiasm he shook off the dust and smells of London. "Well, Sahib," he said with a knowledgeable look at the sky, "it looks as if we've a few pleasant days ahead. It should be a good ride home."

A quiet happiness filled him at the realization that, after a decade wandering the highways and byways and the waterways of the world, he was finally going home. The surprising thing was, it wasn't Hunter's Cove that came to mind when he thought of home; it was the Priory.

Mid May—The Priory

Lady Stephanie dismounted before the stable and patted Aladdin before a waiting groom led him off. She stretched. It had been another long day in the saddle. She'd left the house at dawn and, in the hours since, she'd visited every one of the outlying farms. Now it was late afternoon and Stephanie was both tired and hungry.

But it was a good tired and the hunger was a healthy one. She'd done what she'd meant to do. Her survey had been as complete as she could make it: there were a few repairs to be ordered. There was a hedge or two which needed repair. There was Mrs. Tipper, who, approaching her next lying in, would need help—but that was still some little time away. Last, but hardly least, there was the ongoing argument with Farmer Wilkins about the mangel-wurzels. It was getting late for planting, blast the stubbornness of the man!

But they would be planted. That thought had her mouth firming into an unamused line. Today, the grizzled old man and she had had still another go round. Stephanie had stalked from the Wilkins' kitchen with nothing settled. Obviously nothing was about to convince the recalcitrant old man the new root-crop was a better source of fodder than what they currently used. She'd left to take care of the next duty on her list.

A bit of luck occurred, then. Finding *young* Wilkins alone, she'd ordered *him* to plant the fodder plants. It was not what she liked. Undermining the old man's authority was neither wise, nor was it the way she preferred working with her tenants. The mangel-wurzels, however, had to be planted. Now.

Graham Wilkins the Younger understood Stephanie's plans for the estate and was an enthusiastic supporter of the changes. He'd been pleased to be asked to help with this newest experiment, despite the knowledge he was going against his father's orders. Stephanie fretted for a moment about the repercussions, but shrugged her concern away. Soon enough for that fight when the time arrived . . .

She didn't attempt to fool herself: The time would arrive!

Now, looking forward to a light meal while she awaited the preparation of a bath, Stephanie strolled around the side of the house whistling softly. She was nearly to the terrace when she glanced up, stopped, and, scowling, strode on more quickly.

"You!" she spluttered with something approaching loathing.

The man who had been far too often in her thoughts stood, nearly six feet of solid reality, on the other side of the terrace wall. Worse, he looked as if he belonged there.

"I see you have yet to find your skirts," drawled Anthony.

He leaned a hip negligently against the brick wall separating the flagged area from the first of the flower beds just coming into riotous bloom. The beds spread scent and color everywhere. He'd already discovered that Jane Felton, Lady Stephanie's friend, companion, and occasional chaperon, planned them, cared for them, and loved them dearly.

"Seem to have lost your tongue as well," he added when she didn't instantly respond.

The taunt had her spluttering all over again. "Remove yourself from Priory land! *At once.*"

Anthony shook his head in mock despair. "Still the unwelcoming soul I met under such *very* interesting conditions, are you not?" He grinned, a quick slanting slash of a smile which caused a flickering appearance of the elusive dimple. "Not that you were *totally* unwelcoming . . ." he added suggestively.

Stephanie felt heat in her throat. "Still the unmitigated blackguard who steals from children—"

"Does what, my *child?*" One brow arched.

"I'm nothing of yours. Must I call for help?"

"You mean you've mislaid those useful pistols? In that case, a *proper* welcome is in order!"

He laid a hand on the wall and lifted himself smoothly over it and the narrow flower bed beyond. Bending quickly, Lady Stephanie pulled a gun from her boot. Anthony rose to his full height and stilled.

"I see you have not," he said, regret obvious.

He stood there, arrogantly she thought, his hands on his hips. She couldn't decide if she envied him that natural authority or resented it, but however she felt about it, she realized the man was very likely more than she'd yet learned to handle.

He broke the growing silence. "Why did you suggest you'd call for help when you've your pistols with you?"

"I've no desire to harm a man as badly needed as you must be at Hunter's Cove," she retorted. "Why aren't you there? Or were you unable to prove your claim after all . . . my Lord Blacksheep?"

"I've proved the claim and had time to toss my dearly unbeloved cousin's possessions out of my old home. Unfortunately, he was not in residence or he'd have been out on his ear as well, and," added Anthony in a more thoughtful tone, "very like under threat of the law for the inroads he's made on the estate. You wouldn't believe what he's done." Anthony's brows clashed over his blade of a nose. "Although I'm told he claims my brother will be thought the culprit . . ."

Stephanie stared rather blindly at the heavily laden wisteria which had been trained along the terrace wall. "It seems I must once again be the bearer of bad news," she said softly.

"Now what? Surely you aren't suggesting there's any truth to that claim! I can't believe my brother sold heirlooms!"

"Perhaps not that, but there were rumors about wild gambling, both at cards and on the turf. Shortly before he died I heard a prediction of disaster." Stephanie shrugged. "Still, it was voiced in that indulgent tone indicating there was nothing too desperately wrong. He hadn't sold any land or mortgaged anything yet. Only that there *would* be serious problems if he kept on as he'd begun."

Stephanie raised her gaze to see how Anthony took the news and found he was watching her with something approaching an indulgent expression. Her temper was roused, although she couldn't put her finger on just why.

"I'd check closely," she said, her voice taking on a crisp note, "into just who did exactly what, although I myself can give you evidence Oakfield sold family possessions he'd no right to." Her mouth tipped in the half-smile characteristic of her more sardonic moods. "I've got one of your precious heirlooms myself, my lord. I heard it described and that it was available—for a price. Not that the despicable blackguard *knows* I have it. I used an agent to make the purchase." When Anthony looked a query, she added, "A lovely old tapestry, an Italian garden scene—"

"Which was used to hang in my mother's sewing room," interrupted Anthony making no attempt to hide the bitterness he felt.

"I bought it and have hid it away, a name day present for Jane. Since she hasn't a notion I've got it, I'll return it to you . . ." She eyed him, obviously thinking.

"For a price," he finished when she didn't.

There was a wry note to that which lifted Stephanie's mood. Humor filled her features with a warming light. "Why yes," she agreed. "I do believe there is!"

"Name it."

"Leave," she suggested. "Go away. Don't come back."

"Your price is too high." He tipped his head. "Besides, that demand sounds very like you feared my presence. Are you afraid of me, my lady brat?"

The good feelings fled. "I'm afraid of no one and nothing."

"More fool you," chided Anthony. "A sensible person should fear the vicious and evil people who would harm one."

"Well, I don't fear *you*." Even Stephanie could hear the bluster in that!

"Ah! Then, if you do not, you'll not try again to be rid of me."

"Why not?" she asked, confused by the conflicting feelings racing around inside her. Not the least of them, she realized, was the exhilaration their banter roused in her!

"Because," he responded, in a kindly tone, "if you *do*, I'll think you a coward."

Relaxing, Stephanie chuckled. "Does that trick work for you very often?"

"What trick?"

"Bending someone to your will by making them fear your opinion if they disagree."

Anthony gave her a thoughtful look. "You, my lady, have a very interesting mind. Am I to understand you don't give a damn what I think of you?"

"Not so much as a diddly," said Stephanie, chagrined to discover she lied. Not that she'd allow the blacksheep lord a hint of that!

"Hmm."

He rubbed his chin and, even some feet away, Stephanie heard the faint grating. A vision entered her mind of Anthony standing over his wash basin just as Theo, her twin, would do. Naked to the waist, razor in hand . . . Stephanie shook her head to rid herself of the tantalizing daydream.

"Oh good," said a new voice. "You've met our guest!"

Anthony and Stephanie jumped at the sound of Jane Felton's pleasant soprano. Stephanie shoved the pistol behind her back. When Anthony grinned at her action, she sent a grimace his way before blandly facing Jane.

"He brought a letter of introduction from Sir Francis, Stephie. They met in London. I forgot to ask," she added a trifle wistfully. "Did Francis say when he'd return home?"

"Merely that it would be soon," said Anthony in a gentle

tone Stephanie had never heard. "He didn't know exactly when."

"The sooner the better. I—" A quick look toward Stephanie and she changed that. "We miss him. Stephanie, I've given Lord Huntersham the green suite. Now aren't you glad I insisted we turn the house upside down, as you call it? One should always be ready for guests, you know."

"When have we ever before had *uninvited* guests?" demanded Stephanie.

"Well . . ." Jane frowned, then brightened at an almost forgotten memory. "There was the time Theo came home unexpectedly, with his tutor and those two friends . . ."

"Years ago!"

"Yes, but, even so, one should be prepared."

"I hope," inserted Anthony smoothly, cutting short what looked to become a mild argument, "my unexpected arrival raises no serious problems because . . ."

He paused, his mouth dry with self-loathing as he realized that his very existence would soon be a serious problem. For the first time, he was uneasily and fully aware of the precarious position in which his business with Lemiston had put these women. At the time it had seemed the only way to protect Lady Stephanie, but was it? Or had he done the reverse? Stephanie and Jane stared at him and he realized they were waiting for him to finish.

"I must warn you there'll be *more* company soon."

"Yes, you definitely should warn us," said Lady Stephanie bitterly. "One would think we were nothing more then housekeepers in need of direction!" When a flush rolled up Anthony's neck, Stephanie put it down to her scold. "Oh, don't take my quick temper too seriously, my lord," she said faintly sarcastically. "It appears I've more of a hermit-like nature than I knew. The thought of company arriving, unexpected to say nothing of unwanted, set me off. Not to mention, of course, that I should very much like to know who you think you are to invite not only yourself, but a horde of others to visit as well, whatever Lemiston said about using the Priory as you would." She paused for half a moment. "You'd think this was *your* home!"

The thought *If you only knew!* flew through Anthony's mind and his color deepened. He wondered, even as he swallowed back the words which would reveal the truth, why he'd yet to admit to Lady Stephanie and her companion that, as of some weeks ago, the Priory *was* his home. Surely Chris's prohibition didn't include his daughter and her chaperon! He reconsidered. Knowing Chris, it very likely did.

"Well?" demanded Stephanie when he was slow to respond to her taunt.

"Stephie!" Jane exclaimed, embarrassed by such blatant inhospitality. She turned to Anthony. "Pay her no mind, my lord. I believe it is only tiredness speaking."

"Perhaps I do owe her an apology," Anthony returned. Decidedly ill at ease, he cursed Chris's sense of humor which had put him in this deucedly awkward situation. Lemiston might have been gone for more than two decades, but he should, thought Anthony, retain enough propriety that he'd warn his daughter's household of their change in circumstance. Instead Lemiston had sent the Priory's new owner on ahead with no warning at all.

"How many guests should we expect, my lord?" asked Jane interrupting Anthony's cogitations.

Stephanie scowled at Jane's placid compliance to the situation, her overly accepting, go-ahead-and-take-advantage-of-me attitude.

"Oh, a myriad of couples at least." Anthony was chagrined at his unanticipated cowardice in the face of Stephanie's antagonism. Suddenly he felt relief that Lemiston wanted the sale kept secret! "And a hundredweight of bachelors and . . ."

Her chaperon's infectious chuckle interrupted what appeared, in Stephanie's admittedly jaundiced opinion, a rather forced lightness on Anthony's part.

"A myriad indeed!" said Jane. "You jest, but perhaps later

you'll tell me exactly what to expect. I take care of the arrangements in the house, you see, while Stephie sees to the
management of the estate."

Since Jane turned as she spoke, only Stephanie noticed the
arcs formed by Anthony's brows. "You think I *don't* have the
management of the estate, my Lord Blacksheep?" she asked.

Jane swung around. "Stephanie!" she said, shocked.

But Anthony didn't rise to Stephanie's gibe. "I wondered,"
he said, "who should be complimented on the excellent condition of the land. I'm much impressed by it. You'll have to
teach me how to go on. As you know, I wasn't trained to estate
management. I'll need all the help my friends will give me."

Stephanie, forcibly reminded of the fact he'd only recently
learned of his bereavement and the necessity of stepping into
what must be very ill-fitting shoes, felt a touch of guilt. Besides, her enthusiasm for modern agriculture was strong
enough to dampen even the instinctive wariness Lord Huntersham always induced. "I'll be happy to do what I can," she
said formally.

Jane blinked. "Stephanie, I swear your behavior is more
erratic than usual. First you insult his lordship, who is a total
stranger to you, and then you turn around and agree to help
him. In fact, you treat him very much as you would Sir Francis." She found the pair staring at her, questioningly. "As if
you'd known him forever," she explained.

Stephanie and Anthony turned quick looks on each other
and, just as quickly, both looked away. Stephanie wondered if
he too felt as she did, as Jane had said, as if they'd known
each other forever.

It was very strange.

"I'll help him learn what he needs to know, but I won't
have him staying here."

"Stephie!" said Jane, bewilderment lost in still another
shock. Her voice was a trifle hushed when she said, "The letter
of introduction from Sir Francis, Stephie! Surely we can't turn
him away."

"Sir Francis should have sent him to Warring Heights if his lordship didn't wish to go to Hunter's Cove!"

"Now don't be stubborn, Stephie," soothed Jane. "There are these other guests Lord Huntersham has been kind enough to warn us of. There is to be a house-party, and if his lordship has arrived a little early, well, what of it? It is a good thing, actually, since I'll have time to arrange things."

"Ah yes. The house-party. You're suggesting that Sir Francis invited a party? To come *here?*" Stephanie frowned. "I think not. But, if not, who *would* invite guests to the Priory. . . . I was jesting when I suggested it was you, but was it?" Stephanie glowered at Anthony who shook his head while watching her with a wary eye. "Theo would never do so. In fact, no one we know would treat the Priory as his own, except . . ." Suddenly Stephanie's eyes widened. "No! I don't believe it!"

"So adamant?" he asked softly.

Stricken by the unpalatable thought which had slipped into her mind, she muttered, "Surely it can't be true!"

Jane, again confused, asked, "What can't be true?"

Stephanie looked up. "Only Lord Lemiston himself would . . ."

"Yes?" asked Anthony when Stephanie broke off. "What would your father do?"

Stephanie's skin paled to an ashy white. She stared into the distance. "He's in England?" she asked on a thread of sound. *"That's* why, that day we met, you said he'd told you you could use the estate as you willed?"

"Yes . . ." He paused and, once again reminded that he now owned the place, every stick and stone, he added, "In part."

Stephanie turned painfully widened eyes on her nemesis. "He's coming here?" she asked.

"Why should he not?"

Stephanie turned away. For a moment she stared at nothing at all . . . then she walked away, her tread heavy, her shoulders rounded, her head bowed into a posture of defeat.

"Oh dear. Poor Stephie," said Jane softly, watching her go.

"Why do you say that?" asked Anthony, his gaze also on the subdued figure, so unlike the spirited young woman he'd grown to admire.

"Think, my lord," said Jane, watching as Stephanie wandered away. "How would you feel if your whole life were overturned, the most important part of it removed from your control?"

"Explain."

Jane sighed. "She loves Lemiston Priory with a depth of passion I've never understood. It isn't hers, of course, yet she's cared for it, studied how to improve it, and fought for those changes with the conservative men who farm the property. She'll be devastated if its management is taken from her and she must watch someone else make the decisions."

"Sir Francis—"

"Oh, not for years. The past year or so he's even backed off from pretending to run things."

"I see." Anthony stared at the corner of the house around which Lady Stephanie had just disappeared. Swearing silently, he rubbed his chin between first finger and thumb. Coming to a decision, he dropped his arm. "I can't leave here until I've talked to Chris."

His lips compressed. Chris must be made to understand. He must, if necessary, be forced to buy the Priory back and have it held for his children. He *must not* hurt Lady Stephanie as she'd be hurt by its sale.

"Lord Huntersham?" asked Jane hesitantly.

"There is something Chris and I must do."

"Chris? Oh. Lord Lemiston! Well, you mustn't worry about Stephanie, my lord. She'll come around. Stephie's the most adaptable person I know." A frown drew Jane's fine brows very slightly out of alignment. "I should perhaps warn you," she added, her embarrassment obvious, "that she'll very likely not appear for dinner. She won't do it to be rude, but because her mind will be occupied with nothing but the problem you inadvertently handed her." The frown disappeared and, in a confiding tone, Jane added, "Stephie likes her food far too well to be absent for more than *one* meal. She'll have come to her senses long before breakfast!"

"She'll likely find someone to feed her," he suggested.

"Perhaps." Jane chewed on her lip. "But then again, perhaps not. She'll wish to be alone just now and food will be the farthest thing from her mind." Jane turned toward the house, turned back, her smile an invitation for Anthony to follow. "We don't often change for dinner, my lord, although I suppose it will be necessary once his lordship's house-guests arrive. So, if you do not object, I suggest we eat in the breakfast parlor, as we usually do. We'll just sit down in all our dirt, shall we?"

Anthony smiled. "That sounds the very thing. Although, as to the dirt, I think I'd prefer to remove a layer or two from hands and face first."

Jane laughed. "Very well. You know the way to your rooms, or if you've forgotten, a footman will guide you. I'll have water sent up." Anthony started for the door to the hall. "My Lord," she added as if suddenly remembering something important. He turned. Jane cleared her throat, her eyes never wavering from his, but with a note of apprehension there to be read by a sensitive soul. "Stephie is . . . is a rather *odd* girl, but very special in many ways." Jane bit her lip. "Please don't judge her by what you saw today."

Anthony remembered the slim lad who had shot away the end of his favorite crop and then, when he'd discovered she wasn't a lad at all, had fit into his embrace as if she'd been designed for it. "I've no intention of judging Lady Stephanie by anything that happened today." A wry smile tipped his mouth and a touch of humor deepened creases beside his eyes as he added, "I haven't that right, have I? Blacksheep that I am, how could I think to judge her?"

A blushing Jane didn't—or couldn't—respond.

With a dry laugh Anthony disappeared, leaving Jane to wonder about this stranger Sir Francis had sent them. Either he'd be a very good thing for Stephanie, with his unconventional notions and blunt but not unpleasing ways . . . or he'd be her bane.

The next day Anthony tried his best to locate the young woman about whom he'd become so deeply obsessive. He'd not gotten close. Wherever he went, whomever he spoke with, she'd been there earlier and was then gone.

Worse, Jane was wrong in her assumption that Lady Stephanie would avoid him for no more than the one meal. Although she'd slept in her own bed, as he discovered by chatting idly with the maid who brought his morning chocolate, Lady Stephanie had not joined Miss Felton and him for breakfast.

Nor did she appear for dinner.

Three

Two days later

Stephanie returned from her morning inspection to be greeted with the information that her twin had arrived soon after she'd left the house. "Why do you suppose Theo's come home? I meant to write him about Lemiston being in England, but I hadn't yet done so. He wasn't expected, I don't think?"

Jane, who had made a point of intercepting Stephanie the instant she'd returned in order to give her the welcome news, said, "He wasn't. When I asked why he'd come, he just said, in that irritatingly vague way he has, that he'd felt like it!" Jane shrugged. "Well, I must meet with Cook. And I wish you'd change your clothes before Lord Huntersham chances to see you looking, once again, like a stable boy!"

Stephanie, happy her twin had deigned to return home from the rooms in Oxford where he lived most of the year, pretended outrage. "Jane! You insult me! I do *not* look like a stable boy." The sardonic look so common to Stephanie flashed across her face and, mischievously, she suggested, "A lad about to go up to Oxford perhaps?"

As she spoke the two moved into the entrance hall and separated. Jane trotted up the stairs toward the large and airy office she kept in the back of the house among the store rooms above the kitchens, dairy, and laundry. Stephanie crossed the Great Hall with boyish strides heading toward the broad corridor that led to the library where she was certain to find her studious twin. His nose would, as usual, be pointed toward the pages of an open book.

She'd traversed somewhat more than half the highly polished floor when the Priory butler stepped through the baize covered door hidden behind the stairway. He cleared his throat and she swung around.

"Yes, Abbot?"

Silently he held out a dark beaver top hat.

Impatient to see her twin, Stephanie ignored it, looking instead into the old man's face. "What do you wish of me?"

He pushed the piece of apparel toward her. "Your brother's," he said.

Fretful, wanting very much to speak with her twin, to have the comfort of his presence when she was unhappy and worried about the future, Stephanie took the hat, glancing down at it as she did so.

She froze. Slowly she raised a finger and pushed it through the hole in the high crown. She pulled it out and looked at it. A faint trace of a dark powdery substance discolored her skin. She raised it to her nose, smelt singed fur and a hint of black powder.

Abbot nodded as if she'd said something, turned, and disappeared back into the regions over which he ruled.

Clutching the hat, Stephanie pushed her pace a trifle. She shoved the library doors open more roughly than she might have done and stared around until her glare lit on the unpolished toe of a boot and the corner of a book, the owner thereof otherwise hidden by the high back of a chair pulled sideways, nearer the window.

"Theo!"

The young gentleman, his face as perfect an oval as his twin's, rose slowly to his feet. "Steph," he said, his slow smile lighting up his face. "How good it is to see you."

"You could see me every day if you were to live at home instead of keeping rooms in Oxford all year round!"

"We'll not refight that ancient quarrel, Steph," drawled Theo pacifically. His glance fell on the hat she clutched, her knuckles white. "Don't break the brim," he warned.

"The brim! You're worried about the *brim?* You'll please explain what caused *that.*" She pointed with a slightly shaky finger to the hole.

"Well, at the time," two spots of color appeared on Theo's cheeks, "I thought it an accident and wasn't best pleased, you know? But I wonder . . ." His straight brows drew together in the characteristic Morris frown.

When he didn't continue, Stephanie huffed impatiently. She waved the hat in his face. "Theo, make sense."

"Have I not?" he asked, surprised.

Well aware of her brother's propensity to think he'd spoken the words running through his head, Stephanie glared. "Back up to the beginning and start over. Aloud."

"It's this way, then," he said in his slow considering way. "There was the other accident . . . You see?" His brows arched toward his hairline and, with a hopeful look, he tipped his head sideways as if to ask if all weren't now quite clear.

"I don't see at all!" she retorted on a sharp note. She sighed, wondering how long it would take to dig the story out of Theo, who had little patience for the slow-witted and couldn't seem to pace his own thoughts at a speed which communicated the whole. "Theo, begin again and describe to me *exactly* what has happened! All of it. Begin with the shot that did that." She shook the hat.

Theo nodded, content to follow his sister's lead, as was usual between them. "Let me see. I was out walking with Robinson—my old tutor, you know—when a shot went through the hat knocking it from my head. A friend on horseback rode up just then and nothing else happened and we decided it was a poacher whose aim went wild. It was getting on for evening, you see?"

"There was another shot?"

"Oh no. Not another shot."

"You said there was a second . . . accident."

Theo sighed. "That was later. Several days later, I was walking along the High near Saint Marys on my way to Radcliff's Library. Suddenly a tremendous shove sent me stumbling into the street just as the mail coach came by. You know how fast they come? Even when the streets are rather crowded?"

The sharp note in her voice tended toward shrill. "You might have been killed!" She moved toward him.

"Since I wasn't," he said, holding her off, "don't come over all feminine on me!" His voice was, for the first time, also rather crisp. Warily he watched Stephanie, and when she'd gotten herself in hand, he continued. "I wasn't hurt. More than bruises, I mean. I managed to keep my feet under me and jumped up and fell across the pole between the leaders. The driver thought it a wager and was most unappreciative." Theo frowned. "I *did* explain, you know, but I don't think he believed I'd been pushed . . ."

"Then it was thought a dangerous prank? That's why you've been sent down?"

Theo's eyes widened. "Steph, you idiot, I'm no longer a student. I *can't* be sent down. Besides, Robinson believed me. He knows I'm not one to gamble and, too, that I'd not lie about something of such importance. But . . ." Theo's face expressed his confusion. "Although he pressured me mightily to come home for a space, urging me strongly, he then dawdled and diddled and fussed until it was overly late to begin such a journey. *Then,*" Theo's outrage was vivid in his expression, "he insisted I come anyway."

"So I should think!"

"But Stephie," said her twin, his expression one of mock outrage, "you don't understand. I was forced, you see, to put up overnight at the most inconvenient of inns. You can't begin to imagine the state of the sheets!"

Even as the twins grinned at each other, Stephanie's thoughts flashed at a furious rate through her mind. His tutor suggested he come home? And then made certain he travel at such an odd hour no one would know, immediately, that he'd left Oxford. Did that mean Robinson believed Theo to be in continuing danger? Stephanie's brows seemed almost to have grown together.

"Theo," she demanded, "who did it?"

Her twin reverted to his usual drawl when he responded, "I don't know, do I?"

Her frown deepened. "You must have *some* notion."

"But I don't."

Stephanie's expression silently but eloquently expressed her disbelief.

"Truly, Steph. Robinson asked the same thing and I've tried and tried but can think of no one I've offended to the point they'd wish me dead. Especially in such a way. I mean, it isn't as if someone had suggested a duel, is it?"

"As to that, anyone with any sense would avoid dueling with you," said Stephanie promptly. "You're too good a shot. Think, Theo. There must be something."

A bewildered note entered his tone and expression. "I tell you I can think of no one and nothing." After a moment, he asked, "What are we to do, Steph?" His gaze met his twin's, certain she'd solve this mystery for him. Interested in nothing but his books, Theo had long depended on Stephanie for any problem unrelated to his studies.

Stephanie remembered Anthony Ryder's comment that he'd responsibilities to her father—the father who had finally returned to England. But *when* exactly, and *where was he?*

Had their sire been up to Oxford? Was it true, then, as she'd sometimes wondered, that the man hated his children for existing when his wife was dead? But, would he hate to such a degree, especially after so many years, that he'd stoop to *murdering* them? Why now? Why not at once, right after their birth? And who else might have an interest? Also, if not Lemiston himself, might he have sent Ryder to do the job for him? Stephanie shuddered.

"I don't have the answer, Theo," she said, finally. "But, while you're home, would you not go out alone?"

"I very likely won't go out at all unless Wilkins is free for a little fishing. But now that we're adults he rarely is, is he, working the farm as he must do? Of course, I'll ride now and again, but I can go with you, can I not? In any case, I've work to do," said Theo and glanced at the book he held, one finger marking his place. "Speaking of work," he added, somewhat absently, "order me a tray, Steph, will you please? I'd like to finish this tonight . . ." His fading attention was caught by the slow movement of her head and his gaze sharpened. "Why do you shake your head that way?"

Stephanie, finding something with which she could restore her waning humor, grinned. "You'll insult Cook and have someone else wishing you dead. My guess is that, as soon as she heard you'd arrived, she immediately did all she could to provide the young master with all his favorite dishes. I wouldn't *dare* suggest a tray, Theo! *You* may do so, assuming you are willing to eat the burnt offerings with which we'll be served for the next week or so, but I hope you've a better sense of fairness than to punish the innocent in that particular way!" She grimaced. "Also the not so innocent. We've a house-guest, Theo," she explained, when he quirked his head questioningly. "One who would not, I'm sure, be best pleased by the inedible! And, worse, we're expecting a houseful, including," she rushed on, nearly mumbling the rest, "our nearest if not our dearest relative."

Stephanie's grimace was met by Theo's grin and, mollified, she chuckled. Despite the difference in their sexes, the twins looked very much alike—especially with Stephanie still in male attire.

"I suppose you'll insist I pretend to a great appetite," Theo drawled, "just so the rest of you will eat properly in the near future?"

"*Yes,*" she responded promptly.

"That's plain enough." He nodded judiciously. "All right, then. I'll sit down to a proper dinner. As a favor to you."

"And with Jane. And," she again rather slurred her words,

"Lord Huntersham and, when he comes, Lord Lemiston and . . ."

Stephanie wasn't certain whether the names didn't register with Theo or if her brother simply ignored them. Instead of commenting, he added to his agreement a caveat, warning, "But if I come to table tonight, it is *you* who will owe me, Stephanie Morris, not the other way around."

"Because I'm the messenger bearing the bad news that you must come to table at all?"

He nodded, his grin widening.

"I've never understood why the messenger should be punished, merely for giving unwanted news," said his sister pensively. She turned to the door, stopped, and faced him again, backing toward it as she said, "Theo, if you will, it'd be a nice gesture to change into evening gear. Jane is feeling harassed by the situation and she'd be embarrassed, I fear, if you come to table in all your dirt, a book in your hand, as is your way. Even I will be in skirts." The sardonic touch so often in her voice returned. "On top of everything else I've agreed to do her the favor of dressing of an evening so long as we have guests. Such a bore to dress properly, but she fears our sire may be something of a tartar so . . ."

Suddenly Theo's brows snapped together. "I rather dismissed it as one of your japes, but when you mentioned guests and a relative you *did* mean our father?"

"We've been told he'll arrive any time now. With no more warning than to send one of his guests on in advance." The derisive half-smile which was also a characteristic of Lady Stephanie appeared. "He's invited a house-party, also with no warning, which will arrive at some unknown time, too." She scowled. "From something Huntersham said, I think he's included a number of bachelors. Bah!"

"But won't you enjoy that?" said her uncomprehending twin. "New friends shouldn't be a hardship for you. You've always gotten along with strangers more easily than I. And, as to putting on a gown now and then, it wouldn't be a good idea for you to altogether forget how to act as a female should. I don't suppose the necessity to dress properly will hurt you, either." Having completed his thought to his satisfaction he again eyed his book, but glanced back to his sister when she waved her hands wildly, catching his attention.

"And why should I *not* forget if I wish it so? That is the *true* question, is it not? Why I should have to appear fashionable when the only reason to do so is to catch a husband and, as you know, I've no wish for one of *those?*" Her good humor fled and she scowled. "Since he's bringing along unmarried men, I fear our dearly unbeloved papa may have some scheme in mind to marry me off—and I won't have it!"

Stephanie whisked herself out the door before her twin could think up a suitable reply, to say nothing of new arguments against her oft-expressed wish to remain unwed. Especially since she was no longer quite so certain she *did* wish it! Or at least, no longer certain there'd be *no* advantages in the wedded state.

Drat Anthony Ryder, Lord Huntersham! Blast and bedamned to the stranger who had dared to kiss her with such sensitivity! Why, *why,* had he kissed her in that particularly tender and intriguing and blood-heating way which she could *not,* no matter how she tried, forget! But she *should,* because who knew what the man had become? Her throat tightened as, once again, Theo's danger attacked her mind.

She couldn't deny the possibility their father wished to kill his son, but surely Anthony Ryder's was *not* the hand which had attempted the deed! Still, the chilling suspicion lurked and could not be completely banished. Ryder was wild. He was rash and impulsive and overly willing to take up any dare however dangerous . . .

Or so Lady Eltonson had claimed when she'd visited only that afternoon. She'd had herself driven over the moment word of Lord Lemiston's imminent reappearance became common gossip. Her ladyship had been still more interested in confirming the additional word that the new Earl of Huntersham was already installed as his lordship's guest. She'd drunk tea with Jane and—willy-nilly—with Stephanie who, needing to check a pedigree in her records before returning to the barns with a breeding decision, had been caught out by her ladyship's unexpected descent on the Priory and forced to join them.

Lady Eltonson ignored Stephanie's trousers in the greater joy of what was surely slanderous speculation concerning the two men. Her ladyship had been full of memories of long dead gossip about Lord Lemiston's escape from the Priory at his wife's death and more recent stories about Huntersham's misspent youth. Each tale had been worse than the last, and if even half were true, the men's reputations were black indeed.

So, *could* Anthony Ryder be involved in Theo's near disasters?

But the man who had kissed her had not been despicable. Had he? She recalled his bravery in the face of her gun. Recalled his lack of temper when he'd lost his chance to seduce Mary Wilkins. Could a man with the temperament Stephanie had noted—and liked in spite of herself—be a murderer?

Unlikely. On the other hand, he'd been absent from England for a decade, and who knew what sort of life he'd lived, how he'd survived, in those odd corners of the world to which he'd gone?

Bah. It was all nonsense and must be put from her mind. Far more likely their sire merely *wished* them dead, assuming even that much energy was spent thinking on their existence. Besides, even Lemiston, despicable though he might be, wouldn't set out to murder his children.

Or would he? Someone *had* fired at Theo and *had* pushed him into the street. . . . Stephanie growled aloud in frustration at her circling thoughts, very much startling a maid whom she happened to pass at that instant.

Her mood hadn't much improved when she went to dinner that evening, but at least she had her brother's absent-minded support—until he discovered that Lord Huntersham hadn't forgotten everything he'd learned at university and still had an interest in some aspects of moral philosophy. At which point Stephanie looked at Jane and they silently agreed it was time to leave the two men to their port.

In succeeding days and no matter how early Anthony came to the breakfast room, it was only to discover that Lady Stephanie had already disappeared. Finally, his lordship decided he couldn't force her into his company and, on this particular day he'd good reason not to try. It would, after all, be foolish to discover he *might* indulge himself in her company when he'd an appointment he mustn't miss. So, he'd not chase after her. Not today.

Still, however sensible his decision, he was uncomfortable in a household preparing for its first house-party in decades. Therefore, discovering Theo deeply preoccupied in writing up notes and unavailable, Anthony rode out and, more or less by accident, found himself in the glade where he'd first met Stephanie.

Lady Stephanie. Wary as a wild thing. Lemiston's daughter. Given time, she'd feel comfortable with him and then he'd . . .

He'd what? As he dismounted, visions of all he'd *like* to do with and to Lady Stephanie Morris rushed in to fill his mind and taunt his body. Maybe she had reason to be suspicious of him! The wry thought twisted his mouth into a self-deriding grin. He stared up through the high branches of the copper beeches at the bits of deep blue sky, breathed in the scent of thyme. A lark sang, enthralling him for a long moment.

Finally he asked himself what, beyond the obvious, was it he wished of her? Anthony couldn't answer that question.

Or perhaps it was more that he'd not admit to the answer! The slashing smile of self-derision quirked his mouth, faded. Time, he thought. They'd lots of time to discover each other and what they'd have of each other, but there was nothing he could do about it just now. As he settled himself into the bed of thyme, Anthony put aside thoughts of a situation which couldn't be changed instantly. The problem would eventually reach the stage when a solution would present itself.

Instead of dreaming of what might be, there were plans to make where something could be accomplished.

Dear ol' Cuthbert, for instance. Just how *should* he deal with the bastard! Anthony's first choice, to call his cousin out onto the field of honor, was just as quickly rejected. After all, the man had no honor to defend! So . . . demand payment for the costs incurred while returning the Cove to its previous condition? But Cuthbert was unlikely to have the money even if the courts did decide he owed it.

So . . . have him arrested for theft of Hunter's Cove assets?

The flashing grin again slashed across Anthony's features as he thought of Cuthbert in irons standing before the local magistrate. And then he had another equally vivid vision of his finicky cousin enduring the horrors of a prison ship on his way to Botany Bay! Anthony's grin hardened. It wasn't a nice smile . . .

. . . and broke on a jaw-cracking yawn. Anthony had discovered bedding down under the same roof as Lady Stephanie was not conducive to a restful night's sleep! Knowing she was somewhere in the house, very likely only a few rooms away, roused desires he'd been unable to quench.

Drowsy, Anthony settled himself against the aromatic thyme, pinching off a sprig and holding it to his nose. He nibbled at the edges of a tiny leaf. The soaring lark started his liquid trilling again. The beech kept the breezes at bay and the sun heated the trapped air. Anthony sighed softly, enjoying every one of his five senses. He relaxed, taut muscles unwinding. Perhaps he'd not bother to think about his cousin just now.

Or anything else, for that matter. It was far too pleasant just lying here.

Besides, the recent past had been more than just difficult. "Difficult" he could handle. It had been tedium which wore him down.

Unfortunately, the settling of his claim to the earldom was complicated but lacking in diversion. He'd spent more time than he'd ever thought to spend with the dried up little man who was the family solicitor, and seen far more of the man's office in the Inns of Court than he'd expected to experience in a lifetime! The petty details necessary to becoming confirmed a peer of the realm, reaching an understanding of his financial situation, and setting his tenure in train had been boring. Anthony had never dealt well with boredom.

Worse, everything reminded him his whole family was dead. When he allowed himself to admit it, that too was exceedingly stressful. He couldn't, without pain, think of the father and brothers he'd lost forever before he'd a chance to become reacquainted with them, to prove to them he'd changed, become reconciled with them . . .

Regretting a past he couldn't change, Anthony rubbed tense hands through the thyme, crushing it. Once again, he forced grief away to where it was no more than a tight lump deep inside where he could ignore it—for the most part.

He yawned again and peered, one eye squinted up through the leaves at the position of the sun. There was time enough for a nap before he need ride to the village where he and Chris had agreed to meet at midday today. Anthony stretched, removed a twig from under his buttock, and pulled his hat over his face. He drifted into a deep, restful sleep.

When Anthony awoke, not only had the sun moved well up the sky, so too had a layer of clouds. With no sun the air had cooled, but he wasn't chilled. Setting aside his coat, he rose to his feet. And then he stilled. The coat had been rolled behind Sahib's saddle. How had it come to cover him? Who . . . ?

Anthony looked around but there was no sign anyone had been in the glade. Sahib showed no agitation, merely lifting his head from sweet forage when whistled up. The animal ambled nearer. Anthony frowned. How could he have been so deeply asleep he'd heard no intruder, hadn't felt the coat placed over him. He'd lived in places where he'd be *dead* if he'd been so careless!

So *who?* Had Lady Stephanie, perhaps, come upon him,

found him lying there, vulnerable in his sleep? Felt pity for him and covered him against the chill damp air?

He didn't want pity! Especially *her* pity.

Anthony shivered and put the coat on. A certain scent drifted to his nostrils. Once he was mounted, he held the lapels wide and ducked his head, sniffing. His clothing smelled of the thyme in which he'd lain. A hard grin stretched the skin across his cheeks as other thoughts of Lady Stephanie blossomed. The unmistakable odor would, ever more, instantly and pleasantly, remind him of the interlude right here in this glade! He must remember to put some fresh thyme amongst his clothing . . .

"Well, boy, this isn't getting us on. Besides, I'm tired of dreams. These odd fancies of the elusive chit will very likely die the death reality gives so many dreams!"

Still, thoughts of Lady Stephanie had their usual physical effect and, feeling discomfort, he shifted in the saddle.

"My dear Sahib," he scolded, "you must believe me! That wench cannot possibly be *half* what I remember." He wished he could convince himself of that! "Very likely," he added, "it's the same as when one is months at sea."

Sahib shook his mane, rattling his bit between his teeth.

"You don't understand? Well, let me explain." Anthony lay the reins against Sahib's neck, turning him. "You see, when one is at sea one dreams of the women one will meet the instant one reaches port, but, as you must know, such expectations are rarely fulfilled." The horse's ears twitched. "You still don't follow my reasoning?" Anthony grinned. "Sahib, my boy, think of a sweet little mare and you'll have a notion. Or perhaps not? Poor Sahib! I forgot you'd been gelded!"

He chuckled at the ribald nonsense and then urged Sahib to a canter when a grumbling in his stomach reminded him he'd not eaten since soon after the sun rose that morning. He'd hoped to catch Stephanie at table before she left the house. He'd missed her by just long enough he knew he'd never catch her up and, unfortunately, he'd been too wide awake to return to his bed. At the village inn, he could order a slice of meat pie or perhaps a good south country pasty. He'd break his fast while he awaited Chris's arrival.

Anthony approached the Lemiston estate village just in time to see a burly farmer storm into the small inn. His brows climbed into arches as the man's voice roared out through the open window:

"You may stop ordering my son to disobey me!"

Four

The tavern's door banged against the wall and Lady Stephanie swung around, dipping, reaching automatically toward her boots and the pistols hidden there. That instant response to possible danger was a habit Francis had drilled into her as soon as she reached an age where spending so much time alone might lead her into danger, a lesson repeated until wariness was second nature. Now, recognizing the incomer, angry as he obviously was, she relaxed.

"Farmer Wilkins," she said politely. "What may I do for you?"

"You may stop ordering my son to disobey me!" yelled the irate farmer.

Lady Stephanie grimaced. "Mr. Wilkins," she said, "if your son has obeyed my orders, then it is as it should be."

The old man shook his fist. "I won't have it, you hear me?"

Lady Stephanie smothered a sigh. Well, she'd expected it. And it had come. It was *definitely* to be a fight! But, as she prepared herself, an odd sense of exhilaration streamed up her spine. She discovered she'd no desire to avoid it. In fact, she looked forward to it!

Drawing herself up until she looked the old man straight in the eyes, Stephanie said "I assume, then, that your son followed my instructions for the three-sided field southeast of the stream?" In a satisfied tone she added, "Excellent!"

"Hear me! *You are not to give him orders,*" roared the old man, so angry he trembled with his emotions.

"I've no choice but to hear you," she said, her voice chilling. "The question is, do *you* hear when *I* speak?"

"You make no sense," growled the old man and added the bitter rider: "You would change everything around."

"I would make things better for the both of us," riposted Lady Stephanie, her arms crossed, her eyes narrowed. "I've ordered nothing that . . ."

Ryder stilled, listening outside the open window. He turned to the side and leaned against the old stone of the inn's wall. Jane had said Chris's female offspring managed Lemiston Priory, but he'd rather dismissed the reality of that. Until this instant he'd assumed she did no more than see that orders, probably her guardian's, were fulfilled!

Anthony's lips twitched. Chris hadn't a notion how lucky he was in this odd daughter of his! He returned his attention to the scene inside and the smile widened as the thought crossed his mind that the argument didn't appear to have gotten much further along.

". . . nonsense. What's good enough for my grandad is good enough for me," shouted the farmer. "And for my son and for *you* as well." Graham Wilkins's chin thrust toward her, a glare in his red-rimmed eyes.

"Now there's a problem, is there not?" Steph shifted her position, her stance widening and her hands spread against her hips. She glared right back, her chin thrust toward the old man's. "You bloody old curmudgeon, the old ways are *not* good enough. You'd keep us living in the last century if you had your way."

The old man waved a ham-sized fist. "It's folly, these changes you think so grand."

"I've ordered nothing which hasn't been tested over and over and shown elsewhere to be an improvement."

"Mangel-wurzels!"

The words were half strangled, as if the farmer couldn't quite bring himself to even speak of the fodder plant which had had a fairly recent introduction from the Continent. This time Wilkins's fist shook under her nose, but Stephanie didn't flinch, nor so much as blink.

"Yes," she agreed calmly. "Mangel-wurzels."

"I'll not have them on my land, do you hear?" he roared.

"I should think the whole parish might hear you," she responded in the cool manner Sir Francis had taught her. "I'll not allow Lemiston Priory to stay mired in the past." Eyeing the man, she pushed back her coat and stuffed two fingers of her left hand into the waist of the buckskins she wore with such panache.

Staring through the window, Anthony's gaze was drawn by the movement to her waist, dropped lower. Her breeches left little to the imagination and he felt again the hot wanting this woman could rouse in him by merely invading his mind. But now he had something beyond the memories which had fed his imagination! He couldn't take his eyes from the long flanks revealed by the close-fitting trousers.

Then, a movement beside him drew Anthony's attention. A sideways glance proved the intruder to be Chris. The man's brows arched queryingly. Anthony touched a finger to his lips and Lord Lemiston nodded understanding, turning his attention, as well, to the scene within the inn.

"The old ways are best," Wilkins was insisting still again.

"The old ways," insisted Lady Stephanie, "are unprofitable."

"You're a woman," roared Graham Wilkins. "You can't know nothing about such things!"

"A woman!" muttered Chris. Anthony nodded, never taking his eyes from Lady Stephanie.

"Oh, yes, I'm a woman. But a thoroughly educated woman!" The half-grin tipped her mouth and a reminiscent gleam in her eyes brightened Lady Stephanie's features. "You'd never understand how much I, a *mere* woman, enjoyed those lessons." The smile faded. "But I'm long out of the schoolroom, Mr. Wilkins, and I still read. I correspond with the foremost agriculturists in the country. I learn and I adapt what I learn to what we need."

"You're nothing but a woman."

"And that's the crux of the matter, is it not? You dislike taking orders from a woman."

"Aye." The old man's jaw worked. "I do. I run my own land and I run it my own way."

Stephanie leaned back against the table, giving up the advantage of her height which equaled the farmer's. She stared through him, blankly. "Mr. Wilkins," she said softly, "perhaps Lord Lemiston has been absent for so long you've allowed yourself to forget that it is *not* your land." She tipped her head, her eyelids drooping over her eyes.

A knowing one, which Anthony considered himself, would realize Lady Stephanie's temper was finally roused to boiling. What now? wondered Anthony, anticipation growing. It was like watching a play, but better because there were no theatrically artificial mannerisms to detract from the drama!

"I wonder," said Stephanie more softly still, forcing the slightly deaf Wilkins to bend nearer, "if you are quite happy living on Priory property. Perhaps you wish to find a place elsewhere where you need not be beholden to a mere woman?"

Shock rocked the old man. Bewilderment reddened his unshaven features. "Ye'd have me go?" he asked. A touch of panic made his voice break. "But where would I go?"

"I've no notion and, since there have been Wilkinses on Priory land since time began, I'd dislike to see you leave. But if you cannot accept that I'm mistress in my sire's absence, then perhaps that's the only solution."

From his vantage point outside the inn, Lord Lemiston pulled his brows into a sharp vee. The chit in trousers was his *daughter!* The realization hit him in the gut, twisting it. How *dare* she dress in that fashion? Not even *Meg* wore trousers. . . . His lordship pushed away thoughts of his second wife and his plans for their future in the Antipodes, instead, doing his damnedest to call to mind the features of his long-dead wife, his love, his only love . . .

The mother of this hoyden!

When, for all his effort, he could envision nothing more than a tiny woman, a pale oval of a face, and paler hair, his frown deepened. There was nothing in this daughter's countenance, other than the oval shape, to help him. Suddenly he'd another reason, beyond the fact she was responsible for his lost love's death, to hate this child of his loins: She *should* resemble her mother!

Stephanie's eyelids lifted, as her easily roused temper returned quickly to normal. She sighed with an overly emphasized huff of air. "It won't be easy to replace you, you old grouch! But if you truly cannot accept that I give the orders, that there are changes I insist be made, then I'll be forced to accept your decision to go." She gave him a wide-eyed, innocent-looking stare.

"But," he repeated, confused. "where will we go?"

"Don't willfully misunderstand me! I'm not saying you should go. In fact, Mr. Wilkins, I'll be sorry if you *do* go. I merely suggest that if you cannot take orders from a woman, it would be best if you *did* go."

"But—"

"I very much hope you *won't* go. I know, too," she added, tongue in cheek, "that my father would be unhappy to return home and discover you and yours had left our land."

The old man looked thoughtful.

"Why," Lady Stephanie continued, "it's been home to all of us for more generations than one cares to think on. And think," she deliberately widened her eyes, "if your son were gone, who would fish with Theo? And for myself? I really don't know what I'd do without you, stubborn as you are."

"Mayhap I've been a slight too stubborn," muttered Wilkins, his eyes looking everywhere except at Lady Stephanie.

"If you'll have a little patience, Mr. Wilkins, you'll see it's all for the best. Please decide you can stay," she coaxed. "As I said, I don't believe my sire would like it if you went."

"You've had word from Lord Lemiston?" asked the old man, straightening shoulders rounded with age.

Realizing suddenly that she *had* had such word, Stephanie sighed—silently this time. "He's coming. I've no notion when."

"Ah well. The sooner the better, but what can one do with such a man? Rampaging around the world like a mad bull. But you say he *is* coming?" asked the old man anxiously, needing reassurance.

"No one will be happier about that than *you*." Stephanie's eyes gleamed with unsuppressed irony.

Anthony, who had been there when Lady Stephanie had first learned of Chris's plans, knew the old man would be far happier than *she* would.

"I won't deny it, Lady Stephanie. I won't deny it."

"Whatever happens, he hasn't come today. The mangel-wurzels stay."

Silence followed. Mr. Wilkins didn't agree, but he didn't *disagree* either.

Stephanie saw she'd won. "Those hedges we discussed—see they are well trimmed as quickly as possible and that place mended where the sheep are getting through."

He merely nodded.

"Have a brew on my bill, Mr. Wilkins, before you return to your work."

"Aye. That I will. Thankee kindly." The old man sighed again. He cast her one more pleading glance. "But . . . mangel-wurzels?" Stephanie met his gaze with a bland smile and the farmer sighed once more. Then he brightened. "We'll see what his lordship has to say!" He went with lighter step to the bar where the innkeeper's young wife drew him a mug of her nut-brown ale.

Outside, Anthony took one look at Lemiston's rigid stance and angry features and pulled him away from the window before he could make a scene. They crossed the unswept innyard, avoiding from long practice the worst of the day's accumulation of dung, used straw, and mud until they were hidden in a grove well beyond a noisome pile of manure which had been forked out of the stables. Finally Lemiston stopped, refusing to go farther.

"That . . . ! That *female* is my *daughter?*" Chris barely waited for Anthony's confirming nod before sputtering, "Dressed like a . . . a . . . the *devil!*"

"Why are you so angry? I thought she looked rather good in trousers."

His grin, Anthony realized, was very nearly licentious and he modified it, but the tight-fitting buckskins *did* suit the long-legged, long-backed Lady Stephanie. He'd discovered that, if he looked closely, the neatly tailored coat and smooth vest revealed the merest hint of small breasts. And he remembered the heavy length of braided hair falling down her back to swing gently against the tops of slightly rounded hips.

Too rounded, he thought now, and wondered why, the first time he'd seen her, he'd not immediately realized it was a woman in britches. But what would that long hair look like unbraided . . . ?

Chris stopped muttering and lifted an icy gaze to meet Anthony's milder look. "How dare she show her legs that way!"

Anthony's grin widened.

His lordship's lids drooped. "A well-raised female keeps them covered in proper skirts and decently hid from men's eyes!"

Even knowing it was dangerous when Chris was in this mood, Anthony goaded him a trifle. "I wonder," he mused, "what your wife would think of the style. She's at least as tall and just as slender—I think Meg would look just as good. Did you," continued Anthony before Chris could respond, "arrive in time to hear that your daughter is responsible for the excellent condition of the estate?"

"I left Francis in charge," said his lordship arrogantly. "Whatever she *said,* you may believe my old friend has done his duty by the Priory." A frown drew his brows into a sharp vee. "But he damn well didn't do it by that . . . that . . ."

"Hoyden? Wench?" Anthony searched his mind for another, more insulting term. "Mort, perhaps?"

"All of them. And a bitch as well."

"I remember a woman saying, 'I may be a whore but only a dog can be a bitch!' You've insulted your daughter pretty badly, calling her a dog. Why?"

"I'll have her over my knee! She'll learn to behave as a woman should."

"As your Meg would behave?"

"You leave Meg out of this. Meg is more woman than you'll ever know, but she isn't, and will never be, a lady. You haven't a notion what she suffered. You don't know what a help she is under conditions that would have that play-acting wench crying for mercy!"

Anthony's eyes narrowed. He didn't believe Lady Stephanie would flinch at anything Meg faced in the Australian outback. In fact, he suspected she'd enjoy the challenge. But it wouldn't do to suggest such a thing when Chris was in this mood. Fuming and fretting as he was, his lordship would never agree to buy back the Priory—let alone agree to leave it to his daughter and her twin! Anthony knew he must divert Chris's thoughts away from Stephanie if he were to broach the topic anytime soon. Meg. Keep his mind on Meg. "I thought you told me yours was a marriage of convenience."

"My marriage? *Of course* that's all it is." Chris tipped his head back, narrowed his eyes. "What else could it be, her being who she is?"

Lemiston appeared more the aristocrat than Anthony had

ever seen him look, and he saw no contradiction in the things he'd said. Anthony decided he'd liked the man better when they'd shared command at sea or when he'd visited his lordship's growing household in Australia!

"I needed a woman," added Lemiston, a trifle defensively when Anthony refused to respond with more than thinning lips. "One can't very well have children without one, and I want sons. I needed a woman in a part of the world where no woman of my status would or could survive!"

Again Anthony bit back his opinion. And he didn't have time to remind Lemiston he already had a son since his lordship continued:

"Meg has done her duty by me and I'll do mine by her. But what has any of that to do with what went on in the inn, and why did you drag me back here into the woods when I should have gone in there and blasted that . . . that . . ."

"Tart? Draggle-tail, you think?"

"Stop it! You mean to be sarcastic, suggesting she's no better than a common harlot, but I tell you—" A muscle worked in Lemiston's jaw. "I'll teach the wanton a lesson she'll never forget! *She'll* learn. They'll both learn . . ."

Lemiston's eyes narrowed. He gave Anthony a sharp glance. Suddenly, impossibly quickly, his lordship's temper appeared to cool. "Nothing about which you need concern yourself, Anthony, my boy. We're in no hurry, now, so I'd like a better look at this estate that . . . that female person claims to manage. *Then,* perhaps, we'll go on up to the house. You'll ride with me, of course?"

Anthony ignored the question. Warily he studied his friend and mentor. "I've seen you do that before."

"Do what?"

"Go from livid hot to icy cold in an instant. What are you plotting?"

"Plotting? What makes you think I'm doing anything of the sort?"

"Whatever you've in mind, Chris, don't do it."

"I've no notion of what you speak."

"Don't you?"

Anthony eyed the man who'd been more father to him than his own had ever been. But, whatever the relationship between them, this was too important to pretend it didn't exist.

"Chris, if, for reasons I don't understand, you think to hurt Lady Stephanie, you'd better think again."

Chris sighed. "I never quite managed to eradicate that odd streak of knight errantry that runs through your system, did I?" The two men stared at each other. "You needn't concern yourself, Anthony. I'm capable of dealing with a mere female in a fashion proper to fatherhood."

Still silent, Anthony continued to stare.

"Well?" asked Lemiston, drawing himself up and looking down his nose. "Do you think you'll know me again?"

"I fear I know you too well already," said Anthony slowly.

Chris shrugged his coat more comfortably into position. "You spout nonsense."

"Do I?"

Lemiston didn't respond.

"If I'm wrong, then I apologize. If I'm not . . ."

"You'll not interfere in my plans," said Chris softly, dangerously.

"Won't I?"

Rage filled Lemiston. "Damn you Anthony Ryder! By what right do you think you can tell me how to treat my own! For a farthing I'd throw you off Priory property!"

Anthony's mouth slashed into a broad, hard grin. "But you can't, can you?"

"You think I'm too old to throw you off my—" Chris stopped short, his mouth open. He grinned, too, and relaxed. "Ah well. I can't then, can I?"

"Buy it back and then you could . . ."

"More nonsense. I'm well rid of it."

Before Anthony could decide how to tell Chris it wasn't nonsense, that he *must* buy the estate back for the daughter who loved it, the men heard the sound of shod hooves beating a tattoo against cobbles and turned to stare through the brush hiding them from the innyard. At the sight of a groom struggling desperately to hold a stallion's bridle and barely able to keep his feet, Anthony held back a branch for a better view.

Lady Stephanie stood to one side grinning.

Hers, he wondered? But who else here would own such an animal. Softly, Anthony whistled. *Someone should tell the chit that's too much horse for a woman!* he thought. But, a beautiful animal. One he'd have no shame himself owning.

"Surely Francis doesn't allow her on that devil's back!" growled Lemiston, and something which looked a trifle like alarm, or perhaps it was concern, shadowed his sharp gaze.

Anthony hid a smile at the thought his mentor had a bit of the knight errant left in his soul, too—although he'd never admit it.

Lady Stephanie mounted and the men watched the animal play up, watched his rider grin as she swayed with the movement, watched her gradually bring the beast under control.

"She *enjoyed* that," said Anthony, wondering at the feelings he'd experienced as he'd watched.

There'd been concern when the horse first rose, pawing the air, still more when the creature kicked out. Then, when she'd settled him, there was that warm sensation he finally decided must be *pride* as he watched her ride off.

But pride? Did that make sense . . . ?

"It certainly looked as if she enjoyed it." Reluctantly fair, Lemiston added, "She did it well, too. Maybe wearing trousers, so she could ride astride . . . but she *shouldn't* wear 'em!" The frown was back with a vengeance. "Come on! I want to see what has happened around here. Old Wilkins always was something of a conservative soul, but surely he exaggerated when he said she's changed everything."

Anthony raised his hand, interrupting his mentor and friend. "I'd like another look, too, but let me eat first," he soothed. "I've not had a bite since dawn and I'm gut-foundered!"

Lemiston's answer was to veer away from the stable toward the inn. While Anthony ate his lordship's fingers tapped impatiently against the table. "Anthony, once we've seen what's to be seen, come with me to Southampton. I've had word the Golden Ducat is in port. We've a few days before my guests will arrive. We can settle this last shipment between us before we descend on Lemiston Priory."

Anthony grinned his not-nice grin. "Can't yet throw your heart over the gate, is that it?"

Lemiston bristled. "What the devil do you think to mean by that! I've never been one to hold back from a jump!"

"Oh? I've just recalled a campfire. On the bank of the Ohio River, if I remember rightly. You told me of a vow you'd made—that you'd never again cross the Priory threshold!"

"Mind your own business!" Lemiston's brows snapped over dark blue-gray eyes.

Eyes the image of Lady Stephanie's, thought the innkeeper's youngish wife. A visiting relative, perhaps . . . ?

That evening Stephanie sat by the fire in the library, fuming. Why, when she'd finally decided, while staring down at his sleeping figure, to confront Anthony Ryder, had his lordship had the unmitigated gall to send a bland message he'd be away a day or two! She glared across the room to where her brother sat placidly reading near a patent colza oil lamp. *Was* her beloved Theo in danger? And did Anthony have anything to do with it? A shiver ran up her spine. How could she feel as she did for a man who might, for anything she knew, be a murdering marauder of the most dangerous sort? Murder. Rapine. For all she knew, rape!

She shook her head at such melodramatic thoughts. He'd not been *raping* Mary. The youngster had been cooperating in every way she'd known how. And, later, he'd been close to seducing *her* with his soft touches and gentle kisses. Rape was

definitely one sin into which he did not fall! Blast the man
for being so attractive!

Stephanie brooded, watching her oblivious twin. How was
she to discover exactly what was happening to Theo and who
was responsible? Where did one begin? How did one discover
why someone unknown wanted Theo dead. But she had to find
out who. And why. And stop it.

Too, she had to deal with the imminent arrival of her long
absent and unwanted sire. That was a complication all in itself.
Why had he returned? Just when she'd arranged her life to
suit herself, the blasted man had to come home and unsettle
everything.

The only hope she could see was that he wouldn't stay, that
he'd find settling down in one place boring when compared
to roaming the world as he'd done for a quarter of a century.
Or had he reached an age where settling down was exactly
what he wanted? If that was the case, then would he allow a
daughter, whose existence he'd never once acknowledged, to
continue to manage his estate?

Doubtful.

And what about Theo? Would Lemiston demand Theo return
from Oxford and adopt what the ton would consider his rightful place as the future Lord Lemiston? Theo would hate that.

Or had the man come home to kill his son and wed off his
daughter to the first man who could be induced to offer for
her? Induced? More likely *bought*. And if so, why? What was
in his mind? Stephanie cut off that unprofitable line of thought.
There was no way she could read the mind of a man she'd
never met even if he was her father.

She rose to her feet and paced from one end of the long
room to the other, automatically winding her way around tables
and chairs and the stand on which rested an overly large bible.

The family bible. She touched it as she passed and remembered how she and Theo had once looked for their names in
it, the date of their birth. They'd found them, of course. In Sir
Francis's distinctively ornate hand. Their father hadn't thought

enough of them to record their births before leaving England forever.

Except it was *not* forever. *He was coming home.*

Stephanie whirled around. "Theo," she called. "Theo!"

He looked up from his page, his face that blank uncomprehending facade one presents when totally preoccupied with something else.

"Theo, fence with me," she ordered. "I can't stand this seething mass of nonsense in my head. It goes round and round and gets nowhere. I have to *do* something."

"Fence? With swords?"

"Please?"

He looked down at his book. "When I finish this—" His gaze met hers, sharpened, and he grinned, "—*chapter.*"

"You won't forget?"

"Give me . . . twenty minutes?"

"I'll meet you in the armory." Stephanie strode from the room with lighter steps.

Jane Felton occupied her favorite sitting room off the terrace. Beside her stood a pair of tall work candles as well as another of the ubiquitous colza oil lamps, this one with double Argand burners, that shed a mellow light over delicate embroidery. A sharp knock sounded at the French doors leading onto the terrace and Jane jumped half out of her skin.

Sucking her pricked finger, she looked to the nearby bell pull, wondering if she should call for help.

"Jane!"

She breathed again at the glass-muffled sound of a voice she knew. Sir Francis was home! Rising to her feet, she took a few quick steps toward the windows. But the lightening of her spirits was instantly followed by the wariness she always felt in his presence. Why, believing as she did, did she look forward, always, to his coming? Why had she allowed him . . . but she had. They . . . but they shouldn't.

Why, the anguished thought passed through her mind, *wouldn't the man agree to mere friendship? Why does he persist in persecuting me?* Moving more slowly, another thought followed those. *Why can't I insist he cease doing so?*

Taking in a deep breath, Jane unlatched the doors. "Why won't you go to the front door like a sensible man?" she scolded. "Very likely you shortened my life by a decade!" She turned on her heel and stalked back to the small fire which had been laid to cut the late spring evening's chill.

He glanced around the room. "You're alone?"

She gave him a wary look over her shoulder, discovered he was much too near. "Francis . . . you mustn't."

"I must," he said, gathering her into his arms.

He kissed her and, after the first instant in which she attempted to hold herself still, Jane gave in, as she always did, to his expertise.

"I've missed you," he said softly.

"You could have found a woman," she responded crossly.

"I could *not,* you perverse creature! Just *any woman* would not do when it is you I want."

"Nonsense."

He released her. "Jane, I will never understand you. I wish you'd explain why you will take me to your bed but will not agree to wed me."

Jane turned away, biting her lip. He'd never understand and she . . . well, perhaps the reason he didn't was that she couldn't explain her feelings lucidly even to herself. Oh, not why she'd allowed him to become her lover, because she knew why she'd done that. She'd been unable to resist him.

But why she'd not wed him . . . she wasn't entirely certain, although she had *some* notion. Even if she could get her ideas sorted and clear in her own mind it was doubtful she'd be able to bring herself to tell him. Besides, as she'd said many times, he'd not understand even if she did.

"If you want Stephanie," she said sharply, "I believe she and Theo are in the library."

He stared at her, baffled. "I want *you*—as mistress, yes, but even more, as mistress of my home."

Jane stared, a rather peevish look of wariness combined with reproval.

"But," he chuckled at her expression, "we'll not beat that dead horse, shall we? Something else brings me here tonight. Jane . . ." He paused, uneasy, then began pacing the floor, his eyes avoiding hers. "Jane," he repeated, "I've not come to harass you, but with rather incredible news." He glanced at her, then away. "Lemiston has reappeared. I couldn't believe my eyes when I met him at the home of a friend while in London . . ." His fingers mussed the dark curls his valet struggled to control.

Jane felt a pang at the amount of gray the derangement revealed. "How nice for you, to see him again," she said politely. She seated herself before the small fire and folded her hands.

Francis came toward her, the hint of a frown and barest tightening of lips moving across his features, then gone. He leaned against the mantel, a certain tension denying the relaxed pose. "He'll arrive here any day now," he said, staring over Jane's head.

"We know."

Francis abruptly met her eyes, a question in his.

"Lemiston's friend told us." When Francis still questioned her silently, she said, "Huntersham! You wrote an introduction for him . . . the lost earl?"

Francis, remembering, nodded and relaxed slightly. "I've been so wrapped up thinking about Chris, I'd forgotten about Huntersham."

"He warned us what to expect. I've had everyone working like slaves!"

Francis, not looking at her, twiddled with one of the porcelain ladies gracing the mantel.

When, after a moment he still said nothing, she added, "You

do not seem as happy as I'd have expected. That your old friend has returned?" She tipped her head, questioningly.

This time his lips compressed into a hard line. Finally, ruefully, he met her gaze. "I've discovered I've an element of selfishness I'd no notion existed." When Jane frowned, he went on, his tone derisive, "My dear, my creation is about to be taken from me. I find I don't care for the notion. Not at all!"

His brows rose in an invitation that she laugh with him . . . but his chuckle was too wry to contain much humor and he wasn't surprised when Jane's frown not only didn't clear, but deepened, and that she looked still more perplexed.

"Jane, think! I've raised Stephanie from an infant. I've proven beyond doubt that a female *can* be taught equally with a male. I'm very proud of our Stephie. And fond of her." His eyes narrowed. "Now, with no please, thank you, or you're welcome, Stephie will be required to march to Chris's tune. Don't you see? It is I who love her and encourage her, who have watched her grow, have been responsible for her—but it is he who will reap the benefit."

"Assuming he thinks it a benefit!" said Jane with a touch of acid unusual to her placid nature.

It was Sir Francis's turn to looked a trifle confused, but then he smiled. "Ah! You think he'll expect a conventional miss, but it is not so! My father's overbearing insistence that women were less than nothing ruined any happiness my mother might have had. It spoiled my sisters' lives as well. Chris and I saw all that and decided at an early age that we'd never force our children into molds they didn't fit."

"Which explains, I suppose, why Theodore remains in Oxford among his books, libraries, and friends at the university and Stephanie runs the estate he'll someday inherit?"

"Exactly."

"And what will his father think of Theo's lack of interest in an estate which will someday be his?"

"Theo . . . my Lord above!" Francis slapped his brow. "Something he said in London, Jane. It didn't really register at the time, but now I've a notion he thinks he has twin girls!" He relaxed. "Not that that makes a jot of difference, of course."

"No difference! A son he doesn't know exists? One with little or no interest in the estate which will someday be his? And what of Stephanie, Francis? Our wildly independent Stephanie? Will he be pleased she's still unwed at such an age! Think, Francis. What if his lordship arranges a marriage for her? Will her husband give her such freedom as she's always enjoyed?"

"He and I discussed the sort of men our daughters should wed. I cannot believe he'd force her into an unwelcome marriage. Besides, she'd refuse—"

"And," retorted Jane, interrupting, "if she's disinherited for disobedience and tossed out with nothing more than what's on her back? What then?" A quick smile flicked across Jane's face and was gone, but her voice trembled with suppressed laughter when she explained. "Knowing our Stephanie, it would be excessively unsuitable clothing, at that!"

The humor of that escaped Francis and a muscle jumped in his jaw. "She'd come to me, of course!" He ran fingers through his hair. "This is nonsense! I'm allowing my jealousy and your ridiculous fears to run away with me. Chris will do nothing to hurt his daughter."

Jane continued in a musing tone. "You are very certain of that, but I wonder. I know of no men but yourself and Theo who accept her as she is. Francis, can you not see the problem? Stephanie believes she may run her own life, that she need depend on no one. She believes she deserves, in fact, that she's earned the respect of those around her, and that she has the authority to order the world as she pleases. But you know perfectly well the world disagrees. Very likely, whatever you think, her *father* will disagree."

"Stephanie is as capable of running her life as any man." Jane gave him a pitying look and he ran the splayed fingers of both hands through his hair, leaving a wild tangle. "Our world is so *wrong-headed,* Jane!"

"And you would make it right, all at once, by raising one poor girl to be so different from her peers she'll never in a million years find a comfortable place for herself?"

"Nonsense. She's very comfortable here at the Priory."

"You'd deny her love and children?"

"Why should I?"

Jane sighed. "You are so *blind,* Francis."

He merely frowned, his lower lip protruding very slightly in what the ungenerous would have called a pout. Then a self-derisive expression deepened creases in his face as he stared with hooded eyes at the woman he'd loved for many years now. "You know, Jane, despite my unexpected jealousy, I was rather looking forward to having Chris home again. Now I'm worried. You, my dear, are a kill-joy!"

"I've finally made you understand? Good." Jane nodded. "Having accomplished my goal, I'm ready for the tea tray. Do ring the bell and have Abbot send a footman for Stephanie and Theo. Did I say Theo was home?"

"I'll see him tomorrow. I'm no longer in a mood to be sociable so I'll disappear the way I came and no one need know I walked over to see you." He let himself out onto the terrace and Jane watched him anxiously until he disappeared at the far side of the lawn among the rhododendrons, the huge blooms ghostly in the moonlight.

She wished, again, that she dared feel for him what he insisted he felt for her. But he had such odd ideas, notions which frightened her to the depths of her conventional soul. His theories for the education of children, for instance. She'd never been able to approve of Stephanie's behavior—although she loved the girl, of course.

And wouldn't Francis wish to rear his own children in the same way? Jane couldn't accept that. Not for the children she might have if she were wed with him. So, marriage would never do. A husband had too much power and, as Jane knew to her chagrin, she was far too meek to stand up to him.

Absently, Jane locked the doors. Musing, she returned to her seat where she pretended to stitch, but, instead, allowed her mind to drift among the might-have-beens, the wish-it-weres and the if-onlys . . .

Ten minutes later a scowling Stephanie stalked into the sitting room.

When Jane looked up from her embroidery, Steph pointed. "Put that away, will you?" she asked. "Please? Theo's forgotten he said he'd fence with me, so you come and oblige me with a match, will you?"

Jane bit her lip. "Stephanie, you are very near your twenty-fifth birthday. Don't you think you're a little old for playing games?"

"Games! I don't wish to play games. I wish to *fence.* What has that to do with playing games?"

"You really should stop pretending to be a boy, Stephanie."

"I've never pretended any such thing."

"Look at yourself!"

"Jane," said Stephanie with a patience, self-imposed with some difficulty, "if I were pretending to be a boy, I'd cut my hair and I'd *never* wear skirts. I wear trousers by choice because they are more comfortable and give one far more freedom of movement, and I've far too much to do in a day to fight with skirts."

"And of an evening?"

"Bah," responded Stephanie, unable to think of a better response. Then she added, "Trousers are comfortable. Besides, I wear gowns when we go out of an evening and *especially* when we've been invited to dance. You know how much I love to dance. Do come fence with me," she coaxed, changing the subject with that quicksilver speed Jane had always had difficulty following.

"I never enjoyed it as you do, my dear, and I've no intention of ever playing at swords again."

A tap on the French windows caught Stephanie's attention and she peered into the dusk. "It's Sir Francis! He'll fight me!"

For reasons Stephanie didn't wish to examine—beyond the fact they had to do with Anthony and the ways in which the man unsettled her—she had a strong desire, a deep *need,* to expend a great deal of energy. Now, with her guardian's co-operation, she could do so.

"Won't you?" she asked as she opened the doors.

"Won't I what?"

"Fence with me."

Francis nodded, but said he wanted a few words with Jane first and that he'd be along in a moment. Stephanie knew of Francis's hopes in that direction and approved them, so, taking the hint, she left them alone.

"What is it, Francis? Why have you returned?"

"As I was about to cross the stile into the homewoods, it occurred to me that you may be correct that Chris won't immediately understand about Stephanie. Do you think I should order her into skirts?" Jane gave him a look that had him chuckling. "Well, not *order* her, but ask? At least that she change for the evenings?"

"You think she'll obey?" teased Jane, knowing she was a step ahead of him on this.

He sighed. "Very likely not."

"You may relax. Since Huntersham appeared, she's obliged me by coming down to dinner in skirts every evening. Well, not this evening, but his lordship sent word he'd not be here for a day or two."

"Excellent. In that case you may order the tea you suggested earlier and I'll spend the rest of the evening teasing you until you say me yea!"

Jane blushed and bent her head to her needlework. "Francis, you mustn't."

Footsteps could be heard crossing the Great Hall and Jane breathed a sigh of relief—or was it irritation? *Why,* wondered

Jane, *can I not make the decision that Francis must behave—
and then remember to make him do so?*

"Francis!" said Stephanie, an impatient stride bringing her
into the room. "You *said* you'd be right along!"

She'd removed her coat and cravat and, above her smooth-
fitting vest, unbuttoned the tiny buttons of her collarless shirt.
She stood astride just inside the doorway. Her braid was hidden
behind her back and she stood at the edge of the light, holding
a thin blade in both hands and gently bowing it. To Jane's
distress, Stephanie looked very much the youth.

"Well?" she asked.

Jane and Francis exchanged a glance. "You go along with
Stephanie, Francis. Please." said Jane, too softly for Stephanie
to overhear.

"Jane?" Francis's voice, on the other hand, carried. "Forgive
me? For importuning you once again?" Francis smiled a rueful
smile and, after a moment, Jane smiled back, nodded. Her
smile soothed his concern that he'd finally gone too far in his
teasing and he was able to join Stephanie with a lighter heart.

As she led the way to the armory, Stephanie idly wondered
why Jane was so stubborn. What possible reason could her
companion-chaperon have for refusing to wed Sir Francis? The
thought slipped away as she was soon too busy defending herself against Francis's longer reach to concern herself with her
cousin's marriage prospects.

And, when finally they saluted each other at the end of a
hard-fought match, Stephanie was too tired to think of anything but her bed. She yawned, thanked Francis for indulging
her, and, putting away her blade, wandered off toward a set of
secondary stairs, hoping she'd sleep once she reached her
room.

Once there she discovered that, although so tired she was
ready to fall into her bed still clothed, the persistent memory
of her first encounter with Anthony Ryder still plagued her,
leaving her restless and . . . wanting. Anger at her body's be-
trayal drove all thoughts of Jane and Francis from her mind.

It also replaced her concern that the work she'd set in train be done, that no twig, lamb, or piece of equipment be out of place when the man she'd be expected to call father arrived.

She neither knew nor cared that Francis rejoined Jane and this time accepted a cup of tea which he sipped contentedly while Jane drank her evening coffee. Nor did she know or would she have cared when, later, the pair slipped up the stairs to Jane's room. Eventually Francis left and strolled home through the moonlit spring night wondering if he'd ever convince his love she loved him back, something he knew in his soul was true!

Five

The next morning Jane asked, "Do you think he'll come today?" She looked up from the coffee she absently stirred. Noting Stephanie was engrossed in a letter, she added, "Stephie?" then waited for the younger woman to respond.

"What? Or do I mean who?" Stephanie asked without looking up from the letter she perused. It was from one of her agriculturist correspondents, urging her to come to London for the next meeting of the Society of Agriculture. Stephanie recalled how she'd recently played with the notion that, come autumn, she might journey to London for a meeting. The way things were, she thought bitterly, she daren't plan beyond today.

"You weren't listening!" accused Jane.

Stephanie folded the letter and tucked it under her plate. "You are correct. I wasn't. Now I am."

Jane sighed. "Do you think he'll come today."

"Who?"

The sigh was deeper this time. "As I have said, Stephie! Lord Lemiston. To say nothing of the guests we were told to expect."

"I haven't a notion when they'll come. It doesn't make a jot of difference, does it?"

"Very likely not to you," said Jane. *Someone,* however, has to plan meals, and how can one plan when one has no idea what to expect?"

Stephanie felt a certain sympathy with that since it was very much what she'd been thinking herself, but her own concern was how to proceed with the spring work. Would her father instantly take the reins in hand? Would he overturn all she'd done, revoke her orders for future work?

"Since we've not been told when to expect them, they can't object to pot-luck when they do deign to show themselves. We've enough food on hand that providing generously for every meal from now on shouldn't be much of a problem. Why not do that?"

"I don't know if that's suitable! Perhaps full formal meals are expected. I haven't a notion," Jane fretted, "what tonnish guests expect when they visit! Huntersham, of course, is an easily pleased sort of man so I'm not concerned with him. But your father is an entirely different kettle of fish, or so I fear. Abbot's told me stories, Stephie, about the sort of house-parties held before . . ." She broke off, biting her lip, her eyes flickering toward and away from Lady Stephanie.

"Before I was born and my mother died," finished Stephanie unconcerned. "You can't hurt me by calling to mind the death of a woman I never met! But my long absent sire . . ." She paused, continued a trifle more slowly. "I doubt very much he's kept such state while in the wilds of America! Or in India. Where did our solicitors inform us they next had word from him? The Antipodes?" A muscle jumped in Stephanie's jaw. "Very likely, Jane, he's got out of the habit of it. But, if he *does* insist on all the . . . the elegant trifles or . . . or strict attention to precedence and all that nonsense, then he should be more observing of the common courtesies himself."

Jane bit her lip. "I'd not like him thinking we're showing him the least disrespect."

"In what way has he shown *us* respect? Why should we care if he's insulted when he's insulting us with his lax behavior by not sending word of what to expect and by the arrogant expectation that he'd be welcome even if he did?"

"Oh dear. Stephanie, dear, I don't think you should take that attitude."

"Do you not?" Stephanie laid her knife and fork across her

plate and pushed back her chair. She continued speaking as she rose to her feet. "I'm no hypocrite, Jane. I'll not pretend respect and affection where they do not, cannot, exist."

"Oh, no, not affection. But . . . that common courtesy you spoke of?"

"You fear I'll forget my manners?"

"You've been known to do so."

Stephanie's eyes narrowed, but she stood with casual grace behind her chair, one hand resting on the back of it. "Out with it, Jane. You want something."

Jane drew in a deep breath and let it out with a whoosh. "Put away your trousers? Altogether? Wear your habit? And gowns? Please?"

"I'll wear gowns in the evening. That should be enough!"

"Just while we've company," Jane begged. "People won't understand, Stephanie. Truly."

"And you think it should bother me that they don't understand?"

"I know you don't give a button for the opinion of others, but for *me?*"

Stephanie studied her wide-eyed chaperon. "You'll be embarrassed *for* me, is that it?"

"Yes."

Stephanie sighed. "Whenever I'm in the house I promise I'll put off my trousers and wear skirts. But only so you'll not be mortified by the comments the rude might make. Outside, when I've work to do, it's another situation entirely."

Jane, thinking it was far more than she'd expected to gain, nodded. "Thank you. I know how much you'll dislike it, but I'll feel much more comfortable."

"I do it for that reason only," said Stephanie on a sharp note.

"I know and appreciate it." Jane smiled warmly. "Now, I think I'll take your advice and merely plan meals only a little more generous than those to which we're accustomed. Perhaps two courses with several removes. And a fruit course, do you think, before the table is cleared so that nuts and brandy may be set out . . . ?"

Jane's voice trailed away to a mutter and Stephanie, realizing she was unneeded, removed herself from the breakfast room and headed for the stables. There was that weathercock atop the carriage house which no longer swung with the wind. Someone must get up there and grease the thing. She frowned in concentration, searching her mind for anything else which needed attention.

Mid-afternoon, feeling as if everything which could be done had been or soon would be done, Lady Stephanie cantered up the newly raked drive to the house. Remembering that Jane had mentioned she might work in her rose garden, Stephanie looked toward the well-protected area and saw the top of a parasol bobbing above the bushes. Dismounting, Lady Stephanie turned Aladdin over to a young groom and stalked toward the garden.

"Jane?"

"We're here, Stephie. I've been cutting flowers for the guest rooms . . ."

"We?" Warily, Stephanie rounded a hedge and found Sir Francis patiently holding a flat basket into which Jane tucked the flowers she cut. She relaxed. The "we" hadn't referred to Lord Lemiston or to the blacksheep earl with whom she was again irritated. Why *had* the man disappeared?

"I should have done this this morning," Jane interrupted, her features in the perpetual frown she'd acquired since learning Lemiston was to return. "It didn't cross my mind until a few minutes ago. I've worried and fretted that everything be just right for Lord Lemiston and then to forget something so simple, so welcoming!"

"Don't look as if his arrival were something to be feared," said Sir Francis sharply, his hand on Jane's shoulder. "He's Steph's *father.*"

Stephanie rounded on him, her quick temper suddenly loosed. "Why shouldn't Jane feel concern? He's *your* friend, Francis, but what gives you the notion he'll be mine?"

"Your friend?" Sir Francis ran fingers through the mass of tightly curling hair which, to that point, had lain in controlled waves. "Stephanie, make sense. He's your father. He isn't supposed to be your friend."

Not one of the small, tense tableau noticed when Anthony and Lord Lemiston rounded the nearby corner of the house. Noting the trio standing not far away, his lordship grasped Anthony's arm. Tightly. He motioned for Anthony to be silent as he edged toward a thick hedge.

Anthony, tight-lipped with disapproval, also crept into hiding. Then, recalling he'd done a bit of eavesdropping of his own when he'd listened outside the inn, he shrugged. He could hardly blame Chris for something he'd done himself, although he wondered if Chris would feel a similar shame later! After another look at Chris he sighed and settled himself for more of the same despicable behavior.

"But I don't need a father! Not now. Not years too late!" Stephanie, her voice something of a growl, added, "Besides, Jane has brought it to my attention I'm not exactly what a sire expects a daughter to be. And another thing, Francis, will he come alone?"

"Alone?" Francis frowned, thoughts passing through his mind which had, obviously, never before occurred to him. "A wife, you mean?"

"And children, perhaps?"

"You are asking if he might have remarried?"

Stephanie nodded.

"Steph, how can I possibly answer you?"

"I don't know." Stephanie remained silent for a moment, then turned and stared, blindly, toward the small herd of sheep who grazed beyond the deep haha which separated the meadow from the lawn. "It's just that I've sometimes wondered if you haven't had more *personal* news of him . . ."

"I know nothing more of where he's been or what he's done than you do. You've been told everything his bankers and solicitors passed on to us on those rare occasions he's drawn monies and asked they be forwarded to whatever God-forsaken corner of the world he'd wandered into."

Stephanie cast him a suspicious look. "He has *never* written you?"

"Never."

She frowned. "I don't like it."

The lids drooped again and Sir Francis eyed his ward. "What is it you don't like?"

"That he's been silent for nearly a quarter century and, now, *with no warning,* will suddenly arrive on our doorstep."

Sir Francis eyed her silently. Finally, he asked, "That doorstep?"

Stephanie's face revealed wary tension as she waited for him to go on.

"It's *his* doorstep, Stephanie."

A cold, closed-in look hardened her features. "You know why I can't accept that."

"No."

Stephanie eyed him, noted the implacable expression which would not help her, and struggled for words. "Francis, has it occurred to you that *I've* lived here more years than he ever did! He was what—all of twenty-two, when he left?"

"So?"

Stephanie threw out her hands in an imploring gesture. "Don't you see? He's not a part of our life here. He's a shadowy figure who exists somewhere. Perhaps. Maybe. At least, that's what we've been told all our lives. But he isn't *real.*" She paused. "Don't you see what I'm saying? Francis, he's not *real!*"

"Not real," repeated Francis, and cast a bewildered glance toward Jane.

Behind the hedge, Chris muttered, "She'll soon discover I'm real, all right!"

"You must admit she made one telling point," whispered Anthony.

"Nonsense."

"That she's lived here more years than you did."

"Irrelevant."

"It isn't," hissed Anthony.

Lemiston knew he'd blustered more than enough when he had no real argument. "Hush." He looked to where his daughter spread her hands in a gesture which pleaded for understanding.

"A bugbear, Francis," Stephanie continued, "with which one frightens a child into good behavior! A dragon, dangerous, but watching from afar. A threat, but, even then, no more than a fairy tale. Certainly nothing like a flesh and blood man. And yet," she added slowly, "despite that, I'm forced, by the law of the land, to acknowledge that *he,* who cares nothing for it, owns all this. He may not approve of the changes I made. He's a *stranger,* Francis, don't you see?"

"Stephie," said Jane softly, "I understand what you say, but Sir Francis is correct, too, when he says this *is* your father's home. You accept he has legal rights here. Given that, we must set our mind to making everything as welcoming as we know how . . . think you not?"

Her eyes flashing and a vicious note in her voice, Stephanie snarled, *"Welcome* him? Why should we welcome him? He *abandoned* us. He's left us in ignorance of his very existence year after year the whole of our lives. Welcome? Oh no, Jane. He may come home, if that is how he thinks of it, but will we welcome him? I doubt it very much."

"Come, Stephie," Jane scolded. "You are tilting at windmills as did that Spanish Don about whom you like to read."

Stephanie struggled with her temper and gained the upper hand. She shrugged. "I hope that's all it is, Jane."

"I'm certain of it," said her chaperon soothingly. "Come along now and help me with these bouquets. You do a far better job with them than I do—when I can get you to do them, that is. Please?"

The two women and Sir Francis moved away. Anthony, watching them go, wondered at Lady Stephanie's words. He took a good look at Lemiston and his brow arched. "What's the matter Chris?" he asked softly.

Shock after shock ran through the older of the two men. "I don't believe what I just heard. I feel just like I did when racing that wild fire across the American plains. That chit of a girl feels animosity toward *me?* What right does the murdering wench have to feel anger toward *me?* It was *she* who . . ." He glanced at Anthony and away. "Oh, never you mind!"

Lemiston pushed aside an anger which was so old, so deeply ingrained it was very nearly habit. Having finally returned to old haunts in London, he'd discovered the emotion was far less heated than when, twenty-odd years earlier, it had filled him with such a passion it left room for nothing but the need to escape. Now, to maintain it, he was constantly having to remind himself what had happened, how he'd felt. But, however long it had been, his love was dead. That was all that was important.

He watched the women move away, the one gracefully in skirts and the other with that odd, mannish stride in her scandalous trousers. He turned his gaze on Sir Francis. His oldest friend? Was he *still* friend? Lemiston, unable to face that thought, turned away, motioning Anthony to follow.

"Aren't we going in?" asked Anthony, falsely innocent, his tongue firmly in his cheek.

"Later," snapped his lordship. "Tomorrow maybe . . . or the day after. Never. Blast it, I don't know when . . ."

"What has you in a stew this time, Chris?"

"Francis! That man is supposed to be my *friend*. Would a friend allow a young woman to dress in that outrageous fashion? As a *boy*. Would he allow a woman to manage an estate as large and complicated as the Priory? It's unheard of," he growled. "Scandal making." He stalked on toward where his horse waited.

"But she's doing it very well, is she not?"

"What has that to say to anything?" Steel-gray brows slashed together into a deep vee. "If this excuse for a daughter has become a scandal in society, then how the devil will I get the wench married off?" His voice dropped to a more confiding tone. "I reluctantly concluded I couldn't simply toss the twins, assuming they were still here, out on their ear. I can't make myself leave them to survive as they will. But twins . . . !" A vicious look gleamed in Chris's eyes when he turned to glare at Anthony. "It's just too bad my solicitor never informed me they'd died in childhood, which I told him was the only word I wanted to hear concerning my wretched offspring. Well, since they *didn't* die, then I must deal with them. And that's another thing, Why hasn't Francis already found them husbands and married them off?"

"Husbands? *Plural?*"

"*Twins,* I've told you. Twins."

"But—"

"Not a word!"

Anthony eyed his mentor and decided he'd just let the man discover for himself that one of those twins was male! "I doubt," Anthony said mildly, but with a quick sharp glance at Chris's rigid back, "that there are many men who would know how to handle her. Or appreciate her. Which is likely why she's still unwed."

"*Appreciate* her? Of course no man in his right mind would *appreciate* her. You must be all about in the head to suggest it's possible! What man would marry a female who is more man than woman? None. Not a single one." A muscle jumped in the side of Lemiston's jaw and, staring straight ahead, he didn't notice Anthony's movement of denial. "Blast. What if the other is as wild? I'll be forced to *buy* them bridegrooms. Bedamned to the wenches. I've better things to do with my fortune!"

A muscle worked in Anthony's jaw. He fought and won the battle to relax. "So," he asked. "What do we do now?"

"Anthony, the way I feel at this moment I don't dare show myself," said Lemiston, his tone one of a man demanding understanding. "I'd lose my temper, which, as you learned the hard way, is *not* the way to deal with a difficult situation. Besides, I need time to think."

"And besides," said Anthony very softly indeed as Chris cantered off, "you've discovered still another excuse to avoid the house you once swore you'd never again enter!" He mounted and, in silence, walked Sahib off after Chris's mare. Finally he nudged the horse's sides and the gelding lengthened his pace until they'd caught up with Lemiston.

"I'll admit I'm impressed by the changes which have been introduced on the estate," said Lemiston slowly when Anthony joined him. "But that girl—woman? Lord, who can tell what she is! I don't know what to think of her."

"At the inn, she handled the farmer very well."

"Yes. She won the argument with Wilkins," admitted Lemiston. Reluctantly just, he added, "And she left him pretty much with pride intact."

They rode on for ten minutes or so in silence. "Where *are* we going?" asked Anthony.

"Where I can *breathe*. You'll never know how hard it is for me to ride over Priory land . . ." A muscle jumped in Lemiston's jaw. "I hadn't realized how deep was my aversion to my old home. Lord, how I loathe it!"

"So why do it?" Chris turned his head, casting a sharp glance toward Anthony who added, "Why go there at all? As things stand, you needn't, you know."

"I can't leave them completely destitute however much I'd like to do just that. They have to be married off. That's what I must do and I'll do it. Ah! I can't wait to see those murdering bitches wed! That will settle my last problem very nicely and I can forget England forever."

Anthony's brows clashed together as he thought of the reputations of some of the men invited to Lemiston's house-party. Marry Lady Stephanie to one of those idiots? *Not on your life, Chris!* thought Anthony. What he said, however, was, "Since you've invited people to a house-party, you *have* to arrive soon or you'll not be before them."

After only a moment's hesitation, Chris said, "We'll return for dinner tonight." A bit wistfully, he added, "I hope my old friends and their wives arrive soon. When guests arrive things will be different . . ."

They rode on and Anthony thought more about Chris's plans to marry both his daughters, as he thought, to men who had reputations which were so bad some of them were banned from polite drawing rooms. One would eventually bring himself to ruin by gambling away his fortunes. One had already done so and was desperately in need of funds!

Or a man like Baron Stread! Anthony shuddered at the thought of any woman in the hands of that obnoxious, perhaps evil, man.

It wouldn't do . . . it simply wouldn't do.

Lemiston broke into Anthony's thoughts with one more comment. "Very likely I'll have to dower such a neither-nor creature as that one who wears trousers far more dearly than I wish in order to get *her* wed. What a waste . . ." He glanced at Anthony. "You'll laugh your head off when you finally understand the whole. With your odd sense of humor you'll think it as funny as I do."

Humor? Humor was the last thing Anthony saw in what he feared was a rather diabolical plan. Anthony made a few plans of his own whereby he could counter any which would bring harm to Lady Stephanie.

Perhaps he could offer to sell *her* the Priory . . .

Or, if she hadn't the funds to buy it, then rent it to her on a very long lease?

Or kidnap her and take her away and hide her until Chris gave up and left the country?

Or offer to fight Lemiston for her . . . ? Now, there was a thought! He cast a glance toward Chris and kicked his Sahib to a canter. Actually, if the outcome weren't so important, he'd rather like to match himself against Chris who was a master of all forms of combat.

While Anthony's thoughts were mildly vicious, Lemiston's took another turn entirely. He watched the younger man riding a few paces ahead and a warmth filled him. Anthony was the son he *should* have had. Thank God, thought Lemiston, the younger man hadn't changed his mind about their plans as he might have done when he'd inherited his title and Hunter's Cove! Making new arrangements would have kept him stuck in England far longer than he'd any wish to be.

Because the sooner he could shake the last of England's soil from his boots, the sooner it would be that he'd return to Australia where the future was open to any man with the determination and the will to shape it as he would. Christopher Morris, Lord Lemiston, had grand plans for his future, and they included nothing still to be found in the England he'd left a quarter-century previously. The sooner he was done here, the sooner he'd breathe freely again!

And, if Christopher Morris, Lord Lemiston, had any control over the near future, that would be very soon indeed.

After doing the flowers for Jane, Stephanie went to the stable to check a strained hock in one of the carriage horses. It was healing nicely and, returning to the house, she whistled a cheerful melody—something even Sir Francis thought she should not do. She approached by the south front of the Priory and entered Jane's sitting room by way of the terrace.

Jane, looking up from her embroidery, noticed that grass clippings dropped from Stephanie's boots. "Why, my dear, can you never remember to use a proper entrance so that you avoid tracking in all that dirt?"

"Dirt?" Stephanie raised her hands and looked around herself. "Oh."

Just here the terrace was narrow and, as a result, she'd tracked newly scythed grass in onto the carpet which had, more than half a century earlier, been especially ordered from a French carpet maker. Although it showed wear and had faded a bit near the windows where the sun streamed in on it, the never-ending wars with France made replacing it impossible. At least, if one wished to go to the original source and order the exact same pattern, it was impossible.

"Grass is clean dirt, Jane," she said impatiently. "It'll sweep up when it dries."

"I've invited Francis to dinner this evening," said Jane after indulging in a faint sigh. "I ordered all that extra as you suggested, but I cannot bear to see so much food go to waste—whatever you say about our well-stocked larder's ability to bear it."

"We'll enjoy his company, won't we?" Taking up her normal stance near the empty fireplace, one arm stretched along the mantel, Stephanie eyed Jane's frowning face. "Or will we not? What has made you cross as crabs?"

Jane compressed her lips and stared at her embroidery. She tilted the frame to a slightly different angle, peering at the gradually growing pattern of flowers, leaves, and twigs of an apple tree. "I'm ashamed of myself. I shouldn't have done it."

"Shouldn't have done what?" asked Stephanie, feeling that she'd missed something somewhere.

"Invited Francis to dinner, of course. It encourages him to believe . . . well, it isn't *kind* when he suffers from . . . from . . ."

"Unrequited love?" suggested Stephanie, her brows arching. "But his feelings are not unreturned, are they? You do feel affection for him, do you not? Of course, coward that you are, you don't allow *him* to guess that."

Jane rose to her feet. She glared in a manner totally unlike her gentle self at the britches-clad figure leaning negligently against the mantel. "Must you scoff at everything, Stephanie? Can nothing be sacred in your cynical eyes? On occasions such as this I find it in my heart to agree with the matrons who say Sir Francis has ruined you utterly. You simply don't

understand what it is he suffers. And you are wrong that I . . .
entertain . . . warm feelings for him. I don't. I *won't.*"

A quickly repressed sob and Jane turned, taking overly quick
steps toward the door.

Stephanie scowled. She wasn't wrong. Jane loved Francis.
It was in her eyes when she looked at him, thinking herself
unobserved. In her face. So why wouldn't she admit it? Remembering how often she herself had pushed aside the memory of Ryder's kiss, how often she'd wished to experience again
the treacherous emotions aroused by it, Stephanie discovered
that perhaps she *did* understand. At least some part of it. Perhaps Jane, mouse that she was, feared such heat? Stephanie
reached out a hand—but too late. Stephanie allowed her arm
to fall, her brows crowding each other in the usual vee shape.

"Jane?"

"Don't apologize. Assuming, of course that that was what
you meant to do . . ." said Jane with a touch of acid. She
stopped, stood rigid for a moment, faced around. "Stephie, I
don't know what is the matter with me," she said in a different
tone. "Forgive me?"

"Why do you ask that when it is *you* who have reason to
forgive *me?* I should not sneer at his unhappiness or at yours.
At *anyone's* unhappiness. It is no excuse that I'm unable to
understand why, if you won't wed him, you won't . . .
don't . . ." Stephanie floundered for a polite way of suggesting
Jane bed Francis if she wouldn't marry him! Nor could she
understand why Jane seemed to relax. What had she said now?

"I suggest you not finish *that* sentence," interrupted Jane,
who had feared Stephanie had guessed her darkest secret.
"You'll be asking forgiveness yet again!" She bit the corner
of her lip, her thoughtful gaze on Stephanie who stood straight
and still before the empty fireplace. "I think, since Sir Francis
is to join us, I'll wear my new gown. After all, I've only once
had an occasion worthy of it." She eyed her charge. "I realize
Huntersham has gone off somewhere and that our other com-

pany hasn't yet arrived, but will you, too, put on a gown?" asked Jane. "To please me?"

"Perhaps." Stephanie moved to join her friend and companion. They strolled down the corridor to the main hall. After a moment she sighed and added, "If you truly wish it, I'll dress for dinner, even though we have no company." A grin tipped the side of her mouth. "We'll call it a penitence for my unforgivable behavior!"

"I wish *you* wished it," said Jane. "There are advantages to skirts. Truly," she added when Stephanie cast her a disbelieving look.

"Name one."

"They look good and make one feel good. That's *two* reasons!"

"You mean they make you feel like a woman," suggested Stephanie.

"I suppose I do." Jane's hands gently smoothed the front of the new yellow at-home gown she'd received only a few days earlier from their modiste in Chichester. "There is something about it, the feel of it—"

"But I dislike feeling the way a woman is expected to feel!" interrupted Stephanie from part-way up the main staircase. "I'm neither a mental nor a moral weakling so I've no need of a man's constant guidance." At Jane's reproving look she added, "Jane, you know far too many men consider women childish—except when they think of them as a toy with which they may play. I've no desire to be treated as either a child or as something fashioned for man's amusement and ignored when such amusement is not required!"

Stephanie took the last of the steps in a little run. She turned, arms akimbo, to look challengingly down at her friend who climbed more slowly.

Jane chuckled. "There is far more to feeling like a woman than *that,*" she said and, a trifle smugly, added, "If you'd ever been properly kissed you'd know what I mean!"

Even as she wondered just when Francis had "properly"

kissed her chaperon, Jane's words roused those odd hot emotions Stephanie had experienced in Ryder's arms. They roiled around inside her much as they'd done when she'd first experienced them. A faintly strangled note distorted Stephanie's voice when she retorted, "I've no desire of ever"—she barely stopped herself from adding the word *again*— "feeling *that* way, either." Before Jane could respond, Stephanie moved off, turning down the narrow hall to her room at the back of the house.

Stephanie, cat-like from her earliest years, liked warmth and comfort when she wasn't actively out and around. The smallish room she'd chosen for her own was tucked into a corner where a wing extended away from the main structure of the house. It was a room well protected from sharp winds and easily heated. Too, she'd gradually furnished it in a fashion which, if he'd ever seen it, would have surprised Sir Francis a great deal. Here, finally, was evidence of Stephanie's femininity.

True, the large, well-padded chair could never be called delicate, but it was covered in a dainty floral chintz designed in delightfully spring-like colors from which the drapery and the bed hangings were also made. A soft, smoky pink in the thick carpet was repeated in the panels above dark oak wainscoting. The delicate medallions centered in each panel were white, as was the wide, rather ornate cornice circling the room at ceiling level.

Here, when alone, Stephanie threw off her jackets and vests and pulled on a softened version of a man's banyan, and here, of an evening, she'd curl up in nothing but the heavy, sensuous silk of the robe for a long evening's read.

But not this evening.

This evening she'd agreed to dress properly. Stephanie toyed with the notion of teasing Jane by wearing her presentation gown. She didn't consider it for long, however. The instant she recalled the unhappy discomfort of the necessary stays and the awkwardness of the train, to say nothing of the fact that she must put up her hair if the gown weren't to look ridiculous, she decided it wasn't worth it. Not for a mere jest!

Besides, styles had changed during the years since the elaborate toilet was constructed early in her quickly aborted Season. That was another reason for not wearing the court gown. Because, although it was something she'd never thought important enough to discuss, Stephanie paid more attention to changing styles than anyone was aware. And she'd not be caught dead in anything so outmoded as her six-year-old presentation gown!

Lady Stephanie had hated the strict formality and stricter rules of behavior required by a London Season. When she'd suggested they go home and Sir Francis insisted they stay for several months, she'd instantly threatened to ruin herself utterly by wearing her britches and riding astride in the park during the hour of the promenade. Sir Francis, knowing she'd do it, capitulated to her wishes and brought her home.

Now, whenever she ordered something new, which was far less often than Jane felt she should, it was slap up to the echo—as one stripling, impressed by her tall, slim figure and mahogany colored hair, had informed her. Of course, his mother had instantly removed the young gentleman from Stephanie's contaminating presence, but that didn't diminish the compliment!

So, instead of the old gown, she reached for an evening dress with simple lines which was worn over nothing more than a narrow slip. The gown was decorated with antique-looking braid down the front and with a very wide, straight neckline which bared most of her shoulders. Made of her favorite silk, it had that fluidity she loved to feel as it slid over her skin, an odd, pleasure-giving sensation in which Stephanie secretly reveled.

Unfortunately current designs included a short train which put her into the fidgets when she turned too quickly, the gown wrapping itself around her feet. She reminded herself to move with the necessarily restrained steps. Still, if she could not curl up in the comfort of her banyan as she'd prefer, the delicious feel of the silk was the next best thing.

Sir Francis arrived just as she tripped in properly demure feminine fashion down the stairs. "You look lovely, Stephanie. You should wear your skirts more often."

She grimaced. "Why should I want to do that?"

"Why should you want to wear them more often?"

"Why should I wish to look lovely."

"Because the esthetic pleasure one feels when looking at you is agreeable for those around you," responded Sir Francis promptly.

"Nonsense," said Lady Stephanie, but felt warmed by the compliment and hoped she wasn't blushing. She came down the shallow steps and was on the last when the knocker sounded.

Abbot, crossing the hall on his way to the dining room, changed direction, going to the door instead. Stephanie frowned slightly, curious as to who would be so inconsiderate as to arrive at such an unconscionably odd hour. Just as Abbot reached the door, it occurred to her it would be just like the despicable Oakfield to drop by knowing it was mealtime.

The frown deepened, drawing her brows into the Morris vee. Determined the fool would *not* be allowed entry, her mouth firmed into a belligerent line.

But it wasn't Oakfield.

Six

After an instant's surprise, Francis strode forward. Choked up by the sudden and unexpected meeting, he merely grasped Chris's hand and shook it firmly. Reluctantly, he tried to release his grip so Abbot could remove the guest's hat and coat, but Lemiston retained his hold and would not let him go.

Abbot, who had been at the Priory since a lad in his first place, stared at Lemiston and finally, barely able to believe his eyes, stuttered, "M . . . m . . . my lord?" Even though he'd known his lordship was coming, he was unprepared. "My lord, is it really you?"

"Yes Abbot, I believe it is really I. How are you?"

"You remember my name? But how . . ." The old man shook his head, wonderingly. "I was a mere footman when you left!"

Still not releasing Francis, Lemiston grinned at Abbot. "Ah, but before that you were a rather youngish footman who would sneak me a gingerbread whenever I'd been sent to my room without supper. How could I forget *you?*"

Abbot regained his poise. "It is a great pleasure to see you home again, my lord." He flicked a glance toward Huntersham.

"Ah, yes," said his lordship, finally letting go of Francis. "As you see, Lord Huntersham has returned as well." One of his lordship's brows arched and he cast Anthony a wry look. "He'll be my guest for the duration of my stay, Abbot."

Anthony and Sir Francis eyed each other. They'd not met since they'd been introduced in London. Francis, who hadn't understood then, and didn't now, why Huntersham should wish to stay at the Priory rather than his own home farther up the coast, nodded a short sharp nod of greeting and turned his gaze back to absorb the changes in his old friend of whom he'd had barely a glimpse while they were both in London.

Even as the butler was saying, "I'll check that your rooms are properly aired while you dine . . ." he gave the men's boots a surreptitious glance and noted the dust. "Hmm, come to that, my lords, would you care to refresh yourself before dinner is announced? It can easily be held back half an hour." He looked from one to the other.

Lady Stephanie, the spell holding her finally broken, stepped down onto the floor and strolled nearer, speaking as she came. "Although there is no reason for them to change if they do not care to, I'll show them to rooms where, if you'll instantly order fresh water sent up, Abbot, they may refresh themselves and wash the dust of the road away."

She was glad she'd had a moment in which to regain her poise. Her first sight of Huntersham had raised the echo of those burning tremors which his kisses had roused in her, and she was grateful he'd been preoccupied removing his driving coat and gloves and hadn't witnessed her response.

Or perhaps he had? Stephanie suspected these men had lived lives in which one became exceedingly observant or very quickly dead. It would teach one to notice things, even when it appeared one did not. Stephanie decided it was indeed possible that both men had observed her frown. Anthony wouldn't expect a warm welcome from her, of course, and wouldn't be surprised. Christopher, Lord Lemiston, might not be particularly surprised, but she doubted if he'd be pleased either. Stephanie decided she didn't care.

"Sir Francis," said Stephanie, turning away from the newcomers, "if you would await us in the east drawing room . . . ?"

"No, Francis," interrupted Lord Lemiston, peremptorily. "We'll gather in m'mother's old sitting room, if you'd be so kind." He chuckled. "When in congenial company I've never had a liking for the sort of formality the drawing room imposes on one, and now, after my years abroad, find I've an even greater aversion to it!"

Stephanie felt an instant's sympathy for her sire's position and almost chuckled at his dry humor. That he felt about the drawing room exactly as she did was something she'd no wish to acknowledge, however. Nor would she admit to a soul that she'd suggested that particular room *because* of the nearly oppressive propriety imposed on one. Too, it appeared Jane had been wrong when she said he'd lived in state before leaving England!

From the moment Jane knew there was company coming she'd been in a tizzy, turning the main bedroom floor upside down. It had been a nuisance, of course, but the days of preparation meant Stephanie could take her father to his old rooms and put Huntersham back into the green suite opposite without fearing either man would hang themselves on cobwebs! Although that might be a solution to the problem of their existence, might it not?

For a moment Lady Stephanie enjoyed a mental image of the visitors struggling in the toils of a giant spider web, a monstrous spider closing in on trapped prey. Not that any part of the Priory was allowed to get into that sort of bewebbed state, of course. But the whole of it wasn't kept in constant readiness for guests either, so Jane's recent efforts at housewifery were very likely a good thing.

Stephanie opened the double doors to her father's suite and stood aside. He nodded brusquely as he passed her. Nor did he look at her as he pushed shut the doors with something of a snap. Ignoring Huntersham as her father had ignored her, Stephanie turned to cross the hall to his rooms. And stopped. All too close to the man who'd silently stepped into her path. Her chin raised, she held her ground. She wouldn't give him the satisfaction of backing up.

"You didn't wish us welcome," said Anthony softly.

"Perhaps there's a reason for that."

His left brow tipped at an angle indicating he desired an explanation.

"Perhaps I gave no welcome because I do not wish you welcome?"

"Perhaps. Or perhaps because you fear it?"

"Why should I fear it?"

"Do you think your father will allow you to dress as I found you dressed that first day?" he asked softly.

"I'm fully of age. He can take his wishes and go to the devil. Or should I say, he can go *back* to the devil?" she asked sweetly. Then she scowled. "He can take you with him, my Lord Huntersham."

"I've no desire to go anywhere," said his lordship, his tone mild. "Certainly the devil has no place in my plans." But, even as he spoke, his gaze moved to his host's closed doors, and a thoughtful look could be read in his gaze.

"Hmm, I see."

Huntersham turned back to Lady Stephanie. "What do you think you see?"

"That the devil may have no particular part in *your* plans, although I confess I find that doubtful, but you wonder if Ol' Harry might have some place in *his*." She dropped a derisory curtsy. "Thank you, my lord, for the warning."

Anthony eyed her up and down. "Very quick of you. I really must not forget your exceedingly interesting mode of thought ever again! Very quick indeed, my sweet."

He nodded and, before Stephanie could object to his use of the endearment, he disappeared into his suite. She stared at his closed door, reminded, that this man was not stupid either. As her head groom had once said of a surprisingly intelligent horse, he too was well fitted out in the bone box!

Now, should she warn Theo guests had arrived? Or should she let him stay in the library where he'd dine from a tray as was his preference? She sighed. It would, she decided, be better for her to learn something of this man she was expected to accept as her father before she added still another complication to the pot.

Blissfully unaware, Theo could, for this evening, stay in the library!

Slowly, thoughtfully, Lady Stephanie took herself back down the stairs and, at a quicker pace, on to the small salon where she breathed a sigh of relief that Jane had not yet descended. She didn't need her chaperon's presence. Not when she had words to exchange with her guardian! In a hurry, fearing Jane's imminent arrival, she pulled the door to carelessly and rounded on Francis before realizing it hadn't latched.

"How long will he stay? Why has he come?"

Francis finished taking snuff. He sneezed before putting away the small cloisonné box Jane had given him the preceding Christmas. Then after he'd patted his nose with a pristine white handkerchief, he finally looked at her. "Why do you think I've any answers?" he asked in a guarded tone.

"Because it has occurred to me that you must have met him in London. You must have talked."

The lids of his eyes drooped, a clue to those who knew Francis that he might be hiding something. "I saw Chris in London. Briefly. He was surrounded by friends and acquaintances and we were unable to discuss much of anything. He said we'd talk when he came here"

"He and a house-party. Are there more nasty surprises in store?"

"Nasty, Stephanie?"

"Damn you, Francis Warrington!" Stephanie stamped her foot. Her foot stung through the thin sole of her evening slipper and the thick carpeting made it a silent gesture. Disgusted with herself for indulging in a useless and strictly feminine form of anger, she demanded, "Tell me at once why that man has come home!"

"But Stephanie, I've told you I don't know why *that man*, who is your *father* you'll recall, has come home."

"Recall? But," she said with a dangerously silky note in her voice, "just how could I recall any such thing when I've never known the bastard. You, Francis. *You* are my father."

Outside the door which was slightly ajar, the eighth Marquess of Lemiston paused as he heard: ". . . any such thing when I've never known the bastard. You, Francis. You are my father." His hand jerked back from the door he'd been about to push open. A sharp thrust of angry jealousy burned into his guts and he glared at the tableau framed by the narrow opening. Holding up an open palm, he silently warned Anthony to be still. Even as he did so, common sense returned. His daughter's words had not meant his first wife had been unfaithful, but merely that his friend, Francis, had acted the paternal role to this odd creature.

But her attitude! Why didn't Francis scold the chit for such blatant impertinence? How dare she speak so disrespectfully of him? Realizing his temper was hanging by a thread his lordship carefully, quietly, backed away from the door where he'd once again inadvertently heard his daughter's opinion of him. Losing one's temper was never profitable and, at this stage of his plans, it very well might prove disastrous.

But, for another instant, Christopher Morris stared at the tense figure of the young woman with her magnificent head of hair. He turned his gaze toward the relaxed, cynical expression on Francis's sharp profile and wondered at the odd relationship he sensed between the two. Finally, he moved down the hall, Ryder on his heels.

"The woman has sense, has she not?" suggested Ryder softly.

"I heard nothing but nonsense!"

"She doesn't pretend that something which is *not* exists merely because society says it should."

"She is my daughter," growled Lemiston, his brows pulled into a scowl which would have put off all of his acquaintances and most of his friends.

Anthony, however, was not one of them. "There is more to being a parent then planting one's seed, Chris," he chided, his mouth curled into a wry twist. "As you above all should know! You are far more a father to me than my own ever was or wanted to be. As things have turned out, I'll never have an opportunity to achieve a good relationship with him. I'll regret forever that he and I had no time to come to an understanding of each other. *You* do."

"Have a chance to understand her? I think I understand the vixen very well!"

"How droll. You, the old fox, calling *her* a vixen! But Chris, think. You've a chance to make amends, as I did not."

"Amends! To that . . . that . . . ?" Lemiston growled low in his throat. "Nonsense! It is she who owes me a duty." He recalled the girl's long lean flanks so crudely revealed in the britches she wore with nary a hint of outraged modesty. "Francis has much for which he must answer in the way he reared her. However that may be, she is what she is and I'll deal with it. She'll not enjoy it, but she'll learn her place."

"Will she?"

"What do you mean?"

"In my opinion she knows it." When his friend's brow quirked, he added, "Her place is mistress of Lemiston Priory, Chris, responsible for its prosperity and protective of its people."

"More nonsense. She's a mere female." But Lemiston felt a moment's confusion as he remembered with what self-possession Lady Stephanie had stood up to Wilkins and argued him down. She'd overcome his objections and yet made it possible for the man to retain his pride . . . if not exactly happy with the result, he'd not been demeaned, either.

"I suppose Meg is a mere female," Anthony said suggestively.

Lemiston thankfully dismissed the unwanted softening toward his daughter his sense of justice had prodded into being. His mood shifted quickly with Anthony's sly mention of his second wife. "Meg is herself alone. Don't tell me there can be another like her." The Lemiston brows drew into a vee and his chin rose a trifle as he added, *"Or* that there *should* be!"

"If you mean another with equal independence and equal determination, I've a notion you'll find her standing in that room." Anthony gestured. "And this one has far more sense, as well. Your wife, if you recall, has been known to jump with both feet into situations she can't or won't understand and before she takes the time to learn how to deal with them."

Lemiston's jaw firmed, a muscle jumping there. "Meg was forced to become hard and to take chances in order to survive. You know that. But for all that she's far too impulsive and had too few opportunities in life, Meg has a good heart. She's worth the effort I'm making with her. No woman reared in the ton would encounter the conditions which forced such unnatural growth on my wife."

"But what if a woman *wished* to be independent, to do her own thinking, to run her own life?"

Lemiston blinked. "Why would any woman be so stupid as to want any such thing?"

Anthony shrugged. "Perhaps for the same reason an intelligent man wants it."

For a moment Lemiston stared at Anthony. His eyes lost focus for an instant and then he shook his head. "You've bats in your belfry, my boy." After another moment a wry grin twisted his lordship's features into an unpleasantly sly grimace. "But if by chance you *haven't*, then all the worse it'll be for the chit!"

Lemiston, his temper restored at the memory of his plans for his daughters' futures, turned back down the hall, opened the door, and stalked into the sitting room, wondering for an instant where the second chit might be and then put the question aside. One daughter, especially this particular daughter, was enough to face in the beginning.

Anthony stared after him, just the tip of a corkscrew of worry twisting into him, a twin to the notion which had worried him earlier in the hall upstairs and still earlier when he'd learned Chris planned to marry his daughter off.

"He *wouldn't*. Not to one of his own blood . . ."

But his lordship had mentioned inviting Camberstone, who was a fool, and Baron Stread, who rumor had it was an ugly customer, to his house-party. And Westerwood who would accept any challenge no matter how wild. . . . What other bachelors had Chris invited? A chill raced up Anthony's spine.

"Or would he . . . ?"

Anthony, wary but not certain exactly what it was he feared, joined the others. Given the treacle-thick tensions swarming within the sitting room in the short time before dinner was announced, the meal went off far better than he'd thought possible.

Also better than Lady Stephanie had believed likely!

Jane, arriving soon after the marquess and earl, had instantly fallen into the role of hostess which Stephanie should, but would not adopt, inviting everyone to the dining room. The stories Jane and Francis drew from the two travelers were more interesting than Stephanie expected and far more entertaining. Especially when, as the wine flowed freely, the gray-haired marquess and the sun-bronzed earl fell into a friendly rivalry as to which could be the most outrageous. Some of their tales were full of humor, some of pathos, but all were told with a certain verve which kept one enthralled.

Whether one wished it or not.

To say nothing of a trifle jealous . . .

Stephanie thought she'd hidden her fascination pretty well. She'd kept her eyes on her plate throughout most of the meal and wished she'd not looked up even when she had, because when she did, it was to discover Anthony's warm approving gaze upon her. She couldn't interpret his expression, wondering whether he was remembering their encounter as she did or if he simply liked seeing her in a gown instead of the trousers about which he taunted her. In either case, the knowledge that he watched her did nothing for her equilibrium, to say nothing of her appetite!

She glanced at her father before looking back to her plate. He was gesturing with his knife, answering some question Francis asked about life among the American Indians. The answer was surprisingly complex. Stephanie had had no idea there were so many different nations of Indians. Or, for that matter, that such primitive peoples could understand the concept of "nation."

Perhaps, she decided as she listened, it wasn't that they were primitive, but that they were merely different, because it appeared each tribe had its own rigid code of manners, its own laws, its own way of life, and could feel insult when those codes and laws were broken.

As the stories continued Stephanie came to the decision her father knew a great deal more than was reasonable about all those different peoples. When she raised her face a second time it was to cast him a look of pure disbelief. His description of the ceremony surrounding his adoption into one tribe was utterly outrageous.

Once again only Huntersham noticed, but his probing gaze reminded her to withhold the outburst hovering on the end of her tongue. Which was probably just as well: Francis had once told her that her father was exceedingly stiff-rumped toward those who accused him of lying!

Since none of the three men was the sort who sat long over his port, the trio followed Jane and Stephanie to the sitting room very soon after the meal ended. Lord Lemiston took up a pose in front of the fireplace and Stephanie felt a trifle ill as she realized it was just the way she often stood of an evening as she conversed with Jane. Exactly the same stance.

Did she look so arrogant? Did she have that aura of lord-of-creation which, in Lord Lemiston, set up her back and made her wish to plant this man a good flush hit right square in the nose! If she appeared that way to Jane, how had her friend put up with her all these years?

Her attention was drawn back as soon as she heard the word party. "House-party?" she asked sharply. "Was it truly necessary to invite a house full of strangers to the Priory?"

"I've not been home for a long time, daughter," said her father smoothly. "It might, I'd think, occur to you that I wish to reacquaint myself with old friends."

"You include Camberstone under that heading?" asked Francis, a touch of humor in his voice.

Lemiston cast his daughter an enigmatic look. "I've invited a few acquaintances for Lady Stephanie's . . . sake."

"Baron Stread? Lord Westerwood" asked Anthony, an edge to his tone as he named others Lemiston had mentioned.

"And Lords Hamstead and Rotherwood . . . and Maximilian Lambert." His lordship added the last with something approaching smugness.

There was a moment's silence before, sharply, Francis said, "Chris, I'd like a word with you!"

"Of course, Francis," said Lemiston genially. "Any time you like. Excepting this evening, of course. Miss Felton, I understand I have you to thank for seeing my home has been kept in such exceptional order?"

Jane blushed rosily. "It isn't difficult. I only oversee the servants, my lord. As for the party, Lord Huntersham gave me a hint of what you'd be likely to require."

Stephanie stalked to the windows and pulled back the drapes which Abbot had carefully closed as the sun approached the west. She stared out into the dark garden.

Anthony moved near. "You aren't exactly sociable."

"Don't attempt to hint me into the way of things! I'll behave as I please!"

"Why should I not when I see you about to go off half-cocked and ready to make a fool of yourself? Hmm?"

Stephanie cast him a sideways look but couldn't tell if he was silently laughing *at* her or wished her to laugh *with* him.

He continued softly, "Should you not help your friend entertain your guests? Instead of revealing to the world that you're in a temper?"

"Jane knows me well, in all my moods. If she needs my help, she'll ask for it. And not set up my back when she does so." Stephanie gave her nemesis a scowling look which, it appeared, rolled off his back with no effect. *"She,* at least, knows *exactly* how to deal with me."

"Ah." This time a soft laugh actually escaped him. "I must ask her to give me lessons."

"And why should she?"

His brows arched. "So that I too will know how to deal with you . . . and your tantrums, of course!"

"You expect me to be in a temper with you? So often that you must learn to deal with it? But, Lord Huntersham," Stephanie suggested with false sweetness, "surely you'll not be here long enough for it to be worth your while to take lessons?"

"Will I not?" He pinched a minuscule thumb and finger-full of snuff, shaking off the excess. "I think," he said, "that I will."

She turned to face him fully. "Why would you wish to stay where you're not wanted?"

"I hear real curiosity in that, my sweet. Does it not occur to you that you might lose your prejudice and discover I *am* wanted?" He sniffed and sneezed lightly.

"I see no earthly reason why I might wish anything of the sort," insisted Stephanie, knowing she lied through her teeth. She was glad that, unlike Jane, who in similar circumstances would blush a painful red, her complexion remained unaffected. "I got along quite well before you arrived in England, Lord Huntersham, and I'll do so again once you've become bored with playing at being the new earl and take yourself off for more adventuring." She eyed him. "So, you see that I've no reason whatsoever to wish for your presence, do you not?"

"I can give you six good reasons you'll be glad of my help. At least for the near future," mused Anthony, tossing the snuff box and catching it, over and over.

"Six!" She reached out and took the box out of the air, tossing it onto a nearby table.

He ignored her performance while responding to her question. "My reasons were mentioned only minutes ago," he told her, his brow wrinkling into odd crinkly lines. When Stephanie merely looked at him, he added, "Camberstone, Rotherwood, Hamstead, Stread, Westerwood . . . and Lambert."

"Those men are 'reasons?' Aren't you simply another, then?" she asked, a carefully crafted expression of scorn accompanying her words.

"That, my dear innocent, is an insult. Never again suggest I'm anything like any one of them. I'm neither a gambler nor a rake, nor, for that matter, a fool. Neither am I a man of Lambert's stripe which is none of those, but something *worse*. And, my sweet, I resent any suggestion I am."

Stephanie debated the notion of giving him a critique of his character as it was bandied about the region. But, fair to a fault, she recalled his reputation was based in behavior of over a decade earlier and decided to give him the benefit of the doubt. He *might* have changed. For that matter, he might never have been so lost to shame as the gossips insisted!

"Even I've heard of Lambert's shame," she said, and shrewdly asked, "Will you say that you've never had anything to do with commerce?"

"I feel no shame whatsoever to have been involved in commerce, my lady. When it was forcibly brought to my attention that I was to leave home and hearth or suffer alternatives I'd find exceedingly unpleasant, it also occurred to me I had to make a way in the world, that I had to find a means to support myself. It is thanks to your father that I did very well indeed—but that doesn't put me in a class with Lambert! I've never shipped the sort of cargo in which he deals." Stephanie cocked her head. "I never trafficked in human souls, my sweet," he said softly, "and Max Lambert *does,* which, from what you hinted, I thought you knew."

"You know him?"

Anthony lifted aside the curtain and stared out the window much as Stephanie had a little earlier. "As you learned at table this evening," he said slowly, "I've traveled widely." A muscle jumped along Anthony's jaw. "On one occasion I was in the right Caribbean port at the wrong time. I watched a ship unload. His ship. You don't want to know more!" he added when he saw she was about to ask a question. "We've . . . met once or twice since. Just stay away from him. If you can. He's not, at any level, a decent man."

Stephanie, wondering why Huntersham hadn't asked why Lord Lemiston would invite such a man to his home, muttered, "I can take care of myself."

"I remember once when—"

At his tone Stephanie gave him a sharp look and noted his pensive expression.

"—assuming the gentleman had been another sort, you'd have been well and truly ravished, sweetings."

Despite herself, Stephanie felt a trifling of heat around her ears and hoped she didn't blush fully.

"Do not," he added, still pensive, his lids heavy over his eyes, "be so cocksure!"

"I remember the occasion, too." Stephanie was proud of how off-handedly she managed to say that. "I don't see how you can suggest you're not a rake."

"Because a rake would have finished what was begun whether the lady was so inclined or not. Do you wish," he added, idly flicking her cheek with one long finger, "it *had* been finished?"

This time Stephanie felt hot blood flood her cheeks and cursed softly that he'd managed to get through her barriers. "Of course not!"

"Ah. So speaks your *head,* but your skin reveals another answer, does it not?" Again he flicked her cheek with the same careless finger. "Your body clearly has another opinion. Now what, I wonder, should I conclude that lovely rosy color indicates concerning your *body's* wishes?"

"I don't suppose," she said after a moment in which she controlled herself, "it would occur to you I'm merely embarrassed by discussing something better left decently buried?"

"Embarrassed? Yeesss, perhaps." He grinned wolfishly. "But by *what?* The fact your curiosity was stronger than you admitted at the time? That you *do* wish you'd taken the opportunity to learn more? Perhaps it's *that* unwitting admission which embarrasses you rather than the topic itself?"

"You, Lord Huntersham, are no gentleman."

He nodded. "Excellent. You've no counter-argument, so you make a counter-accusation instead. Well done, my sweet."

"I've no notion what you mean."

"Have you not?" He tipped his head, studying her. "You lie, my beguiling Stephanie. I'm surprised and, I admit, a trifle disappointed. I'd not thought you the sort to make polite evasions!"

"Oh, dear," she said, pretending chagrin to cover an unexpected and unwanted sense of loss and pain. "How terrible that I, a stranger, should in any way disappoint you."

"As to that, we are not such strangers, are we?"

"Are we not? I doubt you've any real notion of me at all."

Not waiting for a response, Stephanie moved to stand beside Francis, tucking her arm through his. He gave her an absent smile and turned his attention back to Chris.

She pretended to pay attention, but her mind was occupied by Huntersham and her hope he *didn't* understand her . . . and her *fear* that he did. The blasted man was too perceptive. Worse, she'd found the banter between them exhilarating—an exhilaration she wished to experience again. And again.

On the other hand, she was certain that to allow Anthony Ryder close in any way would be exceedingly dangerous to her whole well-organized and satisfying life. Stephanie spent the rest of what seemed a very long evening evading any possibility of intimacy with Anthony—verbal or otherwise!

She went to bed exhausted by the effort. She slept late and made only a short day of it, checking that the things she'd recently ordered done had been completed to her satisfaction. She then spent many hours in one of her favorite spots along the coast, a private little nook where she could read or think or just dream. Today, dreams of what might be fought with fears of what would be and, when she finally returned home, it was late and she was so preoccupied she forgot to put on her hated skirts before going down to dinner.

She met her twin as he too approached the stairs to descend and discovered he too had forgotten she'd requested he wear evening gear to dinner. Stephanie, fiddling with the tie to the braid hanging over her shoulder, considered whether they should both return to their rooms to change, then, shrugging, decided to forget it. They continued on, side by side, arriving at the open double doors to the small salon, the room in which the family were to gather before dinner. There they stopped, chuckling at some joke, their laughing faces turned toward each other.

Across the room, before the fireplace, Lord Lemiston straightened. His soft swearing drew Anthony's attention. He followed Chris's starting gaze and, seeing the twins, grinned.

"Been drinking too much, have we?" he asked, chuckling.

"Twins."

"You knew."

"My God of course I knew! But I thought they were both girls. That other one really is male! Seeing them together you can tell."

"Ah. And now?" asked Anthony, softly.

Chris slowly pulled his gaze from the two framed by the door, his eyes moving more slowly than his turning head. "What do you mean, *and now?*"

"The business we did in London, Chris. It appears to me as if it should be reversed. Actually, I've already tried to tell you I wondered if perhaps we'd not made a mistake. I mean Lady Stephanie's love of—"

"Like hell you'll back out," interrupted his lordship softly, an almost vicious note to be heard.

"Chris, I've no particular desire to do any such thing, but obviously you've a son and heir. That changes everything, does it not?"

"Why? I've sons in Australia. If inheritance were an impediment I'd never have made the arrangement with you in the first place." He looked toward the approaching pair and glanced from one to the other. "So."

"May I present Theodore, Lord Riddle, the future Lord Lemiston," said Stephanie proudly.

"I'm very glad you did that," said her father, sneering.

"Did what?"

"Introduced your brother. How else would I have known which of you is the man?"

Theo's brows snapped together. "You will apologize, my lord father."

"I will?"

"I think you will." Theo's expression chilled to ice. "I cannot force you to do so, of course, but if you are truly a Lemiston, you've had bred into you a sense of fairness. You yourself will realize you have done my sister and your daughter a wrong and you will apologize."

"Anthony," said the elder Lemiston, taking snuff, "I cannot believe I bred two such fools. Surely my wife did me wrong!"

Three pair of eyes cast him narrow-eyed looks of disgust. Two spots of color tinged Lord Lemiston's cheeks. His head went up. "For that last comment, concerning my wife, I do apologize, but for none of the rest of it."

Theo nodded. "It's a beginning. Come Stephie, I believe I'll have a tray in the library after all. You'll join me, of course." Turning identical backs, both rigid with disdain, the twins left the salon.

"I'm thinking seriously of joining them," muttered Anthony, casting another look of disgust toward his friend.

Chris put a hand on Anthony's arm. He sighed. "I suppose the boy has something to say for himself in that he's obviously very protective of his sister. That I can like neither of them, the cause of my beloved's death, is surely something you'll understand . . . Anthony?"

Was there the faintest of pleas in that? Anthony wasn't certain. "I've never known you to hold a grudge, Chris. I can't believe you've unjustly nursed one against your truly delightful offspring and for so many years! None of us, after all, ask to be born!" He turned away as Jane entered. "Ah, Miss Felton. Now you've arrived we may, as soon as Abbot announces it, go in to dinner."

Jane blinked rapidly, looking around for the twins.

"Lady Stephanie and Lord Theodore," Anthony explained, "have decided to dine from trays tonight." Ignoring the fact Theo had been home some days, he added, "I presume they've a great deal to discuss since, obviously, they've not seen each other for some little time?"

Jane also ignored the date of Theo's return, gladly accepting the offered excuse. "He's not been home since Twelfth-night, so that would be it, I'm sure," she said. "They are very close, very dear to each other."

Abbot, followed by Sir Francis, appeared in the doorway just then. Jane nodded and the butler disappeared.

"Gentlemen?" she asked brightly, "Shall we adjourn to the dining room?"

Seven

Late June, 1810

The newspaper, arriving two days late as usual, informed them the prince had left London for Brighton. The Season was over and the guests invited to the Priory could be expected at any time. In fact, they arrived gradually over the next several days, the Priory filling with those who had accepted the long absent Lord Lemiston's invitation to visit.

Stephanie refused to conform to society's expectations, which decreed she play hostess alongside her father's role as host. Instead, she rose still earlier than was normal for her, very often greeting the dawn. Dressed, as always, in trousers, vest, shirt, cravat, and coat she was gone before anyone else was up, sometimes even before an early rising servant.

She'd take a set of back stairs to the kitchens where she'd fix a slab of bread covered with melted cheese and eat it as she strolled to the stables. There Aladdin would be made ready for her by a sleepy-eyed groom and she'd set off on her usual rounds of the estate.

If those rounds took longer than usual, well, she'd no particular desire to return to the Priory, where she must don her skirts for Jane's sake, and join the ladies in the second smallest salon. Whenever she did so, much to her surprise, she discovered she didn't object to the women. In fact, she rather enjoyed their banter and gossip and speculation. Oh, not the personal *on dits* about people she'd never met and had no desire to meet, but the conversation of a political nature proved intriguing. There was a great deal of that sort of discussion actually. For instance, many conjectures about the king's worsening condition and the inevitability that, this time, the prince be made regent.

"And then," said Lady Scranton, casting a sly look at a friend, "you Tories will, at long last, find yourselves in the basket. *Quite* out in the cold!"

"I wonder . . ." mused Lady Wheatfield, the one who had been twitted. "I truly wonder if it *will* turn out as you Whigs hope, or if the prince's previous adherence to your politics hasn't been just one more bit of rebellion. I will lay you fifty guineas that, once he has the power to do something, he'll show good sense and return to the Tory fold!"

"Done! The easiest guineas I'll ever take because you speak nothing but the most blatant nonsense," insisted the first, but with a wary sharpness that made Stephanie wonder if the possibility she'd lose worried her.

As much as was possible, Stephanie had ignored the larger world beyond the Priory. What little she had learned of it dealt with the strictures placed on the life of a young lady, unwanted knowledge gleaned from lectures tendered by the disapproving matrons who lived round and about—and the lecture she'd received from Francis prior to their one London visit.

So, because she'd finally adopted a policy of deliberately avoiding her neighbors except for an occasional dance or dinner, she'd not bothered to become aware of things which might have interested her. Listening to her father's well-educated and politically active guests, she discovered how complicated the nation's situation was and the vast differences—to say nothing of the similarities—between Tory and Whig. She found herself fascinated but depressingly ignorant. The next time she saw Abbot, she asked that he bring her the newspaper each day.

"After your father has finished with it, the paper is placed in the library where it is available to all," said the butler, who had, as he'd felt only proper, shifted his loyalties to his lord-ship.

"But I do not wish to read it in the library, Abbot," said Lady Stephanie patiently. Silently, she once again cursed her sire's unwanted homecoming. "Not only would I not be wel-come there, since the library is tacitly a male province, but I do not wish," she cast a meaningful eye toward one of those impertinent gentlemen who was, at just that moment, descend-ing the stairs, "to find myself anyplace where *some* of our guests might find *me.*"

Abbot immediately understood and, briefly, his old protec-tiveness was aroused. "I see." Ostentatiously, the butler waited until the gentleman decided he'd not achieve a moment alone with the heiress. Lord Rotherwood, after a nod toward Stephanie, moved toward the billiards room. Only then did Abbot continue. "I'll have the newspaper placed in your room late each evening, my lady, once the gentlemen have adjourned to their games."

Lady Stephanie nodded.

Both of them knew the twins required less sleep than most people. Stephanie, however late she went to bed, would still have time to peruse the paper. "A maid can return it to you each morning." Abbot nodded in turn and proceeded on his way through the baize-covered door neatly hidden beneath the stairs at the back of the great hall.

So, except for the hated skirts, sitting with the women of an afternoon was less a burden than Stephanie had expected. Joining the whole company, men and women, of an evening was *not* so easy. She wished nothing more than to escape, but the one time she told Abbot she'd not come down for dinner and wished a tray in her room, her father had stormed in with-out knocking.

He towered over where she curled in her chair, a copy of *Tom Jones* open on her lap. "You will dress and join our guests at once."

"*Whose* guests?"

"*Our* guests. You are my daughter—"

"However much you'd like to deny it."

"—and you'll obey me." Lord Lemiston reached for her wrist, jerking her to her feet. For a moment he stared at her. "Disgusting," he said. "How dared Francis teach you to dress as a man!"

"I dress for comfort, my lord. Would *you* appreciate being forced to wear a woman's clothing? Stays, perhaps?"

For just an instant, Stephanie saw a flare in her father's eyes, a twinkle he could not hide. She did not make the mistake of relaxing and, as it faded, knew she was right not to do so.

"A woman should wear a woman's clothing." He looked down his nose at her. "Do you deny you are a woman?"

"I am *me,* a human being with likes and dislikes and dreams and, until you returned, a way of life which pleased me very much."

"You would deny you are a woman."

Stephanie sighed, rolling her eyes. "I do not know how to explain to someone so lacking in logic they cannot understand that being male or female has nothing to do with who one, *anyone,* is, or *what* one is. I've intelligence. I have used that intelligence. It has led to a way of life with which I am comfortable. Why should I change it?"

A cynical gleam lit Lemiston's eyes, making Stephanie more wary than ever. She didn't blink when he retorted, "Because, my child, that life is *over. That* is why you'll change it."

"Over? Because you've returned home? You will *stay* home, then, to manage the estate and make the decisions and see them carried through?" Stephanie felt a painful tightening in her chest. "Is that what you mean?"

Lemiston remembered, just in time, that he'd asked Anthony that, for so long as the house-party continued and his lordship was host, he not reveal that the estate had been sold. Besides, that was a tidbit of news that would wait until just the right moment. His odd daughter might need the shock of that information to push her into the marriage he'd planned for her . . .

"Never you mind what I mean. Just believe you cannot continue as you have done. Believe that that life is ended. In the immediate case, get yourself into a proper gown and do it in the next ten minutes." He eyed her again and an expression of exquisite pain crossed his face. "If you do *not,* I'll return and dress you myself." He stalked to the door and opened it. "I'll not be denied, young woman. You'll go to your destiny as you led your mother to hers."

A chill crawled up Stephanie's spine. "I see. My mother died giving birth to me and you blame me. I asked to be born, of course? I asked to be deprived of the parent most needed by a young child? And then, too, I asked to be deserted by my other parent who might have done something to compensate? You, my lord Lemiston, need your head examined. Perhaps I should call in the king's physicians," she finished in a voice uncolored by any of the anger she felt.

Lemiston's brows snapped into a scowl which should have had her quaking. "You are impertinent and haven't a notion of what you speak!"

Stephanie wasn't very good at quaking. "And if I do not? Then who? Who understands better than I what it is like facing the world with no parents at all?"

Lemiston's eyes narrowed. "You blame me for that, do you not?"

"I suppose I may be as irrational as my sire, may I not?"

Stephanie was almost certain her father was forced to stifle laughter. Since that seemed unlikely, perhaps it was a choked back roar of outrage! He closed the door with a slam before she could decide. She sighed, staring at the book which had lain on her lap when her father jerked her to her feet. With care she picked up Fielding's novel and did her best to return its spine to its normal state.

When she realized the back was broken, she laid it gently aside and moved to her armoire. Although she didn't understand her father in all respects, she'd no doubt at all he'd carry out his threat to dress her himself if she did not do so!

Once again she found herself seated between two of the men her father had invited for her . . . entertainment? Tonight it was Lord Camberstone, who she felt a trifle sorry for, lost as he was among the sharper minds of the other men, and Lambert, for whom she felt nothing but contempt. She ignored the latter, even when it was proper to turn to him, making a point of speaking of simple things with Camberstone, asking about his estate and his interests. The man's slower intelligence blossomed under her gentle attention, becoming positively lively.

When the long formal meal ended, everyone moved to the salon where the women drank their coffee or tea. Stephanie was caught by a change in procedure, resulting from her father's order that the men's port and brandy be served in the drawing room, rather than at table as was the usual custom. She was instantly cornered by Lambert.

"Think you'll avoid me by ignoring me, missy?"

"I'll do my best," she retorted.

"But you'll not succeed. You know why we're here."

"You are here because my father was foolish enough to invite you."

"Foolish? *You* are the fool, my dear, if you believe anything other than that we've been brought here to meet you. I've decided you'll do."

"I doubt it."

He laughed. It wasn't a comfortable sound. "Oh yes. I'll enjoy taming you."

"You'll never have the chance," she said and, from the corner of her eye became aware that not only was her brother approaching from one direction, but Francis was bearing down from another.

She waited until they took up positions to either side of

Lambert and then, when they'd drawn his attention, reached behind an ancient arras, which, appropriately she felt, depicted the Rape of the Sabines. The way some of the men looked at her, she sometimes feared one would pick her up and carry her off as the histories reported the Romans did the Sabine women! But now, silently, she opened the secret door hidden by the hanging and, when next Lambert was forced to look away, she slipped through it, shutting it tightly behind her.

Knowing that, once again, she'd escaped Lambert's attentions, to say nothing of the heavy-handed flirtation which seemed the only way most of the other bachelors knew to deal with her, she didn't bother to hurry through the long passages hidden between the walls.

Originally, in a different sort of era, those passages had been designed for the use of servants, allowing them to disappear at need so as to be invisible to the household. Since it was no longer required of servants to pretend they did not exist, the passages had fallen into disuse—until Stephanie discovered one by accident and she and Theo proceeded to map those running throughout the house.

Almost without thinking she traversed them to an exit into the armory. She shivered slightly in the chill from the old stone walls covered with weapons both ancient and modern. A pale, watery moonlight streamed through the high windows dimly lighting the long room with its bare floor, a part of the original priory ceded to the Morris family long ago. This evening, the cold light gave all it touched an eeriness Stephanie had never noticed.

Because she'd been in the dark passage, time wasn't required for Stephanie's eyes to adjust. She moved slowly, however, a deep sadness filling her, and almost absently chose a foil from the collection racked on one wall. Turning back into the room, she bent the blade gently between her fingers and wished for those pleasant days before her father's return.

If only she could go to Sir Francis, ask him to join her here, ask that he fight her so she could make use of the energy filling her, the tension. She needed, desperately, to rid herself of the tensions riding her and, from long experience, she knew that exercise would help . . .

Additional light spread across the floor from the opening door and she swung around, the foil held ready for defense. "You." She turned away.

"I thought I heard someone. I suppose I might have guessed it would be you," said Anthony, Lord Huntersham. He entered, closing the door behind him. Setting the lamp he carried on a convenient table, he strolled closer. "You know how to use that thing?"

"Should I not?"

"It's unusual, but I don't know of any law that says you shouldn't."

"For most, the fact I'm female is reason enough."

"Perhaps people should travel more widely," he mused. "Then they'd not try to put everyone into narrow little holes." He tested a blade, put it back, and chose a slightly longer one which he whipped through a series of practice moves. He turned and looked directly at Lady Stephanie. "In India I once spent a long week in a society in which women run everything. They do it well, too. My main difficulty was dealing with someone who continually assumed I couldn't possibly know my arse . . . well, that is, as a mere man, that I couldn't possibly have the authority to confirm a deal."

Curious, Stephanie leaned against a sideboard on which stood several decanters. "Were those women fighters, as well?" She poured two glasses of a clever little claret Abbot had discovered when last stocking the wine cellar. She hadn't asked him *where* he'd found it for fear that he'd be forced to admit he'd had dealings with smugglers. If he did, she didn't want to know.

She handed a glass to Anthony as he said, "Fighters? Warriors, you mean? I was never in a situation where I might discover the answer to that, but I'd not be surprised." He drank the wine, set down the glass, and replaced the foil, choosing still another. "Will you show me what you can do with that?" He pointed to her blade.

"No."

His teeth where white in a face bleached by moonlight. "Afraid?" he asked, teasing.

She cast a darkling look his way. "Of course not."

"Then why will you not give me a match?"

"Because," said Stephanie, with obviously false patience, "I am at far too much of a disadvantage dressed in skirts." She replaced her rapier in the rack and turned. "Why didn't you come to the salon with the others? Why are you wandering around by yourself?"

"Am I contravening some unwritten rule concerning guests?"

"It amuses you that you are adept at avoiding answers to my questions, does it not?"

"A trifle, perhaps. But you are quick to guess when I don't *wish* to answer you, and yes, I do find you amusing. Has Lambert caused you problems? I ask because I thought you might have irritated him by your behavior at dinner this evening."

"If I'd stayed in the drawing room I think it likely he'd have made a nuisance of himself. As it happens, thanks to Sir Francis and my brother, I escaped before I said something unforgivable." She bit her lip. Hesitantly, doubting she'd get a straight answer, she asked, "Lord Huntersham, do you know why my father invited such a . . . an odd group of men to his home?"

"I suppose he finds them amusing."

"You know it isn't that."

"What is wrong with my suggestion?"

"He spends his time with the married men, of course, and leaves the bachelors to entertain each other! His reason is something quite different . . ."

"So?"

Again Stephanie hesitated. She turned and faced Anthony squarely. "So I think he means to marry me off to one of them. I'd wondered, and then, something Lambert said to-night . . ."

Anthony's eyes narrowed to glittering slits. "And if that *is* his plan?"

"Then he's in for a disappointment."

It was Anthony's turn to hesitate. "Sweetings, he's your fa-ther . . ."

"But, to act the father in this respect, he's waited too long, has he not?"

"Too long?"

"Lord Huntersham," she explained with just a touch of as-perity, "I am of age! I'll not be forced into marriage to any-one."

"Ah!" Anthony relaxed. "Then you *are* aware he cannot force you?"

"I *can't* be forced?" Stephanie frowned. "You suggest I am *legally* free to decide myself?" He nodded. "*I* merely meant that I'd leave the Priory. I'd work as a scullery-maid rather than be wed to . . . to Lambert, for instance. My education has been thorough, my lord. I could find a way to support myself at need."

"It is far easier than leaving, sweeting. You need only say no and mean it and, if necessary, repeat it again and again until everyone gives up."

"That is truth?"

"For you and for any girl. The law is quite specific."

"It would be nice," she said, dryly acerbic, "if the law were explained to young ladies while they are still in the school room. Perhaps fewer would find themselves married to the wrong man!"

"Yes. My female offspring will be educated as to their rights as well as their duties. Assuming, of course, that I ever have daughters. But, since I have yet to marry and haven't any off-spring at all—"

His words answered one burning question Stephanie had felt she could not ask. She'd ached to know if he were wed.

"—that's not relevant."

"I wish my education had included a grounding in the law. I'm thinking I might like to study it more thoroughly . . ." She cast him a wry look. "I'm finding some bits quite fascinating."

"If any other woman said that I'd assume they were putting on airs to be interesting. With you . . . well, I suspect you not only mean it, but mean to do something about it."

Stephanie chuckled. "I've every intention of riding into Chichester one day soon—or more likely I'll go this winter once the farm work is finished. I'll have a long talk with a youngish solicitor I know. He'll bluster and hem and haw, but he'll eventually agree to set me a course of reading. As the doctor did some few years ago."

"The doctor . . ."

"Oh yes. It was absolutely essential I learn something of medicine and surgery. I should have done so sooner! You see, I came upon one of our elderly men who had chopped into his own foot when splitting wood. I didn't know what to do to help him. He was bleeding to death. I could slow it but nothing I did stopped it. Once the funeral was over I went to Doctor Pritter and demanded he teach me so that something similar could never again happen."

"And has it done you any good?"

"You are snide and, true, it *was* too late for Old Ebert, but I saved the life of a child who cut himself badly only a few months later. I'm glad I learned as much as I could of the doctor's art. Now I'll see what I can find out about the law. Perhaps it too will prove useful at some point . . ."

"I apologize if I sounded disparaging. I didn't mean to. I know only one other woman who could say all that so calmly, with neither a bragging tone nor one of self-satisfaction." Pursing his lips, Anthony thought of Chris's second wife, Meg, and of their rather odd marriage. "I wonder if you'd not like her . . ."

Steph didn't understand the tightening in her throat. She swallowed. "Someone you met on your travels."

"Yes. Someone I met while visiting in the Antipodes, so it's unlikely the two of you will ever have an opportunity to discover if you've a liking for each other—more's the pity. Stephanie," he said, suddenly changing the subject, "if Lambert ever comes upon you when you're alone, you are to remember he's not to be trusted. Don't even pretend to be polite to him. Do whatever you must, but do not let him touch you. Do you, by chance, understand what I mean?"

"He'd not stop short of raping me, you think?"

Anthony opened his mouth . . . closed it. After a moment in which he controlled emotions ranging from surprise to something approaching outrage, he said, "That's exactly what I meant, but you, my sweet, shouldn't speak so bluntly of such things." He frowned. "Actually, you shouldn't even know about them."

"Should I not? And if I *did* not, then why would I have reason to fear Lambert?"

"An excellent question. Perhaps, if you were anything like other women, you'd simply take my word for it that the creature's dangerous!"

"Lord Huntersham, I take no one's word for anything. I wish to *know*. To understand. I do not allow others to do my thinking for me."

"That's what I said. You are not like other women."

There was something of a bite in her voice when she retorted, "I assume that's a compliment and not an insult."

"I don't actually know that it was either. Merely a comment."

"I see."

They eyed each other. After a moment Anthony strolled closer to Stephanie. She moved a step away. He took another toward her. She straightened, stared into his eyes . . .

"As I said," he said softly, reaching for her, "not a bit like any other women . . ."

This time Stephanie knew what to expect, but, even knowing, she was chagrined to discover she couldn't control those incredible sensations aroused by his mouth against her skin. It took every ounce of will power she possessed to bring her hands to his chest, to flatten them there, to ignore the additional sensations flooding through her palms . . . and to push him away.

He didn't release her although he did stop those tormenting forays over her face and throat. He stared down at her. "You tremble."

"Yes."

"With fear?"

"Perhaps. In part. Also with anger that you think you've the right to do this to me. Also with . . . something else. Something I don't understand."

"That something else is called passion, my sweet innocent."

"You are laughing at me again."

"No. Not this time."

"Release me."

He did, holding his hands wide and backing away.

Stephanie couldn't decide just what she felt at that. But, given the opportunity, she took it. And she'd never admit to anyone but herself the reluctance she felt at removing herself from the room. Once again she chose the nearby secondary stairway and went immediately up to her room where, in something of a daze, she prepared for bed.

It didn't surprise her that sleep was a very long time coming that night. When it did, it was restless and unsatisfying.

Having slept badly, Lady Stephanie also slept late. For the first time since the men arrived at the Priory, she took breakfast with Lord Lemiston. She ignored him—except to snarl at his growled good morning.

Stephanie was not in the best of humors. Her mood improved a trifle, as she realized her sire felt little better than she did at what seemed, given her restless sleep, an abominable hour. Having eaten, she strolled into the front hall—just as a demanding ratatattat sounded on the age-darkened front door.

She slipped into the deep shadow where, each a trifle wider

than the last, the bottom three steps and the banister formed an arc behind which she could hide. She watched Abbot cross the polished floor, watched him open the door. She saw the butler's back stiffen . . . and then heard a voice she'd detested from the moment it had first fallen on her ears some months previously.

"I understand," said the high-pitched, rather prissy, voice, "that a man claiming to be my cousin is in residence."

"Your cousin . . . ?" Abbot wasn't about to admit anything. Not to someone his mistress had ordered was never again to be admitted to the Priory.

Lady Stephanie heard an exasperated noise from the unseen visitor. "My cousin, assuming it is he, has recently been awarded the title Huntersham. Since, at an early age, my cousin was disinherited by his father and thrown from his home, I feel there has been a mistake. Assuming, of course, that it *is* my cousin." James Cuthbert Oakfield went on reluctantly, "I suppose one must believe the family solicitor actually checked the man's credentials and proved it's Anthony, but I will assure myself of that fact before seeing my own solicitor. Surely it will be discovered that a man who was once disinherited cannot later inherit."

Abbot was, he decided, completely in agreement with Lady Stephanie. This man didn't have the least notion of his place in the world or he'd not have made such extensive and unnecessary explanations to a servant—even if it were no less a servant than the butler.

"Well?" demanded Oakfield.

Abbot neither moved nor made comment.

"Insolence! I wish discussion with this man . . ."

Abbot still didn't move.

"At once!"

Finally, after another moment in which he silently but eloquently gave Oakfield his opinion of the man's behavior, Abbot spoke in the coldest, most distant voice Stephanie had ever heard him use. "I will check whether Lord Huntersham is, at this unreasonable hour, available."

Abbot then attempted to close the double doors, which he'd opened only a trifle. They were shoved wide.

"How dare you leave me on the steps like . . . like . . . a *cit?*" raged Oakfield, stumbling through the opening he'd achieved. Spittle sprayed from his mouth. "How *dare* you?"

"I don't believe I'd have left Sir Woodhall outside," mused Abbot as he walked away.

The butler spoke just loudly enough it could be overheard but softly enough it could be ignored as though one had not been insulted. Which Oakfield was! Snobbish in the extreme, Oakfield was well aware that Sir Woodhall had received his knighthood only a few years previously, a reward from an appreciative Crown for the extra efforts to which he'd put his agents. His men not only did the work for which they'd been paid, but found and bought art which would appeal to the royal family. Art the mere *Mr.* Woodhall gifted to the nation. Oakfield continued to sputter and fume as he paced the broad hall.

Slightly bent over, Stephanie leaned against the smooth wood of the banister and covered her mouth with both hands, holding in giggles at Abbot's masterful way with an insult. Opening her eyes, she saw boots, straightened, looking up, met Anthony's glittering eyes, the sardonic twist to his mouth. The laughter boiled up still more and she doubled over, moving one hand to press against her stomach. Somehow she gained control—but not until Anthony had stepped closer, drawn her into his arms, and smothered her laughter-shaken body against his torso.

When she stopped shaking, he pushed her slightly away, pointed toward the entrance to a nearby corridor. She nodded.

Silently they moved away from Stephanie's hiding place, staying in the dark shadow thrown by the staircase for as long as possible. When it became necessary to cross a lighter patch, Anthony held her arm, his head twisted to where they could hear his cousin pacing. When Oakfield's footsteps moved away, they raced toward the arched entrance to the corridor that, after it turned a corner, led to an exit which was not too far from the stables.

They were mounted and nearly half a mile from the house when Stephanie realized two things. The first was that she'd accepted Anthony's leadership without one hint of denial or argument. The second was that the horses had been waiting for them, already tacked up!

She pulled up.

After a few paces so did Anthony. He turned and came back to face her. Her Aladdin didn't like Anthony's Sahib so near. He backed a few steps. At Anthony's urging the gelding followed. Stephanie, unwilling to play games, controlled her mount, forcing the stallion to stand.

"I must assume you wish to avoid your cousin?" she said sweetly.

"I never liked him. He was a bully and a sneak and he cheated."

"He still is and I'd guess still does."

"Abbot appeared to know him? Well?"

"He's visited. I've told Abbot he isn't welcome."

"Ahh."

"And just what does that mean?"

"Ah? It means I understand you. He was not merely doing the polite by paying a morning call, was he? He came a-courting, did he not?"

Stephanie grimaced. "He has it in his head that I'll jump at the opportunity to call myself Lady Huntersham. I told him I really couldn't say whether I would or wouldn't. I added that, since he wasn't and never would be Lord Huntersham, it was irrelevant."

"You believed I'd be found?"

Stephanie shrugged. "Whether you were or were not wasn't relevant. Someone would have put a billhook through him before long. They'd not have allowed that blackguard to ruin many more of the Hunter's Cove daughters."

"Not so much a blackguard as a snake in the grass." Anthony's lips compressed. He sighed. "I have to deal with him, of course. I'd thought to do so before I came here, but he wasn't at the Cove when I surveyed the problems there. Knowing he'd eventually return and discover what I'd done, I had his belongings sent in an inn in Chichester. Now he's here, but he'll find we've gone riding and, since I left the impression we'd be gone some hours, it's my hope he'll go away and come another day. I suspect," he mused, "I've a fight on my hands where dear cousin Cuthbert is concerned."

"I thought his name was James."

"James Cuthbert Oakfield. He very much disliked to be called Cuthbert, so of course I did. All the time."

Stephanie smiled. "I try very hard to dislike you and then you say something like that which is just the sort of thing I'd do. In fact, it is something I *will* do when next I have the opportunity."

"You will make him angry."

"Of course I'll make him angry."

"He's the sort who believes any insult must be avenged."

"Let him try!"

"You, my dear, are a hothead."

A wry grin tipped Stephanie's mouth and she pretended to simper. "Why, my lord Huntersham, you'll turn my head with all these compliments!"

He chuckled even as he reached out to settle his hand around the back of her neck. Gently, he pulled her toward him. Leaning, he placed a quick hot kiss on her mouth. Before it could boil higher they were forced apart, their horses playing up at the unbalanced weight on their backs.

Anthony and Stephanie stared at each other.

"Don't," said Stephanie, belatedly rubbing her mouth with the back of her glove, "ever do that again."

"Don't be a fool."

He sounded exasperated and Stephanie didn't understand why. "Fool?" she asked cautiously.

"I don't quite know what's between us, Stephie, my sweet, but there's something. Passion, of course, but that's common." Creases marred his brow with faint lines. "This other thing isn't. Common, I mean. I've every intention of discovering exactly what it is." When Stephanie glared, Anthony grinned. "With or without your cooperation, sweetings!"

He turned Sahib and rode on.

When Aladdin made to follow, Stephanie held him back. She'd no desire to return to the house, because there was no guarantee Jam . . . *Cuthbert* would be gone. But she would not docilely follow in the footsteps of a man who had as much as said he meant to seduce her! And, given the emotions she couldn't seem to control, didn't *want* to control, he just might be allowed to succeed! Or he might if she were to allow him close again. Which she should not. But those sensations . . .

The roiling, impatient desire to give in to Anthony's cajolery, to enjoy what she took from him, fought with the belief she'd lose her independence if she did anything so stupid. It was a conflict Stephanie had no notion how to resolve. Confused, Stephanie did what she always did in that state. She turned Aladdin's head toward a small dell not far from the coast in which a tiny cottage nestled. In it a bent old woman lived alone.

"Grannie Black?" Stephanie called as she ducked and entered the cottage.

"Here child. Why, whatever is the matter, my babe?"

Stephanie wasn't certain how to answer. Nor did she know how her old nurse had guessed she was troubled. Unwilling to discuss her difficulties, but wanting her old nanny's soothing touch, she did as she'd done when a child and on rare occasions since: She knelt before Grannie Black and lay her head in the woman's lap. A hand gnarled by rheumatics gently brushed back the wild bits of hair which, as usual, had escaped Stephanie's braid. For a very long moment Stephanie allowed herself to be warmed by the old woman's love and then she settled back on her heels.

"Are you all right, Grannie Black?"

"Dearie me, listen to her! Of course I'm all right. Why should I not? 'Tis you who are in the fidgets, little one."

Since Stephanie had grown taller than Grannie Black by her

twelfth birthday, this old joke made her chuckle. "You do not change. Thank goodness, you do not change!"

"And why should I, then?"

With seeming irrelevance, Stephanie responded, "His lordship's come home."

"Lord Lemiston has returned?" There was a sharpness to Grannie's tone and an alertness about the whole of her twisted body which drew Stephanie into herself, made her watch warily. "To *stay?*" demanded the old woman.

"I don't know. Somehow I haven't that impression, but . . . no, I just don't know."

The old woman relaxed a trifle. "I thought not . . ."

"Grannie?"

"Bring me the cards."

Stephanie, who didn't really believe and yet couldn't quite bring herself to scoff, retrieved the large hand-painted Deck of Marseilles from the corner cupboard. Carefully she unwrapped the silk scarf that protected it. The silk was old and its once brilliant colors were mostly faded to varying tones of muted gray. She set it aside and took the tarot to Grannie Black. Then she pulled a low table nearer.

"Shuffle them."

Stephanie obeyed. Without being asked she cut them twice and laid the three stacks side by side before the old woman. She watched as Grannie lay out the Past, the Present, and the Future, disliking, as she always did, the figures printed from hand-carved woodblocks which, to her mind, looked either haunted or sinister.

"You're the Fool, then," muttered Grannie as she lay it down.

Since Stephanie, from the moment Anthony arrived on the scene, had often felt the fool, she didn't argue.

"And here. The King of Swords Reversed. That's your father, Stephanie. That with the Nine of Wands and the Seven of Swords—" Grannie shook her head and then glanced up to meet Stephanie's gaze. "That's danger, love. You take care . . ."

As the reading continued Stephanie grew more and more

bemused. She exited the cottage silently mouthing, "The Lovers? For *me?*" She pushed from her mind the King of Cups card. She didn't believe in heroes. Whatever Grannie said, there was no hero who would love her and her alone. A possible love? *A lifetime of love?* No.

But danger. Now that sounded far more reasonable. But to whom did it refer? Herself or Theo? Grannie didn't know someone had tried, twice, to kill Theo. Besides, the old woman had seen nothing specific, only a rather diffuse aura of danger. Too, Grannie insisted she wasn't to trust her father to begin with. Maybe later, when he'd come to know her?

But she'd never trust that impossibly arrogant man! The whole of it was nonsense. *Surely* it was nonsense.

Unfortunately, however silly she professed Grannie's belief in the tarot, Stephanie knew she'd be unable to be anything but watchful, at least for the near future—careful not only for herself, but also for those she loved. Then, exasperated with herself for paying attention to the old woman's ramblings, Stephanie put her booted foot into the stirrup and stepped smoothly up into the saddle. She stared at the little cottage.

Grannie Black was getting old and very likely bored and perhaps needed something to add spice to her life. Surely that was all, and her dire predictions were nothing but a form of entertainment! On the other hand, the old woman's reading matched very closely with Stephanie's anxieties and hopes— except for that nonsense about a lifetime of love, of course.

An irrelevancy, in any case, when there was danger to be faced . . . But no. They were just cards. And Grannie Black had been wrong in the past. Sort of.

But always only *sort of!* Her readings might not come to mean exactly what one thought they should mean, but they nevertheless seemed to fit once one looked back over what happened. But *love?* Men loved another sort of woman altogether. Not overly tall women, with too much intelligence and a better understanding than many and more natural authority then most.

However *pretty* a man might think her, those other traits

made her utterly unacceptable. Some years previously that had been explained to her by one of Francis's nephews. The young man had been sent down from Oxford. He'd thought himself exceptionally knowing to have visited his uncle instead of going home where he'd have had to give his head for his father's washing. Actually he'd so continuously congratulated himself on his acuity he'd become a dead bore on the subject!

But he'd also been an inch or so taller than Stephanie and he'd been good-looking in a rather clean if faintly flamboyant way. Also, he'd found his uncle's ward an interesting oddity and, before she realized what was happening, Stephanie had shyly given her young heart to that silly boy.

Worse, she'd let him know it. It wasn't that he'd not been kind in his adolescent way. But, however kind, he'd been deadly clear concerning what it was a man wanted in a woman. What was wanted would require Stephanie to give up far too much of what she was and who she wanted to be.

So love was out. And Grannie Black was, for once, quite wrong.

A movement caught her eye and Stephanie looked between the trees. Francis and the man she was expected to call father, although she'd not yet done so, approached, crossing the water meadow at an angle.

She pulled up. She didn't think they'd seen her. She hoped not. She'd no desire to join them. Besides, if their expressions and the choppy movements of Francis's hand were an indication, they were arguing and she certainly didn't wish to get into the middle of that. As they approached she could finally distinguish their words . . .

"Besides that, I don't understand how you dared invite the bastard to stay," she heard Francis's frustrated tones.

"Oakfield?" asked Lemiston blandly. "Why should I not? Not only does he wish to speak with Anthony, but he promptly made me an offer for my daughter's hand. It seems perfectly reasonable that he stay where he can both meet with his cousin and woo my daughter."

"He's a known cheat. A fool as well. A *nasty* fool."

"Do you say so?"

Even Stephanie from where she was hidden in the woods could hear the hint of satisfaction in her father's tone. When the men had gone on too far to hear her, she moved out from the trees and turned the other way. She'd go to one of her favorite thinking spots along the water, a low grassy bank beside an inlet, surrounded by heavy growth except for a narrow view across the bay toward Thorney Island. She'd think things through and develop a plan for dealing with the situation so that she'd *not* become the butt of what she'd begun to believe was her father's decidedly skewed sense of humor! And most of all, she'd avoid allowing him revenge, which he obviously meant to gain while amusing himself at her expense!

Stephanie turned into a narrow, nearly overgrown path and took care to avoid the low-growing branches she allowed no one to trim. The difficult passage kept most people from using the path leading to one of her secret places. As the morning progressed, her only regret was that she'd not thought to bring a luncheon! From the lack of progress she made, she feared it might be some considerable time before she came up with the plan—other than simply saying no, which seemed a rather spineless thing to do, and, besides, it would not teach her father the lesson he deserved!

Stephanie scowled. She was *not* one who liked missing her food. But since she wouldn't admit she might *not* arrive at a plan, she stayed on, hungry, going over and over the same ground, trying vainly to discover a solution which would not only save her groats but leave the dictatorial Lord Lemiston gasping!

Eight

The next morning, in the dew-wet dawn, Stephanie strode briskly toward the stables. She still hadn't a notion how to deal with her father's plans. She was still fuming when Theo caught up, striding along in the lazy-looking amble which covered a surprising amount of ground in an even more surprisingly little space of time.

"Wait up Steph. Hot at hand isn't half of it when you're in one of your moods." He cast her a sideways glance. "Want to talk about it?" he asked softly.

"I thought we agreed you were not to go out alone?"

"I'm not alone," objected Theo. "I'm with you." His eyes narrowed. "Tell me?"

Stephanie told. ". . . So you see, I think he means to marry me off to one of those . . . those . . ."

"Shagbags? Ruffians?" offered Theo, his eyes sparkling with suppressed humor.

"Nothing half so polite! Especially that Lambert. I can't think what to do, Theo. Not that I can be *forced* to wed where I do not will it, but simply avoiding the blackguards is wearing me out!" She turned at his chuckle, hands on hip. "Theo, it's not funny!"

Theo sobered. "No, I don't suppose it is. There's a solution."

"You've thought of something so quickly? I've racked my brains for hours and couldn't come up with so much as a single idea. Tell me."

He shrugged. "It's perfectly simple, Steph. Pack a few things

and I'll take you away. We'll go . . ." Theo cogitated for a
moment, eyeing his notoriously home-loving sister. "Where
would you like to go, Steph?"

Stephanie frowned, shaking her head. "The oats—"

Theo put the back of his hand dramatically to his forehead.
"The oats!" he intoned and then, straightening, he scowled at
his sister. "I dare you to *dream* a little, Steph! Think, dear
girl, of all the wonderful possibilities. Italy. Greece. Or farther
east. The Ottoman empire, perhaps? Turkey, I mean. Dream,
Steph! Persia, maybe, or even so far as Madras . . . or Cal-
cutta." He rubbed his chin when she only shook her head. "On
the other hand, we could go west. The Canadas, perhaps, or
the West Indies . . ." He threw out his hands. "Anywhere,
Steph. Anywhere in the wide wide world."

She sighed. "I guess I don't know *how* to dream, Theo. I
don't *want* to go. Not anywhere at all." But, as she spoke, she
recalled the twinge of envy she'd felt that first evening when
Anthony and her father told stories of their adventures. Had
she dreamed then? Could she dream . . . she sighed again.
Even if she could, she couldn't bring herself to leave.

Not just now anyway. Not when the oats should soon be
cut . . .

"Besides," her jaw firmed and she raised her chin. "I'll be
damned if I'll run away! Is that the way of a Morris? No,"
she answered herself. "It is not."

"Oh?" drawled her twin, his eyes again sparkling. "What
about me? Isn't it said I've run from my responsibilities here
at home? And how do you describe what our esteemed father
did when he was hit by something *he* couldn't handle? It seems
to me running is *exactly* the Morris way!"

The twins cast a sideways look at one another and laughter
bubbled up. In perfect charity, arms around each other's shoulders, they reached the stables and were soon mounted.
Stephanie turned Aladdin's head toward the river where she'd
an errand and returned to their conversation as if it had never
been interrupted.

"Maybe it was our sire's way, but you haven't run *from* so much as run *to*. Besides, however apt your logic, Theo, I won't run. And, on top of that, there truly is no place in the world I want to go. I love the Priory, every inch of it. I've never understood why you do not." The look she turned toward him this time was puzzled. "After all, it will all be yours one day."

Theo's brows snapped into a vee. *"Maybe* it will."

"What do you mean?"

Theo's frown didn't lighten.

Stephanie pulled Aladdin up. "Theo, what are you thinking! *Of course* you'll inherit. Think!" she added, trying to lighten the conversation, "I'll have to call you Lemiston!"

"Oh well, the *title*. Of course, there's no way he can take that from me, although," he flashed a quick grin toward his sister, "I wouldn't lose any sleep if he did." Since her brother hadn't stopped Stephanie clicked her tongue and Aladdin moved forward. "Sometimes," he cast his twin a rueful look, "I rather wish he could! But you were speaking of the property rather than the title, were you not?" Theo's sorrel trotted on half a dozen paces. "I don't like to worry you, Steph, but he *could* do something about that."

She cast a sharp glance his way, frowning.

"He could sell that tomorrow," he said gently, "and, from hints he's deliberately let drop, I rather suspect it may be in his mind!"

"Sell the Priory?"

Again Stephanie pulled Aladdin to a stop, She stared at her brother's back. Sell the Priory? Surely not. Could any man be so evil? The very notion shocked her to her toes. Aladdin, catching her nervousness showed his displeasure and she had to put aside her concern to deal with his antics.

Theo, realizing his twin was no longer beside him, twisted around to look at her. He pulled up. "When you are done playing with Aladdin, will you be coming?"

She brought the stallion under control. "Theo," she called, her voice urgent, "you *were* jesting with me, were you not?"

The plaintive tone broke through the scholar's preoccupation with his own concerns and Theo remembered exactly what it would mean to Stephanie if their land were sold, if she were forced to remove from it. He touched his gelding with the reins, turning him, and walked back to join her. "Stephanie—"

"He has told me my life must change, that the life I've lived is over, but I thought it a reference to his intention to marry me off. Sell Priory land? Theo, he *couldn't*."

He stared at her, compassion in his eyes.

"Tell me he couldn't?"

"You know better."

"Surely, the entail—"

"Since I've come of age and we could have instated it, he hasn't been here." Theo spoke gently but firmly. *"There is no entail,* Steph."

Stephanie's pale skin whitened still more. "He could then. Oh God!"

"It means so much as that to you?"

"More than you'll ever know, Theo. More than you could possibly understand."

"Poor love."

"I might as well marry one of those idiots if he means to sell our land!" she said with intense bitterness.

"Don't make bad worse," said Theo with out-of-character sharpness.

Steph smiled. It was a weak smile, but a smile nevertheless. "I'm not quite such a fool! But, what *will* I do?" The smile faded, a rueful look taking its place. "Do you suppose I could hire myself out as a land agent?"

"You'd be good at it, but I've never heard of a female land agent and I'm not certain you could convince anyone you were that able, convince them to give you a fair trial . . ."

"Not as a woman, I couldn't." Her twisted half-smile was almost normal when she added, "I'd have to turn myself into a man altogether, would I not? Put away my skirts for good!"

Stephanie forced herself to set aside her agitation, knowing her brother would never truly understand how deeply the notion of losing the Priory hurt. Besides, if it happened, it would have to be faced, and her half-joking suggestion she turn herself into a man was as good as any.

"Let's see," she continued, a whimsical note in her voice. "What name shall I take? You are Theo . . . Perhaps I'll be . . . Thomas? Or no. Stephen! That way I'm less likely to forget it's me when someone speaks to me. Stephen Morris . . ."

"You're air dreaming, my girl."

She sighed. "Of course I am, because if I *don't* play the fool I'll cry, and I never cry."

"We'll come around."

She gave him a brilliant smile he knew was as false as the words which followed: "Of course we will, Theo . . ."

He leaned toward her, intending to give her a hug, just as a shot startled their horses. Theo's hat sailed from his head. Steph instantly had a pistol in her hand and kicked Aladdin into action, racing toward where she thought the shot had come from. But distant sounds of pounding hooves told her she was too late and that she'd never catch sight of the man shooting at her brother. She returned to Theo.

He glowered up at her from the ground where he stood, the hat in his hand. "Blast and bedamned to it, Steph! How am I to explain this to Abbot?"

He pointed to a hole similar to the one in his own hat. She dismounted and took it from him.

Theo's expression didn't lighten. "It's his Sunday beaver! He'll have my guts for garters!"

Relief at Theo's safety combined with one look at his outraged expression and Steph's overextended emotions broke. She giggled. Catching her brother's still more outraged expression, she explained, "Poor Abbot. He'll be mortified, going to church this Sunday with a great big hole in his hat."

It occurred to Theo that he'd once again escaped severe injury or death. Relief hit him and he too chuckled. Suddenly they fell into each other's arms, laughter welling up and tears running down their faces.

"What's so funny?"

The twins, arms around each other's shoulders, turned with quite differing expressions: Theo smiled at Anthony; Stephanie glared.

Anthony looked from one to the other. "If it weren't for your opposing aspects, I might have difficulty telling you apart. Good morning, Lady Stephanie," he said, smiling down at her frowning face.

"Where did you come from? Why are you here?" she asked. She glanced around suspiciously.

"I'm looking for you, of course, and I came from the stables where a sleepy groom pointed out the direction."

Stephanie's lips compressed, but Anthony got no other further response from her.

"I heard a shot a bit ago," he said after a moment. When there was still no response, he added, "Were you indulging a bit of practice with one of those pistols you carry?"

"It wasn't us," explained Theo. "Someone was using *me* for a bit of early morning target practice."

"You were laughing. You find it humorous someone shot at you?" Anthony frowned. "You *do* mean someone actually *shot* at you?"

"Someone shot at me." Theo offered up the hat, turning a disgusted look on his sister as he did so. "Why'd you do that?"

Stephanie had pinched him. Failing to stop the admission, she grimaced, but shrugged in defeat and turned aside, pretending to check Aladdin's girth.

After a moment Theo too shrugged, turning back to Anthony. "It's become a very bad habit with someone," he said, "and I'm becoming quite bored by it." Theo looked up at the only unmarried man among those now residing at the Priory that he'd decided he liked. "You see, I borrowed Abbot's hat because I've not yet replaced my own. Now I'll not only have to buy *me* a new one, but one for him as well. And, needing to buy him one, I can no longer put it off. Say, there's a notion. Steph, why don't we ride on into Chichester and I'll take care of that this morning."

Stephanie had watched Anthony as Theo revealed the morning's contretemps. His changing expressions went far toward inducing a belief that he knew nothing of the attacks on her twin. Besides, he'd come from the wrong direction, which was even stronger proof he'd not fired that shot. Still, who else could she blame?

When Anthony finally turned his expressive face her way, one brow quirked interrogatively, she said, "This isn't the first attempt, you see. I've been wondering just how *deeply* our father hates us . . ."

Anthony stiffened. Very gradually he relaxed. "If your father had fired that shot we'd be preparing for a funeral."

"That's what I suspected from something you once said, to say nothing of the stories Francis used to tell. But a man might hire a rather more bumbling sort, might he not?" she asked sweetly.

A quick sardonic grin crossed Anthony's face. "Me for instance?" She shrugged. "My sweet," he said softly, "I'm as good a shot as your father any day!"

"Then, assuming that's not mouthy cock-o'-the-walk hot air," she deliberately used the words he'd once used, "I suppose I must absolve you of attempting to kill my brother?"

"That rankled, did it?" asked Anthony, grinning at the memory of their first meeting and his snide words before she'd aimed at his whip and, much to his surprise, severed the end of it.

Theo, however, expressed his outrage at his twin's insults to a guest in no uncertain terms. He ended his diatribe by saying, "Stephanie Morris, you can't possibly have thought Lord Huntersham responsible!"

"Why not? You'd absolve him merely because he's an interesting conversationalist. Because he's willing to talk moral philosophy and metaphysics and can construe a Latin phrase or two. Because he takes you seriously and doesn't brush your interests off as of no account and doesn't laugh at you when you refuse to join our father's guests at the tables of an evening because it's not your way to gamble. Come, Theo! You're not so illogical as to think all that precludes the possibility he might also be a murderer. You *cannot* have concluded anything so irrational, for the simple reason you had the same tutor I had, and he didn't allow such muddled thinking!"

"It is none of that which makes it impossible, Steph. It is the fact he's honorable and trustworthy."

"What makes you think so?"

"A story or two our father has told," Theo frowned at his sister's sardonic snort, "which had nothing to do with our father, but with Lord Huntersham's dealings with others." Steph's lips formed a moue and then relaxed. "Besides," concluded Theo, "he rode up to us from quite the wrong direction. It couldn't have been him. You are wrong to suspect he might wish me ill."

"We'll see." But she'd already accepted that Anthony was no danger to her brother.

"If it is not me and is not your father," Anthony smiled at Stephanie's raised brows which indicated she'd not totally absolved her sire. "Then who should we suspect?"

Theo shrugged.

Stephanie sent a worried look toward Theo. "I've asked my twin that question. He insists he's stepped on no one's toes, that it's impossible anyone should wish him ill. The fact it is happening, that someone is *still* trying to kill him, indicates he's wrong. There *has* to be someone. Theo, *think.*"

"I have thought," he said reverting to his usual drawl. "I tell you, Steph, I've no enemies."

"You must."

"I don't."

"Must!"

"Er, *children,*" interrupted Anthony, rolling his eyes.

Stephanie glared at him but Theo grinned.

When he had their attention, Anthony added, "Do you think we might indulge in a trifle of rational thought rather than the sort of bickering which gets one nowhere?"

Theo shrugged. "The trouble with that, Huntersham, is that rational thought has gotten me nowhere. That is, it hasn't if you are certain our sire isn't the villain. We did, however innocently, harm him. That the loss of our mother harmed us as well cannot alleviate the depth of pain he felt to have left England and never return."

"How," asked Stephanie, "can you be so fair-minded?"

"Perhaps I paid more attention than you to that tutor we shared?" teased Theo.

Stephanie grinned. "No. It isn't that. It's that I have more temper than you. How unfair."

"What's unfair, my sweet?"

Theo cast a quick glance at his sister, wondering why she ignored it whenever Huntersham addressed her in such totally improper form.

"Unfair that he needn't deal with his emotions when trying to think through a problem!"

"Ah. I see."

She ignored that as well, mounting up. "Well?" she asked. "Do the two of you mean to stand here all day or shall we go?" Anthony turned his mount to follow her. Theo, also mounting, following after them both. "Besides," she continued, "I've a strong suspicion the reason Lemiston didn't return to us sooner had less to do with the loss of his wife than that he was enjoying himself far too well."

Anthony's brows rose. "Now that's an exceedingly astute comment, sweetings. Did you think it up all on your own?"

She didn't rise to his teasing, but pulled up, turning toward her twin. "Are you riding into Chichester? Because, if so, this is as far as I go."

"Will you not come with me?" Theo coaxed.

Stephanie shook her head. "I'd like to, Theo, but I no longer go into town dressed in this fashion. It upsets Jane when she must deal with the neighbor's complaints about my hoydenish behavior, insisting I'm setting their daughters a bad example. Such a bore . . ."

"We could," said her brother tentatively, "return to the house where you could change into a habit and *then* we'd go."

Stephanie cast a glance toward the sky. She shook her head more violently. "Far too late. It would become a production. We'd have to ask if any of the guests wished to go. Then we'd have to wait while the female guests changed into carriage dresses or what have you. And we'd be required to harness up carriages. Besides, I might run into one or another of the guests I prefer to avoid and be forced to do the pretty—or slap a face or two. Depending."

"Depending?" asked Anthony, his eyes narrowing.

"On which sort of guest I run into. One like poor foolish Camberstone and Lord Westerwood, who may be under the hatches but is still honorable, or one of the others, those I call my father's means-to-revenge."

"I really must have a word with him about that," said Anthony.

"Don't bother. I doubt it would do any good and might upset the friendship between the two of you if he took umbrage. I'd not want that, since for reasons beyond my comprehension, the relationship means something to you. But perhaps *you* would accompany Theo? Into Chichester?" she finished a trifle hesitantly, not liking to ask a favor of a man of whom she felt so wary.

"I had thought to go riding with you, Stephanie."

She met his level gaze, hers equally true. "I'd rather you went with Theo."

After a moment, he nodded. "I see."

"I suspect you do," she responded tartly, suspecting he saw far more than the partial truth that she didn't want Theo riding alone.

Huntersham was too intelligent not to recognize the additional fact that she didn't dare ride with him, chance them finding themselves so alone he again put her into making the choice between kissing him or fighting him . . . not that that seemed to be the real choice. She wasn't fighting him, but herself!

"Go along with you, the two of you." She shifted her gaze to include her twin who was looking a trifle bemused. "Among other things, I must look in on Mrs. Tipper, which you would not like. She's nearing her time and I must check that all is well and learn if I should send someone to take on her work for a few days."

"Mrs. Tipper? One of your dependents?" asked his lordship.

"One of our tenants, Lord Huntersham. We've five good-sized farms as well as the village and home-farm." No one could miss the pride in her as she spoke of the Priory. "The Wilkins, *one* of whom you've met—"

One of her brows arched as she threw him a quizzing look; he grinned at her reference to their introduction which was due to his fleeting interest in the youngest Wilkins girl.

"—have the largest leasehold and operate the home-farm as well. They've been tenants here longer than Morrises have held the land, which is a very long time indeed. The Tippers work the next largest farm. He's a good man, but he tends to worry himself sick every time his wife is brought to bed of another youngster. I do what I can to ease things."

"But Steph," objected Theo, "can't their oldest daughter take over the work? Surely she's come to an age to do it, has she not?"

"More than of age, Theo! You've forgotten she was wed last autumn to a clerk in Chichester. She's expecting a child soon herself."

Theo did a few calculations in his head. "I swear the last time I saw her, Bitty was still in short coats!"

"Yes, well, time must fly when your enjoying yourself up in Oxford, pillaging one or another library."

"Don't sneer at what you don't understand, Steph," said her

brother pacifically, his usual drawl in evidence. "I don't tease you about your odd interest in the land, do I?"

"Theo," said Steph, her cheeks heating, "I'm sorry."

He grinned. "Good."

She grinned back. "Beast!"

"But such a nice beast, am I not?" Theo turned to Anthony who appeared to be enjoying their banter. "My lord, *will* you ride with me into Chichester? My sister has asked a promise of me that I not go out alone, so if you will not, I must take Abbot's ruined chapeau back to him and endure the scolding he's certain to give me!"

"I've an errand in Chichester myself, although I'd not thought to do it this morning," said Anthony. He met and held Stephanie's gaze for a moment. "Take care of yourself, my dear," he said to her and, not waiting for a response, turned to trot off beside Theo toward Chichester.

Stephanie watched them until they were beyond sight around the edge of a good-sized spinney. Cheap coal had made such woodland less necessary, but it was still harvested each year, the wood distributed to the poor around and about. Stephanie thought about spending a few moments in the quiet of the spinney's glade, but the responsibility of overseeing the running of the Priory, the day's list of things to see to, to check on, to order done . . . it all added up. Her time, since Francis had given her responsibility for everything, was no longer her own. She'd best get on with it.

When Stephanie arrived at the Tipper farm, she discovered Mrs. Tipper was still getting around very well, her youngest hanging on her skirts. Steph, without thinking, picking up the creeping tot and sat down, cuddling the child in her lap. "Is everything going well?"

" 'Cepting Mr. Tipper, o' course," said the woman sardonically. She exchanged a glance with Stephanie and the two women smiled. "You'd think after my eleventh he'd not worry so, silly old man."

"Who you callin' an old man?" growled Mr. Tipper, arriving

just then and stomping onto the flagged kitchen floor with dirty boots.

Mrs. Tipper lifted her spoon from the thick soup she had been stirring and pointed it at her husband. "You get your backside out that door. I already swept the floor this morning and look at all that dirt!"

The farmer lifted his hands and stared at his feet. His ears grew red and, with exaggerated care, he stepped backwards until he disappeared out the door. When he returned, sans boots, his eyes widened at the sight of Stephanie carefully wielding a broom. "Here now, my lady, you can't do that!" He wrested the broom from Stephanie's hands.

Hands on hips, she tipped her head. "I thought I was doing rather well."

" 'Tain't that you *can't*, but that you *shouldn't*," he said primly. " 'Tisn't proper."

Stephanie grinned. "Then, perhaps you'll do it? So your wife needn't do over again something she's already done? In her condition?"

Tipper bit his lip and glanced toward where his wife's back was turned as, holding it with her apron, she pushed the hook holding her soup kettle back over the fire. "Hmm . . . well, why not?" he asked a trifle belligerently, and, raising a dust, swept the dirt he'd dropped from his boots out the door.

Stephanie glanced at his wife who rolled her eyes before pretending to sneeze. Stephanie grinned and also pretended to sneeze. And then the cat, stretched along the wide window sill, basking in the sun streaming in the small high window, really *did* sneeze. It took every ounce of self-control for Stephanie to refrain from bursting into loud guffaws which would not have been appreciated by the man she'd shamed into doing a bit of "woman's work."

Stephanie rode away from the Tippers' feeling the pleasure of the good fellowship they shared. Theo might feel differently about the Priory if he'd ever experienced it, she thought, but set the notion aside to think about her work.

Likely it would be another two weeks, at least, before Mrs. Tipper needed help, but she made a mental note to check again soon. She next rode around the grain fields which were beginning to turn and would soon require harvesting; she talked to Graham Wilkins, the younger, about the mangel-wurzels and was reassured that they were doing well. Eventually she dropped by her old nanny's cottage, but, despite the woman's earnest desire to read her fortune, her insistence she'd seen something worrisome in the cards, Stephanie refused to stay any longer than was needed to assure herself the old woman needed nothing.

Finally, free to indulge herself a trifle, she rode toward her favorite little inlet along the flat shoreline. Today she'd remembered to bring herself a nuncheon of bread and cheese along with a carefully wrapped tart. She'd also brought a pamphlet, a recent study on the use of burnt lime in the refreshment of tired land.

The cove, when the wind remained from landward, was well protected, would be sun filled, and, best of all, free of her father's guests! Stephanie had every intention of remaining there most of the afternoon!

She finished her study long before she started home and was on her way to the stables when she recalled that the first thing she'd meant to do that morning was check a tree reported badly undermined by spring run-off. Chagrin filled her that she'd not noticed it herself, but, now that she knew, she must make a decision. Either the bank of the drainage ditch must be strengthened just there or the tree must be cut since, if it fell the wrong way, it would take out the footbridge her grandfather had had built some yards upstream.

Reaching the stream, Stephanie dropped Aladdin's reins over his head and strolled toward the water. She touched the trunk of the ancient oak which had been old even when one of the old kings was purportedly climbing trees all over southern England in order to hide from his pursuers. So far as Stephanie knew, this one was *not* one of those celebrated trees, but even if it had no such historical value, she didn't like the notion of cutting short its life if it could be saved.

Carefully, her hand on the trunk, she stepped from one gnarled root to the next until she was on the river side of the tree. She bent down . . .

. . . and a huge patch of bark exploded from the tree just above her, right where she'd been standing an instant earlier. Stephanie dropped flat, lying across the roots. She crawled to the side, sliding through reeds lining the water, feeling the chill of muddy moisture seep through her clothes.

A second shot slapped into the water not far from her face, splashing her. Stephanie squirmed faster. She looked ahead. In moments she'd be where she'd have to show herself for an instant until she could get behind the tree and then she'd have the trunk between her and whoever was shooting at her.

The bastard's aim has improved a great deal, she thought sourly. A chill raced through her which had nothing to do with damp clothing. If she'd not stooped in just that instant to look at the bare roots extending into the stream, she'd be dead. Or, if not dead, then badly wounded.

But she couldn't dither another moment. She had to gain the shelter of the tree trunk. Gathering herself, Stephanie drove herself to an upright position and slid around the bole. Another shot and a gash appeared in the bark beside her, a flying shard catching her in the cheek, grazing it. She heard pounding hooves coming from her right and, for once, she didn't care which of the Priory guests might be approaching.

Someone. Anyone. Because a witness of any sort would chase away the villain firing at her. This time he'd come far too close. All three times, in fact. Stephanie, who had believed herself afraid of nothing, felt exceedingly odd sensations. They ranged from a rapidly beating heart and sweat running down the side of her face, to chill tremors shaking her whole body. She concluded she was very much afraid of the man stalking her. Even with a gun in her hand, her ears cocked for the slightest sound of footsteps on the other side of the river or, worse, on the footbridge, she knew she was afraid . . .

"Steph!"

"Theo?" Stephanie collapsed against the bole of the tree. Then it occurred to her that the assassin might have mistaken her male-clad body for her brother's. He must be warned. "Theo! Don't come any closer. Stay away!"

"You needn't worry," called Anthony. "Whoever it was has once again escaped us. I saw underbrush moving over there as he ran away, and listen . . ." Once again Stephanie heard the sound of a rapidly moving horse. The two men dismounted. Anthony strode nearer and pulled Stephanie away from the tree. He looked her over, his hand on one shoulder, and touched her cheek softly where blood oozed from a scrape. "He hit you?"

"Tree bark."

He looked to the side where the tree had been notched. "He's improving, isn't he?" was Anthony's sardonic comment.

"After missing so often, I'd guess he's finally realized his pistol shoots high," agreed Stephanie, trying very hard to repress the shudders which, despite telling herself there was no more danger, continued to run down her spine.

"Hey, Tony, look at this! Damn if he didn't take a huge bite out of this side of the tree, too, so maybe he only got lucky?"

Stephanie shivered violently in spite of herself. "I was standing there an instant before he fired. He'd have hit me, I think. Hurt or killed me . . ." Considering where the bark had burst away from the tree, Stephanie decided "dead" was the likelier choice. "I'd be dead," she said, the words no more than a thread of sound.

She could no longer pretend she wasn't affected. She gasped, putting her hands to her face, and bowing her back. She took in huge breaths, shuddering them out, and a moment later, found herself in Anthony's arms, found her head pressed to his shoulder. She clutched him, her fingers clawing into the material of his coat, grasping at his lapel.

"What are you doing with Steph?" asked Theo when he returned to that side of the tree. "Do you think it entirely proper for you to hug her like that?" he asked in exactly the same questioning tone.

"Your sister was standing where that chunk of bark is missing on the other side of the tree. Would it have hit her?"

Theo's eyes widened. "She was standing? Oh, he'd have hit her, then! *Right square in the heart.*"

"Then I think she has reason to feel a trifle unnerved. Get the horses, Theo. I think we'd better get her back to the house and maybe a drop of laudanum—"

"No!" Stephanie didn't relax her grip on Anthony's clothing, but she did push far enough away to look up at him. "I won't!"

"Then a hot bath, perhaps, and sweet tea," he said, soothingly. "Sweetings, it is no shame to feel fear when one has come that close to death. Relax and let it come. Once your mind and body accept the fact you haven't actually been hurt and that you are all right, then you'll be fine. Crying helps, my dear. Believe me. I know. Just relax and cry a bit . . ."

"I can't. I can't cry. I've never cried."

"That's true," interjected a worried Theo. "Even when she broke her arm she didn't cry." He bit his lip, eyeing his sister's trousers. "You know, I think that shot was meant for me. I think whoever fired didn't know it was Steph."

"I agree," said Anthony, his hand firm around Steph's head, still holding her close.

"Then I'd better go away. I won't have Steph in danger just because some idiot wants me dead."

"No," muttered Stephanie into Anthony's cravat.

"No? But Steph, you'd do the same if it were different. You wouldn't allow *me* to be in danger."

"But," said Stephanie, turning her head so she could see her twin, "you wouldn't allow me to go, and I won't let you. We must find out who it is and why and stop it. Running away won't help."

"We can still discover who and why with me somewhere

else," said Theo stubbornly. "Now if I announce at dinner that—"

"Theo," interrupted Anthony, "do you think we could debate this another time. I want to get your sister back to the house. She's wet and chilled and needs to change."

Theo took another look at her muddy clothing and nodded. "You aren't exactly pristinely clean, now, yourself, Huntersham. I told you you shouldn't be holding her that way!" He whistled. Three horses lifted heads from the grass.

Anthony whistled. One horse trotted closer and the other two followed.

One of the two men watching from a hilltop viewpoint chuckled. They'd been headed toward the sound of shots, but stopped when Anthony and Theo arrived on the scene, and now the grayer of the two looked at the other. "You taught the twins that trick?"

"Of course. There was a period they wanted to know everything I could tell them about you. *About their father.*"

"Don't start, Francis. I can now think clearly enough to see where, from their point of view, I abandoned them, but it isn't relevant and I don't give a damn about that. Whatever they feel, it is no less true they caused my love's death. They caused pain you can't begin to understand . . ."

"If you'd not run away, the joy of watching them grow would have eased that pain, Chris."

A muscle jumped in Lemiston's jaw. "Perhaps it would. We'll never know, will we?"

"Just stop blaming them for your own idiocy!"

The muscle jumped again. "Don't push it, Francis. Instead, tell me who was shooting at her. Why would anyone wish to kill either of them? Even I," he finished bitterly, "don't particularly want them *dead*. That's far too easy."

"I haven't a notion. It depends very much on *why* the murderer was shooting at her. Did he, for instance, know it was a *her,* or did he think it was Theo standing there?"

"Theo?"

"One of those bastards you invited down to seduce your daughter," said Francis quite as bitterly as Chris had spoken, "might have the notion that the girl would inherit a great deal more if only her twin were dead."

"Nonsense." Lemiston frowned. "I made it clear she'll get no more than what I settle on her. I've said I'll make a generous settlement, but that's the end. No inheritance."

"You told all of them that?"

"They knew it before they accepted their invitations. They are, for one reason or another, one and all, quite desperate to marry immediately and marry well. Even poor old Camberstone has an uncle driving him hard to wed and fill his nursery!"

"You think it a great joke, don't you?"

"Oh, the very best jest in all the world. And if you knew the whole of it, you'd understand why I'm enjoying every minute of watching how it'll turn out."

"The whole of it?"

"Forget it, Francis. You'd play spoilsport. As you've done already. Did you *have* to explain to my unbeloved daughter that she needn't wed unless she wished it?"

"I didn't. Someone else must have done it for me, although I would have if I'd guessed at your intentions! She is my *much beloved* ward, and I've sworn to protect her, have I not?" He cast a sardonic look at his old friend and added, "Even against *you,* Chris."

"You've taught her well in some ways, Francis," said Lemiston thoughtfully. "I only know one other woman who would have had the nerve to escape that assassin as she did just now. Any other would have been screaming or fainting or who knows what."

"If you mean your wife, then your memory is playing you up. She used to set up a screech at the sight of a mouse. I can't imagine what she'd have done if someone had shot at her."

"I didn't refer to the twins' mother. Forget I mentioned it," said the marquess dismissively, his second wife, Meg, very much on his mind. "Just someone I . . . met on my travels."

Francis wasn't particularly interested in anyone Chris had met while roaming the world, and changed the subject back to his favorite preoccupation. "Stephie was trained as you and I decided we'd train our daughters. Or have you forgotten that as well as so much else?"

Chris Morris frowned. "We decided . . ." He tipped his head. "Just what did we decide?"

"You *have* forgotten. Remember my sisters? When we saw how my father ruined *them,* we spent hours planning how we'd prevent that from happening to our children."

"Ah. Yes. I do recall some such thing. But I *don't* recall that we planned to turn our daughters into additional sons!"

"We agreed to allow our children to follow their interests . . . whatever those interests might be."

"Ah! That explains why my son has become a sniveling pedant and my daughter a hoyden. Or worse."

"Don't sneer. Theo may be more interested in his books than in crops, but he doesn't snivel. He rides like a centaur and he shoots nearly as well as you used to do. He's an excellent swordsman, as is Stephanie, by the way."

"Nonsense. A woman hasn't the strength to be a swordsman."

"The Italian form of duello doesn't require brute strength as much as it does stamina, finesse, and dexterity."

Christopher's eyes narrowed. "So you took the time to learn that form in order to ruin the girl in still another way?"

"I hired an expert to teach us all. Stephanie and I still practice."

"And my sniveling son?"

"If you stay around long enough, you'll learn," was the disgusted answer. Francis stared at Chris until the marquess dropped his gaze and turned back to stare at the now mounted riders. "You'll note how straight-backed Stephanie is? After what she's just been through? She'll be down to dinner this evening and no one will ever guess she was very nearly killed today."

"And you think that good?"

"I do."

"Why?"

"It shows strength of character, greater strength of mind, and an ability to adapt to whatever is asked of her. That's good."

Lemiston was silent for a moment. "Are you suggesting she'll adapt to whatever marriage she makes? That she'll not be made to suffer by it?"

"She'll not *make* a marriage from which she'd suffer."

"She'll marry when and whom I say."

"She won't."

"Then she'll find herself destitute and living by her wits, because I'll not see her growing fat off my land." His voice iced over as he added, "She *can* suffer. She *will* suffer."

"You've grown cold and hard in the years since you left, Chris. I don't know you anymore." Francis pulled on his reins, backing his mount a few steps before turning away. Then he stopped. "She *won't* suffer, Chris. Not while I live. Or will you kill me so no one will interfere in whatever you think to do? Perhaps I'd better warn you my death won't help. You see, she and Jane inherit from me since Theo and my nephews are well provided for and there's no one else to whom I must leave what is mine. Killing me won't get you any satisfaction unless you are willing to transfer your desire for vengeance away from your offspring and take it out on me."

Chris scowled at his first friend, his mouth pursed into sharp lines of dissatisfaction. He growled deep in his throat.

In a cool voice, Francis added, "I'll see you at dinner, assuming I'm still a guest?"

"You are, of course, still a guest, whatever you've done or will do to spoil my pie." Lemiston growled, then almost snarled, "I'll make a bet with you, Francis. The chit will *not* come down to dinner."

"Our usual?" asked Francis casually.

For a moment Chris frowned. Then he crowed with laughter, his ill humor flowing away. "I'd forgotten that! Very well. Our usual." A wry quirk to his mouth and a twinkle in his eye, Lord Lemiston watched his friend trot off toward Warring Heights.

A moment's further thought and the frown returned. Just *what* would Francis ask of him if he lost their bet? According to their old rules, he'd have to do whatever was asked, although there were restrictions to just what or how much was involved by that asking. Francis, if he hadn't mistaken the matter, would very likely ask for something involving a change in Chris's plans for his daughter . . .

Blast and bedamned! Francis Warrington had tricked him nicely!

Assuming he won, of course.

Just as Lemiston felt certain *he'd* won the bet, his daughter, looking more lovely than ever, strolled into the drawing room, apologies on her lips for keeping everyone waiting. She smiled blandly around the room but, even as several men converged on where she stood, she moved into a circle of women and quickly determined they were discussing the king's physician's latest announcement which had been printed in full in the latest *Times* to reach the Priory. She inserted a comment which brought a laughing protest from several ladies and, fully occupied with the resulting controversy, managed to ignore her frustrated wooers once again.

"Well, Chris?"

"You've won. What's it to be."

"I'll think about it."

"Remember, you can't ask the moon!"

"I suspect I remember far better than you do. She's become rather deft at avoiding your suitors, has she not?"

"Very deft indeed," said Lemiston dryly. He turned to where

several of the married men were discussing much the same problem as their wives, although they were more interested in discovering who would be in the new government which must be formed if Prinny were indeed made Regent.

At dinner Stephanie couldn't avoid the men, because she was forced to sit between two of them. This time, it was the rather gross Baron Stread on one side and, on the other, Lord Westerwood, a Byronic looking man, but a gambler to his soul—a man whose interest in the tables and turf were well known. Stephanie couldn't decide which was worse: the Baron's insinuating comments about her person and his innuendoes about his intentions, or Lord Westerwood's egocentric meandering tales about past coups.

Stephanie finally asked, "And have you never had equally interesting losses?"

Westerwood's eyes opened wide, his mouth dropping open as well. "Losses? Losses are *never* interesting."

"Except, of course, to the person to whom you lose?" she asked sweetly.

His lordship's response was to turn to his other partner and ignore Stephanie for the remainder of the meal, however rude that might be. Which, decided Stephanie, was *not* the result for which she'd hoped, since it left her to the baron's mercy, and the baron wasn't known for showing mercy when in pursuit of his pleasure . . .

"Excellent strategy, missy." The baron's high, grating titter had Stephanie wincing.

"Strategy?" she asked as coldly as she knew how.

"Aye. Ridding yourself of that popinjay so you and I could have a sweet little coze."

"Coze, my lord? I believe that implies talking nonsense. I don't talk nonsense."

"You'll learn." Stread leered. "You'll like it, too . . . The nonsense," he hinted when she gave him a blank look. Stephanie blinked and Stread scowled. "Now, then, missy, you needn't pretend to me. Don't like missish behavior. At your age, one assumed you'd not stoop to pretending you don't know what's what."

Stephanie stared him in the eyes and said, "I haven't a notion of what you speak." She then turned her gaze on her plate and wished the next course would come. Ignoring Stread, she was intermittently conscious of Westerwood's deep chuckle as he teased Lady Winston. She realized that nearly every other thing his lordship said involved a gamble.

And then she heard him say, "Oh yes. What you've heard is true. I've never been known to turn down a bet. Never. It's become so much a part of my reputation it is something of an embarrassment."

"You could, perhaps," teased his dinner partner softly, "suggest to the next idiot who proposes such an absurdity that he's lost his mind."

Stephanie heard a certain amount of bitterness in Westerwood's voice when he said, "I couldn't. You don't know how ugly men can be. I'd be a laughing stock. No one would ever again take me seriously."

"Because you were *sensible* no one would take you seriously?"

Stephanie had to force back a chuckle at the woman's shock. But Westerwood's comments had given her a notion. Now if he'd also give her the opportunity to put it into effect . . .

Nine

The next day as Stephanie returned from a quick trip into the village she was accosted by a stranger. The flamboyantly dressed woman drove a gig which Stephanie recognized as coming from a livery stable in Chichester. "Yes?" she asked, staring at the incredible bonnet worn by the driver.

"You know that big house back there?" The scowling, sun-burnt, and richly but badly dressed woman tipped her thumb toward the Priory gates.

Stephanie nodded. "Yes."

"Then, m'boy, you just tell me this. Is a man they call Lord Lemiston living there?"

"And if he is?"

"A big man? Tall?" asked the woman, staring intently. "Gray hair? A sun-darkened complexion?"

"I've seen a man fits that description," said Stephanie carefully.

"Then," the scowl deepened, "you tell the bastard his wife wants words with him and that he'd better tell that argy-bargy stiff-rumped butler to let me in when next I come!" She turned and lightly cuffed the boy sitting beside her. "Leave your brother alone."

"You said we'd see Papa," he said, scowling.

"Wan' Papa. Wan' Papa," wailed the younger boy.

"You shut your map." The woman looked back to find Stephanie staring at the elder boy. "Well? You want a half crown to take my message?"

Startled, Stephanie chuckled. "I'll take no message even for a *whole* crown." A slow smile spread in a crooked fashion and her eyes twinkled. "I've a *far* better notion." As she spoke her gaze drifted back to the elder lad who glared, frowning in very much the Morris fashion, his brows drawn into a well-defined vee above distinctive gray-blue eyes.

The woman's voice brought Stephanie's attention back where it belonged.

"Here now! You think I'm not good enough for the big house? I tell you I'm Lady Lemiston—assuming the cock wasn't bamming Ryder when I heard—" She cast a shrewd glance at Stephanie, "—what I heard. And if I *am* her ladyship, then my boy here is going to be a lordship one day, and I won't let that Hades-born sea scum cheat me of our rights. My boy'll be a marquess one day!" she said, pride obvious.

"He's already a lordship," said Stephanie politely, "but I'm afraid your son can't inherit. There is already an heir."

"Is there then!" The woman bristled. "You tellin' me his blidy lordship's already married? You tellin' me m'boys are bastards?"

"If you married Lord Lemiston after he left England," Stephanie checked the elder boy's age, "which I'm sure you did, then you are legally wed and the children legitimate. His lordship was widowed over twenty years ago when his first wife bore him twins."

The woman's glance sharpened. "You then? You're the heir?"

"My brother is heir."

"Ah." Meg Morris, Lady Lemiston, looked into the distance, obviously thinking furiously.

"You haven't asked about my grand notion," prodded Stephanie.

Meg gave her a sharp glance, but turned back to the quietly squabbling boys before speaking. "You boys settle down now or I'll give you what for! Now—" She turned a suspicious look on Stephanie. "What's this notion you got lurkin' under that fancy lid you're wearin', then?"

"I'll take you up to the house myself. We'll settle," Stephanie took one more look at those Morris eyebrows, "my brothers in the nursery in which my twin and I grew up and set a maid to watching them. I'll find you a room and—" Stephanie again eyed the woman's astonishing bonnet which was far more suitable to a lady of the evening than a lady of the manor, "some clothes since I see you've not brought your trunk. You, Lady Lemiston, will surprise my—" Stephanie hesitated only a moment over the word, which, so far, she'd avoided giving voice to, "father at dinner tonight." She couldn't quite repress a grimace.

A slow smile spread across the ruined complexion of the woman in the gig. "You don't like 'im."

Stephanie equivocated. "Since he left at our birth, my lady, and only just returned, I don't know him."

The boys giggled, nudging each other.

"Now what is it?" asked their mother.

"M'lidy, m'lidy . . ." they chanted and, succumbing to chuckles, hugged each other.

"Perhaps you'd introduce the boys?" suggested Stephanie.

"Ah! Yes. Now boys! Straighten up and show you've been taught proper manners and weren't raised like your ma was in a back slum." Meg turned to Stephanie. "My lord, this is Richard Morris who is seven and his brother John, who turned four just yesterday."

"Well, Lord Richard, Lord John. Welcome to the Priory, the ancestral home of the Morris family since a rascally fellow *didn't* support the Louis brought to England from France after the Baron's War against John Lackland way back in the thirteenth century." She grinned as the boys looked at each other, obviously uncertain what to think of a person who read them lectures in history before they ever knew a name. For good measure, she added, "Henry III rewarded that particular Morris with the title and this estate."

"So, who are you?" asked the older.

Stephanie grinned. "Me? I'm your half-sister, Lady Stephanie Morris."

The woman reared back, her hat pushed over her forehead by the back of the gig. Meg, Lady Lemiston, straightened it with a rough gesture and then stared at Stephanie. *"Lady Stephanie,* did you say?"

"Yes, but," she turned to the boys, "you may call me Steph, as your older brother does."

"Stuff?" asked the elder, holding both hands over his mouth to hide giggles.

"Lady Stephanie," corrected their mother sternly. "But you . . ." Her voice faded as she stared thoughtfully at Stephanie's trousers and boots. Looking up, she caught Stephanie's eyes, humor vivid in her own. She pursed her lips for a moment. Then, slyly, she asked, "Don't suppose you'd introduce me to your tailor, would you now? I like the style of your ham cases, y'see."

Stephanie chuckled, deciding she liked this odd woman. "I'll do so quite happily for a price—which is that you tell me what ham cases might be?"

"There, now, if I didn't go and do it again. Chris don't like it when I use cant, so I try not to. But ham cases. Breeches, of course."

"Ah! Of course. I don't know him well, but I'd guess my sire's conventional enough he'd be shocked to find his wife in, er—" Stephanie winked, "—ham cases, so how can I resist helping you to tweak him?"

The women grinned at each other in complete understanding.

"Can you turn the gig here?" asked Stephanie, gesturing at the rather narrow lane. "If so, we'll go along to the stables by way of the secondary gate. A groom will return the rig you've rented and another follow. The men can collect your belongings before returning from Chichester." Meg nodded. "Come along then." She walked Aladdin out of Meg's way as the woman, with the intense concentration of the newly trained, awkwardly but safely turned the gig.

After giving orders to the head coachman, Stephanie took her guests to the large suite on the top floor of one wing which, for the last century or so, had been set aside for Morris children, their nannies, maids, and teachers. It included bedrooms, nurseries, a playroom, and a schoolroom. She opened a cupboard she remembered once contained toys her brother had enjoyed and, when she saw it still did, stood back to watch the boys dig in.

Only then did she ring the long unused bell.

When Abbot arrived, half curious and half angry at being forced to climb so many stairs, Stephanie scolded him. "I didn't ring for you. I rang for Sissy Ebert. Now please go along and send her up to the nursery."

Abbot looked at the children and then cast a look of loathing toward the oddly dressed woman. "You!" He turned to Stephanie, "I already told that one the likes of her isn't welcome here no matter who may be in residence. She can just wait for her fancy man somewhere else."

Stephanie casually introduced Meg as Lady Lemiston and then faced down Abbot's look of disbelief. "You needn't go gossiping about her arrival, either," she finished.

"I won't then," said Abbot promptly, "because you'll come a cropper with this start, my lady." Abbot's nose rose a notch as he added, "No Lemiston marries his bit o'muslin!"

Meg leaned very slightly toward the butler, her chin jutting belligerently. "You hold your guff, you slubberdegullion. I got my marriage lines and, by your gizzard, his lordship can't say me nay. He can't make me go neither, so you just treat me proper like and we'll get along just fine . . . Sauce box!" she added, tauntingly.

To prevent Abbot from responding to such blatant provocation, Stephanie took his arm and turned him toward the door. "I think you'd better go before you put your foot in clear up to your knee. A woman doesn't claim marriage unless she can prove it. Not when coming to a place like the Priory! Send up Sissy and keep your, er, map closed, you hear me?"

"I hear you, but you've no call to go talking like someone raised in a back alley. You may have grown up, Lady Stephanie, but I still have ways to punish you!" He brightened at the thought, but puckered his lips tightly when Stephanie merely grinned. "You'll see!"

"What, then? Burnt toast and overly hard eggs, or maybe no hot water of a morning? Poor me."

Abbot merely smiled knowingly and departed.

Sissy appeared soon after, pert and curious and an instant hit with the young gentlemen whom Stephanie introduced as Lords Richard and John, the boys again falling into giggles. "What is it?" asked Stephanie when the older boy looked as if he might manage a response.

"We ain't lords. We're just boys."

"Yes, but since your father is a marquess, you must be called lord. It's a rule."

"Never have before," said Richard, a suspicious look in his eye.

"Never knew your father was a marquess before," said his mother. "Now you behave like you been taught. You do like this girl tells you, 'cause you're in a new house with all sorts of new rules. Tomorrow your pa—" She cast an embarrassed look toward the maid, "I mean your father will have a talk with you, but you don't cause no trouble tonight. Understand?"

"Papa's here?" asked the younger, a hopeful look in his eye.

"Somewhere," admitted Meg, "but don't you go lookin' for him! You'd get *lost* and, as big as this place is you'd starve afore you was found. Johnny-boy," she added, her voice far more gentle, "I'm sorry, but you probably won't see him tonight. Tomorrow, though, for certain sure."

She put a hand against the boy's head, the first softness Stephanie had seen in her. For a moment Stephanie wondered if she'd demand to remain in the nursery with her sons.

Then, squaring her shoulders, Meg turned to Stephanie. "I'm ready."

"Good. Because we've a deal to do." Stephanie had noticed they were much of a height, both being overly tall, and, for the first time ever, rued the skimpiness of the feminine portion of her wardrobe. Once she'd chosen clothing for her guest, there'd be very little left for her own use.

But if the brightly colored and overly decorated carriage gown and pelisse currently on Meg's back were examples of the sort of thing she had in her trunk, then it was important the unexpected Lady Lemiston be dressed in something more suitable. Stephanie might wish to embarrass her father, but she had no intention of making it harder on *Meg* than she must!

And that it *would* be hard couldn't be denied. None of the guests would treat this rough woman, however good-hearted, with anything better than tolerance. She'd suffer slurs on her character, rudeness to her person, and perhaps ostracism. Actually, thought Stephanie ruefully, that last might be preferable.

"Come along," she ordered. "Let's see what we can do."

Meg, her eyes darting here and there along the way, said nothing until they reached Stephanie's room. She gave it a disparaging look. "I'd a thought you'd have a bigger room, being you're a daughter of the house." She cast Stephanie a suspicious look.

"I chose this room the day I was released from the nursery and have never regretted it. You see, Lady Lemiston, old houses are, as a rule, rather hard to heat. I'm a bit of an oddity in that I like warmth and want my surroundings cozy. I tend to freeze to death at my neighbor's homes where they think it unhealthy to keep a room at this temperature."

As she spoke, Stephanie added still more coal to the fire which burned most of the year round in her grate. She lit every one of the multitude of candles set on the mantel, in wall sconces and on flat surfaces around the room. Finally, she went to the windows and, after closing shutters which had been designed to keep out every draft, she pulled her curtains shut as well. And, last of all, she yanked the bell pull.

"We'll have hot water for baths," she said and then laughed at Meg's very expressive grimace. "You don't believe in bathing?" she asked.

"Just like your pa, you are! Always wanting a body a washin' of itself. Can't be healthy!"

"It has never caused me to take ill, and surely you'll admit it's far more pleasant to be around people who bathe than those who smell to high heaven of body odors and the eau de colognes and sweet waters used to mask them."

"Nothing wrong with the smell of good honest sweat," Meg contradicted.

"I don't myself object to the honest sweat of hard work. It's the other, far more unpleasant, body odors to which I object. And the perfumes. And too, the odd, sour smell that comes from nervousness or fear. That isn't pleasant at all."

Meg cast a suspicious look at Stephanie. "Here now! You think I'm afeared of facing down that hell-born lad I took to husband?" A silent laugh shook the woman. "Well, then, maybe I am, a bit, but you don't need to think I'll ever let him know it!"

When Stephanie expressed her approval of that attitude, Meg subsided. She strolled around the room, poking at the mattress, feeling materials between her work-roughened fingers and, finally, slid open the small drawer in the bedside table.

"Here now! A pistol?"

"Careful. It's loaded."

Meg frowned. "Why would you be needing a loaded pistol by your bed?"

"Actually, at night it's under my pillow. Once you meet the men my dearly unbeloved sire has invited into his home, you'll understand why I lock my door and keep a pistol handy." Stephanie spoke with a dry note in her voice which had Meg eyeing her. "My sire blames me and my brother for the death of our mother. He left home before she was buried, returning for the first time only recently. We don't know him. He doesn't know us." Stephanie's brows lowered over her eyes. "But, even though we don't know each other, *someone* is trying to kill my brother and there is *no doubt at all* my father wants me married to one of the rakes, rogues, or the one merely foolish gentleman he's collected for this benighted house-party."

"You think *he's* the one trying to kill your brother?"

Stephanie sighed and turned away. "Actually, from everything I've learned, I rather doubt it, but there doesn't seem to be another candidate for the role of murderer, so I keep coming back to his dislike of us."

"Don't you believe it. He'd never kill his own blood! Besides that, if he wanted you dead, you'd be dead. And then, too," said Meg, her gaze steady, "you mustn't say bad things about Chris to me. He's done right by me ever since we first met."

"Just where *did* you meet?" asked Stephanie after losing a struggle with her growing curiosity.

"In the Antipodes." Meg's chin came up and her eyes burned with an emotion Stephanie wasn't certain she understood. Watching her stepdaughter closely, the woman added, "You might as well know first as last. He bought me out of my sentence when I was transported to one of the penal colonies there." She compressed her lips, waiting, obviously, for expressions of horror. Or worse.

All Stephanie did was blink. Once. "Were you? Why?"

"Why? 'Cause I was caught stealing a loaf of bread, that's why." She held herself well up. "It were the third time I were caught, you see, and the judge said enough were enough."

"I'm sorry you were caught," said Stephanie and added, musingly, "I can't imagine being so hungry I'd steal. It must be pretty awful."

Meg blinked. "That's all you gonna say?"

"Should I say more?"

"You ain't, aren't I mean, gonna . . . going to give me a lecture on my sinful ways?"

"Is that what I'm supposed to do? Not me," Stephanie demurred. "I'm not the vicar. It's *his* business to lecture us on our sins. Besides," said Stephanie thoughtfully, "in my opinion, the sin is letting people get so hungry they must steal."

Meg stared. "That's what your papa said!"

"He did? Then perhaps I'll change my mind and give you that sermon after all," said Stephanie lightly.

"Don't want to be like him in any way, do you? Contrary, that's you! And *that's* like him, too, if you only knew! Contrary, I mean."

Stephanie turned away. "I suppose I am. I've resented his leaving us as he did and yet . . . yet, if he *hadn't* gone, then Francis, Sir Francis that is, wouldn't have been responsible for raising us. And if he'd not, then I'd not have been allowed to live my life my own way, would I? So, if I were the logical creature I think myself to be, I shouldn't resent his running off." Stephanie smiled the brilliant smile which drew people to her on those rare occasions it appeared. "In fact," she said, "I must remember to *thank* him."

"You're an odd one, ain't you?" asked Meg. After a moment she gave Stephanie a shrewd look. "Doubt me anyone else will think the way you do. About me, I mean."

Stephanie sobered. "You are likely correct in thinking the other guests won't react to you as I do. Perhaps it would be best if we tell no one about your past? Merely that you and Lord Lemiston met in his travels. That should be sufficient. If anyone is rude enough to ask for more, look down your nose and tell them to ask his lordship. I doubt if anyone would have the nerve, but if they do, then let *him* tell them what he wants known."

"That one will tell the truth and shame the devil, he will!"

"Then let him. But don't you offer more information than you must. You are aware your English isn't quite what you'd like. I've heard you correct it occasionally, you see. But don't apologize for it and don't explain it. All right?" Stephanie didn't wait for an answer, but turned to let in the maid for whom she'd rung some time earlier. "What took you so long, Sarah?"

"We're that busy, my lady, what with all the company and all, and then you calling Sissy away, well! That was outside of enough, my lady." She cast a curious look toward the stranger.

"I will have to see about more help if you are all so overworked no one has time to answer my bell."

The maid blushed, but grinned with it. "Ol' Abbot set me a task to do before I came up."

"Hmm. He said he'd punish me! But perhaps it's just as well you are all so occupied, since it appears the servant's grapevine hasn't yet managed to pass on word that Lady Lemiston and her sons have arrived . . . or has it?"

Sarah cast another quick look at Stephanie's guest, noticed the hat, and couldn't remove her gaze from it.

"Her luggage was lost," said Stephanie smoothly. "The things bought to replace what was needed were *not,* perhaps, just in the style she'd have liked—"

"Here now! What do you mean I don't like—"

"—and *so,*" insisted Stephanie, firmly interrupting, "she'll need to borrow some of my things for tonight and until we replace her wardrobe. Which reminds me. We must have Miss Hammer *immediately.* She's to bring a selection of material and take measurements and hire as many seamstresses as necessary to fill an order instantly. I'll write a note and you must have a groom ride in with it at once." Stephanie discovered her guest was glowering at her and she grinned before turning back to Sarah. "We both require baths after which Lady Lemiston will try on the blue gown with my mother's lace on it and you'll see if adjustments are needed before dinner this evening."

Sarah curtsied and left the room.

The door was barely shut before Meg demanded, "What do you mean my clothes ain't all the crack? Bought them in Lunnun, didn't I? Right up to the mark, every bit of it!"

Stephanie pointed. "If that hat's an example, it *will not do.*" She shook her head. "Oh, dear, I'm sounding exactly like Lady Eltonson! But, please, take my word for it. Even I know that hat would never be seen on a lady's head." She cast Meg a wry glance. "Someone from the demimonde would wear it, perhaps."

"A whore, you mean. A doxy what's come into a bit of money . . ." She sighed lustily. "It's the hat, then, makes that snooty-nosed bibble-babbler think me his blidy lordship's ladybird? That's why that old rumguzzler wouldn't let me in?" Meg spoke with deep bitterness. "Jist one more indication I don't belong here, isn't it . . ." Her chin came up. "Well, I *do* belong. I'm Lady Lemiston all right and tight and no one can say me nay! I'll have m'rights."

"You most certainly will, beginning tonight when you'll sit at the head of his lordship's table, right where you belong."

Meg chuckled. "And you can't wait to see Chris's face when he sees me, can you?"

"Exactly."

"You think he'll care, that he'll be embarrassed?"

Stephanie's eyes narrowed and she responded in a slow thoughtful manner. "No, Meg, I *don't* think that's what's in my mind. What I *do* think is that he'll be chagrined you followed him to England when, or so I suspect, he told you to stay home, and even more chagrined that you've discovered his title. At least, something you said earlier made me think he isn't aware you're here or that you know?"

"He blidy well didn't tell me!" She lowered her voice. "Had to overhear him talking to Ryder—"

Stephanie's brows arched.

"—Anthony Ryder, that is, his partner."

Stephanie's eyes narrowed. "Anthony Ryder is Lord Lemiston's partner? In what?"

"Their shipping company, o'course. Hasn't his blidy lordship mentioned where he gets his gold? No, he wouldn't, would he? Not the thing for a blidy lordship to dirty his hands in trade, is it?"

"I dirty my hands every day, working with my tenants, but you are correct to think that isn't the same thing. He sails his own ship, then?"

"Chris stopped sailing years ago, liking the bit of land he got in Australia. He turned his ship over to a captain like they done the others. But Anthony. He likes it. Regular poet when he gets going. Says there's nothin' like takin' the helm and navigatin' the wide reaches of ocean and all that sort of thing. He's also got a knack for knowing what to buy and where to sell it for a profit. Chris trusts him."

"So that's what he meant by responsibilities . . . ?"

"You know Ryder?" asked Meg when Stephanie didn't go on.

"He's staying here," said Stephanie shortly, and turned to her armoire where she searched out the blue gown. Holding it up to her length, she turned and looked at Meg, whose pursed lips and disgusted look made the woman's reaction obvious. "You don't like it," said Stephanie, grinning.

"It's so plain. An' so dull a blue," Meg complained. "I like bright colors, I do. I like more lace than that narrow stuff and flounces and, to tell you frankly, a more womanly cut to the thing."

"More womanly?"

"More bosom."

"You'd prefer something resembling that which a Covent Garden doxy wears?" suggested Stephanie, tongue in cheek.

"Not like those trulls. None of that fake satin and worn silk for me. My new clothes are all of the very best. Not a remade gown in the lot."

"Meg . . . I may call you Meg?" Stephanie's stepmother nodded. "Meg, it isn't the *quality* of the *material* that's the problem, but the *style* which, believe me, isn't right for the society you'll join downstairs."

"You're trying to help me," said Meg, "and I'm not helping

back any." She sighed. "But I do like a bit o' color . . ." she added on a wistful note.

"When your trunk comes, we'll see if anything can be altered so it won't offend."

"I don't like pretendin' I'm somethin' I'm not."

"But you don't have to pretend. You are Lady Lemiston, are you not?"

Meg squared her shoulders. "True. I'm a lady and better act the part." She reached for the dress and held it up to herself, looking in the mirror hung on the inner side of the armoire's doors. "Don't look atall like me. You dress me up like a duchess and I won't know myself."

"Oh, no," laughed Stephanie. "Never like a duchess!" Meg cast her a look. "Merely like a marchioness!"

They were still laughing when Sarah returned leading a retinue of male servants who carried two hip baths and several pails of hot water. Sarah directed the work and then shooed the footmen away, turning to lean back against the closed door. She cast a look toward Lady Lemiston, then toward her mistress. "Lady Stephanie, the oddest rumors . . ."

"Which means everyone knows that Lady Lemiston has arrived?" Stephanie sighed, regretting she'd not surprise her father after all.

"Oh, no, my lady. They are saying a London whore has come to chouse his lordship out of some money, pretending to be what she isn't. Or, perhaps, she's looking for one of the other men. No one is certain quite what's afoot."

"Blast Abbot! How dare he?" Stephanie relaxed. "Sarah, all those rumors are wrong. Do you understand? This is indeed Lady Lemiston, but we won't explain that to anyone, will we?"

"Why?" asked the servant who had been Stephanie's childhood friend and her confidant long before entering service at the Priory.

"Because I say so," said Stephanie.

"Up to mischief, *you* are," said Sarah and sniffed.

"Not at all."

Stephanie took off her coat and cravat and then undid the button at the neck of her shirt. Slowly, Meg followed suit and soon the two women were sitting in hot water, Meg still in her shift which she'd refused to remove.

" 'Tain't right, going naked."

"It isn't? Hmm." Stephanie wore that attractive laughing look again which could win over even her more fervent detractors when directed their way. "I suppose that means you won't go swimming with me sometime?" she asked.

"Swimming!" Meg straightened, sloshing water over the rim. "You *swim?*"

"It's great sport. Our guardian taught us when we were younger than your boys. Lemiston and Sir Francis swam in the Chichester Bay as lads and Francis has let us try everything they did, allowing us to follow up with what interests us. Swimming is wonderful fun. Just *swimming* is very enjoyable on a warm day, but along the coast on days when the waves are just right, one gets out beyond them and rides them in. It's indescribable . . ."

Meg, thinking of the surf around the Australian coast shook her head. "Too dangerous. I don't want my boys doing anything so foolish. But what has swimming to do with nakedness?" Again she straightened, her eyes widening. "You don't mean . . . ?"

"Of course. The feel of the water flowing over and around one's body is unbelievably nice. But if you won't, you won't." Stephanie laughed at Meg's wry look. "Do you ride? I thought you did very well with the gig, by the way."

"Thanks to his blidy lordship's teaching, I both ride and I drive. Don't do neither all that well, though," she said, determinedly truthful. "It'll never come natural like, but I had to know. Out where we live, in the bush, we're miles from our nearest neighbor and even farther from any town."

"Why do you call him that?"

"His blidy lordship?" Meg grinned a rather vicious grin. "I call him that because the bastard would never a tol' me I was a ladyship. Because he's kept me out there in the wilds all alone except for occasional trips into Newcastle. Because he'd have me think he couldn't do any of it without me, but when anything *fun* happens, it's where were you?" Meg glowered. "Blidy men. They're all alike. All the world made for men. Women can come along for the ride so long as they keep their place and wipe their noses and don' forget who's master!"

"Did you say Newcastle! But surely that's up north . . ."

"A brand-new Newcastle. Taint *too* far from Botany Bay, really. But he never took me there. His blidy lordship!"

Stephanie chuckled. "Is that, perhaps, why you want to meet my tailor, to even the score?"

"Hmm. If we go back there, which I'm pretty certain Chris means to do, or he wouldn't a left the boys behind . . . well then, I'll take me some trousers along. He don't need to know I'm doing it, though." Meg cast a sharp look first toward Sarah and then Stephanie. "Don't you go crying rope on me!"

"I've no intention of spoiling your game and neither will Sarah, will you?" asked Stephanie. Sarah smiled and shook her head. "Besides, I think it a wonderful idea. You've no notion how much more freedom one has wearing trousers! I do it all the time. Well," Stephanie corrected herself, "I *did* it all the time until 'his blidy lordship' showed up with a houseful of equally blidy guests!"

"Why would he want you to marry some rake or gambler? Isn't that what you said he wanted?"

"What he wants is revenge," said Stephanie. She shrugged wet shoulders and repeated the movement to feel, again, the lovely sensation of warm water sliding over smooth skin. "I told you. He blames me for the death of his first love. My mother, you know."

"Men!" said Meg, thoroughly disgusted. "Don't he know who plants a babe? It's himself who caused his wife's death if anyone caused it and so I'll tell him!"

"Meg, you'd better not—"

Take a Trip Back to the Romantic
Regent Era of the Early 1800's with

4 FREE ZEBRA
REGENCY ROMANCES!

(AN $18.49 VALUE!)

4 FREE
BOOKS
ARE
YOURS

PLUS YOU'LL SAVE ALMOST $4.00 EVERY MONTH
WITH CONVENIENT FREE HOME DELIVERY!

See Details Inside....

We'd Like to Invite You to Subscribe to Zebra's Regency Romance Book Club and Give You a Gift of 4 Free Books as Your Introduction! *(Worth $18.49!)*

If you're a Regency lover, imagine the joy of getting 4 FREE Zebra Regency Romances and then the chance to have these lovely stories delivered to your home each month at the lowest prices available! Well, that's our offer to you and here's how you benefit by becoming a Zebra Home Subscription Service subscriber:

- 4 FREE Introductory Regency Romances are delivered to your doorstep
- 4 BRAND NEW Regencies are then delivered each month (usually before they're available in bookstores)
- Subscribers save almost $4.00 every month
- Home delivery is always FREE
- You also receive a FREE monthly newsletter, *Zebra/Pinnacle Romance News* which features author profiles, contests, subscriber benefits, book previews and more
- No risks or obligations...in other words you can cancel whenever you wish with no questions asked

Join the thousands of readers who enjoy the savings and convenience offered to Regency Romance subscribers. After your initial introductory shipment, you receive 4 brand-new Zebra Regency Romances each month to examine for 10 days. Then, if you decide to keep the books, you'll pay the preferred subscriber's price of just $3.65 per title. That's only $14.60 for all 4 books and there's never an extra charge for shipping and handling.

It's a no-lose proposition, so return the FREE BOOK CERTIFICATE today!

The woman cast a shrewd glance her way. "You think to tell me not to interfere, hmm?"

Stephanie's chin lifted. "You *mustn't*. If you make him see the error of his ways he'll just transfer his dislike of me to you. Few men will take the blame when something goes wrong. He'll take it out on you if you're the means to making him do so!"

"You're a good girl. Didn't think I'd like any of you proper sort, the ladyships and lordships—" A muscle worked in her jaw, "but I won't be cheated of m'rights. I won't!" She cast her stepdaughter a thoughtful look. "Maybe it won't be so bad if there are more like you."

"There's a problem! I'm a scandal to my rank, you see. I was raised exactly as my brother was up until he went to university and, for that matter, he like me! I've been allowed to pursue interests a woman isn't supposed to know anything about. I not only wear men's clothing, I manage the estate. My twin isn't interested in the land, you see, and I am. We both fence and I'm a better shot than he is. I ride astride on a stallion I trained myself from a colt. I swim. I do all sorts of things a woman shouldn't do. And so you'll be told by all the old biddies from around and about."

"Hmm." After a moment Meg struggled to get up. "Had enough of this. Can't be healthy sitting around in hot water. Here now, what's to do?" she demanded when Sarah approached and, soaping a wet rag, tried to wash Meg's back.

"It won't hurt," said Stephanie, stifling laughter.

"You can't know that! Let be, there," Meg added, when Sarah pushed her back into the water and reached down with the rag. "Stop that. At once! Dratted lubra . . ."

"Lubra?"

Meg subsided, sighing. "Maid, I mean. In the bush, the native women are called lubras. Ain't you done? You'll have the skin off me."

"Not through that shift I won't," said Sarah and helped Meg stand. "No, don't get out. I'll just pour the rinse water over you and get rid of the soap . . . there." She handed Meg a towel and pointed toward a screen she'd placed near the fire. "You can undress and dry off back there, since you're such a shy one. I've laid out a clean shift and petticoat. Your stays can wait 'til later. Now, for you, my lady," she said, turning to where Stephanie patiently awaited her.

After the gown had been fitted and the necessary alterations determined, Stephanie left her guest lying on her bed in her petticoats where, Meg said, she'd just have a little cat nap.

"It's been a worrying time, following his blidy lordship, and then finding out where he is, and then trying to get past that sapscull at your front door. Well, I'm done to the bone, Lady Stephanie."

"You rest. I'll be back in time to see you dressed and take you down."

Ten

Lady Lemiston's Grand Entrance

Stephanie moved gracefully down the stairs, preoccupied with gleeful thoughts of her sire's coming shock. She couldn't wait to see his expression when he looked up from his place at the end of the table and found his wife sitting opposite him at dinner. She hoped he didn't hear any of the rumors, because he'd be warned, at least in part, and Stephanie didn't want him warned. As she stepped to the hall floor, a group of laughing, jostling men bustled out from under the arch into the corridor leading to the library and billiards room.

"You couldn't do it!" insisted Hamstead.

"Hit all the pips in a three spot playing card?" drawled Westerwood. "Sure I could."

"Bet you a pony you can't!"

"A bet!" said Rotherwood. "I think he just *might* do it. I've seen him shoot, you see. What will you bet against him, Camberstone?"

"Don't bet," mumbled his lordship. "Never bet right, so just don't do it, but," he brightened. "I'd like to see Westerwood shoot out the pips. All of them."

"Who will organize the shoot?" asked Baron Stread.

Stephanie stepped forward. Here was the opportunity she'd wanted. Westerwood's penchant for betting on anything and everything had just handed him to her on a platter! Or if not he, then another, perhaps?

"We've an excellent shooting range out beyond the orchard," she said, calling attention to herself. "I'll have tables set out for the shot and powder. Why don't we organize a *real* competition, not just the one round that's been suggested?" She glanced at the suddenly silent group of men and smiled. "You think I don't know how to organize one?"

"Lord Lemiston—"

"Lord Lemiston has been away from home so long it's not impossible he's forgotten where the practice range lies," she retorted with a touch of astringency. Stephanie drew in a deep breath and donned her most brilliant smile. "Now then, does anyone need the loan of pistols? The armory can be opened so you may choose what you like, once I've removed my brother's." After a brief pause and in an offhand manner, she added, "My own are kept in my room, of course . . ."

"Your pistols?" interrupted Baron Stread. He looked her up and down in that way she hated. "You shoot?"

"Yes." Again that smile which lit up her soul. Or it did when real and not adopted for a hoaxing reason such as this. "I was taught as a matter of course. I enjoy it."

Anthony joined the group just in time to hear that and chuckled. "I've seen her shoot. She's good."

"A woman? Nonsense." Baron Stread sneered. "A woman is good for only one thing, and then it ain't *her* doing the shooting!"

A few chuckles and a few frowns followed the baron's comment.

Stephanie, after noting which man did which, pretended she hadn't a notion of the ribald side to the baron's jesting, and said, "I much prefer to do the shooting myself, thank you."

This time there were more chuckles, mostly muffled, and of a more kindly nature. Anthony, his eyes slightly narrowed, gave her a knowing look which she returned with a bland, questioning gaze. Then she turned back to the men, wondering how she might prod one of them, most likely Westerwood, into a competition—with her naming the bet, of course!

"I'm very likely better than most of you," she added, again
with that innocence which anyone who knew her would have
guessed couldn't be real. Luckily, these men, except Anthony,
didn't know her. She got no more than supercilious looks. "I'm
very good."

"Nonsense," snorted the baron.

Stephanie wished it would be he who offered to match her,
but knew she hadn't a hope of that. She'd already discovered
the baron never bet on anything that wasn't a certain win. She
glanced around. "Is that what everyone thinks?"

"If Huntersham here says you can shoot then I'll believe
him. But can you shoot well enough you'd back yourself?
Would you lay a bet on it?" asked Westerwood with a slyness
he obviously thought well hidden.

"I might. Depending on the bet, of course. *Some* things a
lady simply couldn't allow." Stephanie feared she'd rather over-
done the simper she added to the words, but again she got
that kindly if rather muffled chuckle from several of the men.

"I'll bet you, then, that I can best you in a match. So that
we may be certain it'll not offend," Westerwood bowed, "you
can have the privilege of naming the bet."

"Hmm." Stephanie eyed his lordship. "What if I said that,
if you lose, you had to leave the Priory, bag and baggage, and
not return?"

Westerwood's brows climbed his forehead, nearly meeting
the carefully combed Brutus-style curls arranged on his forehead. "And if I win?"

"Oh but, you won't will you?"

"I believe I will." A muscle jumped in the side of his jaw
and his eyes narrowed. "Name my side of the bet."

Stephanie pouted, a look which would have had Sir Francis
or her twin, if either had been there, feeling wary about what
was to come. Anthony, who was beginning to know her well,
straightened. She eyed Westerwood, glanced around the waiting men, and suddenly relaxed. Letting her gaze settle on An-

thony she said, "Lord Huntersham can name what I lose. *If* I lose. Which I won't."

"I think, my lady," he said in a calm voice, "that if you lose, you must listen to Westerwood's proposal of marriage."

For half an instant Stephanie felt rejection flow into her. Luckily, it occurred to her that Anthony had merely said she must *listen,* not that she must say yes. She smiled a slow cat-eating-cream smile and nodded. "Very well."

There were growls from among some of the other men. "No fair!" said a bass voice. Stephanie heard a tenor, "Gives him the advantage in the heiress stakes." And a baritone, "Can't have that!"

Other such comments flowed around and over them, but Stephanie and Anthony barely heard them, their gaze locked, and everything and everybody seeming to cease to exist. Stephanie was only aware of the trembling in her limbs and the shivers running up her spine that his mere look induced. What if he touched her . . . ?

Westerwood, preening, touched Stephanie's arm and then her hand, lifting and turning it, to press a kiss to her wrist. It took an instant to realize the man was the wrong man but, when she did, she tolerated the touch for a further moment. She glanced around, wondering what the men had thought of her rudeness in staring at Anthony that way. It seemed impossible, but no one appeared to have noticed.

"Tomorrow, then," said Westerwood. "Early, I think. About one, perhaps?" he suggested.

"I'll give orders tonight. The gun room will be opened from eleven on for anyone who wishes to enter the organized competition. And any servant can direct you to the grounds. I must join the women now." Once again she flashed that glowing smile, letting it linger for just an instant on Anthony. "I'll see you at dinner, of course," she said and knew *he* knew she referred to him rather than any or all of the rest of the men.

But mentioning dinner reminded Stephanie that she was looking forward to it for once. It also reminded her she must

find Jane and have a little talk with her so that her chaperon
didn't, automatically, take the place at the head of the table—
the place which should, and *would,* be Lady Lemiston's.

Stephanie wanted that chair quite empty when she brought
Meg in at the very last instant! She wanted to guide her new
acquaintance directly to her place, and stand there, introducing
her ladyship from a position where she could watch her father's
reaction!

Oh yes. Stephanie would, she thought, enjoy her dinner tonight.

For a change.

But, later, Meg Morris took one quick look through the open
doors to the dining room and backed into Stephanie who stood
behind her. She turned and pushed her stepdaughter down the
corridor. "I can't go in there," she hissed.

"Why not?"

"That blidy table! Never seen anything like it. What the
devil does one do with all that stuff?"

"The silver?" Stephanie's eyes narrowed and with great effort she avoided a grin. "That could be a problem," she said
thoughtfully. "Ah! I have it. Anthony is seated only a couple
of chairs down the table from you. You watch him. Use the
utensil he chooses. I'd suggest you watch Lord Lemiston, but
Abbot insisted on putting the largest epergne we own in the
middle of the table. It's such a nuisance. Oh, another thing I
forgot to mention. You are supposed to talk to only those people seated beside you, changing with each course. Start with
the person on your right. Lord Emmerville, I think. He's married and not a bad sort. Ask him about salmon fishing in Scot-
land. He'll do all the talking. On the other side is Lord
Scranton. He's in politics. Ask him what he thinks of the pro-
posed Regency."

"Regency?"

"Never mind. Ask him what he thinks of Prince George."

"Ol' Florizel?"

Stephanie chuckled. "The same, but I wouldn't call him that.

He's no longer the slim golden prince who deserved that particular pet name! He's usually called Prinny these days." She
gave Meg a kindly look. "Ready?"

Meg drew in a deep breath. She squared her shoulders and
firmed her chin. After only the briefest of hesitations, she nodded.

"Then let's face down the . . . the nobs."

"Let's," agreed Meg through gritted teeth.

Stephanie, this time, led the way into the room. An apology
tripping off her tongue for keeping everyone waiting, she
strolled toward the head of the table, stopping just to one side
where she could still see her sire. "Good evening everyone.
Lord Lemiston?" Her father slowly rose to his feet, his eyes
on Meg. "We thought to surprise you. Have we?"

Chris left his chair and paced slowly and silently, dangerously, to their end of the table. "Meg, m'dear. Oh, yes, you've
surprised me all right."

He grasped Meg's arm and Stephanie's eyes narrowed. She
pulled the chair away from the table. "You can introduce your
wife to the company later, my lord, since I see Abbot is anxious
to begin serving." She spoke with a warning note in her voice
and, almost finger by finger, Lord Lemiston let Meg go. There
would be bruises, thought Stephanie.

"Wife, Lemiston?" asked Emmerville. "You didn't tell us
your lady was coming."

"I didn't know. I saw her last just before Huntersham and
I left Australia." He transferred his hold to Stephanie. "Our
sons, Meg?"

"Upstairs. John wants to see his papa."

"I'll look in on them before I go to bed, of course," said
Lemiston smoothly. "Stephanie, my dear, I think I'd like you
beside me this evening. If," he turned to Abbot, "you'd be so
kind as to move Lady—" He cast a quick glance to his end of
the table. "—Winston to Lady Stephanie's place?"

Stephanie lay her hand briefly on Meg's shoulder, urging
her to take her place. She squeezed gently, encouragingly, then,

freeing herself from her father's too-firm grip, moved to where Anthony sat back in his chair, his eyes narrowed. "Exaggerate which utensil and glass to use at any given time," she whispered into his ear. He nodded and she walked on to where Lady Winston had, pouting, abandoned a place beside her father.

"You," he said softly as he seated her, "are a minx."

"Also a handful, a hoyden, or a blot on creation . . . depending on who's speaking," she retorted.

To her surprise, Chris chuckled. "You've set the cat among the pigeons." He frowned. "But it isn't kind of you to subject Meg to this lot."

"She wants her rights."

"So you'll see she gets them? Don't take out your anger at me by hurting her."

"You will probably find this difficult to believe," said Stephanie softly, "but I like your Meg. She knows her mind and what she wants and she's not so stupid as to think she'll be taken to the bosom of the ton simply because she has her marriage lines to prove she belongs there. But, to quote her, she won't be cheated."

Chris paused before speaking, obviously taking Stephanie's subtle warning seriously. "I don't believe I ever had a notion I'd cheat her of anything by leaving her home," he mused. "And, although it may surprise *you,* I, too, rather like Meg."

"She thought her son your heir. That and her position in society are what you'd cheat her of."

"Ah." The Lemiston brows curved into an arc. "I wonder how she learned who I am . . ."

"If I understood what she said, and—" Stephanie smothered a quick grin, "—I'll admit occasionally I do *not,* 'my blidy lordship,' then you told her yourself."

Again Chris chuckled.

Stephanie knew she shouldn't have said that! She felt a faint heat in her ears and hoped her face wasn't too red. "As she calls you."

"Yes, that sounds like Meg. Did you also like your new brothers?"

Stephanie heard something she thought might be pride in her sire's tone. "I haven't had time to discover whether I will or not. They seemed good boys, neither too wild nor overly cowed."

"All too soon, now, I must see to their education." He frowned into his wine glass which Abbot had just refilled.

Since he didn't seem to require a response, Stephanie didn't answer. She had too much to think about. The first surprise was that her father hadn't reacted at all as she'd expected, except for that first too-firm grip on Meg's arm followed by that on her own. That had been all.

But, she wondered, was that instant response a clue to what he'd do when he had Meg alone? Obviously, in that first instant, he'd been angry. Would he beat his wife or laugh at the trick played on English society? Most likely, if nothing more, Meg would suffer an awful tongue-lashing.

But not tonight.

Stephanie would, she decided, take Meg to her own room. She reminded herself she must tell Abbot to have a trundle bed made ready. She'd not allow her sire to take his temper out on the woman until Meg had recovered enough to stand up to him!

"Are you sure you'll be comfortable?" asked Stephanie, suddenly unsure that she did the right thing putting Meg in her room. Would it, perhaps, only make her father's reaction worse? "Should I have had the other room in the master suite prepared for you?"

"You haven't a notion what it was like growing up in Spitalfields, do you?" asked Meg and yawned. "I'm not only entirely comfortable, I've no desire to face Chris tonight when I'm done to a bone. He and I can have our row when I'm feeling up to snuff." She yawned again. "It's work being a she-marquess. Even harder than I thought it'd be."

"You don't have to do it, you know. There are plenty of places we could place you if that's what you'd prefer."

"Here, now!" Meg sat up, silhouetted against the light of the fire. "I thought you was on my side."

"I am. I just want to be sure we know what that side *is*. You want to face down those 'blidy' women, we'll face 'em down."

"That's all right then." Meg lay back, crossing her wrists over her head. "I'll have my rights if it kills me and," she added in a thoughtful tone, "if tonight was an example of what it'll take, it may blidy-well do just that!"

"Nonsense, you did very well. But," even Stephanie could hear the smile in her voice, "if it *should* do you in, why, just think! You'd have your rights for eternity when they bury you in the family ground!"

"Won't be leavin' my bones in English soil. Chris says we'll lay them in good red dirt under a blue gum tree and generations more after us."

"Do you like it in the Antipodes?"

Meg was silent for so long Stephanie decided she'd gone to sleep and wouldn't answer. She was beginning to drift off herself when Meg responded, her words spaced out with thoughtful slowness. "It ain't what I'm used to. Not atall. And it ain't green enough . . . I'll never get used to the odd color of the trees there, or their eerie shapes. Some look like something out of your worst nightmares, their bark dripping off and their branches all which way . . . but, I'm part of it there . . . I'll have done something. You see, don't you? I'll've helped make a new country grow . . ."

When it became apparent Meg had no more to add, Stephanie said, "That may be more important than whether you like it."

The response was a faint snuffling snore and Stephanie raised herself on her elbow. She smiled. Meg, Marchioness of Lemiston, had dropped into a sudden, deep sleep. Stephanie hoped it would be restful as well. She curled up, snuggled into a vee formed by two large pillows, and lay there, quietly, waiting for the sleep into which, earlier she'd been about to drift . . .

And decided she wouldn't. She rolled onto her back and sighed.

She was still wide awake when she heard the soft, metallic sound of a key inserted into her keyhole. Stephanie instantly eased out the far side of her bed, taking her pistol with her. On bare feet she moved into the shadow formed by her armoire and sent up a prayer of thanks that Meg was there. Because if the woman hadn't been, more than her *feet* would be bare!

Perhaps, for the duration of his lordship's "blidy" houseparty, it would be best if she *continued* wearing a long shift to bed. Swearing silently at her naive belief a locked door would keep her safe at night, she watched the door ease open. From now on she'd pull a chest across it, too!

A man peered into the room, listened. . . . In the dim light of the dying fire, Stephanie couldn't decide who it was. She waited, watched him tiptoe toward her bed. He'd almost reached it when he realized it was empty and, stopping, he straightened, glancing around a trifle wildly.

Stephanie stepped into view. "You'd better leave."

The man stiffened. "I won't. Tomorrow Westerwood gets to propose. That's not fair to the rest of us."

"The rest of you?"

"Me, then," he said sullenly.

"So you think you'll compromise me and get me that way?" The man snickered. "What choice will you have?"

"All I have to do is say no."

"You won't do that."

"You don't know me very well, do you?" Stephanie stepped another step forward and light from a spurting flame flickered off her pistol. "Where would you prefer to be shot?" she asked, in a conversational tone. "The thigh? Or perhaps your shoulder? Your right or left arm? Name your spot."

The man backed up. "Here now, where'd you get that?" He relaxed. "Not that it'll be loaded, of course."

"How wrong-headed a man can be," muttered Stephanie. More loudly she said, "Of course it's loaded. What's the use of an unloaded pistol? Come one step nearer and you'll discover that the hard way. I think the shoulder will be best. A thigh wound might put you to bed and I'd just as soon you left the Priory."

"You wouldn't do it. No woman would."

Three things happened then. The man started toward Stephanie; Stephanie pulled the trigger; and Meg, approaching from the side, hit the man over the head with the porcelain night pot.

Meg lowered the pot and looked into it. "M'ol' auntie had one with a head painted in it," she said absently. "Forget who it was or what she called him, but we all thought it funny to squat on, you know?"

"There's one of those in the attic. A Dr. Sacheverel, I believe I was told. The potter was said to have made a fortune . . ." Stephanie, her gaze riveted on the man she'd shot, realized she was babbling and closed her mouth. She forced herself to relax.

Then footsteps in the hall caught her attention. Meg, also hearing, turned and raised her odd weapon as the door burst open. She lowered the pot. "About time you're getting here, my blidy lordship. What took you so long?"

Chris leaned against the doorjamb. He looked from his wife to the man on the floor and on to where Stephanie held her pistol pointed downward. "Why do you need me?" he asked. "It appears you've taken care of it all by yourselves."

"I only hit him over the head. Our daughter put the bullet in his shoulder."

"Did she? Well done, I suppose. But having taken care of this little problem yourselves, I don't see why you want me."

"To clean up the blidy mess, o'course," said Meg waving

the pot. "You just get him out o'here and tucked away safe so we can go back to bed and get our beauty sleep."

"You made the mess, you clean it up."

The butler, half-dressed, appeared, his shocked face peering over Lemiston's shoulder.

"Abbot," said Stephanie, her voice not quite normal, "you will order Lord Hamstead carried back to his room and send for the doctor. You will also see his bags are packed and that he removes from the Priory at the earliest possible hour."

"Yes, my lady," said the obviously subdued servant.

It hadn't occurred to Abbot that any of the men invited to the Priory would go so far as to attempt to rape his young and well-loved mistress. Perhaps it had gone to his head to have Lord Lemiston home again, to say nothing that he'd felt betrayed that Lady Stephanie had flouted his decision concerning the so-called Lady Lemiston—except, thought the confused man, it appeared she truly was Lady Lemiston. In any case, Lady Stephanie Morris had been mistress here for a very long time now.

"I'll see that everything is done just as you'd wish it," he added.

Chris cast a wry look toward his daughter and grimaced, but then turned to stare icily at the crowd gathered in the hall. "It seems one of our gentlemen guests was too much in his cups this evening and forgot himself. He also forgot that my daughter is well trained to defend herself with her pistol. The drama is over and I would be pleased if everyone would return to their beds."

The crowd drifted away, wondering who was lying, face-down, on the floor of Lady Stephanie's bedroom. A couple of gentlemen who had toyed with notions of a similar invasion of her ladyship's bed chamber decided they'd better think again. One or two, desperately in need of funds but, still retaining most of the gentlemanly standards with which they'd been reared, were shocked and disgusted. They might be addicted to play, but they'd never stoop so low as *that* to make

a recovery. It was a despicable ploy and so they told each other
as they returned to their rooms.

The next morning Anthony caught up with Stephanie as she
strode toward the orchard. She sent a fuming glance his way
and, although he grinned, he remained silent. For the third time
in as many yards, she kicked the skirts of her detested riding
habit out of her way. If it had been Francis and her brother
with whom she'd be shooting, she'd be comfortably dressed in
trousers and boots and she resented feeling as if she had been
forced to wear the much disliked habit.

Especially since nothing and no one but her own conscience
had made her don it. She sighed.

"Feeling better?" he asked softly.

She glanced at him. "No. But I'll not bite off your head,
either. Not for something that's my own fault."

He chuckled. Grasping her arm, he slowed her pace. "You'll
get along better if you don't rush so." She glared, but, with
him holding her, she had no choice. Once it became obvious
to both of them his assessment was correct, that her slower
pace meant her skirts didn't get so much in her way, he said,
"I hear I missed a great deal of excitement last night."

"Excitement!" Stephanie grimaced. "You think it exciting
to shoot a man? I don't suppose I'll ever forget . . ." She drew
in a sharp breath at the memory of bullet hitting flesh and
shivered slightly. "Well. Never mind that. The worst part is
that it wasn't necessary. If only I'd waited half an instant, Meg
would've crowned him and floored him and I needn't have
done it."

"Yes, but no one would have heard her hit him, whereas I
understand half his lordship's guests heard the pistol shot."

"Including my unrespected sire. If he heard it, why did you
not?"

"I doubt if he could have done. Our rooms are too far away.
In my humble opinion, he was roused," his brows arched, "per-

haps by the gentleman's valet? I'd guess he was *sent* to your room, the idea being that you'd be caught in such a compromising situation you'd be forced to wed the villain. Which villain was it, by the way?"

"You mean that isn't common gossip?"

"Your father seems to be doing his best to protect the man, deeming it his fault the fool got himself shot."

"I'd say that's taking responsibility too far," Stephanie said with a touch of acid. "Lemiston didn't have a hand in forming the imbecile's morals. And it's a lack of morals that drove the simpleton to my room. He knew I had pistols there, too," added Stephanie thoughtfully. "They were all standing in the hall when I used the excuse of planning this shoot to give out that bit of information. Now, did he forget, or did he believe, as our dearly unbeloved Baron Stread so obviously does, that a woman wouldn't have the will to shoot even to defend herself . . ."

Anthony cast her a thoughtful look. "Now you've done it once, *could* you do it again?"

"It would, I think, be more difficult the second time . . ." Stephanie frowned. "As long as I live I'll not forget the sound of that bullet hitting flesh! It was awful . . ."

Again he sent a quick glance her way. This time he spoke more sharply. "You'll not let that stop you if the need arises?"

Stephanie turned to look at Anthony who strode beside her, his eyes forward, his mouth grim. "You think I'll have reason to shoot again."

Even though it was a statement, he answered. "I think, through no fault of your own, you've been set in the midst of a hornet's nest of trouble, my sweet Stephanie." He glanced down at her, touching a loose tendril of hair. "I don't want it to be *you* who is stung."

"In future I'll not only lock my door, but pull a chest across it. And I'll have both pistols loaded."

"It wouldn't hurt to have your maid sleep with you, as well.

A servant's word isn't the best in the world, but it wouldn't hurt if it came to real trouble."

"The room really isn't large enough for two. Meg slept there last night because she was too exhausted to face whatever her husband might have wished to throw her way, but she'll not be there tonight."

"But it isn't only at night you're at risk," he objected.

"No?"

"I suspect that shooting the man in your room may deter anyone else from trying to harm you there, but what about when you are out and about on your morning rounds? These men are stronger than you, my sweet, and one of them might be able to sneak up on you. Then, too, we mustn't forget that someone has the bad habit of mistaking you for your brother! We don't want you killed by mistake, my love."

Stephanie pushed aside a branch heavy with small green fruit and moved forward before speaking. "It *is* a hornet's nest, is it not?" She pushed aside one more branch and stepped onto the green which had been made into a shooting gallery. It had originally been laid out for bows and arrows and only in the last century adapted for guns. At one end was a man-made hillock, formed in the shape of an ancient barrow. The sod grassing the alley was well scythed, well rolled, the footing even. At the near end were two long tables on one of which were placed supplies for loading the pistols, mugs and pitchers set out on the other.

"We'll be shooting pistols only today?"

Stephanie checked that all was as she'd ordered and looked thoughtfully at the table ready to hold liquid refreshments. "I thought it best," she said absently. "If we were to attempt a general shoot involving a variety of firearms it could take days, and that isn't the point of this little charade, is it?"

"The point is to get rid of another of the men pursuing you?"

"Of course."

Anthony nodded. "You managed that with a great deal of

finesse, my sweet, tricking him into betting with you. I did think, just for a moment, you'd give it all away . . ."

"It was only for an instant that I thought you'd betrayed me," she said, with the hint of an apology in her tone. "I don't think I'll lose, but, if it happens, I can *listen* to a proposal, can I not? Ah, Theo!" she said sharply. "You came out alone?"

"No. Several of the guests stopped to see if there were any apples near enough ripe to eat."

"They'll get the stomach ache."

"I doubt they'll find any large enough to tempt them," said Theo as he strolled toward the tables where he calmly loaded his pistols. "When will you shoot, Stephie?"

"Not until later." A mischievous smile making her face glow, she added, "No sense in spoiling everyone's fun too soon."

It was that glowing face her father saw as he pushed aside the last branch and stepped into the alley. For an instant he was caught by it. The life and humor and intelligence revealed there!

His plan would kill that. Was that what he truly wanted? An instant's confusion settled over him, but Lemiston shrugged it away, turning to greet the first of the men who would participate in the contest.

Much to Stephanie's disgust, her father took over the organization of the afternoon's entertainment. She sat on one of the tables, swinging her legs and watched him. He did it rather well, she decided, the choosing of lots to begin and the setting of paces for the first round. He also took the bets in hand, writing them into a betting book, something Stephanie had not thought to provide—but an excellent guard against arguments if, later, a man tried to renege on a bet, or truly thought it other than it was.

Stephanie had ordered the refreshments to be brought out at a later hour. She was chagrined when she realized she'd been over-ridden: Abbot arrived and directed several footmen in preparing a keg and setting out bottles, which joined the mugs and pitchers already on the smaller table provided for that purpose.

Finished, Abbot gave Stephanie an apologetic look and she shrugged, telling him silently it wasn't his fault. Besides, very likely her father knew what he was doing, and that was an admission she didn't really care to make.

Anthony leaned against the table near her. "They seem quite happy, do they not?"

"Will it last?"

"Not beyond your contest with Westerwood!"

"You are so certain I'll win?"

"Oh yes. I haven't forgotten that I was required to buy a new whip!"

"You haven't told that story?"

"No."

"Why not?"

He cast a thoughtful look her way. "I hold the whole experience too precious to make a tale of it, my sweet."

Stephanie turned to stare at him, discovered he was eyeing her with a sober expression she didn't understand, and turned quickly away, rather wary of both his intense study and the serious expression which accompanied it.

"Sweetings?"

"You shouldn't call me that."

"Why do you object now when you never have before?" he asked quietly.

Stephanie wondered that herself. It had something to do with the fact she sensed he wasn't teasing now, but was that logical? Besides, it wasn't something she could use as an explanation. Before she'd determined an answer, the baron approached, and she was almost glad because it meant she needn't answer the unanswerable.

"You aren't shooting in the competition?" Baron Stread asked Anthony. He cast a sneering glance at Stephanie, a glance that induced a steadying anger as it skimmed down her figure.

"No," said Anthony easily, drawing the man's attention away from her. "Chris and I decided it would be unfair for us to compete. Taking candy from babes, that would be!"

"You talk big, Huntersham," the baron said, glaring at Anthony, "but I've yet to see any reason for it."

"You will." Anthony smiled wolfishly. "After the general contest is over, then we'll have Westerwood shoot his playing card to settle that bet, and then Chris and I will give a demonstration of real shooting."

"Ah. You've decided your little girl here isn't to defend *her* bet? She is to renege?"

"Hardly. That's the high point of the afternoon, wouldn't you agree?"

"You mean, of course, that by *that* time Westerwood will be so drunk he couldn't hit the side of a haystack, let alone a target!"

"Hmm. We hadn't thought of that. I must remind Chris to take away all alcohol in plenty of time that everyone will be sober, must I not?"

The baron scowled, perceiving he'd just made impossible a complaint which might, later, have been used to cancel or delay that particular competition. He scowled, stared thoughtfully at Stephanie who looked back levelly, and, without another word, stalked off.

"He doesn't love you, sweetings."

"I know. How sad." The cynical half-smile tipped her mouth, faded. "So, since he does *not*, why doesn't he go away and leave me be?"

"Because he wants your dowry, and the only way to get it is to take you, too."

"He won't get it."

"No. I don't think he will. Even if he manages some trick to compromise you, you'll say him nay, will you not?"

"I wouldn't wed that one for all the tea in China." Her chuckle lightened the air. "If you've recently had reason to buy a pound of tea, you'd know just how serious I am!"

Anthony laughed. "Since I just brought in a cargo, much of which was tea from China, and it sold in London for even more than I expected, I think I've a glimmering of exactly how seriously you'll object to having our dear baron to husband. What about taking me instead?"

Stephanie stiffened, then forced herself to relax. "You shouldn't tease about such things, Anthony. Obviously you've been gone from England far too long. An English girl," she said in a falsely kind tone, "particularly one who is as ancient as I, should jump at the chance of wedding anyone so foolish as to drop such words into a jesting conversation."

"Ah. Then you accept?"

"You know I don't." Stephanie drew in a deep breath. "You may as well know that I determined long ago that I've no wish to wed. Anyone. Ever. Ask Theo if you don't believe me! You see, I like my life just as it is and I'm damned if I'll have some man around who has the right to order it otherwise!"

"But," said Anthony in a thoughtful tone, "what if the man did *not* order it otherwise? What if he liked you just as you are? What then, my sweet?"

Stephanie felt warmth flowing up into her cheeks and wished her hair were free of its braid so she could hide her face in it. "Don't push me, Huntersham." To cover her embarrassment, she spoke more sharply than she might otherwise have done. "This is not a subject in which I find the least bit of humor, especially not now—given my father's fell intentions."

Anthony eyed her firm little chin and resisted sighing. Instead he looked around for a change of subject. "Ah! I didn't know Theo dropped his lot in the hat. See who he drew for partner . . ."

Stephanie *did* sigh. "The blidy baron. He won't like it when Theo beats him. It'll only make him more determined than ever to win the dowry stakes! Blast Theo!"

"Theo will win?"

"Unless the baron is a far better shot than I'd guess him to be. Actually, it would take a surprisingly good shot to beat either of us. From what you say, you or my sire might do it." She turned when a bright flash of color caught her eye. "Oh lord. That must be a gown she bought in London!"

Anthony chuckled. "Dear Meg. She'd shame the devil before she'll be other than she is."

"I truly thought she'd be busy forever and forgot to warn her. I left her with the modiste and Jane, too, since she understands fashion. But something tells me Meg didn't like the advice she was getting!"

Chris strolled toward his wife, glanced once at her flamboyant hat and dazzling gown, and then ignored her dress, except for the low-voiced comment, "No wonder Abbot wouldn't admit you!"

"Meg, I thought you were choosing a new wardrobe," said Stephanie when the two approached. She noted she'd not avoided an accusing note and could have kicked herself.

"What's to choose? Once that seamstress took m' measurements, I left it to your Jane. Nice girl, Jane, but not just in my style, you know?"

"And my daughter is?"

"Your daughter is the only real lady in that house," said Meg, faintly belligerent, and turned back to Stephanie. "I warned you I wouldn't like the colors or the fashions, and since I don't, well, it don't matter what they choose, does it?"

"I suppose that makes sense. I told Sissy to bring the boys out when their father and Huntersham have their demonstration shoot."

"That's kind of you. They'll like that."

"You didn't ask me if it were all right," said her father.

Stephanie responded in a sweet voice. "Lord Lemiston, do you have any objections to your sons witnessing you show the idiots you've invited into your ancestral home exactly how one puts a bullet into a target?"

"What makes you think I'll show them anything at all?"

"From what Sir Francis has said and Anthony confirmed, how can it be otherwise?"

"You can take that innocent look from your face, daughter. I know you hope I'll miss every shot."

"You're wrong. As much as I resent your presence here, upsetting everything as you've done, I dislike those gentlemen—the unmarried ones, anyway—still more. Show them up with my pleasure!"

Lemiston gave her a thoughtful look and then, when she chuckled, glanced at his wife.

Meg nudged him in the ribs. "She's a better woman than most, is she not, my blidy lordship? She'll roll you up, foot and guns afore she's done with you!"

"Where did you learn the military talk?" ask Lemiston.

"From Colonel Lord Winston. Last night. He told me he thought I'd rolled up the company, foot and guns, when I came into dinner last night, so I asked him what he meant and he kindly explained."

"Winston, hmmm?" Lemiston turned to look at his old friend, his eyes narrowed. "Yes, he always was a gentle and perceptive soul. Too soft for the military, I thought. I wondered how he'd do in the army, but he seems to have done well, colonel and all."

"Poor man," said Meg, her eyes on the colonel. "He done well there, but he's got pain deep within him he'll never be rid of nonetheless," she said softly.

Lemiston gave her a sharp look, nodded once, and turned away to get the competition started.

"How do you know Winston is in pain?" Stephanie asked Meg, when Lemiston began giving orders to the men. "Does he have wounds which didn't heal properly?"

"I don't mean his body, although 'twas a saber cut sent him home and has him limping. 'Tis his soul, like. More'n his *words* last night, 'twas what he *wouldn't* say . . ." Meg trailed off.

"You liked him?"

"Oh yes. And feel sorry for him. He's in love with that little wife of his'n, you see, and that can only give the man pain."

"Is he? It will?" Stephanie was gaining a new picture of her stepmother; one that surprised her a great deal.

"Deep in love and she nought but a flighty piece. He left her at home while he was in Portugal and Spain—to keep her safe-like. Mistake that . . ."

"Hmm." Stephanie noticed Meg's eyes darting from the colonel to Lord Lemiston and wondered if, perhaps, Meg's understanding was based on her own feelings for her husband. But Anthony's touch on her arm drew her thoughts away from her stepmother.

"Watch! Theo's up to the mark," he said.

The two women turned.

Each round was to involve three shots taken in turn. A flipped coin determined that Stread shoot first. He was obviously pleased when his ball went through the ring just to the side of the center. He smiled patronizingly at Theo and stepped aside. When Theo's first shot went through the exact middle, his smug look changed to a scowl. When Theo's second did likewise, following another merely decent shot from the baron, Stread said something sneering about the luck of babes. *His* third shot went wild and, again Theo's hit a bull's-eye.

Stread threw down his pistol. "Fires erratically," he growled. "Not my usual gun. Weight's different." He looked around at the others and scowled. "Nothing but a fluke," he blustered. "Do it over and you'd see."

"I'd be happy to do it over if that's your wish," said Theo calmly. "Would you care to practice with that pistol before we do so?"

The baron growled something incomprehensible and removed himself to where he could relieve his temper by shouting at a footman for not anticipating his need of a bumper of brandy.

Theo looked after him frowning. "Now why did he do that? I thought he wanted a rematch . . ."

"Did you really?" interrupted Lemiston. "I thought you were pushing him that way to show him up."

"Why would I wish to do anything of the sort!"

"Because he's a bully and a blackguard."

Theo was silent for a moment. "I see. I suppose the deed is as good as the wish, in this case."

Chris smiled at his eldest son. "You twins continually surprise me."

"If you'd not run off in a snit," drawled Theo without even the faintest trace of heat in his voice, "you'd have helped us grow as you wished and we'd be no surprise to you at all."

"Ah. You too resent that I left you to Francis's tender mercies?"

"Oh no not at all. Where did you get such a strange notion?" Lemiston blinked.

"For my own part," continued Theo as the next paired contenders flipped a coin, "I'm perfectly content as I am. I discovered at an early age I'm happier with books than with people, so living in Oxford suits me right down to the ground. You, if you'd remained in England, very likely would not have allowed your heir to develop such an irregular life."

"Very likely I would not."

"Which," said Theo, his eyes on the first contestant, "would have been a great pity. I suppose I'd have gone the way of many young men I know of that went down to London from university. There they waste the ready, get the pox, drink too much too often—wastrels merely because they've nothing better to occupy them."

"And you think you are better occupied, do you?"

"Ah, well shot!" said Theo, when the colonel hit the bull's-eye. "Better occupied . . . ? Why yes, I do. Do not you?"

"Why not occupy yourself with the estate if you don't care to join friends in their London revels?"

Theo grimaced. "Pigs. Hay. Thatching. *Mangel-wurzel,* for Heaven's sake! They may interest Stephanie, but I find it all a dead bore . . . Hmm, I wonder if I can best Colonel Winston," he said, breaking into his own thoughts as the colonel finished his round. "He's very good, is he not? But then a military man . . . one would expect him to know how to shoot, wouldn't one?" he said of the man who would be his rival in the next round. "I don't know that I can outshoot him."

Abruptly, Chris asked, "What would you do if you could never return to the Priory?"

"You mean if you were to sell it as you've hinted you might do?" Theo cast a sad glance toward his sister before lowering his gaze to his boots. "I would apply for and get a position at my old college. Or, if they had no position open, at another college. I would do very well."

"What would your sister do?"

Theo flashed a grin. "Very likely put on trousers permanently and apply for a job as estate agent somewhere. She'd do well too, you know."

"You can laugh at the notion she'd pretend to be a man?"

"If the world were a more sensible place, she wouldn't have to pretend, would she? She'd be judged on her ability and good sense and given the job she's suited for. But the world isn't sensible, so, very likely, she'd do what she had to do to do what she wanted to do."

"Nonsense. She'd never get away with it!"

"I hope she never has to make the attempt, but, my lord father, I must beg to differ. If it becomes necessary and she does as I suggest, then my bet would be on her!" Theo gave his father a straight look, turned on his heel, and strolled to where Stephanie and Anthony still rested, one against and the other on the table.

"What was that all about?" asked Stephanie.

"Another hint he means to rid himself of the Priory." Theo reached out a steadying hand, holding his white-faced sister in place. "Here now! Don't you dare!"

Stephanie rested against the palm of his hand for a moment then straightened. "I'm all right, but surely he'd not be so cruel . . ."

Neither twin noticed Anthony's frown. "Cruel?"

"As to sell the Priory . . ."

"That would be cruel?"

"It's been Lemiston land for so long, you see. It's part of us. Bred into us. I don't see how he can even think of such a thing. Surely he is merely trying to frighten Theo. Theo inherits—"

"Theo inherits." When she didn't speak, he added, "Not you."

"But you must understand that if I inherit," said Theo softly, "then Stephie wouldn't be driven away. You see?"

Guilt filled Anthony at what his buying the Priory had done to this intriguing woman. Although she didn't know it yet. "And if you don't inherit?" he asked Theo.

Stephanie drew in a deep breath and straightened her shoulders, but her pallor was still such as to worry Anthony. "In that case I'll do what I have to do."

"Marry one of those idiots?" suggested Anthony, his words soft, but his glance sharp.

Stephanie cast him a look of dislike. "You jest. I've alternatives."

"If you think to pretend you're a man and find a position somewhere as someone's estate agent, you should think again!"

"You think I couldn't do the work?"

"You could do the work, but could you bear to never again be the woman you are?"

"Being a woman has never done anything but cause me problems. When I play the man, I enjoy myself hugely and I needn't fear someone like the baron or Lambert—men who have nothing but contempt for women." Stephanie nodded. "I think they are ready for your next round, Theo."

The afternoon progressed. Westerwood did shoot the pips from his playing card, which gave Stephanie pause, but then she remembered how erratically he'd shot during the rounds before when he was only third in the contest. She would win.

Westerwood was accepting the congratulations of the men who had bet on him when, with a whoop, two youngsters broke from the trees into the alley and raced toward Lord Lemiston. "Papa, Papa!" squealed the younger throwing himself at his father who turned and caught him up just in time. The elder approached a trifle more warily.

"Well, son?" asked his lordship. "Have you no hug for your papa?"

With that, Lord Richard, too, threw himself into his father's arms.

"Why did you not come to me at once?" asked Lord Lemiston when he'd set the boys down.

"Didn't know if it were proper like," said Richard, digging a toe into the turf. "You a lordship and all."

"I'm exactly the same person I was when you last saw me, son. The title means nothing."

Richard grinned suddenly. "Should'a known that! I'm no different and that lady says I'm a lord, too."

Anthony chuckled. "So you are. Ah, Theo, may I introduce you to your brothers?"

"We've met, haven't we imps?" The boys nodded and went to stand beside their half-brother, looking up at him trustfully. Theo turned to his father. "May I see to them while you and Anthony shoot?"

"If you don't mind . . ." Lemiston gave his eldest son an odd look. "You *don't* mind?"

"I like them," said Theo, and grinned down at the boys who smiled back. "Come along out of the way, now. I'll stand you on that table and you'll be able to see every shot."

Lady Lemiston trailed along to where she could keep a close eye on the boys and also watch the exhibition. She soon decided Theo was to be trusted and moved to where Stephanie, her arms crossed, ignored the compliments, both real and snide, directed toward her by several of her suitors.

Meg deftly separated her stepdaughter from the men. "Why

does your brother want to pay attention to my brats?" she asked straightaway.

"Because he likes children," responded Stephanie just as straightly. "It's unlikely he'll ever have any of his own, so I suspect he is especially pleased to find he has younger brothers."

"Why don't he wed and breed himself a houseful?" asked Meg, suspicious.

"If you fear he has a particular interest in little boys," said Stephanie sharply, "you can, er, stubble it!"

"But would you know?" persisted Meg.

Stephanie sighed. "It's no particular secret, so why don't I simply explain. My brother, you see, is in love with a married woman who is true to her husband. I doubt very much he'll ever love another."

"The Morris way? To love once and never again?"

At the bitter words, Stephanie tore her eyes from where her father had just made his first shot which Anthony was to match exactly. "You do love him," she said softly

"To my sorrow."

"He'll not be a good husband to you?"

"I've no regrets *that* way." But the sorrow of which Meg spoke was obvious in the eyes with which she stared hungrily at her husband. Stephanie had no solution to the poor woman's problem and didn't offer platitudes.

Lemiston and Huntersham gave a show that would have gone down well at Astley's circus. They not only shot at such impossible targets as a piece of black thread placed across a white background, but they aimed back over their shoulders, using a mirror and other stunts of a similar nature. Then Anthony turned to Stephanie and held out a crop. He grinned, but there was a dare in his eyes.

Stephanie, realizing what he wanted, didn't hesitate. She took the whip, an old one she noticed, and walked toward the targets. There were cries of outrage, one or two of encouragement, and only one question. "Stephie, are you sure?" called Theo.

"Of course I'm sure."

She stood against the mound and flipped the whip sideways, her hands on her hips. Anthony raised his pistol, hesitated, lowered it. "Hold it higher, my lady. I find I'm more a coward than I thought."

Chuckling, Stephanie raised her arm. The whip extended across one of the used targets. She didn't even flinch at the twitch she felt when the bullet severed the narrow end of the crop, merely looking around for the tip which lay some feet away. She picked it up and took the two pieces back to Anthony.

"Don't you ever do anything so foolish again," hissed her father.

She glanced up at him, her brows in the Lemiston vee.

"You might have been killed!"

"That would bother you?"

"Of course it would bother me."

"Why?" Stephanie's frown deepened. "Because I'd no longer be available for your revenge?" For an instant his lordship looked confused and Stephanie wondered if, for the moment, he'd forgotten his resentment for his offspring.

All too soon confusion passed into anger. "Stop putting words in my mouth."

Stephanie watched Lemiston collect his young sons and stalk away to where Meg talked to Colonel Lord Winston. He didn't break into their conversation, but she noticed how closely he hovered, casting the occasional glare toward the colonel.

When Winston drifted away, Meg cast her husband a wry look. "Fool!" she said.

"Fool? Or careful?"

"He's a very pleasant man and willing to speak to me as if I were a real person. That doesn't mean I find him anything more than friendly, or *want* him to be anything more than a friend. What's more, he wouldn't."

"Why not?"

"Because of his *wife,* something you might not understand."

Meg collected her sons to her side and moved to join Stephanie who had realized she was eavesdropping and had turned away to unlock a square wooden box. Carefully Stephanie checked her pistols. As she loaded them she explained to her stepbrothers exactly what she was doing and why, and when she'd finished, she stood beside them, waiting for the word that her match had begun.

Stephanie was some feet from where they were to shoot her first round, but when told to come to the line, she lifted the first gun and, giving away the advantage of moving closer, placed her shot exactly in the center of her target.

Startled by her casual attitude which, if he'd only known it, was the object of her stratagem, Westerwood was a trifle off when he shot.

They moved back and Stephanie put another shot in the center, and again her opponent was a hair off. Her third and last shot was from a still greater distance, but the result was the same, except that Westerwood's shot was still farther from the bull's-eye. When Stephanie's win had been verified, he bowed to her, his mouth a grim line. Turning on his heel, he moved rapidly away and disappeared among the trees.

"He'll leave?" asked Stephanie of nobody in particular.

"He'll go," said Rotherwood. "That was the bet. Besides, I suspect from something he said earlier, he'd realized sometime during the night that you'd only promised to listen to his proposal, not accept it, and he'd have gone after your refusal anyway."

Stephanie glanced up into Rotherwood's face. "I don't suppose you'd care to make me a similar bet?"

"Oh, no, indeed not. I've seen you shoot, you see!" Rotherwood cast a thoughtful look around the group of men that was now allowed back at the keg and taking advantage of it.

"I think perhaps you've frightened Camberstone to the point he's about to shear off as well."

"Frightened him?"

Rotherwood grinned. "Even his uncle doesn't *shoot* at him, and he's afraid you might!"

"Poor boy."

"He's at least five years your senior!"

"He's a boy and will never be anything else. I feel sorry for him, but not to the degree I'd be so foolish as to wed him!"

Anthony joined them and Rotherwood cast him a wary look. "Sweetings," said Anthony, "Meg wondered if you are ready to go and if you'd walk back to the house with her and the boys."

"Certainly."

Stephanie had wondered how she could gracefully leave the shooting party which would, she suspected, rapidly drink itself into a condition she'd not wish to see. However that might be, she'd not wanted to simply slip away, particularly since she didn't trust either Stread or Lambert not to stalk her. With Meg and the boys as chaperon, she should be all right. When Anthony and Theo joined the little group, much to the boys' joy, she knew she could relax and forget her fears. For the moment.

Life, thought Stephanie, was no fun anymore. She had to worry every instant about who was near and what they'd do next! And given the last look she'd seen on Baron Stread's face, she knew that whatever it was *he* had in mind, it would not be pleasant. Lambert hadn't worn a particularly benign expression either . . .

Ah well, this day was about done. Tomorrow was another. With any luck, it might be better . . .

Eleven

The next morning Anthony joined Stephanie as she walked to the stables where Aladdin, already tacked up, awaited her. "You'll not stop making your rounds while this farce continues?" he asked.

"I've responsibilities. Would you shirk yours simply because it was a trifle dangerous?"

"It's the 'trifle' I object to. It's become common knowledge you ride out each morning, my sweet. Early. And that you only return when you feel you must."

"The 'early' saves me, does it not? Who, besides yourself, gets up at this hour? Actually, Anthony, my lad, you look as if you could do with a bit more sleep yourself."

"Since you insist on rising early, then I'll do likewise."

"Protecting me?"

He nodded.

"Why?"

"My future wife should not suffer the indignities to which a couple of her suitors would subject her. I protect my own, sweetings."

Stephanie didn't understand the emotions flooding her at his words. "But I am not yours," she said a trifle belatedly.

"Yet."

"I've sworn to remain unwed."

"And told me why. You'll eventually learn your reasons don't exist. Not with me."

Stephanie cast him a bitter glance. "That's what you *say.*

But you were shocked to find I was a woman dressed as a man. That shock tells me you lie."

"I freely admit I was shocked. I'd allowed a mere woman to shoot the end off my crop! At that time I'd no idea of just what a woman you are."

"Lady Eltonson had you cornered for some time last night, did she not?"

Anthony grinned. "She doesn't like you, little one."

"You turned her up sweet."

"I merely agreed you are everything she says you are. The difference between us is that I *like* what you are and she doesn't."

"Did she try to push you toward her friend's granddaughter?"

"Oh yes, but I cut off any attempts in that direction, or, come to that," he rubbed his chin, "any other."

She was distracted by the fact there was no grating noise. Again that vision of Anthony, shaving, filled her mind. Belatedly, she asked, "How?"

"I told her frankly I was secretly engaged and not free," he said promptly. He flashed a wicked grin her way. "She wanted to know the name of my bride and I responded, politely, of course, that if I told her it would no longer a secret be."

"Poor lady. She'll go quite mad attempting to discover who is to be the next Lady Huntersham."

"We can put her out of her misery anytime you say the word."

"Stop that!"

"Stop suggesting we'll wed? But we will, my sweet. Having found you, do you truly think I'll let you go?"

Stephanie didn't respond except to put her heels to Aladdin's sides. She was far ahead of Anthony's gelding when she turned up a lane between two tall hedges.

At that inopportune moment, a bird rose to one side of the path and Sahib played up. Anthony lost sight of Stephanie and missed the turn. When he realized he'd lost her, he swore.

Fluently. Then he set himself to tracking her down. For the next two hours he managed to just miss her at every point she stopped to talk to someone.

For her part, Stephanie almost immediately regretted riding away from Anthony. When the impulse leading her to do so subsided sufficiently and she could think rationally, she realized she'd felt safe with Anthony beside her—even if he did insist on teasing her unbearably.

It had never occurred to her she'd be sensitive to teasing. Certainly Theo's never bothered her. She merely gave as good as she got. Francis's teasing was, occasionally, a bit of a problem, since all too often there was a bite to it, a lesson she didn't wish to learn. And the only other person with whom she'd the sort of relationship that resulted in bantering was Jane, and Jane, a trifle lacking in the proper sort of humor, rarely jested.

But it was done and not to be undone, and, alone, Stephanie settled to accomplishing all she'd set herself to do that day. She went first to check on Mrs. Tipper. The farmer's wife was doing fine although she looked uncomfortable and was obviously sleeping badly.

"Not long now," said that motherly woman placidly. "Maybe I wouldn't object if you'd send me a girl in a day or two?"

"I'll do that," said Stephanie, and, as she rode away, wondered who was available. Obviously no one. She grimaced. As much as she preferred to avoid hiring casual help from the agency in Chichester, Abbot must go into town and do so. Now, he'd need even more then she'd forecasted. As much as she'd miss her, she'd have to send Sarah to help Mrs. Tipper because Sissy, who would normally have done it, was needed in the nursery.

After leaving the Tipper farm, she headed for the Eberts' where she wished to see how near the oats were to cutting. Very close she decided, chewing on a few grains. Mr. Ebert agreed. He'd been about to send word, he said, that he'd need all the help he could come by since he didn't like the feel of the weather and wanted the scything and shocking done as quickly as might be. Stephanie added hiring day laborers to her list of things to do.

She next rode over to see old Graham Wilkins. He grumbled and grunted, disliking that he must agree with Stephanie in any way shape or form, but he too admitted it was time for oat harvest. Worse, he, who was the area's best weatherman, also disliked the smell of the air and asked, offhandedly, if extra help might be found.

Stephanie sighed softly, wondering if she'd put it off too long, so that every other landowner in the region was already hiring up all the readily available day labor. One *more* thing to worry about.

She was ambling along a lane not far from her private place along the shore when all thoughts of field work, of Mrs. Tipper's impending labor of quite another sort, and the weather dropped from her mind as a man on horseback burst from a clump of wild rhododendron and held a gun on her. She faced Lambert's pistol with her back straight and her face expressionless.

"Coward," she said, working methodically at one finger after another of her glove.

"I prefer to think myself cautious," said the slaver, sneering. "Take your feet from your stirrups."

Stephanie obeyed.

"Now turn that fine animal and guide him between those trees. Since you appear to know every inch of Lemiston property, I'm sure you're aware of the pleasant little glade perhaps a hundred yards in. Stop when you reach it."

"Would you shoot, I wonder?"

"Of course." Lambert shrugged. "It would merely be a great accident, would it not? Whoever is trying to murder your pretty little brother would have made a terrible mistake, would he not?" The sneer and all other expression dropped from his face. "You'd better believe I'd shoot."

Stephanie did. A slaver, who trafficked in human souls,

many of whom died in the holds of the ships transporting them to the new world, would certainly not quibble about murdering an uncooperative female.

As Stephanie turned Aladdin she dropped her glove. Until she was certain Lambert hadn't noticed, she held her breath, relaxing slightly when he followed Aladdin into the grove. Would Anthony see it? And would he read its message? Stephanie hoped so. And then she wondered at her belief he was following on her heels as fast as he was able. Because she did believe it.

"Dismount."

Stephanie did. She turned to face her tormentor who didn't let his gun waver. "Now what?" she asked.

"Now you strip."

"You'll enjoy that, won't you?"

"Oh yes." Watching her, never moving his aim, he too dismounted. "More so," he added, "since I know you'll hate it."

"How did you get so wicked? Were you born that way or did you have to work at it?"

Lambert chuckled. "Tart-tongued wench, aren't you? I'll take care of that when we're wed. Either you'll learn to hold your tongue or I'll have it from your mouth."

"We'll never be married."

"After I'm done with you, you'll be glad to marry me."

"I don't think so."

Lambert scowled. "Woman, haven't you any notion what I intend?"

Stephanie forced her brows to arch. "Of course. You'll rape me and take me to my father who will insist I marry you. But you see, there's a very interesting but not well-known law in this land: You *can't* force an unwilling woman to the altar and I'm damned if I'd put myself permanently in your power for any reason whatsoever."

"So, merely raping you won't be enough." Lambert's scowl deepened and for a moment Stephanie thought his attention would falter and she could take advantage of his distraction to reach for her own pistol. Then his gaze sharpened. "So. What if I threaten that milk-and-water brother of yours as well?"

"That horse won't run. Someone is *already* threatening my brother, as you seem to know." She gave him a thoughtful look. "It isn't common knowledge, however. I wonder how you learned of it?"

"It doesn't matter how, does it?" He gestured. "Get that jacket off. Now."

"Ah!" she said. "I must conclude you've *already* threatened Theo, must I not?" When he motioned she unbuttoned one button, than another. "How else could you know?"

"I've no intention of spoiling sport for the idiot who's doing it." Lambert grinned wickedly. *"I'll* not tell."

"I see. You know the person responsible and will allow him to continue trying to kill my brother?"

"Something finally shocks that insensitive and unfeminine soul of yours?" He laughed loudly, but cut it off, glancing around. "Don't want to catch the ear of that watch dog of yours, do I? Why, by the way, did you go riding off away from him this morning?"

"Huntersham? He made me angry. I don't even know why now," she said, preventing what she foresaw to be the next question.

"Huntersham's a damned nuisance," growled Lambert. "If I weren't preoccupied with *you,* I wouldn't mind if he did show up. I've a bone or two to pick with the bastard, myself."

"Oh?"

"He's gotten in my way once or twice, that's all." Lambert mused on the wrongs done him by Ryder—Huntersham that is—and then realized Stephanie hadn't removed her coat. "Off with it."

She shrugged out of it, making more of a difficulty of the procedure than there truly was. Her heart pounded with a fear she was damned if she'd let this creature know. Where the devil was Anthony!

"Now the vest."

Again she attempted to make a slow thing of it, but this time he was watching like a hawk and prodded her on.

"The shirt."

Stephanie sighed. The shirt followed the vest to the ground and she stood tall and proud in only the thinnest of shifts which was tucked into her trousers.

Lambert motioned with his gun. Stephanie could see sweat beading his brow and watched his other hand stroke up from his crotch, pressing hard against the weapon she feared far more than the gun he held on her. "Now," he said, his voice thick, "the trousers, my dear lady. Oh yes, the trousers."

"I'll have to remove my boots first."

"Do it."

Stephanie sat on a fallen log and reached into her left boot. And stopped. Cursing silently but with more fluency than she'd ever done, she moved her hands, preparing to remove the boot. Idiot that she was, her guns were still in their locked wooden case. She'd forgotten to return the pair to her boots where they usually lived! She scowled.

"You're afraid," he gloated.

"Merely having a bit of difficulty with this boot. Do you find it easy to remove yours?" she asked politely.

"Get on with it, damn it. I can't wait much longer." He unfastened one side of his leathers as he spoke, letting the flap fall. He reached inside to touch himself. "Come on!"

Stephanie dropped the first boot, reached for the second. Where the devil was Anthony?

"Finally," he said when the second boot hit the ground. "Now stand up."

He licked his lips when Stephanie obeyed.

"Come here."

She hesitated.

"Come here," he growled.

She moved toward him.

"Faster."

She continued the same pace.

"Damn you!" He reached out and yanked her up against him. Shoving the gun into a holster on his saddle, he pressed a hand against her bottom, pulling her hard against his aroused body, rubbing against her and crooning softly, his eyes half closed. Stephanie reached around him toward his gun, stretching toward it. Her fingertips touched hard metal . . .

Not so involved as she'd hoped, Lambert flung her away and she fell. Standing over her, he glared down at her. "Think you'd shoot me with my own gun? Not this man! You've shot one already and that should be enough for any woman."

Stephanie raised herself on her hands, pressing them into the ground, hard. "I shot to defend myself. You'd do the same."

"Well, you won't shoot me," he said, stalking nearer.

"No. I've something else in mind," she muttered. Thrusting upward with one leg and the full force of her hips, she shoved one stocking-clad foot straight into Lambert's crotch.

He screamed, doubling up and falling to the ground where he moaned and groaned and rolled back and forth clutching himself. He half crouched and vomited, still holding his privates with one hand. He'd just rolled back into a hunched position when Anthony strolled into the glade.

"You might have gotten here a bit sooner," growled Stephanie, who had her shirt back on and half buttoned.

"You might have stayed with me this morning and not gotten yourself into this fix," he retorted, his eyes on the still groaning Lambert.

"Oh, yes, of course. It's all my fault," said Stephanie, and found she was shaking so much she had to sit down.

Two more men rode roughly through the woods, breaking branches as they came into the clearing.

"What's toward?" asked Colonel Lord Winston. "We heard a scream."

"That animal decided to see if rape would win him a fair maiden," said Anthony, thrusting his chin toward Lambert.

"Low blow that," said the other, eyeing the writhing man.

"Shouldn't hit a man that low, Huntersham. Maybe you've been gone too many years. Just a word? Not good ton, m'boy."

"You think *I* laid him out, do you?" Anthony chuckled. "My sweet lady there did that to him."

"Did she now?" The second man's brows arched. "Strange, someone teaching her that old trick. We don't teach ladies such things, you know? Or perhaps . . . *did* you tell her?"

"I suspect her guardian was the culprit," mused Anthony. "Sir Francis seems to have taught her a great deal more than any woman is supposed to know about all sorts of things."

"Hmm. Glad my lady isn't that sort. I much prefer a dainty woman," said the colonel, and the other men, even Lambert— or perhaps Lambert was still too preoccupied to care—were politely silent about some of the colonel's dainty wife's preferred activities which, since she didn't like women, most often included some deluded male.

"It takes all sorts," said Anthony finally, and his eyes told Stephanie *he* preferred her more independent style. "Well, I suppose someone must clean up the trash. Lambert!" he said, his voice demanding attention. "The latest word I've received is that you've a ship refitted and ready to sail from Bristol waters. We'll see you there and you'll leave England. Forever."

"Damned if I will. That she-devil may have ruined me for life." The slaver was still exceedingly pale and looked as if he might cast up accounts all over again, but he was no longer curled into a tight ball. "I'll see her hung for this."

"Oh, no you won't. You'll go quietly and, if you know what's good for you, you'll never touch this island again." Anthony moved to where he could stare straight into Lambert's glowering gaze. "Believe me, Lambert, I'll have covered every port and every free trader. I'll have word of it if you try to return. It isn't only what you tried to do to Lady Stephanie just now. It's your whole way of life I object to."

"I'll have you killed," growled Lambert.

"Will you?" Anthony eyed him. "Thanks for the warning. If I die anywhere but in my bed, and you'd better hope I do, a couple of very good men will hunt you down and kill you whether you were responsible or not. Don't think you can bribe them. They think they owe me a very great deal for one reason or another. Besides, they hate slavers and will enjoy the opportunity of torturing you a bit before ridding the world of you forever. Forget you ever saw me, Lambert. Forget there was ever anyone named Lady Stephanie Morris. You'll be exceedingly sorry if you don't."

"Needs an escort to Bristol, Huntersham," said Colonel Lord Winston, much impressed by Anthony's tone and his stance, both of which radiated authority.

"Are you offering?" asked Anthony bluntly.

"I and my valet, who was my batman when we were with the army, could do it. We'll set off as soon as *he's* packed," Winston thrust his chin toward Lambert, "and we've shoved a few things in a portmanteau. You can trust us."

"You can take my coach," said Stephanie quietly.

"Good thought," said Anthony nodding. "Your coachman and a couple of outriders will assure that slippery devil causes no problems. You realize you'll have to wait to see he actually leaves port, don't you?" he asked Winston.

"Yes," said the colonel. Then after a moment, he asked, "But what's to prevent him sailing right back in again?"

"Don't worry about that. I'll have my man on the road right behind you. He'll contact agents I've used in the past and they'll pay others to spread the word. Lambert's too wary of his skin to ever come back, are you not?" Anthony nudged Lambert, who, head hanging, nodded. "Up with you."

"Can't."

"I'd suggest you try," said Anthony blandly.

"You don't know . . ."

"You will move. Now."

Lambert glanced up, saw something in Anthony's features which convinced him he'd no choice, and, moaning, groaning, wincing, and holding himself in an awkwardly strained sort of way, he minced to where the colonel waited to help him on his horse.

"I can't ride!"

Anthony had followed closely. He'd no intention of giving this villain an inch. "Then you can walk," he said, no sympathy whatsoever in his tone.

After another moment's hesitation, Lambert grabbed his horse's reins and, with an occasional moan, made his way through the trees toward the path.

Silence filled the glade. After a long moment in which she strained to follow the sounds of the retreating trio, Stephanie finally relaxed. It was over. She hung her head, breathing deeply—and realized tears were running down her cheeks.

She was *crying*. She never cried. She never *had* cried.

"How odd," she muttered, rubbing her sleeve over her face.

Anthony sat beside her, turned her gently into his arms. She wept, her face hidden in his jacket, one hand clutching a lapel. "He's gone, my brave girl," he said gently.

"I didn't know I was so frightened until you showed up."

"You'd already saved yourself at that point, my love. It was all over the instant you hit him."

"I'm not certain that's true."

"What do you mean?" asked Anthony when she didn't continue.

"I'd been thinking, *dreaming,* of shooting him the whole time he held his gun on me." Even as she'd buttoned her shirt she'd stared at the pistol Lambert had shoved into a saddle holster, wondered if she had the nerve, thinking that just perhaps she did. "Shooting him *dead* with his own gun," she added.

Stephanie's muffled words brought a chuckle. He tipped her head up and saw tears, which, starting all over again, dripped over her lashes and ran down her cheeks. "Is that something to cry about?" She nodded. "Where, by the way, were *your* pistols?"

"My stupidity," she wailed. "My blidy stupidity!"

He chuckled again. "How so?"

"I forgot to put them back in my boot holsters! They are in their case where I left them after taking them back to my room yesterday. I was playing with my half-brothers and never reloaded."

"Yes, that was a bit stupid, was it not?" He grinned and ducked to put a kiss on her lips. Finding it far too brief, he tipped her head up and, after sipping the last of her tears from her cheeks, kissed her again, a long solemn kiss.

Somehow, in the heady moments which followed, Stephanie found she'd been turned, that she lay across his lap, her head on his other shoulder and his hand doing very odd things, having, somehow, found its way up under her shirt. Odd things she found she liked very well. *So* well she couldn't bring herself to ask . . . *order* . . . him to stop.

Sometime later she discovered she'd managed to unbutton his vest, pull his shirt from his trousers, and insert her hand against warm skin where she discovered a rather unsteadily beating heart.

"You've too many clothes on, love," he whispered into her hair and gasped when her curious fingers found, played with, a tiny sensitive nubbin hidden in the mat of hair covering his chest.

"Theo doesn't have this much hair here."

"And how," he murmured, his eyes closed, "do you know that?"

"From when we swim," she muttered, her fingers raking through the intriguing mass, the feel of the stiff hairs against her palm sending tremors up her arm. "Sir Francis has more, but not this much."

He grasped her shoulders and pushed her away. "What do you know about the baronet's bare hide?"

Stephanie blinked, tried to get back close to him, felt herself lightly shaken. She frowned. "Know . . . ?"

"How the devil do you know your damned guardian has more hair on his chest than Theo?"

"He taught us to swim. Of course I've seen his bare hide." She scowled and pushed a strand of hair loosened from her braid back behind her ear. "What did you think? That he's held me and touched me as you've been doing? You swear at Francis for undone sins and you use Lambert's real attempt on me as an excuse to exile him for reasons of your own, and then you attempt the same thing yourself?" She struggled to free herself. "You just let me go, you . . ."

"Damn!"

It wasn't as easy to subdue Stephanie as it had been the farmer's daughter, but Anthony was larger and stronger, and Stephanie found herself on her back, the backs of her hands held against the ground above her head, and Anthony sprawled across her body. She glared up at him.

"You certainly know how to ruin a mood," he said, smiling down at her.

"You were seducing me."

"You weren't objecting."

She turned her head to the side, stared at a tiny pink flower almost hidden in grass. "I wasn't thinking."

"Neither was I. Thinking only interferes with the pleasure, you see." He released her and rolled away, covering his eyes with the back of his wrist. "But I am now. It was unfair to you. You were in no state to decide anything, and what we were about to do is a big decision for a woman . . ."

Stephanie raised herself on one elbow and stared at him. "That's it?"

"Hmm?" He lifted his arm enough that he could see her with one eye.

"That's all you have to say?"

"What more can I say?"

She picked the flower and twirled it. "Damned if I know, but it seems like there should be *something.*"

"I could tell you I love you to distraction and got carried away by the feel of you warm and pliant in my arms . . ."

"You *could,* but I don't think you should." She stared at the tiny petals, marveled at the wonderful combination of form and color and the faintest of subtle scents; surprising scent, given how small the flower was.

"Put that down and look at me."

Stephanie slowly raised her eyes to meet his stern gaze.

"Why should I not tell you I love you?" he asked.

"Because I won't be lied to. You like women. You like bedding them. I was here, available, and you are not such a slow-top you'd pass up an opportunity. Any opportunity whatever and whenever."

"I am not a rake."

"Are you not? I think you must be. Think of our first meeting where you kissed first Mary and then me. And, then of course, there's today. You used the situation here once you'd rid England of that evil man to use me, did you not? No Anthony, the one thing I'll not allow is lies."

"I've never lied to a woman in my life."

"Have you not?" Stephanie reflected that he had not truly said he loved her, only that he could have told her that. "No I don't suppose you have," she said, a sad look to her drooping figure.

Anthony sat up, his ankles crossed, and gave her a baffled stare, his wrists resting on his knees and hands hanging loose between his legs. Stephanie couldn't keep from looking at where tight trousers pressed against his evident arousal. She was fascinated. If he hadn't spoiled things by asking questions she would very likely be experiencing the pleasure she was sure he'd give her if she'd only give in to the wonderful sensations he could induce all over her body. What if . . .

"Stephanie, *don't*," he said softly. She glanced up, felt warmth flow up from her breasts into her neck and face. He grinned but there was a wry twist to it. "I'm having enough trouble keeping my hands off you. You keep looking at me in that heated way and I don't think I'll manage it much longer!"

She looked away. "I'm sorry," she said in a tight voice.

"So am I," he said and there was no missing the truth, or

the self-deriding humor. It made her glance back. "Smile at me, sweetings. Please?"

"I don't know that I can."

He tipped his head, queryingly.

"Yet."

"Too much happened too fast, didn't it, my love?" he said, his voice gentle.

"Between Lambert's evil intentions and your very personal attentions, I'm not exactly feeling my normal self."

His eyes brightened, but he didn't laugh this time. "Yes, a rather hectic day, altogether, was it not?" After a moment he asked, "Stephanie, is there somewhere you could go for the *rest* of the day and also tonight? A friend's house perhaps?"

Stephanie instantly thought of Grannie Black. "Yes." She had, on very rare occasions, stayed the night in Grannie's tiny cottage, rolled up in a blanket before the fire. She could do it again.

"Then let's get you dressed and I'll escort you there. I'll make your excuses to Jane who can make up some reason why you are gone for the night. You needn't face that crowd until you feel more the thing. Besides, since I want to make absolutely certain Lambert can't play games he shouldn't, I'll be gone myself for some hours and I don't like leaving you unprotected." He rose to his feet in one graceful move. "If no one knows where to find you, then no one is likely to cause problems." Approaching her, he held out his hand.

Stephanie, pretending she didn't see it, looked around for the clothes Lambert had forced her to remove. They were only a few feet away and she stretched, reaching for her boots. She scooted to the log and pulled them on. Then, still not looking at Anthony, she buttoned her shirt. Her cravat, a narrower version of what men wore, was dangled before her nose and she hung it around her neck, not bothering to tie it. The vest was handed to her next and she stood to put it on, buttoning it. The coat was held for her and she turned, slipped her arms in the sleeves, and pulled it onto her shoulders properly.

"What an excellent valet you make."

"And why not? I was one once for a brief period. I was at exceedingly low tide just then."

Stephanie ignored the teasing hint she should ask when and why he'd become a valet. She was perfectly sure there was a story and also certain he'd tell it with humor. She wasn't in the mood for humor.

"Are you ready?" asked Anthony quietly when it became clear she'd not ask.

She looked around the glade and the random thought crossed her mind that there was no thyme growing here, that there should be thyme. She wondered why she'd thought of something so irrelevant. Then she remembered her introduction to the man who stood quietly behind her. There'd been the scent of thyme. And this man. Then she recalled finding him there, asleep, his face innocent of guile. She'd covered him with his own coat that time . . .

She turned. "I'm ready."

"Good." He whistled and both his gelding and Aladdin raised their heads from their grazing and looked across the glade. Stephanie whistled more softly and Aladdin obediently trotted to her side, Anthony's horse following along behind.

"You needn't come with me," said Stephanie, when they'd mounted.

"I'll see you to your destination, my sweet, and come get you sometime tomorrow. I've several things to do, each of which will take some time, so I can't tell you when, exactly."

His stern expression didn't invite questioning his intentions and Stephanie, more drained than she wanted to admit, didn't probe. They soon arrived before Grannie's wee cottage. The bent old woman came to the door and stared at where Anthony and Stephanie sat their horses facing each other.

"Have you any orders for Theo?" asked Anthony. "Is there anything he can see to while you're absent?"

Forced to think of practical things, Stephanie recalled her earlier activities, the conversations and decisions which were made so long ago as to seem irrelevant. But they weren't irrelevant.

She sighed. "Yes. Oat harvest is upon us. Tell Theo to contact the families we usually hire during harvest and to ask around for any other help he can find. I'll take every man I can get. Women who want to earn money tying up sheaves and forming shocks will be paid a shilling a day and any child who helps with the shocking will earn six pence, while the men get the usual per day for the scything."

"Which is?" He hurried on when her brows began to crowd together. "You forget. Theo won't know and I've not been around to learn."

"The men have been getting two shillings a day. It's excessive, but work is scarce and, as a result, common day labor has been leaving the land and is hard to find."

He nodded. "Anything else?"

Stephanie's frown deepened. "Yes. Abbot must go into Chichester and hire three extra, a footman and two maids, to help in the house for the duration and he's to send Sarah to Mrs. Tipper. They'll know."

"And?"

After searching her mind, Stephanie drew in a deep breath. "I think that's all. If I've forgotten anything . . . well, if it's important, I can always come home, can I not?"

"I'd rather you didn't. Be very certain it is truly important before you put your head into that lion's den a moment before you're ready. Especially since I won't be there."

Stephanie chuckled and the sound was very nearly her old sound. "But I'll never be ready, whether you are there or not! I'm not at all fond of the scavengers skulking around my father's den!"

Anthony reached out and touched her cheek lightly. "You'll do, my sweet. You'll do."

He turned and trotted off, the gait changing to a canter where the path widened. Stephanie stared after him until he disappeared around a curve and then, finally, walked Aladdin to where Grannie Black impatiently awaited her.

"Thought I taught you better manners, girlee," stormed the old woman.

"I'll introduce him when he comes back. Tomorrow," promised Stephanie, not pretending ignorance of her one-time nanny's meaning.

"Hurumph! So that's the man, is it?"

"I haven't a notion what you mean."

"The one you'll lose if you don't have good sense. And you were never known for your good sense, were you then?" said the old woman a trifle sourly. "You all right?" she asked sharply when Stephanie didn't respond.

"I've been very nearly raped by one man and then just as nearly seduced by another and you ask if I'm all right? I don't think so."

"So why'd he stop seducing you?"

Stephanie thought back to the scene which had gone from sensual delight to bickering in the blink of an eye. "I don't know."

"Probably some stupidity on your part," said Grannie and stalked back into her cottage where she went straight to her chair and gathered up her cards. "Come here."

"I don't think so. I'm very tired of people giving me orders. It seems to be all I've heard this morning."

"You come here, missy. The cards have been laughing at me this whole morning and I'll have it right or know why not."

"What does that mean, laughing at you?"

Grannie ignored her. "First all seemed well with only a tiny cloud lurking."

"I rode out this morning with Huntersham for escort."

"Then that cloud blew up into a brief storm."

Stephanie grinned. "He and I had an argument."

"Your fault no doubt," scolded Grannie, who had been feeling worried for hours and now took her irritation out on the cause of it all. "Then that blasted cloud blackened and got bigger and bigger."

"I suppose that was Lambert, tracking me down and getting me alone." Stephanie wished her old nurse hadn't forced her to think of Lambert.

"That the man that tried to rape you?"

"Yes."

"Don't go shivering now when you didn't then!"

"How do you know?"

"I know *you.*" Grannie looked at the cards in her hand. She shoved them toward Stephanie. "Be a good girl and shuffle them."

Stephanie sighed. She knew she'd have no peace until she did as Grannie demanded. Shuffling them efficiently, she laid the pile down before the old woman crouching over the board. She cut them into three piles. And then she strode to the door.

"Where you going?"

"You don't need me and I must see to Aladdin."

Putting her hands flat on the board, Grannie straightened. "See to Aladdin?"

"Something you haven't foreseen, Grannie?" Stephanie spoke over her shoulder without stopping. "I'm your guest for the night, my darling old beast! So—" She stuck her head back in the door, "put *that* in your cards and tell me what comes of it!"

Twelve

Late that night, long after Grannie went to the bed in a narrow alcove built into the wall next to the chimney, and even after Stephanie had rolled herself into a quilt and laid down on the braided rug before the fire, loud knocks thundered through the cottage. Mumbling, Grannie sat up and rubbed her eyes.

The knocking started up again. Hunching a coverlet over her shoulders, the old woman limped slowly toward the door, only to stop partway there and hiss at Stephanie, who was once again swearing at herself for not having her pistols. Grannie pointed toward the ceiling. Stephanie grabbed up the poker and climbed the ladder to the loft where she lay along the wide floor boards and peered through the hole into the room below.

"Hold your buttons," growled Grannie as the raucous knocking once again resounded. "Just hold on there . . ." Grannie unbarred the door and, for a moment stared through it. She stamped her cane to the floor. "You." There was blatant disgust in her tone.

"Yes, Grannie Black, it is I." A faint hint of apology might have been imputed, by the generous, to *his* voice.

At her father's words Stephanie lay her head against the backs of her hands. Whatever danger he was to her, he would neither try to kill her nor rape her, and what else could he do to harm her at this hour?

Grannie straightened to her full height, such as it was.

"Didn't think you'd come see me. Thought you knew I was that ashamed of you I wouldn't admit I'd a hand in rearing you. Thought you'd stay as far from the scold you deserve as you could get!"

"Let us in, Grannie."

"*Us,* is it?" Grannie stretched her neck, peering around Lemiston's broad shoulders.

"I'm here, too," said Sir Francis. "Grannie, did Stephanie come to you this afternoon? Is she here?"

Grannie was silent, merely backing up and letting the men into her home. Stephanie realized the old woman was leaving it up to her. If she said nothing, Grannie would lie for her. She sighed and, urging her tired body to one more effort, raised herself and crawled back down the ladder.

She leaned on the rounded top of the fireplace poker. "Of course I'm here, Francis. Where else would I be?"

"It was in my mind," he said gently, "you'd go to Warring Heights where there'd be servants to protect you. But you didn't. They'd no knowledge of you." He nodded to the old woman. "No shame to you, Grannie Black, but you couldn't stop a determined man, could you?" He turned back to Stephanie. "You know you'd have been welcome there, Stephie."

"I didn't even think of it." She turned toward her sire. "Well, Lemiston?"

"Well, daughter?"

"I assume you are pleased with yourself."

"You assume wrong."

Stephanie's eyes narrowed and her mouth twisted very slightly in disbelief.

After a moment in which his own lips compressed and he quite obviously fought for self-control, Lemiston sighed. "Did he harm you?" he asked after a further moment.

"Which *he* do we discuss?" asked Stephanie sweetly.

"Now then," hissed Grannie. "None of that then. She warn't hurt, my lord, no thanks to you. When you going to be done playing games, then?"

"I haven't played a game."

Stephanie glared.

Lemiston stared back steadily. "Come home, daughter. It's late and Francis has something of a ride ahead of him since he insisted on helping me find you, wishing to see that you were all right, but he insists he won't stay at the Priory."

"He probably thought his presence necessary to protect me, since you'll want to beat me for not, in proper feminine fashion, succumbing to the vapors or fainting and allowing that rope-ripe thatchgallows to rape me."

"If he didn't succeed, then Anthony got there in time," said Lemiston, waving a hand, a sign he was losing patience. "Don't make a drama of the nothing it must have been."

"Anthony got there after it was all over," she said dryly. She turned to Francis. "I have you to thank for that bit of advice, old friend. It worked very well." Her mouth quirked in a rather vicious smile. "Actually, far better than it ever occurred to me it would work."

"You kneed him?" asked Francis, his head tipped to one side.

"When he stood over me, I shoved my foot into his crotch." Both men winced. "It worked at least as well as what you showed me."

"Yes, I'd think it would," said Francis with some heat. "Poor Lambert!"

"If you've sympathy for him, you're no friend of mine!"

"Stephie, love, any man would feel sympathy for another who suffered what you describe."

"Yet it was you who taught me!"

"There are *degrees* of defense, my child. I suspect you rather over did it," said Lemiston and eyed his daughter with new respect. "You are not at all what I expected, you know."

"It seems I'm not what anyone expects," said Stephanie and turned away. Dropping to one knee she put a scoop of coal on Grannie's dying fire.

"Find your coat and come along now. I'll saddle that moun-

tain you insist on riding when any sensible woman would know
he was far too much horse for her."

"Don't bait me!" Stephanie straightened her back, but neither rose to her feet or turned to face him. "I raised Aladdin
from a colt. He's gentle as a lamb. I've ridden so-called lady's
mares with harder mouths and far fewer manners than Aladdin!" Then she rose and turned. "I'm staying here tonight and
perhaps tomorrow as well. When I'm ready to pretend the necessary hypocrisy, I'll return to the house and your fool party.
Good night—" she glanced from one man to the other, "to
the both of you."

"Now one little minute here!" inserted Grannie, moving forward when it looked as if the men, after a look at each other,
had agreed to leave without Stephanie. She put a hand on the
girl's wrist and added, "You may go to sleep, my little one,
but I've a few words to say to his lordship—"

"His blidy lordship," inserted Stephanie under her breath.

"—and I won't be denied. You, my fine gentleman, just
come right over here and sit yourself down!"

Stephanie had a fleeting vision of Grannie, a much younger
and bustling nanny, with a finger and thumb around an un-
fledged Lord Lemiston's ear. The scene played through
Stephanie's mind, one which might have happened forty-five
years in the past. Lemiston, if the sheepish look he cast Francis
was an indication, seemed to feel much like the nursery brat
she envisioned. Whatever his emotions, he joined Grannie in
the corner, sitting across from her with a narrow table between
them.

For the next twenty minutes Francis and Stephanie conversed quietly, Stephanie reluctantly revealing to Francis more
details of her ordeal, while both pretended they weren't interested in what Grannie said in an intense but low voice to Lemiston. However curious they were, they knew they'd never find
out unless his lordship himself told, and, to their equal but
unadmitted regret, each doubted he'd reveal one word.

His lordship pushed away from the table and joined the two

at the door. "You can come home freely when you will, Stephanie. You'll be glad to know that in order to pay off a bet I lost to Francis, I'm sending away all your suitors. Actually, I'd decided to do so before Francis's urging, but I'm just as happy to have that debt out of the way." He tossed a grin toward Francis who grimaced. "Of course, Camberstone had already made an inane excuse about another party. *He* meant to leave anyway."

"Which will leave only your *real* house-party?"

"Yes." As an afterthought he added, "And Anthony's cousin, of course."

Stephanie crossed her arms. "I think I'll stay here. Permanently."

Lemiston's brows arched. "Why?"

"Anthony's cousin," she explained carefully, as if to a witless child, "is almost as big an idiot as the others combined."

Lemiston stroked his chin. "I, on the other hand, tend toward feeling rather sorry for him. Think, daughter. He believed he'd a title and goodly inheritance and then finds the true heir isn't dead after all!"

"Yes," retorted Stephanie, "and then, such an unlicked cub as he is, he accepts the hospitality of the house where that same heir is staying and all the time contemplates taking that heir to court to have from him what he believes he lost—although he never truly had it, of course."

Lemiston chuckled. "Put that way, he does sound a trifle lacking in grace, does he not?" He sobered. "Well, however that may be, you needn't worry I'll try to make you wed him. I've learned things since I returned that have forced me to change my thinking. I doubt I'll ever love you and your brother as I do Meg's children, but I no longer blame either of you for my Elizabeth's death." A frown creased his brow in a totally un-Morris fashion, the creases running horizontally across it. "I wonder, now, if I didn't feed my hatred of you two so as to have an excuse, something to soothe the guilty feelings I occasionally suffered for avoiding my responsibilities. You see—"

His look invited the others to laugh at his foibles, but Stephanie couldn't see the jest.

"—my adventuring suited me right down to the ground!"

"I'm glad you enjoyed yourself," she said rather bitingly.

At that he stared at Stephanie, shook his head, and then sighed. "One can't turn off emotions one has held dear for a quarter-century. I find, however, that they fade. And now I've met you, the *both* of you," another sardonic smile and he interrupted himself again, "Were you aware I thought you were twin girls?" Before she could answer, he continued, "Well, now I've met you, I find you are merely human and not the monsters I'd made of you in my mind. You've suffered, daughter, because of me, but no more. My word on it."

He held out his hand. Stephanie stared at it. When she didn't accept it she heard someone draw in a sharp breath. She ignored that too and transferred her gaze to meet her sire's. "Pardon me if I wait to see just how good the word of a Lemiston is—in your generation."

"You speak very coldly, child . . ." Grannie moved restlessly and Lemiston remembered he'd sold the Priory and that this odd daughter loved it deeply. He sighed. "Perhaps I deserve your suspicion. Sobeit." He turned. "Come Francis. And do," he coaxed his old friend, "accept a bed at the Priory tonight! It is much too late to be riding all the way from here to the Heights."

"I'd rather go to my own bed." Francis glared at Stephanie who glared right back. "You are abominably stubborn, Stephanie Elizabeth Morris! It's the one thing I could never cure in you!" Turning on his heel, Francis strode toward where his horse patiently awaited him, head hanging, one hoof cocked.

Lemiston chuckled. "You do have a way of setting up people's backs, do you not, my child?"

"I must live by my own precepts. Which is something *he*,"

she shoved her chin in the direction Sir Francis had taken, "taught me."

"Don't be angry with him, my dear, for being upset in my stead. He and I were friends from the leading string. He's done his best for me over the years and done very well. He is still my friend, however torn his loyalties have been since my arrival."

"You needn't apologize to me for Francis's behavior. We know and understand each other very well. I know exactly what he's thinking. He knows my thoughts. Soon, we'll either agree to disagree or we'll come to a compromise. Good night, my lord."

Reaching for the door, she closed it in her father's face.

Late the next morning, just as the sun shortened the cottage's shadow to where it no longer touched the tidy garden a few feet from the west side of the house, a tired but satisfied Anthony, Lord Huntersham, rode into Grannie's little clearing. He dismounted and, quickening his step, hurried to take the heavy pail of water Grannie carried. She shook the dipper at him, then subsided. "Oh. It's you. She isn't here."

He set the water near the garden and watched as Grannie carefully soaked individual plants. When the bucket was nearly empty, he poured the rest along a row of young cabbages and went to get more from the streamlet that flowed across the clearing hidden under water loving greenery. He returned and set the bucket convenient to the next plants to be watered.

"Told you," said Grannie. "She isn't here."

"She isn't at the house, either." He waited but got no response. "Where is she, Mrs. Black?"

"Why you want to know?" asked Grannie after a moment during which she poured water over another cabbage.

Anthony grinned. "I intend to wed that girl, Grannie Black. She isn't making that an easy task, but I'll win her to my way of thinking yet."

Grannie straightened, one hand going to her back. She studied Anthony. Finally she plopped the ladle into the bucket and headed for the house. When Anthony didn't immediately follow, she gestured, calling, "Come along, then."

The cottage was very dim after the unusually bright sun outside, and Anthony, after ducking under the lintel, paused, letting his eyes adjust. When he could see again, he discovered Grannie seated near a low table. On the table was a stack of cards.

"What do I do?" he asked, chuckling. "Play you for her? I must warn you, it is said I'm a dab hand at the pasteboards!"

"Not these *pasteboards*." She said the word as if it tasted bad to her. "You come here." She pointed imperiously to a spot across the table from her.

Going forward, Anthony discovered a flat cushion on the pounded dirt floor. He sank down gracefully, ankles crossed and wrists on knees, hands hanging loosely between his legs. "Now what?"

"Now you shuffle these." Grannie gestured.

Anthony obeyed.

"Lay them before me."

He did and then turned them when she wanted them set the other way.

"Cut a pile and lay it there and another and lay it there."

Again Anthony obeyed.

"Now . . ." She laid out the Past and stared at it. "Someone hurt you. Or you hurt someone else." The Three of Swords was combined with the Five of Cups. Grannie looked up. "The relationship is dead."

Anthony paled. "You speak of my father . . . ?"

"I don't know. I only tell you what I see, what the cards tell me."

"Well," he said a trifle bitterly, "I'd say he and I hurt each other again and again. Any possibility of a relationship died when he did."

She nodded and lay out the three cards signifying the present. "The Nine of Swords, reversed . . . the possible ending of bad dreams? Of regrets? The Five of Cups strengthens the idea that regret is involved . . ."

"I definitely regret I'd no occasion whereby I might have come to some understanding with my father."

"Not your father. Now. Something recent . . ."

Anthony's ears heated and a rueful laugh escaped him. "Well, there is something recent I *definitely* regret." A thoughtful look narrowed his eyes. "In two contradictory ways, actually. That it wasn't finished . . . and, on the other hand, that it happened at all. At that particular moment, anyway."

"Yes. The Ace of Cups reversed says it was a bad step or an unfinished step."

"Or both?"

"Maybe . . ." She laid down next two cards, the Future. "The Eight of Wands, Reversed and the Ten of Cups. Ahhh."

"What . . . ?" Despite his natural skepticism, Anthony found he'd become curious as to what this haggish-looking old woman would say next.

Grannie didn't respond immediately merely muttering, ". . . So . . ." She gazed into the low-burning fire. Finally she turned back to Anthony who waited patiently if a trifle warily for anything else she had to say. "You'll find her along the shore in a little cove not far from here." She gave directions for getting there and Anthony rose to his feet. "And, young man—" She shook her head impatiently when he began searching his pockets. "No! I don't take pay for this. What I wanted to say, young man, is that you started something and didn't finish it. If you start it again today it is *very important you finish what you begin.* If nothing else is clear in the cards, *that* is. There is hope . . . The Ten of Cups . . . yes, a great deal of hope, but the warning is clear."

Anthony smiled sardonically, his usually elusive dimple very much in evidence. "Mrs. Black," he asked in a soft voice, "have you any notion what I started yesterday and didn't finish?"

"I've a notion," she said, broodingly, "but it makes no difference. I merely read the cards and the cards say it's important that, if it's started, then it must be finished."

"And if it isn't?"

"I'd guess there will be delays and anxiety and perhaps failure . . ." She peered up at him. "I don't have that wrong, do I?"

"I don't know, Mrs. Black." He bit his lip, looking down at the now scattered tarot. "I must live my life in the way I feel is right." He glanced at Grannie, grinned. "Perhaps the best solution is if I don't start something which *requires* finishing?"

She frowned. "That *might* solve the problem. Assuming you've the right problem in mind . . . ?" She peered up through a wild tangle of hair which she'd not bothered combing that morning.

He shook his head. "How can I know? I *can* think of something else . . . but did I do anything about it yesterday? I can't recall . . . No, I'm sure I had no conversation with Lemiston on that particular subject."

"Well then, that's all I can do for you." She sighed, getting stiffly to her feet. "Almost all, anyway. Just let me cut you a sandwich and you can be off to find her . . ."

Once freed from Grannie's strangely compelling influence, Anthony looked back on her words and chuckled. He put the whole scene from his mind when he reached the shore, concentrating all efforts on moving slowly and silently along the gentle coast.

Grannie said Stephanie liked a little cove just to the south, a sheltered inlet where the trees ran down a spit and turned back on the grassy shoreline. Centuries of rushing spring waters had dug into the earth just there and the resulting pool was hidden by the trees from the traffic along the waterway leading to Chichester. At this time of day Grannie thought Stephanie would likely be ready for her lunch.

While looking ahead, Anthony nearly fell when a stone twisted under his foot. He picked a still more cautious route, determined Stephanie would not hear his approach and run off before he'd found her. . . . And she took a bit of finding! The waters of the narrow rill running around the end of the spit of land hiding her pool were well enough banked to tempt one to step over them. He'd nearly done so and gone on before he realized it was, likely, the very stream Grannie had mentioned. Anthony peered between the trees.

"Very nice," he murmured, his eyes feeding on the serene magic of the tree-enclosed pond which was considerably larger than he'd expected. He glanced along the sun-dappled grassy bank and his gaze stopped. His breath rasped in his throat and his heart, after a moment's halt, pounded in his breast.

"Stephanie . . ." He breathed her name on a mere thread of sound.

Everything—the beauty surrounding him, his recent experience with Grannie, the whole of life and living, all he'd done, all he meant to do—*everything* blanked from his mind leaving only the golden-skinned figure lying on a hunk of moss carpeting.

Mesmerized, he stood stiffly silent. Then, slowly, piece by piece, he removed his clothing, dropping everything just where it would go. As naked as his love, he stepped from between the trees onto the narrow sward. His eyes never leaving her, he approached, knelt, discovered she slept.

Silently, carefully, he lay down beside her, holding himself on one elbow, enjoying every line and curve, every soft swelling, intrigued by every lovely inch. He waited with the patience he'd learned in hard lessons all over the globe . . . but a patience he was glad, now, to have acquired, knowing that if he woke her, startled her, she'd be up and gone in a flash.

Probably into the water, was his rueful thought. Swimming was the one thing Chris hadn't managed to teach him to enjoy! And, worse, he'd not learned how to swim *well*. Or perhaps that fact explained the other?

At long last Stephanie stretched. She scratched her thigh where a lady bird beetle had landed and crawled across her skin. She yawned—and stretched again, her arms above her head. Anthony couldn't quite suppress a sharp intake of breath at the long lithe lines revealed by the movement and her eyes snapped open, meeting his, instantly alert.

The tension drained from her as she recognized him . . . only to return as she remembered her state of undress. She glanced at him, away, back, noted his encouraging look. Then her eyes drifted to his chest, on down. . . . A faint blush underlay the sun-touched skin the instant she realized he, too, was as bare as at his birth.

Stephanie stared up at the sky. She couldn't think what to do . . . and then discovered she didn't really want to do anything. She was here. So was he. And there had been those exceedingly interesting dreams.

Dared she discover the reality?

"Hello," he said softly, breaking into her indecision.

And, for the moment at least, his voice tipped the scales against him, embarrassment gaining the upper hand. "You shouldn't be here." She reached out one finger and poked his chest. "How *did* you find me?" But, before he could respond, she answered her own question. "Grannie!" A frown marred the smooth skin of her formerly serene brow. "I wonder why she told you . . ."

Stephanie sat up, looked around for her clothes before she remembered they were neatly folded and laid in the low crotch of one of the trees.

"You shouldn't be here!" she repeated, wondering how to hide her embarrassment.

When he lay his hand softly on her thigh, she jerked and stiffened, but didn't otherwise move. As he ran that hand up and then back down, up and down, she gradually relaxed.

"Would you kiss me? Again? As you did yesterday?" he asked as softly as he'd touched her.

"If I said no?"

"Then I'd have to accept that, would I not?"

"You shouldn't be here."

"You've said that," he said. "You're not usually so lacking

in conversation, my sweet." There was a smile in his voice that drew her eyes to his face. "You are very beautiful, you know." She shook her head. "Lovely, enticing, intriguing, tempting . . ."

"You are . . . rather tempting yourself."

"Not lovely, enticing, or intriguing?"

Again she heard the smile. "Oh, perhaps not *lovely.*"

"Ah." His hand continued the gentle caress, dipping occasionally below her knee. "If you won't kiss me, may I kiss you?"

"And if I say not?"

He sighed. "Such a waste."

"Waste?"

"Of a beautiful day, a beautiful woman, a beautiful, wonderful, incredible hour of dalliance."

"And that's *all* it would be. Dalliance."

"But how could you want more than that?" When she turned aside, his eyes narrowed very slightly. "You'll never wed, you said, but will you also deny yourself the wonders of lovemaking?" He moved his hand to her waist, slid it across to the other side and turned her slightly toward him. "I would love to love you, sweetings," he murmured and lowered his lips to hers.

Tentatively Stephanie lay her hand on his hip. She felt more than the heat of sun-warmed skin; she recognized a subliminal heat coming from within her own sensitive body, the simple touch of palm to hip drawing forth an incredibly seductive desire for *more.*

And why should there *not* be more? Why should she deny herself the pleasures she was certain would be hers if she only had the nerve to accept, to enjoy, what he wished to teach her? To allow his hand to wander as it willed . . . as it did . . . touch, arouse, draw forth sensations such as she'd never imagined . . .

Stephanie gave herself up to sensation.

"So sweet." His hand moved to cup her breast. "So right."

"Too small," she muttered.

"Who said so? I'll offer challenge to anyone who says anything so stupid."

"Most women . . ."

"My love, you are not most women. You are you, my rare delight"

Even as she gained confidence and her own hand began its own exploration, she demurred. "I've told you. Don't lie to me."

"I wonder," he said with just a touch of humor, "what it will take to convince you I do not lie." He reached for her braid, untied the ribbon and eased the strands apart. "Ah . . . I wondered what it would look like, spread around you."

Stephanie lay back, looked up at him. "Why?"

"Why what, love?" he asked absently, his eyes drawn to her breasts, his neck bending, his mouth approaching . . .

She caught him, pushed him back up. "Why do you find me, in all my oddity, attractive when no one else has ever done so?"

"Perhaps I'm as odd as you and it takes an oddity to know an oddity?"

She smiled and, giving in to the yearning she always felt in his presence, reversed her hold and pulled him down, found his mouth and, remembering how he'd kissed her that first time, brushed his lips with her own, brushed his again, touched her tongue to where his mouth softened, opened, accepted her hesitant exploration . . . and then returned the favor.

This time she wasn't at all startled. This time she welcomed him. The world faded. Sensation after sensation flowed into, around, over, through her, driving her wild, wilder, wanting, needing . . .

Thirteen

An ungentle boot against his bare hip jerked Anthony around to see who intruded on an interlude such as he'd never before experienced. Immediately aware of Stephanie's nakedness he swung back, half covering her.

"You will instantly release my sister!"

Anthony raised himself slightly and looked down at Stephanie who stared at him blankly, then, sharply and wide-eyed as she came abruptly back to reality. His wry look told her he regretted the interruption as much as she did, told her that he understood her embarrassment, that he would handle the situation . . .

An utterly silent communication that missed its mark! Stephanie definitely regretted the interruption, but she wasn't particularly embarrassed and she much preferred handling situations herself!

"At once!" insisted Theo in a growling voice his twin had never heard. "Stephanie, get into your togs . . . Now!" he added when she didn't move. "Leave this rutting bastard to me."

"You sound like the outraged father in a melodrama, Theo," said Stephanie wearily. She lay back, her wrist over her closed eyes. "Why the hell did you come and spoil everything?"

"You will thank me eventually," said Theo, a hard note that made her raise her wrist enough to stare at him with one eye. "I've brought *your* clothes, Huntersham. Get them on and leave the Priory. We'll speak of this outrage again, but not here and now. Stephanie, will you get yourself up and cover your shame!"

"I was enjoying the sun before Anthony arrived. I'll enjoy it again when you both leave."

"Francis has much to answer for, that you can lie there naked under the eyes of a stranger and feel no shame!" growled Theo.

"Go dress, sweetings," urged Anthony, who realized Theo's intent. "Our moment here is spoiled, but there will be others," he soothed.

He held his hand to her and, reluctantly, she put hers into it. She stood up. Only then did she, too, realize how angry Theo was. Hands on hips she glared at her twin. "You will have words with *me* Theodore Morris! Don't you dare say one more word to Anthony, do you hear me?"

"This is between Huntersham and myself and none of your business."

"It is if you mean to propose a duel. Just whose business if *not* mine? Do you think I want either, or for that matter, *both* of you dead or even wounded?"

She stamped her foot and wished she hadn't, her bare sole hitting a rather sharp-edged rock which bit into the arch. She sat, sighing, and nursing the bruise. "Blast and drat!" she muttered. "This too is your fault, Theo! You made me lose my temper. And don't you dare laugh, Anthony Ryder! None of this is the least bit funny."

"I won't duel with your brother, my sweet. Now, as he says, get dressed." She glared at him. *"Go,* sweetings. Please?"

The frown remained, but, after a hesitation during which his look encouraged her to do his will and a glance at Theo indicated she could say nothing which would help, she went.

When she was beyond range of their voices, Anthony chided Theo. "The proper thing to have done, my boy, was to go away and leave us alone."

"I will have satisfaction, do you hear me?"

"Very likely *Grannie* can hear you. Theo, I wish very much

to marry your sister, but she's making that a damned difficult goal to achieve! Or are you unaware she's sworn she'll never wed?"

Theo, about to rant about careless rogues, stilled, his eyes narrowing. "She's said so for years," he said slightly less belligerently.

"I swear I'll win her, but I'll have to do it my way. Will you not leave me to my eccentric wooing?"

The warily thoughtful look changed to one of scorn. "If you think seducing her will send her to the altar," drawled Theo, his tones closer to normal, "you don't know her at all."

"She'd at least learn to enjoy our loving, and, as you must know, once experienced, good loving is hard to forgo! However that may be, I agree that alone won't turn the trick. What I must prove to her is that I like her just the way she is. Every single idiosyncrasy. I must show her I'll not attempt to change her. I must have time in which she can learn I'd allow her to live very much as she's lived all her life." Anthony sighed. "I'll do none of that easily. Your sister isn't a very trusting soul, Theo."

After a moment's thought, Theo asked, "You truly wish to wed her?"

"Oh yes."

Another moment. "Does our father know?"

Anthony picked up a handful of pebbles and dribbled them through his fingers as he stared out over the water, a muscle jumping in his jaw. "I decided I'd not discuss it with Lemiston. You and your sister are of age. She need ask no one's permission to wed and I'm under no obligation to ask anyone's permission to woo her! Besides, I'm convinced I must pursue her in what will seem a very odd way . . . or I'll lose her. But, however that may be, she will accept it is marriage she'll have, whether or no, at the end of things."

Theo remained silent, the Morris brows slightly veed, but thoughtfully rather than in anger. Anthony decided the scholar, surprisingly hot to hand where his sister was concerned, had laid to rest the emotions which would lead to shooting him out of hand. He reached for his drawers and pulled them on. He put on his shirt and then his trousers, tucking in the shirt before buttoning the flap at his waist.

"Did you come for a swim?" he asked, setting his socks and boots to one side.

"Yes. Francis and I went to Grannie's to talk to Stephanie. The dear old soul—"

Anthony's brows went up as he wondered if that were sarcasm or if Theo knew a different side to Grannie then he'd yet met.

"—wouldn't tell us where my sister was to be found. Francis, knowing her over-developed sense of responsibility, thought perhaps she'd gone to oversee the oat harvest which began today and, since it seemed oppressively hot, I came down here for a swim."

"Alone?"

"Oh dear." Theo sent a worried glance toward where his sister was hidden among the trees.

"I thought you promised to do nothing alone."

Theo flushed. "I forgot."

"Well, if you mean to swim, then do go in and enjoy it," urged Anthony. "We'll eat, I think, and just sit here enjoying the sun."

Theo glanced at the trees. "You'll soon have to move or you'll lose it. Actually, I prefer the shade. My skin burns. I've never understood why mine does and Steph's does not."

Anthony chuckled at the hint of muted jealousy. "The sun is the one thing I miss from my travels. That and the heat of the tropics. I'll readjust, I suppose, but I may never again think it proper that a house be kept as cool as are all the English houses I've ever been in."

Stephanie stepped from the glade, fully dressed, just in time to see her brother throw back his head and laugh.

"You should visit Steph's room some time," said Theo. His tone was completely free of any innuendo one might expect to color such a suggestion, and Stephanie wondered just how Anthony had managed to turn her stubborn brother up sweet.

"She is never without a fire," he continued, "even in the middle of the summer. She would agree with you that the temperatures *sensible* people agree are healthy are deuced uncomfortable!" Theo grinned.

"You seem to have gotten over your fit of temper," said Stephanie with a touch of pique she didn't understand.

"Yes," he drawled. "Anthony reminded me you mean to remain a spinster and convinced me it would be a shame and a waste if you were to also remain a virgin," teased her brother.

Theo smiled a quick and rather wicked smile. It was not an expression Stephanie had ever been privileged to see. Her brows arched.

"It isn't, of course, something I'd normally have thought to discuss with a mere sister," he continued, "but, Steph, my love, I'm convinced you've made the right choice."

She waited. When it became clear he'd not continue, she prodded him. "The right choice."

"To take a lover, I mean . . ." Then, suddenly, the grin faded and he frowned. More slowly, Theo added, "Except, it's a bit different for a woman, is it not? What will you do if there's a child?"

That Stephanie hadn't thought of that was revealed by the sudden scowl, the hard line of compressed lips and quick speculative glance lashed in Anthony's direction.

Anthony smiled gently although he felt very like kicking Theo; it *had* occurred to him that she might, if she were to conceive, wed him in order to keep her child from carrying the taint of illegitimacy. It wasn't the way he wished to win her, but, as someone once said, all's fair . . .

So, instead of showing his irritation, Anthony chuckled. "Come Theo, surely you don't think I'd allow a child of mine to suffer, do you? I'd see it had every chance in life. Stephanie need not concern herself about such things."

"But the scandal . . ."

Stephanie scowled. "I'm already a scandal. Why should I care if I become more of one?"

"Steph—"

"Theo, let it be. I make my own decisions."

"Yes," he said, "you always have, have you not? But usually I don't know what they are until it's too late to argue. This is different. I *do* know. I *should* argue you out of the possibility of utterly ruining yourself!"

"Be consistent. A moment ago you were practically congratulating me and urging me to enjoy myself!"

"That's because I only thought of the moment, not the repercussions!"

"Easy now, the both of you!" said Anthony, stepping between brother and sister. "There are methods of preventing conception. I'll see your sister is taught what she needs to know. Well, Theo?" he added when Theo still frowned.

"The French envelope?" Theo looked faintly shocked. "I don't know if that's at all proper. This is my *sister* we're discussing!"

"There's also the sponge and . . ."

Finally Stephanie felt embarrassed. "We aren't!" she interrupted. "Discussing me," she explained when both men looked her way. She drew in a deep, steadying breath. "Not another word," she insisted in a tone her brother knew. After ascertaining her twin had given up, she asked, in an entirely different tone, "Did you bring a lunch?"

"Yes, but I'll not eat until after I swim." Theo looked from one to the other, back to Stephanie, and sighed. "Steph, would it be too hypocritical if I go into the trees to undress?" he asked on something of a pensive note.

"You know it would."

"Then turn your back as you are supposed to do."

She gave a wry look toward Anthony whose brows climbed his forehead, and, obediently, turned her back. "We started doing this," she explained, "when Francis realized I was showing signs of becoming a woman. I think I was nearly fourteen."

"If it's just she and I, we don't bother," added Theo and grunted as he pulled off a boot. He smiled gratefully when Anthony offered to help with the other. "For years it simply never occurred to us to do so. Then, once, when Jane came along—"

"Just for the outing," inserted Stephanie. "She doesn't swim."

"—we realized she'd be utterly embarrassed by our undress and even more so by the fact we undressed in each other's presence, so *we* now get a little embarrassed, I suppose, when anyone but just ourselves is here." Theo quickly stripped the rest of his things.

Anthony finally understood why she'd not run screaming the instant she'd realized they lay, both naked, on the moss.

A moment later, Stephanie heard the faint splash of her brother's shallow dive and turned back around. "I'll share my luncheon with you, Anthony," she offered in a slightly muffled tone.

He looked to where she was stalking toward the trees among which she'd dressed, a thoughtful look was still on his countenance when she returned after far longer than it should have taken her to pick up her lunch. "His words made you self-conscious of me, did they not?"

"Yes."

"Nothing is different from before he made his thoughtless remark."

"My feelings are different."

Anthony nodded, hiding a sigh. "Wait here. I've bread and cheese somewhere if the gulls didn't find it. Your Mrs. Black fixed it for me."

He went to the spit of land where he'd undressed and returned with the sandwich Grannie Black had wrapped in a piece of oiled paper. They sat on the carpet and watched Theo swim the long way of the pool, back and forth, again and again . . .

"He may be a scholar, but he's not an altogether bookish man, is he?" asked Anthony.

"Not at all. When his intellectual interests first became obvious, Francis had a talk with us about living a balanced life so one's health wouldn't suffer. Theo will spend hours, *days,* occasionally, on a problem, but usually he exercises some part of each day." She grinned. "Part of Francis's lecture was about some ancient Italians who were naturally well-rounded men— artists, engineers, businessmen on the one hand, but not forswearing hunting, fencing, or taking up arms in time of war—and managing it all to perfection."

"Da Vinci?"

"And Michelangelo, for instance."

"Was it because of the Italians you were taught to fence?"

"Theo first got the notion. But anything Theo learned I learned as well. Francis hired a tutor who worked with the three of us." About to bite into her ham and cheese and bread, she lowered it. "I think, in the end," she said, slightly pensive, "I enjoyed those lessons more than Theo did, actually."

Anthony nodded, but after a moment's thought he slid a querying look her way. "You learned what he was taught. Did Theo learn the things you were taught?"

Stephanie smiled, her eyes alight. "I framed our first samplers and hung them in my room." The smile edged into a grin. *"His* is *much* prettier than mine—but he no longer stitches, I think. Jane, however, doesn't disdain to ask his advice when her work isn't going well."

"Sweetings," he asked after a long, peaceful silence, "can we speak now of our loving?"

Stephanie felt heat flooding up her neck. She looked around her for an excuse, stared at her brother and, thankfully, realized he'd soon return to shore. "We'd be interrupted in only a few moments," she said, indicating why they must postpone their discussion.

Anthony sighed. "The longer we put it off, the more difficult it is likely to be."

"Even so, it must wait. See?" she added, vindicated. "Theo is swimming in." She ostentatiously got to her feet and turned her back as her twin reached the shallows and began to find his footing.

Anthony chuckled obediently as he knew, by her playacting, she'd meant him to do, but he was deeply disturbed. He should not have allowed her to put him off even if they were forced to go elsewhere for their talk. Remembering Grannie Black's Cassandra-like warning of disaster, he wondered if finding another occasion for speaking about it, or, indeed, for doing something about it, might not be more than just *difficult*. It might, in fact, be next to impossible . . .

He was very nearly certain of it when Stephanie avoided being alone with him, keeping Theo nearby, for the rest of the day . . . even holding her twin at her side during the long boring hours in which she watched the men and women working in the fields, occasionally warning a man he needed to hone his scythe or carrying water to a woman who flagged. And off and on she'd cast a wary eye toward the far west where dark clouds billowed, their tops glowing white while their bottoms looked heavy and dark.

Nobody, including Graham Wilkins, was more relieved than she that they drew no nearer.

Stephanie stepped casually down the front stairs on her way to the salon where the much reduced party would collect before the dinner hour. She'd almost reached the bottom when she realized Oakfield stood, half hidden, where the banister curved away from the steps. She slowed to a halt. "What do you want?"

"You," he said. Preening, he came out of the shadows and around to where he could face her. He grinned, revealing one broken tooth, the rest badly discolored. "It is obvious, now,

that I'm the favored suitor. Why else would your father send
the rest away? So you might as well accept the situation and
get it over. We'll announce our engagement at dinner."

"You may do so—"

He smiled complacently.

"—if you wish to look the fool."

The smile faded like magic.

"I'll simply deny it, you see," she said, with false sweetness.

"Your father—"

"—is irrelevant, is he not? I'm of age, remember?"

He reached out, grabbing her wrist and yanking her down
the last few steps to the floor. Stephanie, not expecting it, just
barely managed to keep her feet under her.

She jerked at her captured wrist. "Release me at once!"

His grip tightened and it took every ounce of control
Stephanie had not to cry out at the pain.

"You are mine, do you hear?" he said, viciously.

"I think not!" she answered, scorn dripping.

"You will see."

Voices could be heard in the corridor leading to the library
and game room and, with a glance in that direction, he threw
her hand from him, turning to climb the stairs. Stephanie absently rubbed her wrist which would, she feared, soon show
bruising. She smiled at Colonel Lord Winston, nodded to the
other married men whom she'd not gotten to know, slid her
gaze over Anthony without acknowledging him, and strolled
away toward the corridor leading to the salon.

Anthony separated himself from the others who started up
the stairs to their rooms and their wives where they'd have a
little time apart before changing for dinner and rejoining each
other in the salon. Anthony caught up with Stephanie before
she reached the arch to the hallway. He reached for her shoulder, halting her. "What is it, sweetings?"

"What?" She pushed his hand away, turning as she did so.
"Did you want something?"

"You, love," he said with a wicked look.

His playfulness drew a smile—and then a frown when she recalled Oakfield had said much the same thing.

"That, of course, will wait," he said, misinterpreting her look. "I asked you what was wrong, and if you tell me nothing, then I'll be forced, my sweet, to inform you that you lie!"

"It *is* a nothing. Truly. Your charming cousin," she didn't try to keep the sarcasm from her voice, "informed me just now that he has obviously become my favored suitor. Why else, he argues, would my dear father have turned off all the rest, but not him?" Absently she again rubbed her wrist.

Anthony lifted her arms, holding up the one she'd been rubbing. "Red. I can see his fingerprints. You call this a mere nothing?" Angrily he glared, catching her gaze and forcing her, by pure will power, to admit there'd been more to her talk with Oakfield than she'd admitted.

"I deal with my own problems, Anthony."

"In the past you've *had* to do so, have you not? Theo has been absent. Your Jane, though a very pleasant lady, is not the forceful sort, is she? And Sir Francis, who should have protected and cosseted you, has, instead, encouraged your independence, has he not?"

"I have *wished* to be independent."

Anthony sighed. "Yes. And, when not taken to excess, it makes you an excellent woman. An interesting woman. A woman who will never pall on a man. But you haven't learned your lesson quite properly, my sweet one. All good generals learn it early on or they don't long remain generals."

She tipped her head to the side, watching him, waiting . . . and lifted her chin as her patience slipped. "Well?"

"You are asking for instruction? It's simple, my sweet. The general makes the decisions, yes, but then gives orders to others who see all is done as it should be. You've learned to do that with the estate, Stephanie, and do it well. But, when it is something personal, you forget."

"Ah. I see. I should order you, for instance, to give dear Cuthbert a slap around the ears?"

He grinned. "Perhaps not quite that. But you might suggest I tell your father my cousin is unwelcome and should be told to go as the others were told."

"My sire feels sorry for your cousin."

"Sorry for that bullying prig? Nonsense."

"Ask Francis. He was there and heard Lemiston's comment."

Anthony frowned. "I still say nonsense. Perhaps it's some misplaced sense of hospitality since Oakfield is my cousin. I'll have a talk with him."

"But not at my orders!"

He grinned. "I too have a mind of my own, my sweet. I don't need your orders. Besides, I'm tired of doing the polite to dear Cuthbert myself. He's a nuisance with his constant complaints, his insistence he'll take me to court, his equally irrational insistence I owe him an allowance."

"If he's your heir presumptive you do owe it, don't you?"

"He isn't. And even if he were, as, against all logic, he persists in thinking, he's demanding an unreasonable sum—the amount approaching what Prinny claims is an inadequate royal grant!"

Her eyes widened. Everyone, even she, knew that Prinny received an incredible allowance.

"You begin to understand? So, perhaps I'll have that talk with Chris on my own account. It needn't have a thing to do with you."

Looking both ways, discovering they were alone, he pulled her into a quick embrace, giving her far too brief a kiss. Setting her away, he grinned, nodded, and, using that odd ground-covering stride Stephanie admired, he returned to the stairs and disappeared up them, taking them two at a time.

Stephanie, wandering on toward the salon, noted with surprise that the double doors were wide open. As she neared them, she heard voices. Meg's rather harsh and sarcastic tones stopped her. "Oh then, right you are, gov. I should certainly have stayed at home and minded my blidy needle."

"I don't believe that is exactly what I said," Lemiston objected in a much milder tone. "I *said* you were left to mind the property and see all went well in my absence. And I *asked* why you decided you could flout those orders and follow without my permission. Especially why you brought along two very young children for whom the journey must have been particularly difficult and dangerous!"

"You know very well Ol' Jem wouldn't have heard any order if I'd've dared give him one. I was no more in charge of our property than our Richard! As to the dangers and hardships of travel, your sons are not such little darlings they must be coddled and watched over every moment. They did very well and hugely enjoyed themselves, my blidy lord."

Christopher, Lord Lemiston, sighed. "When do you think you'll cease using that exceedingly irritating appellation when referring to me."

"Damnitall, the man's breakteeth words will kill me yet!" muttered Meg, but loudly enough that her words would not be missed.

"Did I do it again? I apologize, Meg. I believe I once promised I'd not use words you didn't know unless I explained them. What was it this time?"

"Apple-something."

"Appellation? It means the name by which one is called. Meg, I've still to have an explanation of the real reason why you followed me."

"You *know* why," she said and Stephanie heard a faintly sullen note.

"I believe something was said in that tirade immediately after you arrived of rights, and that you felt you'd be cheated."

"Not just me," said Meg, a defensive note in her voice. "Our boy, too."

"Except he *isn't* my heir. There is Theo."

"I didn't know about Theo, did I then? And it's my understanding, my blidy lord, *neither did you.* So you meant to keep it a secret, dinnit you, then? You believed our boy had rights to a title and all this and you weren't to let us know? Bah!"

Chris sighed. *"All this* brought me nothing but unhappiness, Meg. I want nothing to do with it. I meant to see done what had to be done and to be gone from these shores long ago. If things had gone as smoothly as I'd expected, I might even have been back on the ocean headed for home before you reached England!"

Meg paced into Stephanie's range of vision and, kicking the short train to her proper new gown, turned. She stood, arms akimbo and glared back toward where Christopher must be posed by the mantel in that irritating fashion Stephanie had once realized was her own usual stance.

"You'd have cheated us, you blidy bastard! Of our rightful place in the world, my blidy lordship! I won't have it. Hear? You don't know half what it was like when I was young, watching the swells, well fed and dressed to the nines and starin' down their noses at us poor folk in our rags and goin' to the opera or climbing into fancy carriages or goin' into fine shops and saying I'll have that and that and that and that . . ."

"Ah . . ." Christopher too strolled into Stephanie's line of sight. He reached for Meg's rigid shoulders. "I think I begin to understand." He shook her, very gently. "Well, my dear, you've had a taste of the fancy dress. Does it satisfy?" He tipped his head at her quick frown. "You want more? Perhaps it's time you saw something of the opera and the shops, to say nothing of the fancy carriage! What do you say? Shall we take Stephanie and Theo, if he wishes it, and go to Brighton for a couple of weeks? Would you like to meet the prince?"

Meg's eyes widened and her skin paled. "What? Me? Meet ol' Florizel?"

"He's now called Prinny."

"That's what your Stephanie said."

"Did she?" He shook her again in that oddly gentle fashion. "Well, Meg? Shall we?"

"I don't think I want to meet the prince. People from Spitalfields who bin transported don't talk to princes!"

"You needn't if you don't wish it. I'll see to it."

Meg looked up, her gaze sharp. "You can't disobey him if he orders you!"

"If he gives a direct order, we'd have to obey, would we not? Except, I could say you were sick. He'd thank you for *not* obeying, if you were ill. He has an abhorrence of illness, you know."

"Another breakteeth word."

"Abhorrence? Fear and hate all mixed up together, my dear. Come now. Do you wish to go? I'm uncertain if there'd be an opera, but there is sure to be a decent theater where you can see a play or two and there are certainly shops! Not quite so lavish as in Bond Street or Piccadilly, but far better than anything one can yet find in the Antipodes!"

Meg flashed a quick grin. "And I kin go in and say I want that and that and that and . . ."

"And, within reason, *that and that!*"

"We'll take your daughter?"

"And Theo and Sir Francis and . . ." He hesitated. "I guess that's all."

"Ryder. Huntersham, I mean."

"If you wish."

"Nice offer, my blidy lord, but you won't trick me that way." Meg twisted from his grip and turned her back. "I've heard the women talk. There'll be nowhere to stay. Brighton'll be as full as it can hold and you'll go all apologetic like and say it's impossible so let's go home instead."

"Not at all. I'll send an agent. He'll find something even if he has to buy it. More likely bribe some poor fool who is in over his head, but we needn't worry *how* he finds a place. Assuming you want to go." She didn't respond, only raising her nose another notch. "Meg, you know I do what I say I'll do, so is that what you want?"

Again Meg moved away and, this time, she was silent for

a long moment. She turned, came back to face him closely. "Yes, my blidy lord, I believe I'd like to go. Even if I have to go an' make m'bow to the blidy prince!"

"Then we'll go." He touched her cheek and, when she didn't move, bent to kiss her forehead. "I've missed you, my Meg," he said meaningfully—and reached for her.

Realizing she'd eavesdropped was bad enough, but when she also realized her father meant to kiss his wife and that, given the way Meg melted into him, she'd no objections, Stephanie found herself exceedingly embarrassed.

Very softly she turned and moved back down the hall, finding a spot where she could lean against the wall and think over what she'd heard. Brighton. The shops didn't interest her, but the theater did. She'd seen every traveling troupe to play in Chichester and, bad as some of them undoubtedly were, she'd enjoyed each and every one.

Besides, although her father hadn't mentioned them, there would also be libraries and bookstores, both of which Stephanie thought she might like to patronize. Once the summer's work was done and her days less hectic, it would be nice to have some new reading matter.

So, when her father mentioned his plan to remove the family to Brighton, she would simply nod, which ought to surprise him no end! And, she thought, a half-grin quirking one side of her mouth, she'd begin tomorrow organizing everything so that all would be well while she was gone. It would be unnecessary to demand a delay to their leave-taking while she did it.

"What a very interesting little smile, my lady," said Colonel Lord Winston. "Could one ask, little cat, just what particular cream you've been in?"

Stephanie straightened away from the wall. "Cream? The whole pot, I think! You didn't wait for your wife this evening?"

"Lissa has the headache," he said shortly, frowning. "She has asked for a tray in her room."

"Should I send for the doctor?"

"She says not." Winston made the effort to put his concern

aside and offered Stephanie his arm. "If you can safely stop propping up that wall," he said, his tone whimsical, "perhaps you'll join me in the salon while we wait for the others to come down?"

"Ah. The salon. Hmm . . ." Stephanie cast a pensive glance down the corridor. "Do you think we might speak rather loudly as we approach it?"

"Why? Ah! A stupid question, was it not? And I now see why you prop yon wall. Someone one is there and you believe we'll interrupt . . . something?"

"Well, I almost interrupted . . . something . . . some minutes ago, but perhaps, by now, all is well."

He grinned. Hearing someone come, he turned. "Miss Fenton! Lady Stephanie is reluctant to continue on down the hall. She says someone is already using the salon and that we should not interrupt. What do you say?"

Stephanie grimaced. "Very likely I've made something of nothing. Let me see."

"Perhaps if we stroll slowly and talk rather loudly we'll give your truants time to make themselves presentable?"

"But I didn't say there was anything objectionable going on! I merely said I didn't think the couple should be interrupted."

"Ah. And I jumped to conclusions?" He quirked a brow. Stephanie compressed her lips. After a moment when she made no explanation, the colonel continued, "Now then, of what should we speak?"

"Perhaps," suggested Stephanie, "you would be so kind as to explain to me why some of our guests are so scathing about Viscount Wellington's conduct of the war in the Peninsula?"

"Ah. Now there is a subject about which I *may* speak at length and with some heat! Ignorant souls here in England, who have no knowledge of the sort of impossible ground our armies must cover, the sort of odds they meet, insist Wellington is a coward who retreats at the first sign of trouble."

"And is it not true that he retreats?"

"It's true enough." Winston eyed the two women. "Ah! Perhaps this will help you understand. If you, Lady Stephanie, along with Miss Fenton here, faced ten or twelve ruffians with a clear way out and no help in sight, but a place in mind where you might better defend yourself, would you not retreat?"

"I would indeed. It seems far the better part of valor," mused Stephanie.

"Exactly. Wellington is a genius at choosing the ground on which he's willing to fight. And he *won't* fight unless he's evened the odds against the enemies' larger forces by adding the lay of the land into his side of the equation! I do not consider that at all cowardly. Merely sensible."

They reached the salon. Curious, Jane stepped into the room, looked around. She turned and gave Stephanie a glance that asked exactly what it was that had roused her to such odd behavior.

"No one is here. But if you were in the corridor, then how did they leave? Or do I see?" Winston gestured toward the neatly covered windows over which Abbot had drawn the drapes.

Stephanie, however, moved toward the fireplace where, just to the left of it, there was a black line alongside one panel. She snapped shut the secret door and turned. "I don't think so," she said and grinned.

Jane's eyes widened. "Theo was in here?"

"Lord Lemiston was here," responded Stephanie. "He and his lady."

Winston blinked. "They left by way of a secret passage? But why?"

"I'd not care to hazard a guess." Her most wicked grin flashed across Stephanie's features. "Of course, if one or the other disappears forever, then we might lay bets on how the murder was done."

"Stephie, don't jest about such things!"

"Sorry Jane. They *were* arguing, but when I realized I shouldn't be listening, they had finished with that."

Soon everyone but Lemiston and Meg arrived. Abbot glanced in the door, looked around, frowned, and backed away.

He came again. When he came the *third* time, he motioned to Jane who excused herself from a discussion of her current piece of needlework, and went to him.

"Cook is tearing his hair. Where's his lordship got to?"

"Abbot, you will speak more respectfully when referring to Lord Lemiston. As to where he is, I haven't a notion."

"Unless I was right, and one of them did the other in," said Stephanie joining them in time to hear Abbot's complaint.

"If you can't help, then go away," scolded Jane softly. "Abbot, I don't know what to tell you . . ."

"Simple," said Stephanie. "Tell him to announce dinner. You and Theo can play host and hostess. And you," she said to the butler, "can have a tray prepared which you'll take up and quietly leave in the sitting room in the master suite."

"You can't be suggesting . . ." Jane began, but stopped, shocked.

"Can I not?" Stephanie again grinned the wicked grin. *"Why* can I not?"

"But in the middle of the day? Just at dinner time?"

Stephanie's grin widened and Jane moaned softly.

"Please, Stephanie . . ."

"In what way is my daughter upsetting you now, Miss Fenton. Shall I take her to task for you?"

The three who had stood with the heads together, turned at Lord Lemiston's voice. Meg graced his arm, her head high.

"I don't believe I will, though," his lordship mused. "I'm feeling much too benign just now. Abbot, why do you stand there with your mouth agape? Shouldn't you have announced dinner before now?"

Abbot gathered his composure and very soon the company was seated to what the cook insisted was a ruined meal. No one seemed to notice, so eventually Abbot was able to partially smooth that temperamental creature's ruffled feathers . . . but not entirely, until Lord Lemiston was thoughtful enough to send down a commendation of a fruit confection he said was quite delightful.

Fourteen

A messenger from Arundel Castle arrived while the guests were dining. Much to Lemiston's obvious irritation the groom hadn't awaited an answer, since the Duke of Norfolk plainly assumed his invitation to Lemiston and his guests would not be refused. Watching Abbot explain to her father, Stephanie wondered if he *would* return a denial—out of pride and a feeling of insult. But Lemiston controlled his pique, relaxed, and nodded. He rose to his feet.

"Everyone," he said. "I've an announcement."

Although he raised his voice only slightly, there wasn't a person at the table who didn't, immediately, turn to listen, the last clink of fork to plate loud in the silence.

"Norfolk has kindly sent an invitation to all of us. It is for dinner three days from now, a hunt and a steeplechase arranged for the men in the days following. Given we'll be partway there, I think we should all continue on from Arundel to Brighton where I wish to spend a week or so. The time has nearly arrived when I and my wife and children must return to the Antipodes. I'd have Meg enjoy something of our city society before we leave, so must ask you all to forgive my rudeness in telling you this house-party is about to end."

Sir Francis, sitting beside Stephanie, bent near and murmured in her ear, "That's just the way *you* look when you've decided to set the local matrons' on their ear! I should have recognized it long ago, but I'd forgotten Chris's mischievous look."

"My features are nothing like his!"

"The eyes and brows are the same, but it isn't a question of features. It's the expression. Don't you agree, Huntersham?"

Stephanie hadn't realized Anthony, seated on her other side, was listening. She tensed, but immediately forced herself to relax. She turned.

"Definitely." Anthony watched her, head to one side. "He's managed to insult half his friends and amuse the other half. I'll bet a monkey that, before the evening ends, he'll have insulted the amused and have the presently insulted eating from his palm! I've seen him in this mood."

"I wouldn't touch that wager for anything!" chuckled Francis.

"Perhaps the guests should be warned?" suggested Stephanie.

Anthony shrugged. "Why spoil his fun?" His gaze met hers and, after a moment, Stephanie lifted her shoulders in silent agreement. Anthony lowered his voice. "I've not had enough exercise today. I don't suppose—" His voice became a thread of sound so no one would overhear what he said to her. "—that you'd give me a match?" He watched her half shake her head. "Later this evening, I mean?"

Sir Francis's hearing was better than Anthony had known. He was startled when Francis leaned forward. "Do you fence?" asked Sir Francis. "So few do these days," he said, faintly apologetic, at Anthony's instant, if faint, frown.

Anthony sighed, wondering if Stephanie would have agreed if they'd not been interrupted. "We'd a young man who . . . Let's just say he joined our ship on a whim? It's a long journey to the East Indies. We passed the time by his teaching me the Italian duello. Since he was a nearly penniless stowaway it was the only way he could defray the cost of his passage!"

"Why had he hidden on your ship?" asked Stephanie. "Was he a criminal?"

"Merely a coward who was forced to leave Naples in something of a hurry." One brow arched in sardonic humor. "An outraged husband, you see. Having met us at one or another social gathering, he'd assumed ours an English ship and that we'd be sailing from Naples to London. He was something surprised when, instead, we bent sail for the south once we'd passed Gibraltar!" Anthony grinned. "A charming rogue."

"Perhaps it wasn't that he'd met you but seen your English flag?"

"I think not," said Anthony dryly. "There wasn't one, you see."

"Were you not sailing under our flag?" Francis asked.

Anthony shrugged. "Chris bought his first ship from a shipwright in the colonies. He won his second from a French privateer in the Caribbean. That came complete with a French flag. The next was constructed in Holland, I think and . . ." Anthony broke off as Sir Francis indicated a certain amount of surprise. "What is it?"

"I'd no notion he'd such a fleet."

"Ten ships at last count. Perhaps," Anthony frowned, "it's nine now. We've not heard from the Santa Carissa for far too long. On the other hand, that particular captain tends to run his ship, buying and selling, very much as an independent matter and has, in the past, managed to lose himself for great lengths of time."

"And Chris allows him this freedom?"

Anthony's rare dimple showed for a moment. "Allows? He encourages it. The man is honest as a man can be. Better, he makes more in a year than any other two ships. He's a genius when it comes to buying and selling. He taught me a lot, the ol' pirate!"

"Pirate? Surely you don't mean that literally."

"Do I not? Perhaps I don't. . . . Sweetings," he added, again lowering his voice, "you've not said you'll give me a match."

Stephanie itched to match herself against this man who in so many ways was her equal, or, although it gave her a strange feeling to admit it, perhaps, at least in some ways, her superior. He made her stretch both mind and skills, and, for that matter, her emotions. She hadn't quite decided whether she liked the fact he made her use every sense, every bit of her intellect. Or, alternatively, whether he merely irritated the devil out of her.

He didn't, however, bore her. And that outweighed many of the disadvantages of an association with him. Besides, she'd not decided, yet, whether to accept what had been another sort of a challenge. Should she learn how to avoid conception so that she could enjoy the pleasures of the marriage bed, while avoiding the responsibilities? It was ironic that she'd accused young Mary Wilkins of wishing to do just that the day they'd all met!

"My sweet Stephanie, can ye say me neither yea nor nay?"

"Not now, but later . . . ?"

"Not immediately after dinner?"

Stephanie shook her head. "I find I enjoy the company, now most of my problems no longer plague me." She flicked a glance toward Oakfield who sat just beyond hearing, indicating the type of problem to which she referred.

"Poor fellow," said Sir Francis in a dry tone. "He can never make up his mind which he wants more—" Meg indicated the meal was at an end and Francis, along with everyone else, rose to his feet. "—whether to join Stephanie or to avoid you, Huntersham!"

"I believe you have that right," said Stephanie, her chuckle joining Anthony's bark of laughter.

The laughter brought Oakfield hotfoot to join their little group. "At what do you laugh, Lady Stephanie?" he asked in his irritating, high-pitched, voice. "Do share the joke with the rest of us."

"I don't think so."

"Come now!" He tittered. "You mustn't deprive your guests of any enjoyment." The unwanted suitor smirked at her, his eyes traveling in an objectionable fashion over her figure.

"It isn't the sort of thing which can be repeated," said Stephanie dismissively and turned her shoulder.

"Nonsense. You are such a wit you'll make it quite humorous," insisted Oakfield.

"Cuthbert," said Anthony. "You do *not* want it repeated."

"Do restrain yourself from using that abominable name!"

"But *Cuthbert,*" said Stephanie, "it *is* your name, is it not?"

"I much prefer James. I make you free of that name . . . Stephie."

Stephanie lay a restraining hand on Sir Francis's arm and gave Anthony a look which had him shutting his mouth with a snap. "I have not given you leave to use my name. You will not do so again."

"You would prefer that I call you Mrs. Oakfield once we're wed?"

"I would *prefer* that you remove yourself from my presence and never again come within sight or sound of me!"

"As I said, a wit." But there was a strained note in Oakfield's high-pitched, cackling laugh. "And you've not said what amused you."

"What amused me," said Stephanie clearly, in a low but carrying tone, "was the observation that you could not make up your mind whether you wished to be in my company or avoid that of your cousin. Unfortunately, on this occasion, you made the wrong choice."

Oakfield's complexion darkened and he straightened to his full height which was still an inch or so less than Stephanie's. "You will discover, Lady Stephanie, that you cannot insult me with impunity. As your only remaining suitor, you are foolish to do so." He tittered. "I might, you know, change my mind about wedding you."

"Let me see . . ." Stephanie pretended to think.

"You are thinking how to phrase an apology?" Oakfield again smirked, smoothing down a minuscule wrinkle in his sleeve.

"I am thinking how best to insult you so that you will, finally, *leave me alone.*" Stephanie was very near to losing a temper which, when, on those rare occasions she'd given free reign to her tongue, fueled it to flay the hide off of a man.

Seeing what was coming, Sir Francis decided this was not the place for such an exhibit. He stepped to Oakfield's side. "Come along now. I think you and I should adjourn to the billiards room instead of the salon. *Now,*" he added when the young fool would have objected. "I assure you, you do *not* wish to go on with this conversation." His hand tightened on Oakfield's arm.

"Here now! I say!" he blustered. "Really, Sir Francis!" Still muttering, Oakfield was firmly led off.

"Why does he persist?" fumed Stephanie.

"Sweetings," said Anthony, a touch of laughter in his voice, "it is the only sign the man has any taste at all."

Her expression was stormy but questioning.

"That he woos you, I mean."

"But he doesn't even like me!"

"Does he not?" asked Anthony, a lazy look about him like that of a big tom cat, a seasoned warrior at rest. "Then I was wrong."

"Wrong?" Stephanie cast Anthony a wary look.

"No taste whatsoever! The man is, as I'd thought, a total blot on society."

"Then make him go away."

"Didn't we have this conversation?"

"You offered to tell Lord Lemiston to make him go."

"But you were adamant I not do so. I decided I'd obey your wishes after all. Are you now suggesting you've changed your mind and don't wish to handle the man yourself?"

Stephanie sighed. She glowered at Anthony for a long moment. "You, my lord, are impossible."

"Am I? I merely wish to ascertain your exact wishes."

"I don't think I know my exact wishes," she muttered, glaring at him with a sidelong and rather suggestive look. Before he could frame a response, she walked away, leaving the dining room and the men impatiently waiting for her to do so before they lit up cigars.

Stephanie went to the salon where she joined a group arguing about what it said about Napoleon's character that he'd set aside Josephine and married Marie-Louise of Austria. Some said he'd done so reluctantly. Others were adamant that his need for a son ruled his heart. Stephanie, although she refrained from saying so, wondered if his need hadn't ruled his head and that, in his heart, he'd been reluctant!

Anthony didn't approach her again until he saw her make her excuses to the guests and leave the room. He followed, catching her as she stood at the foot of the stairs lighting a bed candle chosen from those awaiting the guests.

"Half an hour?" he asked.

"Half an ho . . . Oh." Her lower lip pursed out a bit. "May I have your promise that we will merely duel?"

"More. I'll promise we'll duel only with swords!"

Stephanie bit back a laugh. "I'll see you shortly."

"As proof of my word, I'll bring Theo."

"Theo? By this hour Theo will have his nose deep in a book."

"Then Sir Francis?"

Stephanie nodded. "Francis will, if he is still shepherding dear Cuthbert, appreciate the rescue."

"Half an hour."

Stephanie watched him return to the drawing room where he'd tactfully make certain, she thought a trifle cynically, that everyone knew she had gone and he had not! But when he again removed himself from company, what then? Would there be speculation concerning an assignation?

As she climbed the stairs Stephanie wondered if she were truly perverse. After all the years of not caring one whit whether she roused her neighbors to gossip, she suddenly discovered she didn't care for the sort of gossip a liaison with Anthony would provoke!

Nevertheless, whatever might be said, a half an hour later,

redressed in trousers and shirt, she used the secondary stairs near the armory and descended to meet her match.

Meet my match.

The words echoed round and round Stephanie's head and, she was embarrassed to discover, it was necessary to wipe sweat from damp palms. Surely Anthony Ryder was prevaricating when he said he liked her just as she was, that he wouldn't attempt to change her.

But what if he meant it?

She opened the stair door and stepped into the lower hall just as Lord Lemiston, Sir Francis, and Anthony turned into it. Almost, Stephanie stepped back up onto the first step. Almost. Then it occurred to her that to do so would be running away and, instead, she strode forward, reaching the armory just as the men did.

"I am told you fence," said Lemiston, his voice cold.

Stephanie shrugged.

"I would see such a miracle."

"You think it a miracle a woman can do such a thing?"

"Such a warlike thing. Women are not warriors." Anthony cleared his throat and Lemiston, still looking down his nose, turned the glare away from his daughter toward Huntersham. "You've something to say?"

"I think you met women in America who had fought Indians alongside their men. I know *I* did."

One could almost see Lemiston grow smaller. His eyes lost focus for a bit. Then he turned a wry grin Anthony's way. "I think it is that I have difficulty imagining *my* daughter in such a role. It is," he added, adopting a prissy tone which was totally out of character, "not *at all* the thing for Lady Stephanie. Her ladyship will cause a scandal with such behavior!"

"*You* concern yourself about scandal? That'll be the day," said Anthony.

"I know," admitted Lemiston in normal tones. "It's inconsistent of me, is it not? I cannot understand my contradictory feelings for you, my girl. I'm usually a very logical creature,

I believe. I apologize." He burlesqued a formal bow, pretending to hold a handkerchief which he waved in a series of dramatic arcs as he did so. "Lady Stephanie, let us proceed to this bout you've arranged."

He offered his arm. After a quick glance toward Anthony who, with one jerk of his head, nodded, she placed her fingertips on her father's arm and swept into the large room with the elan of a duchess entering a grand entertainment.

Twenty minutes later, panting slightly, Stephanie looked to where her foil had come to a stop after skidding some yards across the wide planks of the wood floor. "How did you do that?"

"Pick up your sword and I'll teach you," said Anthony.

Stephanie did so with alacrity. A little later she crowed with laughter. "Like *that!* I *see.* Now I want to know how to defend against it!"

Anthony picked up his foil and turned back to her only to discover her father, his jacket off, standing there instead. "Chris?"

"I'd like a turn."

"She's tired," said Anthony quickly.

"You misunderstand." Lemiston nodded and Anthony turned to discover that Sir Francis was removing his coat.

Stephanie wouldn't have admitted it to a soul, but she was ready for a rest. As Anthony had known, she was tired out by their endeavor and then the period of instruction had involved some really fancy footwork to say nothing of intense concentration. She put away her foil and lifted herself onto one of the long tables. Anthony came to her carrying two glasses of claret. She took hers and drank half without stopping, but never taking her eyes from the two men carefully testing each other's strengths.

"I'll teach you the defense another time." He too watched the men. "Unless Sir Francis is very good indeed, he'll very soon find himself in hot water," said Anthony softly.

"Hmm."

"Does that mean he's good?"

"He's good," said Stephanie with a frown, "but . . . oh, *well done!* But perhaps not quite good enough." She turned a quick look toward Anthony, turning back as she felt heat rise up her throat. The white shirt and stocking-covered feet, the tight breeches . . .

Stephanie admitted she could not continue to resist him. That she didn't *wish* to refrain from learning more about that body, learning more of what his could do to hers. Heavens! If she felt this way when merely sitting beside him, what feelings would he rouse when . . . If!

Stephanie stifled a sigh. Definitely *when.* But she'd have to find a moment of privacy in which to inform Anthony of her decision, and there was very little time left in which to act. In a few days they all left for Arundel. From there the Lemiston family would go to Brighton. So, just when *would* she see Anthony again, once the company broke up and went its various ways? Or was it decided that Anthony go, too? She couldn't at this moment recall.

"I don't believe this," muttered Stephanie, as she rode beside Anthony under the Arundel's portcullis and through the gates, walking Aladdin up the castle's curving drive.

The long expected storm had held off until the harvest was done, finally bursting over them the evening before. It had beaten itself out before morning and the ride, dust free, had been far more pleasant than one of such length might have been. And now they'd arrived. Above them rose the stark, dark lines of the ancient castle.

"It's truly incredible, is it not?" she added after a moment's awed silence.

"You've never been here?"

"Norfolk isn't interested in sweet young women. Luckily, he never learned I am not particularly sweet, because I'm still the sort of woman in whom he has no interest!"

"Because you are virginal?"

"Yes."

"More fool he!"

Her eyes scanned the looming ramparts.

Anthony followed her line of sight. "Impressed?"

"I admit it. I've never imagined anything so massive."

"You *should* feel awe. Arundel has survived everything thrown at it for six centuries. It looks likely that it'll survive another six!"

"Or forever." She gaped at the changing view.

Anthony chuckled. "Close your mouth, sweetings. Even as fascinated as you find yourself, you should pretend to a proper boredom."

"No. Not if you mean the fashion that one pretend to no emotions, pretend life is something one must force oneself to endure."

"Why not? In London I saw that everyone does it."

"Perhaps that *is* why," said Stephanie thoughtfully, the wry self-deriding half-smile in place, "If everyone does it, I won't."

"In other words, your reputation among your neighbors has been deliberately fostered?"

In no hurry, the carriages far behind them, the other riders somewhat ahead, they allowed their mounts to mosey around the last curve and up another rise where they faced the great sallyport into the inner court of the castle.

"You don't answer," he said, prodding her. "Was it deliberate?"

Stephanie glanced at him. "My reputation as a hoyden? I suppose so. For a very long time I didn't realize how seriously people disapproved of me. After all, who do I hurt by acting as I do? Why should anyone think anything about it at all? When I realized they *did,* I felt both hurt and perhaps something one might call rejection. Since I'd already been rejected by my father—" Stephanie nodded toward where Lemiston was dismounting among a crowd of other riders and Arundel grooms "—who was not around to be told what I thought of him, well, perhaps I thumbed my nose at the world in general?"

"Sounds reasonable to me. Except there are things about the world you've rejected that can be very pleasant indeed."

"I wouldn't know, would I?" she said.

"You've the opportunity now to discover all you've missed. Your father's house-party was a beginning."

She gave him a wry look.

"I don't refer to your unwanted suitors, my sweet. Remember, you've admitted to an enjoyment of his more intelligent guests. At Arundel, you'll find that house-parties can be fun when you're a guest instead of hostess." He chuckled as she cast still another look his way. "All right. You refused the public role of hostess, but I know, that behind the scenes you did much to keep the household running smoothly." Stephanie quirked an eyebrow. "I was listening the day you settled a dispute between your butler and housekeeper. You did it very well."

They'd arrived in the courtyard by then and Stephanie, knowing she blushed at the compliment, was glad of the opportunity to ignore Anthony's praise in the process of dismounting. She wore her hated habit and was a trifle chagrined to realize that, after riding sidesaddle for so long, she'd be glad of his help—when Norfolk himself appeared to aid her dismount.

"Ah! Lemiston's rebel daughter!" he twitted her, the faintest of leers twisting his smile. "Welcome to my home, m'dear."

Anthony strolled up and stood perhaps just a trifle too close to Stephanie's side. "We are happy to be here, Your Grace. The invitation was very welcome."

Norfolk drew in a deep breath and let it out. "So. Ah, well." He pouted slightly, his plump cheeks forming jowls, but then, after a slight bow, he turned away, muttering, "I didn't really suppose the chit would favor me tonight . . ."

Shocked, not quite believing her ears, she look sideways,

up at Anthony, silently asking if she'd heard what she thought she'd heard. His head gave the barest hint of a nod.

Norfolk, stalking toward Lemiston, raised his hand, making a grasping motion with it. Instantly, a footman appeared at his side and extended a tray. The duke picked up a large bumper, drank it down in gulps, and wiped his mouth with the back of his hand. Stephanie noted her father's sardonic expression and looked from him to Norfolk. Surely Lemiston had been too far away to hear that comment? Perhaps, since Lemiston was rather abstemious, the look was directed at the duke's drinking?

Anthony took Stephanie's arm and strolled off through the sallyport and along the drive toward the duke's private chapel which stood some way off.

"You weren't surprised that Norfolk insulted me. You expected it, did you not?"

"Are you insulted?"

Stephanie's mouth compressed into a thin line.

"I see you are," he answered his own question when she remained silent. His amusement was obvious.

"You laugh, but why do I deserve such treatment?"

"In the first place, my dear, you must keep in mind the duke is well known for heavy drinking. He's rarely completely sober. Then, too, he's a sporting man. In fact, his nickname is The Jockey. Which reminds me! If by ill chance you find yourself cornered by him, ask which of his horses will win at Newmarket this year. He'll talk your ear off, but he'll leave your person alone." She grimaced. "He doesn't give a damn for conventions!" continued Anthony, "and thought, I presume, that you didn't either—having, obviously, learned the gossip about you. Since a lack of conventional behavior would, to his mind, include your attitudes concerning the bedroom, he hoped to have the honor of a tumble with your perfect self. Especially when he saw you and how lovely you look in that much despised habit."

With something approaching a wail, Stephanie said, "All I want is to be left alone to live my life as I wish!"

"All you want is to forget the world has rules by which one must live or find oneself ostracized."

She glared.

"For the most part, I agree," he continued, not noticing her look and, by his very obliviousness, soothing her anger at his scold. "Our world, far too often, isn't worthy of much respect. But that isn't entirely true either. There are many people within it whom I'd wish to call friends." He paused. "It is not impossible, you know, to live very much as one wishes *without* stepping on the toes of convention."

"Is it?"

"You know it is."

"But, such a bother." She tugged at her train, lifting it out of her way as she turned to look at the castle. After a moment she asked, "Arundel is incredible, is it not?"

"Are you ignoring me?"

"Have you finished lecturing me?"

He chuckled. "I was hoping to slip that wee lecture in in such a way you'd not realize that is what I'd done!"

Stephanie sighed. "I wore the habit today, did I not? In fact, I didn't even pack a pair of trousers. I couldn't disgrace myself if I wished."

"You can't disgrace yourself *in that particular fashion*," he said, teasing.

"I do know the proper modes."

"I'm sure you do."

"If that was to suggest you think I'll not obey the strictures laid down for me, the unwed daughter of a peer, then you may just think again."

"You intend to play the proper young miss?"

Stephanie's most wicked grin slashed across her face. "I thought it might be amusing to confound all my neighbors who, once they know we've arrived in Brighton, will instantly spread the word that I'm such a one who would tie her garter in public!"

Anthony chuckled. "Come along my perversely sweet

Stephanie! The carriages are arriving and it is time we allowed ourselves to be shown our rooms so that we may change for dinner."

"But it is early, only two!"

"Don't be naive. Norfolk is an old-fashioned host. Dinner will be early, of course, but he also wishes to allow those couples who enjoy liaisons time in which to pursue them before they dress." His brows rose at the speculative look she turned his way. Rushing his words, his voice urgent, he said, "Stephanie, if that expression means you've decided—"

Sadly she shook her head. "Not now. My initiation into the bedroom arts is not something which should be rushed or done when we might fear interruption!" She heard the soft intake of a sharp breath. "Don't pretend surprise, Anthony. You knew how I'd eventually decide."

"I thought I knew. I must have had doubts, however." His breathing was a trifle ragged when he continued. "You take my breath away, sweetings." She cast him a smile which should have been carefree, but a bit of strain showed. He stopped her. "Stephanie, I'm honored."

"Don't discuss it." She caught his gaze, held it steadily. "At some instant it will be the right time and place. Let it simply happen." He nodded. "Then," she said, "let us go on. My stepmother is motioning to me."

"And you think she very likely needs you since Chris is nowhere in evidence. Not that he would be. I suspect Norfolk has already passed the decanters more than once! He'll not let his male guests go upstairs anything less than half-sprung, preferably well-to-go."

"Why? *Why* does he drink so much?"

"It's part of his generation's style, Stephanie. Our parents and more particularly our grandparents were, a large number of them anyway, exceedingly hard drinking. Go along now. Lady Lemiston has that wrinkled forehead which, I've noted, means she has a particular question for you."

Stephanie went. Some hours later she exited her room to

discover Anthony leaving the room across the hall from hers. Her brows rose. He grinned.

"How did you manage that?" she asked, suspicious.

"I didn't. My valet has been complaining the whole time I've been up here that he had to repack and move rooms after he'd just nicely settled in to the room to which I was first assigned. It seems," said Anthony with a falsely sober look, "that Lady Wheatfield didn't like the view from her room and demanded another. Mine was thought to have a particularly pleasant prospect."

"Hmm."

"Yes, I wonder, too. It seems odd that after giving the duke the impression we are lovers, I am suddenly changed to a much more convenient milieu for such activity!"

"It *is* convenient, is it not?" she asked, her words a trifle slurred with repressed emotions.

After half a moment he quirked a brow. "Tonight?" he asked, a certain brusqueness contrasting sharply with her unusually lax tone.

Stephanie hesitated only a moment. As a door farther down the hall opened, she nodded. Then she bit her lip.

"If you change your mind, slip a note under my door with some innocuous comment about the hunt which is planned for tomorrow," he said softly.

"Does the duke expect women to hunt?"

"If you don't take a gun out, neither will I," said Anthony promptly. "Don't you agree, Lady Crighten," he asked a woman with a youngish face belied by hair thickly sprinkled with gray, "that it would be perfectly proper for Lady Stephanie to join the shoot tomorrow so long as her father and Sir Francis are there to see to the proprieties?"

"It would be unusual, but I don't see how it can be improper. You are Lady Stephanie? I am Lady Crighten, since our new Lord Huntersham seems to have forgotten the proper forms. I've been hearing the most ominous things about you, Lady Stephanie," said her ladyship with a cat-like smile. "Do come along and enlighten me!" She hooked her hand through Stephanie's arm and drew her along the hall. "Tell me, is it true you outshot young Westerwood and sent him to the right about by winning a bet to that effect?"

"Lady Crighten, you cannot expect Lady Stephanie to blow her own horn!" said Anthony, pretending horror. "Allow *me* to tell the tale of Westerwood's defeat!"

"So I shall," said her ladyship, not releasing Stephanie. "But I've other questions as well," she said, her eyes twinkling.

They reached an arched opening to a set of circular stairs and, in single file, went carefully down the worn steps. At the bottom Stephanie and Anthony allowed Lady Crighten, who knew the way, to lead them through the long, narrow double library, through an anteroom and then to the right along the connecting hall to the salon where the company was to meet before dinner.

Stephanie, who liked a neat if slightly frugal table, was overwhelmed by the number of courses and excessive number of removes in each course. Luckily, she'd had the sense to watch the behavior of her new friend, Lady Crighten, and noted how little she was served and then only from a few of the many dishes, so that she didn't sate herself in the first course. She was too far from Meg to give her the hint, but decided Lemiston must have had the foresight to do so, because she too ate sparingly.

Long before the meal ended, Stephanie was wishing herself elsewhere, even though she much enjoyed the conversation which, at her side of the table, was of Perceval. Most of the comments were scathing denunciations of the first minister's attempt to unite the country by forming a government composed of both Whigs and Tories.

"I don't understand how it's survived this long!" said one.

"He's a stubborn man," said another, raising another contentious subject. "I can't think why he continues pursuing that lost cause in Spain, however. I feel strongly our best move would be an early peace."

"You are wrong," said Colonel Lord Winston, his strong feelings on the subject compelling him to enter the conversation although he sat across the table and should *not* have done so. "The war is *not* a lost cause and you would be exceedingly foolish to appease Napoleon. The man is mad for power and, if he *were* to sign a peace agreement with England now, it, like the Peace of Amiens, would last only so long as it took him to use the troops freed by it to consolidate his power elsewhere. Then he'd be right on our doorstep demanding we too capitulate to his rule."

The argument became general, continuing over the heads of most of the women. But not only Stephanie paid attention. Lady Scranton, whose husband was a radical Whig, actually had the nerve to make her opinion known!

The meal ended eventually and the women trailed through the door into the adjoining salon where there were comfortable chairs both near the fireplace in which a small fire had been lit, and well away from it for those who preferred a cooler clime. Stephanie found herself taken in hand by Lady Crighten who introduced her to those she'd not yet met, deftly finishing their tour of the room at Meg's side where she sat alone by one of the windows, staring through it into the dusk.

"You must tell me about living in Australia," suggested Lady Crighten with a sly grin.

Her ladyship's insinuating tone was the first thing about her that Stephanie found to dislike. "Yes, Meg," she inserted quickly, "I've wanted to hear more about the house you and my father live in. Is it comfortable?"

"The first house warn't," said Meg, casting Stephanie a look which revealed both resignation that she must speak to a woman who obviously meant to show her up and thanks that Stephanie had introduced a topic which was unlikely to become a source of too much embarrassment. "That first was a rough place altogether, but the new house is built in a style that was invented in the American colonies—or so his lordship tol' me. It allows for the circulation of air so one isn't so hot, you see."

"Hot? One hears how awful the heat is in India, of course," said her ladyship.

"Believe me, it can get pretty blidy hot where we are, too."

Lady Crighten laughed lightly. "Blidy hot. What a . . . quaint turn of phrase."

"You'd prefer damned hot?" asked Stephanie. She was ignored.

"You live in Botany Bay, or Newcastle, of course?" asked Lady Crighten.

"We don't then. Our land is near fifty miles inland from Newcastle."

"Oh?" Lady Crighten's brows arched. "An *estate* you'd say?"

"No more'n ten thousand acres," said Meg with a touch of embarrassment.

Lady Crighten sobered instantly. "So much."

"Lemiston says we'll help make a new country great."

"I'm certain he will," agreed Lady Crighten, this time inadvertently offensive in excluding Meg from her assessment!

Stephanie noted that Meg gritted her teeth and, in order to avoid a biting comment, of which Meg was certainly capable, she asked another question which drew a calm response after a moment in which her stepmother very obviously fought and won an inner battle. Soon others gathered around, pelting Meg with questions. It wasn't that they accepted her as one of them, but most of the women who made up this particular circle were intelligent and interested in discovering what they could of the Antipodes from someone who lived there.

All went well until someone asked, "But the prisoners! Don't you fear them? Are they not dangerous?"

Meg looked at Stephanie. Her lips twitched but she shook her head. Just then the door to the dining room opened and several men came through—including Sir Francis. Stephanie sent him a silent signal and he immediately joined the group. When the woman repeated her question, he took over.

"You are aware, are you not," he asked, "that the greatest

number of transportees are guilty of nothing more than—oh, for instance, stealing a loaf of bread?" His brows rose. "Desperate rogues indeed!" The laughter was general. "There are, of course, *some* hardened criminals among them, or so I hear, so one may not be perfectly safe. But then it isn't perfectly safe in the streets of London."

Francis then offered a change of subject which was followed up, and, soon the group around Meg broke up. Meg looked up at Stephanie. Stephanie winked and Meg grinned. It was a brief smile however and broke on a yawn.

"Tired?" asked Stephanie.

"I don' know how it is. I can work from dawn to dusk when we're home. Here, seems like the least little thing makes me tired these days."

"Very likely it's the strain, knowing you might at any moment find someone who will insult you to the quick, or will snub you, or . . . whatever."

Meg's jaw firmed and her chin came up. "I've rights."

"Yes. Are you enjoying any of them?"

Meg turned a startled glance on Stephanie and a bark of laughter escaped her. "Between you and me, Stephie, m'girl, no. Not even the fancy clothes." She plucked at her gown, one chosen for her by Jane. She wrinkled her nose. "So pale and plain, I *will* be glad to get back to my own home. I were surprised to discover it *is* home." she added, a hint of that surprise evident in her expression. Thoughtfully, she added, "Do you suppose that woman knew I'd been transported?"

Stephanie shrugged. "If she did not, I'm certain someone will enlighten her. Does it matter?"

Meg's chin rose. "No. Not a smidge."

"Good. That's the way you should feel." Stephanie stayed near Meg for the rest of the evening but was glad when people began drifting away—some seeking privacy, some the card tables which were set up in one end of the long library, and some, including Meg and Stephanie, their rooms.

Once there Stephanie remembered she was to expect Anthony to join her. For a long moment panic engulfed her and she thought seriously of slipping the suggested note under his door that would tell him, without the words being said, that he was *not* to come to her.

But if not tonight then when? Having decided to take him for a lover, Stephanie feared her nerve wouldn't hold if she must wait for days, weeks perhaps, for another opportunity. She paced back and forth across the soft carpet, pulling pins from her hair and letting it down as she walked. Sitting at her dressing table she pulled her brush through it with long soothing strokes.

A little later, calmed, she went to her armoire and pulled out the silk banyan-like garment. Undressing completely, she put it on and took up John Christian Curwen's book, *Hints on Agricultural Subjects and the Best Method of Improving the Condition of the Labouring Classes,* which had come out the preceding year but that she'd only recently purchased. She curled up in the nearly adequate armchair and settled down to read. Unfortunately, she discovered her ability to concentrate was not as full as usual—or perhaps she was tired?

Nonsense. She was as nerve-ridden as a new recruit facing his first battle! Whenever she heard voices in the hall, her head came up and she'd strain to hear, attempting to determine who was outside her room. Finally she was rewarded: She heard Theo say, "Good night Tony. If, then, you'll ask your valet to wake me, I'd appreciate it."

"He must wake me so I see no reason why he should not wake you, as well."

"In the morning then."

"Good night."

Stephanie set aside her book and, her heart beating only a trifle rapidly, she composed herself to await her lover's arrival.

And she waited.

Fifteen

And she waited some more.

Occasionally she'd hear hints of someone moving along the corridor. Once, half-stifled laughter reached her ears. Again, the querulous tones of a nagging woman. Finally she set to pacing her room.

Had *he* changed his mind? she wondered. Or were there rules to this game of which she'd no knowledge? Stephanie choked back a panicky laugh of her own as it occurred to her that perhaps she should have applied to her father for lessons. Or perhaps Lady Crighten? Her ladyship seemed the sort to know exactly how this particular ton pastime was played.

A new sound in the hall brought her to a halt, had her swinging around to stare at the door. Again she was disappointed. If he didn't come soon, she'd write that note! *Anything* to get beyond this . . . this awful anticipation of the unknown.

Another long wait while she pressed herself flat against her door, one ear straining against the wood—and finally she was rewarded. The click of his door had her scurrying toward the bed, then, nerves not so steady as she'd have liked, toward the window. She held her breath, letting it out as her door opened and Anthony slipped through it.

Stephanie relaxed. Suddenly and completely. Why she should, she didn't know, but she did. Perhaps, she thought, watching him turn and lean back against the closed door, it was that she trusted him. How strange. She'd never before

totally trusted anyone but Theo, Francis, and Jane—and sometimes she'd wondered about Jane!

Did she trust him? She nodded.

"Yes?" he asked.

She felt heat flow up her throat. "I . . . was thinking, a
question . . . answering myself. That's why I nodded that way.
It's a bad habit."

"Can I know," he said in the whimsical fashion Stephanie
had come to love, "what it was you said to yourself?"

"I . . ." Could she tell him. Her chin went up. "I decided
I trust you."

He choked back a laugh. "I should hope so. It would be . . .
inappropriate to take as a lover someone you could *not* trust."

She felt the heat blossom still more, rising into her cheeks.
She turned her back, the silk of her robe swinging against her
skin as she did so. She heard a restrained gasp and looked
over her shoulder.

"You are unbelievably lovely," he said softly.

"You needn't lie," she said, turning and facing him.

"Haven't we had this conversation? I've told you, I don't
lie. I will never lie to you."

"That rare thing, an oddity among men . . ."

He frowned. "That I find you lovely?" She nodded. "My
dear delight, what nonsense is this?"

"I was told long ago that men do not find women as tall
or as independent-minded as I the least bit attractive."

"You think I'm not attracted to you? That I only pretend?"

Stephanie frowned. On more than one occasion she'd been
close enough to verify the physical results of his attraction.
"You *admit* to being odd, then."

"Perhaps the cretin who told you such an idiocy was not
so tall as I?" He moved slowly closer. "Or perhaps he was
rather unsure of himself, as I am not?"

"He *was* considerably younger . . ."

"Ah. Let me inform you, my dear, that a man's tastes mature
along with his body. He reaches an age where the merely su-

perficial, the facade, the public face is not enough. He wants more in the woman he loves. And you *are* more. Much, much more, but what an ass he must have been if he didn't at the very least think you attractive in form and face."

"Me . . . ?"

"You wish words, my sweet?" He chuckled at her quick nod and wide eyes. "Let me begin with your hair."

He lifted it from behind her and lay it over her breasts, allowing a curl to wind around his wrist. Holding her gaze, he lifted it to his mouth, kissed the tress, rubbed it gently against his cheek.

"Magnificent, my love. Thick, long, and alive, your hair is a glorious crown. Your features—"

As he spoke he touched her forehead with a finger, running it down the length of her nose and dropping to touch her lips.

"Those wonderful blue-gray eyes with their sleepy look—as if you'd just finished making wild and satisfying love. You'll never know how intriguing that is. And the skin, perfectly fresh, perfectly clear, perfectly tinted with the roses of health. Your lips, my sweet."

He ran his finger back and forth across them until Stephanie opened them, leaned slightly, and nipped the tip.

"Lips that laugh," he said softly, "and pout and smile and speak. Wonderful lips, my sweet life."

She nipped again and he smiled, shaking his head.

"Not yet, my dear," he said, tapping her mouth lightly. "If you begin such things I don't know if I can finish and I've so much more to say."

He lowered his hand slowly, the other joining it at her waist, and tugged gently until she rested lightly against his torso.

"Where was I? Ah yes. Tall. Tall enough I needn't break my back to reach that tempting mouth." He touched her lips briefly with his own. "Do you know," he added, the whimsy very much in evidence, "that I once thought of wedding a wee creature." Again his lips barely touched hers. "Then it occurred to me I'd need a stool to put her on whenever I wished to kiss her. I decided that wasn't the best notion I'd ever had." Again, teasingly. "I'll never need a stool with you."

Still another time his lips brushed hers, even as his hands moved at her waist, caressing her, pushing the soft silk back and forth against her skin. Stephanie couldn't quite repress a soft moan.

"No, no, my sweet!" he said, laughter not far below the surface. "Not yet. There's more. Much more . . ." His palms rose to cover her breasts, burying into long tresses to do so. "So perfect. Ever since that day by the water I've wanted to touch you again, here, mold you, hold you . . . kiss you . . ."

His fingers had been busy in ways Stephanie hadn't noticed and suddenly the robe fell apart. He bent to her breast. Stephanie's hands rose of their own accord, cradling his head, feeling his hair beneath her palms, running the fingers of one hand through it, even as she held him close with the other. Her eyes half-closed at the ecstasy his playful mouth induced. "Anthony . . ."

"Soon, love," he murmured, slowly lowering himself to a kneeling position. "Oh Lord," he muttered against her skin. "Words, my dear heart, will have to wait!" His hands slipped down to cradle her hips as his tongue explored . . . discovered the dip of the navel, played there, mouthed from one hip, across to the other, dipped a trifle lower, back . . . still lower.

Stephanie's knees turned to water. She leaned over him, her hands sliding down his back . . . and found herself lifted, carried to the bed where he pulled open the covers and laid her gently onto the sheets.

"I'm in awe," he said, his voice a deep rumble, emotion filled. He stared at her body, framed by the wild color of the open robe. "I am humbled by your perfection and come to you the supplicant, my love." He raised his eyes and met her wondering gaze. "I need you."

"I think I need you, too," she managed and lifted her arms.

Anthony rested one knee on the bed and set his hands carefully to either side of her head. Still holding her gaze, he lowered himself slowly until his mouth met hers in the softest of kisses.

Soft teasing kisses turned heated. Arms entwined, tangled with hair and robe, hands moved, explored, touched, teased, tempted . . . until, with a groan, Anthony reached between her thighs . . .

And felt her tense.

"Trust me . . ." he whispered and breathed again when she relaxed enough he could touch that most secret and sensitive center of a woman's pleasure. He smiled when she gasped at the feelings he induced.

Then, covering her mouth with his own, he slipped one hair-roughened leg between hers, spreading her a bit wider. His fingers continued their play and her arms tightened around him, her body moving restlessly.

"Good girl. That's the way, my sweet," he murmured. "Let go, my love. Feel all you were meant to feel, what you were made to feel . . . Yes!"

Stephanie gasped, moaned into his mouth, felt him moving over her, widened the vee between her thighs, made room for him, wanting him there, feeling the first gently probing touch of flesh against damp flesh . . .

And felt him jerk away as the wall-muffled sound of a loud scream, a sound of horror or of pain, reached their ears.

"My god, what was that?" he asked, looking toward the hall.

Stephanie had a hard time coming back from the emotional experience which had accompanied her physical release, but the scream reminded her of Theo's danger and she struggled from beneath him, sliding off the side of the bed. She reached for her robe, pulled it from under Anthony, and slipped into it. She listened as she tied it tightly.

"Was someone being murdered?" she whispered.

"I doubt it." Unhappy at the interruption which had come at such an inopportune moment, Anthony tried to be glad that at least Stephanie had the opportunity to learn what her body could feel, that their loving had not been a total waste. "That sounds like groans, but I'd better go see."

He started for the door, only to find Stephanie grasping his robe which swung free around him. The sound of feet racing down the hall, of voices requiring information, of others asking what had happened, and still others calling out that this person or that must be careful!

Simultaneously with another sharp call that someone should be careful, there came a muffled yelp and then the clearly heard instruction in another voice that anyone coming down the stairs was to beware: "There's a cord stretched across them!"

"Someone has fallen," said Anthony softly. "But a cord . . . ?"

"I knew it was Theo . . . !" breathed Stephanie, a hand going to cover her throat.

"Why do you think of Theo?" he whispered. "Oh . . . of course . . . But here?"

Time had cleared his head and Anthony was conscious, now, of what would be said if he were caught leaving her bedroom, something Stephanie had managed to remember so that she'd caught and held him back.

Anthony stifled a chuckle: If he'd been caught leaving her room, he'd be forced by convention to ask her, again, to marry him. She, contrary soul that she was, would *not* be forced by that same convention into a proper response. She'd be ostracized, and he didn't want that! He had too many plans for their future, so it was just as well she'd not allowed him to leave the room.

"Why would Theo be up and around," he asked softly, leaning against a heavily carved bed post.

"My twin and I need far less sleep than most. Often, when he's lying quietly in bed, as is his habit while others sleep, a question will occur to him and he'll get up and go to the library where the servants may find him in the morning, asleep over a book. If he went down those stairs to find a certain book . . ."

Anthony, seeing how she unconsciously wrung her hands, knowing how worried she was, wondered what to say to ease her. The solution, of course, was obvious. "Stephanie, it has occurred to me that, although *I* daren't be seen leaving your room, you may freely do so."

She gave him a startled look, followed by one of gratitude, and slipped out the door. There were others in the hall. Meg joined her stepdaughter. "Woke you too, did he? Someone screamin' blidy murder?"

"Whoever it is, he isn't dead. At least I assume all those moans and groans mean something," answered Stephanie. She'd relaxed as soon as she realized it was *not* her brother's pleasant baritone, but a high tenor voice loudly revealing its pain. Then she was certain she heard Theo's low drawling voice and relaxed still more.

Sir Francis appeared at the top of the stairs. He glanced from face to worried face. "Mr. Oakfield fell. He has either a broken or a badly sprained wrist and a very bad bump on the head which must be watched for concussion. He is a very lucky man since there is nothing more to concern him but what will surely be a multitude of bruises. A servant has gone for a doctor and, in the meantime, we will get him to his bed." Francis smiled. "Not, however, up these stairs! We'll take him around by the main staircase. Everything is under control and you may all return to your beds with no fear of housebreakers or that Napoleon's army has arrived or whatever other thought may have frightened the ladies."

"But, did someone say a cord crossed the stairway?" asked one gentleman who had a night cap pulled rakishly over one eye. "Why?"

Francis's mouth tightened into a line. "His Grace will make a full inquiry, of course, but that will take time. You'll be informed when more is known." Stephanie caught her guardian's eyes, and arched a brow, asking silently about Theo. "No one was hurt but Oakfield and we must give thanks for that," said Francis with a touch of piety which tipped one side of Stephanie's mouth and brought a twinkle to her eye.

"Must have been a madman," muttered one woman. "Why, someone might have been killed instead of just bruised."

"Mad indeed. Or an evil sort who couldn't care less who was caught by the trap. A good man would have thought of that . . ."

At the women's words, Stephanie's desire to chuckle faded. Had it been another attempt on Theo? If so, then it was someone who had access to Arundel, and that must mean someone of the house-party surely. Unless a servant had been bribed? But even so, it must be someone who knew of Theo's odd habit of walking the halls in the dark. But if Theo was the villain's quarry, the man had once again failed. There was no sense thinking more of it now.

Stephanie slipped back into her room, leaning, as Anthony had done earlier, against her door. She stared at him. He'd returned to the bed, propping himself against the head with all her pillows stuffed behind him. She felt the heat of a blush flow up into her face.

"I was afraid of that," he murmured and turned his gaze toward the ornate embroidery decorating the tester over her bed.

"Afraid of what?"

"You want me to return to my room as soon as the way is clear."

"How did you guess?"

"Stephanie . . ."

"What you haven't guessed is I don't think it would be fair . . ."

As she spoke, she moved to his side and deliberately laid her hand just above where the shape of his robe indicated he was still somewhat aroused.

"Not fair at all . . ." she repeated softly.

Still more deliberately she let her fingers stray over the material hiding the bulge. He groaned and her fingers stilled. His eyes snapped open. "Don't stop! Whatever you mean to do, my unbelievable love, *don't stop*. Please." He rolled his hips slightly, moving against her palm and she pressed down lightly.

"You must tell me what to do, Anthony."

"You don't need telling," he managed through his gritted teeth.

She sat beside him and pushed aside the robe. "I like this," she said, rubbing her palm against the soft pelt of dark chest hair.

"So do I," he muttered.

She leaned forward and ran bared teeth along the skin of his shoulder. His arms snaked around her, one hand pulling her hips close. He reached down and bent one of her bare legs up over his thigh and pressed her close, her lower body hot and damp against him.

They kissed, deeply, and he rolled them over. "Stephie?" She nodded and once again he prepared her for his first invasion of her body. "Trust. Trust me, my love," he murmured as he felt his way into her, stopping as her eyes widened. "Trust . . ."

She bit her lip, but, even as she did so, she very slightly lifted her hips, taking him further in and very nearly taking his self-control, as well. After a moment, slowly, gently, allowing her body to adjust, he came home.

"I expected pain . . ." she whispered.

"You've led an exceedingly active life, my love. Sometimes that takes care of that particular problem. I rather thought it might be all right, hoped it would."

Anthony, supported on his elbows, pushed her hair back from her face. He kissed her, sliding out, in, slowly and then, as control once again receded, took her fast and hard and more quickly than he wanted. She held him tight when, spent, he fell against her.

When his breathing evened, he again raised himself. "I'm sorry."

She blinked. "Why?"

"I should have given you pleasure as well as taken my own."

"But you did, earlier . . ."

He grinned, a wicked pirate grin. "However naturally adept you are, I see there is still much I may teach you. There's no law, my sweet Stephanie, against it happening again, you know."

"Hmmm . . . ?" Stephanie moved her hands against him, lazily exploring wherever she could reach . . .

"Ah, but there *is*," he added, at the speculative look she gave him, "a law that applies to me. It'll be a while before I can—" His eyes widened as she made a particularly interesting foray. "Well, I'll be damned!" he said softly.

This time their loving climaxed almost simultaneously. Anthony lay his forehead against hers and for a long moment just lay there. Then he rolled to one side, taking her with him and snuggling her close. "I knew it would be good with you, sweetings, but believe me, this has been pretty damn exceptional!"

"I have this rule," said Stephanie, teasing, touching his chin with one finger.

"Rule?"

"Hmm. I don't do a thing unless I can do it well."

"And how did you know you'd do this well?" he asked and she could hear the smile in his voice, even if she couldn't see his face.

"Why, because I knew I'd have an exceptional tutor."

"And that makes all the difference?"

"Oh yes. A bad tutor may actually make things worse than no tutor at all. If one is going to take instruction, one must go to the very best."

Anthony stilled. "And is that what you've done?"

"Hmmm?" Languidly, her finger traced a path along his jaw.

"Is that what you've done?" Anthony grasped her hand, held

it tightly. "Have you come to the best instructor you could find for tutoring in something you wished to learn?" he asked.

The smooth, even, almost crisp tone of his voice jerked Stephanie from the relaxed sense of warmth and quiet satisfaction which had held her nearly inert. She struggled away from him and sat, cross-legged, beside him, her arms crossed before her. "What are you suggesting? That I decided to take you for a lover merely because I wished to learn a new skill?"

There was a note of suspicion in his look when he nodded. "I sincerely hope I'm wrong, sweeting, but it was your own words that raised the question!"

"Damn you Anthony Ryder!"

He reached up and covered her mouth. "Shush!"

For a moment they remained absolutely still, listening, Stephanie rigid under his hand. She pulled it away, continuing in a softer but vicious voice: "I don't see how you can think such a thing of me. You are a monster to say such a thing. You are horrible to spoil one of the most precious experiences of my life. You are—"

Once again he stopped her words, but this time by pulling her down and kissing her. When she'd relaxed, he released her and held her so he could look at her. "Was it really precious to you?"

"Very."

"That makes me very happy."

"Good."

"And I don't really think you made a decision to *use* me." His eyes twinkled with humor. The humor faded when she didn't respond. "Stephanie?"

"As you have me?"

Grim faced, Anthony removed himself from her bed. He found where his robe had fallen, put it on, and finally tying the wide sash, he forced himself to look at her. Instantly he softened slightly, but only a bit, at the confusion he read in her face. "You forget, Stephanie, I've asked you to wed me. I've agreed to second best because it is all you'll give me, but the offer is still open. I would much prefer to be your husband to being your lover."

"Why?"

"Why? Because as your husband I can still be your lover, but the reverse is not true. As your husband I could give you so much more than my body, you see. Good night." He turned briskly and, without checking to see if it was safe, crossed the hall to his own room. It was luck alone that no one else happened to be in the hall at just that moment.

The next morning, Stephanie wasn't particularly surprised to discover she was a trifle sore in places which had never before bothered her, but she *was* surprised to find she felt a trifle shy. In fact, so shy she hesitated just outside the door to the dining room, wondering if anyone would notice if she skipped breakfast altogether. But, just as she was about to turn away, her brother came around the corner from the anteroom to the library. His appearance reminded her of the previous night's accident and gave her an excuse to avoid the breakfast room . . . and her first meeting that day with Anthony.

"Theo? What happened last night?"

"Last night?" he drawled. "Oh. Oakfield's fall. It was my fault, Stephie. I feel really terrible about it, but it never occurred to me anyone else would be wandering around. I don't think I'll ever forgive myself if Oakfield doesn't recover properly."

"You still haven't told me what happened."

"I haven't?" He ran splayed fingers through his hair.

"You haven't. Begin at the beginning, Theo." Stephanie took his arm and moved toward a couch set near the windows at the end of the hall. She pushed her brother down and sat beside him. "The *beginning*," she repeated.

"I suppose that was when I got to wondering about . . ."

"No, Theo. I don't want to know what you were thinking. I want to know what you did."

"Hmm? Oh. Well, I needed to check a reference, you see. I wanted to know the exact phrase when—" He noticed her growing irritation. "Anyway, I'd noticed, yesterday, Norfolk had a copy so I came down to find it."

"Didn't you have a candle?"

"Stephie, you know I rarely carry one. I can't exactly see in the dark, but my *feet* seem to . . . to . . . I don't know how to say what I mean, but in a strange place, I guess I must walk in an odd fashion, because *they* seem to see where they're going! When I came down those stairs last night, I felt that cord. I didn't think about it, really, except that it was an odd place for such a thing. I wanted that book, you know, so I just stepped over it and came on down."

"But how could you find the volume you wanted if there was no light?"

"There was a lamp on that table there." Theo pointed to one which sat against the hall wall across from the door to the anteroom. "It was turned very low, of course. I was making my way toward it when suddenly Oakfield screamed and came tumbling down. It was rather awful, Stephie." He gave her a speculative look. "I was surprised you didn't come see what had happened. In fact, I rather hoped you would, since you've learned something about medicine . . ."

"There seemed plenty of people already on the scene and I didn't want to intrude. Why did you say you were responsible?"

"Because I very selfishly didn't take the time to remove that cord before coming to hunt my book. If I *had*, Oakfield would not have tripped over it."

"Hmm. I wonder why *he* was up and wandering around . . ."

"I think someone asked him that. He just moaned and groaned and whined and . . . you know how he is."

"So he didn't explain why he wasn't tucked up snug in his bed?"

Theo shrugged. "The general guess is that he was meeting someone, don't you see? Or perhaps you didn't notice?" He eyed his twin thoughtfully. "There was an awful lot of coming and going, I thought, after everyone had supposedly found their rooms."

"But *Oakfield?*" Stephanie looked skeptical. "Well, perhaps a maid?"

"I don't know. I thought it all a nuisance; it was exceedingly distracting, all that tip-toeing around."

"I'm informed," said Stephanie, tongue firmly in cheek, "that it's one of the benefits of a house-party: The coming and going, I mean."

Theo eyed her. "A benefit you are indulging?"

"Theo!" Despite the protest she put into her tone, she was unable to control a blush.

"Ah. You are. I did wonder."

Stephanie was silent for a long moment except for her fingers which she discovered she was twisting. She carefully straightened them and lay them in her lap. "Theo?"

"Hmmm?"

"Do you think I should not?"

He frowned. "It is your decision, is it not? Isn't that what we were taught? And, too, isn't it what you told me when I thought to interfere?"

"For the first time in my life I'm not certain I'm doing the right thing."

Theo smiled. "Probably good for you."

"Taking a lover?"

"I've decided it's best if I've no opinion on that particular subject! I referred to your uncertainty. Usually you are far too sure of yourself."

Stephanie didn't know whether to laugh or scold but, in the end, did neither because the door to the dining room opened just then and Anthony stepped into the hall. She stared hungrily during the instant he was unaware of her presence, lowering her gaze the moment he turned and saw her. He approached and, undecided whether to run or not, Stephanie rose to her feet. He lifted her hand and kissed the palm warmly, holding it and staring into her eyes as if he'd read her mind. "Regrets?"

"No!"

"But something."

"She says," offered Theo, "that for the first time, she isn't certain of herself."

For a moment Anthony, his head on one side, studied Theo. "You know then."

"We are twins, Huntersham," said Theo softly. "We often know . . . things."

"Uncertain, is she?" When Theo nodded, Anthony turned back to Stephanie who was obviously beginning to simmer. "Hmm . . ."

"What," asked Stephanie a trifle angrily, "do you mean by *that?*"

With a gentle fingertip Anthony traced her lips. "I am pleased you are unsure of yourself. I can work on that insecurity, argue with you and convince you, perhaps, that marriage would be the answer to everything."

"Everything?" She eyed the color that appeared in his ears. "What, exactly," she demanded, "do you mean, everything?"

Anthony grimaced. "Just *everything,* my sweet life. Leave it at that. Now, are you meaning to breakfast before we leave for the hunt?"

"I've decided not to go out."

His brows rose. "A trifle out of character, would you say?"

"I mean to stay here and protect Meg from all the cats."

"Ah. An excellent excuse." He paused and then added, "Is it an excuse?"

Stephanie grinned, her unwanted shyness fading to nearly nothing now she'd seen him and talked to him. "I'll never tell." She retrieved her hand, stepped around Anthony, and headed for the dining room. She turned, pacing backwards. "You might attempt to make Theo repeat his story concerning what happened last night. I found it a trifle intriguing."

"Why?"

She stopped. "I'd very much like to know why Oakfield was prowling around."

"I'd rather know who set that trap and for whom the trap was set."

"That, too, but Oakfield should have been tucked neatly into his bed, should he not?"

Anthony grinned. "Perhaps *you* can't guess why he was not, but *I've* a notion. My nasty little cousin likes to *know*, you see." The twins glanced at each other and back to Anthony. "It is a sort of power if one knows something about another the other doesn't wish known. I've no proof he indulges in a spot of blackmail now and again, but it wouldn't surprise me to discover he does."

"The gall of the man! He's truly a blot on creation."

"Oh, entirely," agreed Anthony. "I was rather surprised to return home and discover someone hadn't done him a mischief years ago for one of his petty—or not so petty—villainies."

When Anthony casually moved in her direction, Stephanie discovered that perhaps she wasn't quite over that odd skittishness after all. She removed herself from the hall, whipping into the dining room in a somewhat unladylike fashion! Luckily, the few people there were preoccupied with a variety of newspapers and didn't notice.

The rest of that long day Stephanie found herself unable to settle to anything. No matter what she did, how she tried, she couldn't keep her mind off Anthony. No matter what, very soon she was remembering the night before—or thinking of the night to come.

Coming so slowly. All too slowly.

Halfway through the afternoon she concluded she'd made the wrong decision: A thing should not take over one's life as this had done, making one incapable of anything but the long wait until the next time! Unfortunately, having experienced Anthony's loving, there was no way she could deny it had happened, no way to return to the way things were before. Because now she *knew*, and knowing . . .

Well, *knowing,* she could not bring herself to deny them the pleasure they gave each other. But surely, once the experience became commonplace, it would not loom so large in her mind?

A tendril of panic invaded her at that thought. *How* could it become commonplace? After the few nights they were to spend here at Arundel there would be the problem of meeting again, of finding a time and a place in which to indulge their passion. Which meant she might spend the rest of her life thinking up ways and means of getting Anthony available and naked!

Stephanie groaned.

Sixteen

Brighton—Briefly

Several days later, Stephanie tried to see everything at once as she and Anthony strolled along Brighton's promenade. As she watched one of the bathing machines pushed into the water, she said, "I wonder why I feel more relaxed knowing your despicable cousin remained at Arundel."

"Hmm?" Anthony's attention was on the water, his gaze searching the horizon.

"Never mind. Not important . . ."

Stephanie, too, was absorbed by the view and understood something of his preoccupation. Besides, she'd discovered an unbelievable degree of contentment that Anthony had not gone from Arundel to Hunter's Cove, but had come to Brighton when she and her family left the castle. She was glad she had more time with him and it didn't matter that he didn't pay her attention at every moment since they'd come directly to the house her father had obtained—by means better left unknown—right on Brighton's Marine Parade. He was here and that was the important thing.

So. Could they . . . ? Perhaps tonight . . . ?

Stephanie ducked her head, hoping her detested bonnet hid her face. Whenever she thought of the preceding nights, the hours she'd spent in Anthony's arms, a warmth started at her toes and flowed right on up her body. It would happen at any time and anywhere.

Meg, noticing, had asked if she were sickening and had cast a worried glance at her boys as she did so. At the time Stephanie, Jane, and Meg had been riding in the carriage, the boys taking turns riding with one or another of the men. Stephanie smiled at the memory although she'd found it difficult to soothe Meg's concerns while not revealing the true cause of her flushed features! Remembering brought a renewal of heat . . .

Think of something else! she scolded herself.

She'd been speaking of something. She cast her mind back to her last words. "Ah! Your oh-so dear cousin is . . . Oh, I don't know. He bothers me."

"Cuthbert? But all your suitors bothered you." said Anthony idly as he greedily watched a gun ship beating a slow way northward against the wind and wondered if it bore dispatches from the Peninsula. "Dear old Cuthbert." He analyzed Stephanie's words and her tone. Concluding she had serious concerns, he asked, "Why does he in particular upset you?"

"I've always felt uneasy in his presence. There is something . . . wild? Untamed?" She frowned. "That isn't it. I just don't know. He doesn't exactly *frighten* me, but . . . oh, the devil." Stephanie thought for a moment. "Perhaps this will make it clear how I feel about him. Recently I read a description of Whinnygate's rockets, a scathing commentary on the fact they are so uncontrolled. They are said—" She tugged at his arm drawing his attention which had strayed back to the vessel. "—to go off in any direction. That's how I see your cousin Cuthbert."

"Yes, well, he isn't here to bother you, so let's forget him, hmmm? Just enjoy the view, why don't you?"

"As that young person is doing?" Stephanie motioned with one finger toward a serving maid who, mouth open and eyes bulging, stared, disbelievingly, at the expanse of water.

Anthony's bark of laughter drew eyes. "I'd guess that one has never seen the sea, but it is nothing new to you, is it? Living as you do on the bay and only a few miles from the Channel." His own gaze rarely left the water, was caught now by a new sail near the horizon. "I think that's why I like the Priory so well. Hunter's Cove is situated in such a way you can't see the Channel. Or, rather, you once could, but the trees have grown to such a degree it is no longer visible. Perhaps I should have some cut—"

"You love it. The sea, I mean," said Stephanie, casting him a enigmatic look.

"Yes. I love it and I'll miss it."

The words soothed a fear Stephanie hadn't known she had. Because, if he believed he'd miss it, then he'd not be sailing away any time soon, and that was good! "You'll no longer sail for my father?" she asked rather diffidently, wanting to be certain.

"I was a bit more than a mere captain, Stephanie. We were partners."

"Were?"

"I've sold my share to him."

"Then you'll not be going off on long voyages," she clarified, stating the obvious, but again from the need to be sure. Their exchange soothed the niggling concern still further and she felt generous. "You could," she suggested, "purchase a yacht."

"I may. But not immediately. It would be far too tempting to simply take off for . . . oh, anywhere."

The irritating suspicion disappeared altogether. "Theo would like that, too, I think. Myself, I can't seem to raise a great deal of interest in anything but home. The Priory is . . . very special to me." When Anthony didn't say anything in response she turned to look at him and found a muscle jumping wildly along his jaw. "What is it?"

"What? Oh, just something I have yet to settle with your father."

"Would it help to discuss it?"

"No."

"That was definite enough even for my poor, weak feminine brain." A trifle hurt by his vehemence and still more so when he didn't respond, she took a moment to control her volatile temper which she knew could be self-destructive. "What *may* we discuss?" she asked, finally.

He ignored the hint that she'd felt rejected and would like him to explain. "That lady's bonnet, perhaps?" He nodded toward where a hat with an extra wide brim carried an overabundance of flowers, fruit, and feathers, nodding over a plump woman's eyes. "Have you ever seen anything to match it?"

Putting aside her pique, Stephanie reluctantly decided Anthony was like most any man, thinking she wouldn't understand, or if she did, wouldn't be interested and therefore he'd keep secrets from her. Stephanie vowed she'd teach him better—but not just now.

She studied the bonnet. As she did, its complete horror came clear to her, and she chuckled. "Meg would like it above anything, would she not?"

Anthony grinned. "So she would. Shall I buy it for her?"

"Right off that poor woman's head?" Stephanie cast him a mockingly scandalized look. "I should think not!"

"Ah well, just a notion. Ready to go back?"

"I guess I've got the cricks out. I swear, riding in a carriage is harder work than making a journey on horseback!"

"Since you mention it, I'll admit I was surprised you didn't ride."

"Jane asked that I keep them company. She *said* it was because it would cause a scandal if anyone realized I'd come so far on Aladdin's back, but I think it was more that she's still uncomfortable with Meg. It is too bad of her that she cannot see beyond Meg's lack of education to the intelligence and kind heart."

"Your Jane is a conventional soul. Meg, most definitely, is *not.*"

"Jane? Conventional?" Stephanie thought about that. "Then how has she put up with *me* all these years?"

"Has she never tried to make you conform?"

"Not . . . exactly."

Anthony chuckled. "So?"

"So," said Stephanie on a sigh, "I've been a trial to her, have I not? And perhaps I understand why, although I'm quite certain she loves him, she refuses to wed Francis!"

"Has he asked her?"

"Over and over and over and over . . ."

"And she's never explained?"

"I'd guess not. I mean, would he not have tried to be different, or tried to make her different or something?"

"Not if he's any sense, and I think he does."

Stephanie thought about that. "You mean one can't, at any basic level, make oneself different than one is," she said slowly.

"Exactly. Nor can one change another to please some ideal one has of them. Character is what it is, and one must accept it, warts and all, as Cromwell is reputed to have said when his portrait painter asked how he wished to be portrayed. No one is perfect."

"I think," she murmured, "I vaguely recall you telling me *I* was perfect." She cast him an impish glance. "Of course I was somewhat distracted at the time, so perhaps . . ."

Anthony glanced around to assure himself that no one was near enough to overhear her. "Minx! *Dub your mummer,* as your coachman said to a mouthy stable boy at one of our halts today!"

"I knew no one was near. You needn't fear I'll say anything of the sort to, or even *near,* anyone else. Ah, is that not our temporary home?" She nodded to a house across the width of the Marine Parade sited near the Royal Crescent. At that moment the street was filled with carriages and people on horseback. "Where did everyone come from? I don't think I've seen so many at one time, even in London, except, perhaps, in the park at the hour of the promenade!"

"I assume, then, that this is the time and the place one promenades when in Brighton. When were you in London?"

"Some years ago. Francis insisted I be presented. I managed to get through the ordeal of the Queen's drawing room, but the one soiree we attended was more than enough of *that* sort of thing!"

"Surely he insisted." Stephanie nodded and, chuckling, Anthony asked, "So how did you make it impossible to continue your visit?"

"Threatened to ride astride in the park during the promenade," Stephanie responded promptly.

"You'd have done it, too, would you not?"

She cast him a surprised look. "Of course. One should never make threats unless one is prepared to carry them through. Francis knew."

"And took you back to your beloved Priory"

"Yes."

Anthony sighed very nearly silently. "I think we can cross . . . now!" He took her arm and hurried across the broad street. "We go to the theater this evening. You'd best check to see if you've anything you are willing to be seen in."

It was Stephanie's turn to sigh. "Yes. Leaving Sarah behind was, perhaps, an error, but I don't know what else I could have done. She was needed there more than I need her."

"Won't Jane's maid have seen to your wardrobe?"

"Perhaps." A strange footman, hired with the house, opened the door and Stephanie nodded absentminded thanks. "But Helena is more disapproving of me than Jane is and rarely does anything for me unless it is directly requested. I'd best see if I must have my yellow gown pressed." She sighed. "Such a bore . . ."

Anthony nodded. "While you see to your boring problem, I must see your father about another boring subject . . ."

They parted and Anthony found Lemiston seated, head back and eyes closed, in a small room which, thanks to a few ladies magazines, a Gothic novel or two, and a pile of sporting news, was called a library. The main thing in its favor, however, was the decently man-sized chairs. Too, from the odor clinging to the draperies, someone had recently used it for smoking which meant the women were unlikely to want to sit there.

"Tired, Chris?"

"What? No. Just wishing we were on the sea and headed back where I belong."

"You've come to know the twins better. Won't you change your mind before you leave?"

"I suppose I have." Lemiston sighed. "It was very difficult to alter notions I've carried around like excess baggage for far too many years, but it's happened. I've settled a large sum of money on Theo, a trust which will be passed to his offspring, if he has any. If not, his sister's children will inherit and, if Stephanie has none, then it will be returned to our children, Meg's and mine, or their heirs."

"Have you told Theo?"

"No. And you are not to do so. I've composed a letter which my solicitor will forward to him after I've gone. I suspect he'll feel a certain amount of relief he need never worry about the Priory."

"Which brings us to the question of your daughter . . ."

"No."

"You didn't let me finish."

"You want me to buy back the estate and settle it on her. No."

"Why?"

"I have my reasons."

"Chris . . ."

"Will you have it in so many words? I'll not buy the Priory back from you, Anthony, because," said Lemiston sardonically, "I firmly believe you yourself will make it possible for her to live there. You may, however, need that added inducement, the capacity to bribe her with the estate, stubborn wench that she is."

"*. . . I'll not buy the Priory back from you. Anthony . . .*"
Stephanie shut the door she'd just opened and leaned against it, the blood running from her head and making her dizzy.

"Stephie? What is it?" asked Theo, coming along the narrow hall just then. Even mired in his usual preoccupation, he could not miss that something was wrong with his sister!

"Take me away," she whispered.

"What?"

White of face, Stephanie stumbled toward him, clutched at him. *"Take me away,"* she repeated in a low trembling voice. "Now. At once."

"Why?" Since she whispered, so did he. "We just got here."

"I can't . . ." She put a hand to her forehead. "Theo, please? Help me?"

Succumbing to his sister's helplessness, something he'd never seen before, he agreed. "We'll go." He put an arm around her, guiding her up the stairs, his expression grim. "Get into your habit. I'll have Aladdin and a horse saddled for myself."

"Do it yourself. I want no one aware we've gone."

"Stephanie, you can't do that!" He eyed her stubborn expression. "At least leave a note for Jane," he coaxed. "She'll worry herself to flinders."

For a moment Stephanie rebelled even at that. The notion of having anything to do with anyone but Theo made her feel ill, but then she sighed, silently acquiescing. Jane couldn't have had a hand in her father's machinations and shouldn't be punished for what she'd not done. But the Priory . . . Her loss hit her again, a physical sensation she felt in the solar plexus, a deep nagging pain.

The Priory was gone forever.

"A note," she muttered. "Fine. I'll do that." Stephanie gulped, swallowing hard again and again, as she headed down the hall to her room.

As the twins rode out of Brighton with the lowering sun in their eyes, Theo glanced at Stephanie's cold, marble-like face. He bit his lip. Tentatively, he said, "I don't know how far we can get tonight, Steph, and I've not much money with me. I didn't think of it when we left for Arundel and I've not had time to get any here."

"There'll be a moon." Stephanie stared straight ahead at nothing at all.

That was all. She continued riding with habitual ease, automatically varying their pace from a resting walk to a slow canter and back again since they'd nearly forty miles to cover and they wouldn't want to change horses. Her mind, however, was not on what she did.

Theo was glad Aladdin had had a long day trotting behind a carriage, exercise which had taken any surprises out of his system. Given her inattention, Theo wasn't certain that, if the stallion *did* act up, Stephanie wouldn't be caught unaware.

When he could stand it no longer, Theo asked, "Won't you explain, Steph . . . ?"

"I can't." She made a chopping movement with her hand. "I can't talk about it. Not yet."

They rode on for several more miles, Theo casting the occasional worried glance toward his twin. Suddenly she pulled up.

"What is it?" he asked. More hopefully, he added, "Have you changed your mind? Shall we go back?"

"No, of course not. But where are we going?"

"You said to take you home."

"Home?" A wild laugh broke on a sob. "But we have no home. We can't go home."

Theo froze. "He sold it."

"He . . . sold it."

"I'm sorry."

Knowing how totally inadequate his words were, Theo dismounted. He went to Stephanie and pulled her off the sidesaddle, holding her close while the woman who had never learned to cry sobbed the great gulping noisy sobs of a hurt child.

When she finally stopped, he pushed her a little away, cradling her with his arms around her waist. "Feel better?"

"I'll never feel truly good again, but I think my mind will function now. At least enough to discuss where we should go. Theo, I didn't say to take me home, but to take me *away.*"

"I guess you did, but we *should* go to the Priory, Steph."

"No!"

"Steph, we've all our own things there. Our unbeloved sire cannot have sold our personal possessions along with the estate! We need to pack up what we'll want immediately and give orders that the rest be packed away and stored . . ."

"Sent to Warring Heights."

". . . all right then, sent on to Sir Francis. Too, it will give us time to decide what to do. My offer of travel is still open, Steph. I can afford it. You've been very generous over the years, but I've spent very little of the funds you've remitted to me quarterly. We could circumnavigate the world a few times with what I've saved!"

Stephanie smiled. It was a weak smile, but it was a smile, and Theo wanted to pull her close and hug her tightly from relief. He resisted the impulse, wanting nothing to change her improving mood.

"You wouldn't wish to be gone *that* long from your precious libraries! But travel . . ." Stephanie pushed out of his comforting arms and turned away. "Perhaps. I don't know. I just don't know . . ."

"Let me help you back into the saddle." He made a step of his hands and tossed her up. "We can talk as we ride now you are no longer acting the ninnyhammer!"

When she didn't smile, Theo's earlier relief faded. His twin was *not* herself and he didn't know what to do to turn her around. He felt bereft and unsettled. For the first time in their existence he was responsible for the two of them. *He* had to care for *her.*

"I do wish . . ."

Stephanie didn't even turn her head and Theo finished the thought silently in his mind:

. . . I knew more about people. Which is why, perhaps I prefer books . . . ?

Dinner waited.

Finally Lemiston looked at Jane. "Where are they?"

"Your twins?"

A muscle jumped in Lemiston's jaw. "The twins."

"I don't know." A frown furrowed Jane's forehead. "I'll send a maid to see why they've not come down yet, shall I?"

"Please."

Lemiston bit off the word, recalling that, when he'd been talking to Anthony, he'd thought someone had opened the library door. But no one had come in, and when he'd twisted around to look, the door was shut so he'd assumed . . . But *had* one or the other twin heard part of that conversation?

Just what had he been saying when that nearly silent double click caught his attention? They'd gotten beyond his explaining about the trust for Theo, had they not? So it must have been when Anthony once again suggested he should buy back the estate.

Jane returned to the elegant salon. It was the only room in the house into which one could, without shame, allow guests entry. The others were furnished from the tolerably well done to the clean but excessively simple. Stephanie was to be found in none of them.

"She isn't here. Neither is Theo."

A chill ran up Lemiston's spine. His volatile daughter was unpredictable. What would she do if she knew her beloved Priory was no longer Lemiston land? He thought of the Channel just beyond the front of the house, remembered Francis telling him the chit could swim . . .

Would she? Swim out and not come back?

But suicide . . . Surely not. No. It wasn't the vixen's way. She'd fight. She'd survive. But she just might be stubborn enough she'd avoid her old home. So where. . . .

Grannie Black? Doubtful. Not when Grannie lived on Lemiston—*Huntersham*—property. Warring Heights, then?

"Send to the stables," ordered Lemiston. "See if that beast she rides is there."

"But she'd not go riding at this time of day, surely? She knows we attend the theater tonight . . ."

"Do it, Miss Felton," Lemiston ordered, sighing. "Just do it."

Offended, Jane whisked herself back out of the room.

"What is it, Chris?" asked Anthony quietly.

"I suspect Stephanie may have overheard part of our conversation this afternoon. If she heard what I think she heard, she's gone."

"Gone!" Anthony straightened away from the table against which he'd been leaning.

"Do you think she'd stay under the same roof as the new owner of the Priory?" asked Lemiston sardonically.

Francis rose from his chair. "What did you say?"

"Anthony owns Lemiston Priory. He has since we were in London."

"You bastard. You unmitigated . . . bastard! How *could* you sell your children's birthright? And you." He turned on Anthony. "How could *you* have bought it away from her."

"I notice you don't say away from *them,*" Lemiston jeered.

"You know as well as I do that it's Stephanie who loves the Priory!"

Anthony interrupted what threatened to turn into a useless argument. "Of course we do. Now. But I didn't when I purchased it. Since I've learned how much it means to her I've tried more than once to get Chris to buy it back. He won't."

Again Francis twisted around. "Damn you to the deepest depths of Hell!"

"I've my reasons," said Lemiston coldly, "and they stand. Do come down out of the boughs! We must discuss this sensibly and leave emotions to when there is time for them. Soothe one fear, please. Do *you* think she'd commit suicide in her first despair, before she'd given herself time to think?"

Francis's angry red skin paled to an ashy white and Anthony, his eyes suddenly unfocused, turned to stone.

Chris bent an impassive look on his fingernails. He looked up, met Francis's fixed stare. "Well?"

Francis relaxed. "I don't know why I felt that sudden panic. Of course she'd do no such thing."

"What *would* she do?"

"You're right about one thing," he said slowly. He glanced at Anthony, a look of loathing. "She'd not stay in the same house as the new owner."

"She'd blame me," said Anthony stonily.

"However irrational, yes, you'd carry a portion of the blame."

"I didn't know of her existence when I agreed to buy it! Or I did. But she was just a child when I left and I'd forgotten. We'd discussed my buying it often, Chris and I. Once he knew an estate of my own was what I dreamed of having and he knew he wanted to rid himself of this one, well we made plans. That's all."

"I never cared for the late Lord Huntersham," said Chris thoughtfully. *"Far* too high in the instep. I thought he might find it a trifle galling if his despised son owned a larger and better estate than he did himself."

Francis grinned as he perceived part of Chris's motivation for selling to Anthony. "I remember a time we had quite a run-in with him. That occasion we managed to lay a false trail for his hounds? Remember?"

"He didn't care for it, did he?" said Lemiston, a gleam in his eye. It faded. "Too bad he isn't still around to see his youngest son master of the Priory! Where has Miss Felton gotten to?"

"The stables are some distance from the house . . . Ah. Here she is. Jane?"

"I don't understand it. Stephanie and Theo rode off not long after you and she returned from your walk, Lord Huntersham."

"Hours ago," said Anthony, bitterness unhidden. "Did they say where they were going." He looked at the note in her hand. "Is that from Stephanie?"

Jane cast the twist of paper a startled glance. "Oh! I don't know. My maid handed it to me a moment ago."

"I suggest, Miss Felton, that you read it."

At Lemiston's words, Jane blushed. She moved closer to the table on which a lit lamp stood. As she read she put out a hand. Francis immediately took it in his.

"Jane?"

"She . . ." She looked up. "She thanks me for all the years I've seen to her comfort and asks that she be forgiven."

"And?" asked Lemiston sharply.

"That's all."

"Oh my God," whispered Francis. His hold on Jane firmed to the point of pain. He didn't even notice when she tried to free herself. "Oh . . . my . . . God . . ."

"I don't believe it," said Anthony, his harsh tone breaking into the silence.

"Nor do I." Meg had stood quietly near the empty grate throughout, but now she strolled into the middle of the room and joined the conversation. "That woman's no quitter. I don' *know* what she's asking forgiveness for, but my *guess* would be it's for spoiling our evening."

Francis, for the second time, recovered himself. "Yes. It would be very like her to think of others even when her own world had fallen into ruins."

"I doubt very much if she were thinking at all," said Lemiston coldly. "And you forget she isn't alone. Theo will see she does nothing foolish and will take care of her."

"Theo?" asked Jane a trifle diffidently. *"Can* he?"

"Don't be a fool," said Francis harshly and didn't notice Jane's surprised and hurt look. "You've always had it in for Theo, Jane, because he has left Stephanie to do what you consider his work and you think she'd have been a different sort of woman if he'd done it himself. However badly you think of him, he is certainly capable of escorting Stephanie back to the Priory."

"Except she won't go to the Priory, will she?" asked Anthony.

Everyone was silent. "Warring Heights," suggested Francis.

"Oxford?" asked Jane, diffidently.

"Lunnun," suggested Meg. "If'n she wants to disappear and lick her wounds, she'll lose herself in Lunnun."

"No. I think you're wrong," said Anthony. "I think *I'm* wrong. They've personal possessions at the Priory. She'll go there to get what she needs and order the rest sent on somewhere. Theo, I think, will suggest they leave England altogether for a time and I won't have that! I must get the word put out now, before they've time to leave, that the ports are to be watched . . ." He strode from the room, calling for his man.

"Stephanie won't go," said Francis thoughtfully, once the door had shut behind Anthony.

"You think not?" Lemiston asked Francis. "But all has changed, has it not? She no longer has reason to remain."

Francis frowned. *"Surely* she'll go to Warring Heights."

"That would be the sensible, conventional thing to do," said Jane bitterly, "but there is nothing conventional about our Stephanie. She'll bring down shame and scandal and . . . and I told you and told you you were making a mistake letting her believe herself capable of managing her own life! I *warned* you." She beat on Francis's chest and then, whirling around, ran from the room, sobs breaking free at last.

"Meg . . . ?" asked Lemiston. "Should you go after her?"

"Not me. She don' like me above half," said Meg. "Sir Francis better see to his woman himself." She smiled a falsely sweet smile at Francis who left the room extremely startled by the implication Meg knew Jane and he were lovers. She

watched him go before turning back to Chris. "Are we goin'
after them, then?"

"We, Meg?" asked Lemiston, a touch of whimsy lightening
his expression.

"You think you'll leave me here?" she asked belligerently.

"We'll be riding. Riding hard," said Chris softly, going to
her. "I need you here to care for the boys."

She sighed and turned away. "Right you are, but I *like* that
girl. I like Theo, too. He offered to take our boys in hand when
the time comes you send them here to school, did you know
that?"

Lemiston gave her a startled glance. "And you'd trust him?"

"You blidy well better believe I would. He's a good lad and
he likes our boys. So does your Stephanie. You'd better find
her, hear me, my blidy lordship?"

"Will I have that thrown at me for the rest of my life, whenever you are irritated with me?"

She eyed him. "Likely you will."

Lemiston chuckled. And then, surprising himself as well as
Meg, he leaned closer and kissed her. "Be good, Meg," he
said softly. "When I return we'll buy you the most godawful
hat in the whole of Brighton to take back to Australia with
us. And maybe another sort of hat, as well. One to match up
with the trousers and coat I suspect you've hidden in the bottom of one of your trunks!"

Meg grinned. "More'n hair about *your* cockloft, ain't
there?"

"I never was thought a stupid man," agreed Lemiston, his
normal sardonic expression returning. He looked around. "I
wonder if Francis will come or will he take your advice, Meg,
and see to Jane? Anthony will have ordered the horses and I
don't know about him, but I want to change. I'll be damned
if I'll ride halfway across the south of England in my evening
clothes!"

Half an hour later Anthony and Chris left Brighton. Francis,
who had appeared as they were about to mount, was torn first

one way and then the other, until cornered by Meg. "You want to lose her forever?" asked Chris's wife.

"Jane? No! But she wouldn't see me."

"*Make* her see you. I'm warning you, you'll lose her."

"I—"

"For once, you'd better put Jane ahead 'a Stephanie and let Chris see to his daughter as it's right he *should* do."

After another moment's thought Francis headed again for the stairs. A moment later, the sound of a door banging against a wall could be heard throughout the house.

"Jane . . . !" they heard, and then, the door closing, no more.

At about three in the morning Stephanie led Theo to a barn distant from any house, a wooden structure in which bedding straw had been stored over the years.

"It isn't as comfortable as your bed, but far better than a hedgerow," she said.

"So it is. We'll do. Except I wish I'd thought to pack some food. I don't know about you, Steph, but I'm starving!"

"That's another reason I chose this place. There's a bramble patch in the hedges along the lane loaded with fruit. We'll be able to see to pick them soon."

The eastern horizon was lightening, proof of her words, but Theo grimaced, obviously thinking wild fruit less than satisfactory when he'd missed his dinner and it was nearly breakfast time.

"Is there a well?" he asked.

"Water. Yes. There should be a pail hanging inside the barn door and then you have to go around back. I'll meet you there, and after we've watered and seen to the horses, we can have a drink ourselves. By then perhaps we can see to find us our breakfast!"

"Steph?"

"Yes?"

"Have you decided what you'll do?"

Stephanie sighed. "I think that once we've slept a bit we'll have to go to the house, as you said. Then, once I've packed up what I need immediately, I'll do the sensible thing for once in my life and go to Warring Heights. Francis will simply have to help me find a position somewhere. Surely there is *someone* in the world who would give a female a chance at managing their estate! And if not? Well, then I guess—" She cast him a mischievous glance that almost matched her former self. "—I'll have to put into practice that plan I once suggested in jest."

"Plan?"

"Stephanie Morris will disappear and Stephen be born in her place."

"I can't like it, Steph."

"Because I'm female and shouldn't behave like a man? Do you think I can't?"

"Of course you could, but the question is whether you'd be happy."

Stephanie looked up from where Aladdin had his nose deep in the bucket. "I will not live as a demure young woman, holding my hands when I'm not working at my embroidery or seeing to my roses."

"Don't sneer at Jane. She enjoys those things."

"Well, I don't. Nor will I live the rest of my life at Francis's expense."

Theo was silent for a long time. "I suppose you'd also dislike keeping house for me? I could buy a manor near Oxford . . ."

"I think not. You couldn't afford any *land,* Theo, and I'd be bored to tears. One way or another, Francis *must* find me a position."

"Maybe Anthony would hire you," suggested Theo, tongue in cheek.

Stephanie turned away. Any thought of Anthony's perfidy brought a wetness to her eyes which she could not like. She never cried. And, since the blacksheep lord had appeared, she'd cried *twice*.

"Never mind, Steph. I shouldn't have said that. I'm sorry." Once again Theo held his sister close, his hand cradling the back of her head. He tipped her head so he could see her face. "No tears?"

"I think I cried them all."

"Just as well. I don't know you when you cry."

"Don't tease, Theo. I'm not ready for teasing yet."

"Ah. That 'yet' gives me hope!"

"Don't . . ."

Seventeen

The Priory

Hours later, rested but stomachs rumbling, Theo and Stephanie left their horses at the stables where the head groom informed them in a scolding tone that they'd missed Lords Lemiston and Huntersham by a short hour.

"I thought you promised to leave Jane a note," said Theo, as they walked toward the house. "Did you forget?"

"I didn't forget."

"Then why are they looking for you?"

"What difference if they hunt?"

"The point is, if they knew what you were doing, then I'd think they'd not be worried and Chad just insisted they are both very concerned about you. Even though it is known that I'm with you! Which is *not* flattering," finished Theo.

"They can hunt me all the way to hell and back for all I care. I've a life to arrange."

"Steph." Theo's hand on her shoulder stopped her stalking progress. She stilled, staring straight ahead. "Just what *did* you tell Jane?" he asked.

"I don't remember. Yes I do. I apologized, I think. And gave her thanks for all she's done for me over the years." Theo's brow arched. "I tell you I don't remember."

"You didn't give any indication of our plans?" he asked gently.

Stephanie grimaced. "Did we *have* a plan?"

Theo, remembering he'd simply assumed they were coming to the Priory, realized that indeed, at that time, they had not. The twins were silent as they strolled the rest of the way up to the house. There they discovered Abbot had promised to send word to the Brighton establishment if the twins arrived.

"What game you playing now, Lady Stephanie?" asked the butler crossly.

"Game? No game, Abbot."

His sister's skin was still too pale to please Theo and he drew Abbot's attention away from it. "I don't know if his lordship thought to tell you, but Huntersham is the new owner of the Priory. Steph and I are here to sort out our personal possessions and give orders for their disposal."

Abbot's eyes bulged. "Sold . . . The Priory? But—"

"It's all right, Abbot," Theo soothed. "Anthony doesn't seem the sort to summarily relieve good servants of their place. You may pass that word on, Abbot, so that there will be no unnecessary panic. Or perhaps you should wait and allow his lordship to explain himself?"

"But, the Priory. Lord Lemiston . . . He couldn't have *sold* it."

"Perfectly within his rights, Abbot," said Theo sharply.

Abbot looked at Stephanie and dropped his gaze. "Yes," he said. "Of course." Another quick glance at Stephanie's stony features, and he drew in a deep breath. "Now then," he said, "just tell me what must be done and I'll give orders to help you."

"Thank you, Abbot. We depend on you and I knew you'd be the rock you've always been. I'll let you know the instant we decide exactly what is to be done." Theo dismissed the butler with orders to bring a large breakfast to the library. He drew his sister, who had the appearance of a hungry wolf as she appeared to try to eat her surroundings with her eyes, on down the corridor to his favorite room.

"We must make plans, Stephanie," he said quietly after they'd silently wolfed down enough eggs, bacon, and fruit to make up for a missed meal. "We can't simply order our things packed, because how will anyone but ourselves know exactly what is ours and what is not?"

Stephanie didn't seem to have recovered very much. "It doesn't matter. Find what you need while I throw a few things into a trunk and we'll give Abbot some sort of orders about the rest. I must be gone as soon as possible."

"I don't see why you are in such a rush."

Stephanie turned a wild look his way. "Don't you understand? We don't belong here anymore. We don't belong anywhere." Her skin paled again. *"We don't belong,"* she whispered.

Theo studied her. His steady gaze steadied her and she drew in a deep breath, letting it out slowly, but her despair was obvious and it ate into her twin. "I know it goes deep with you, Steph. I'm sorry I can't fully appreciate how much pain you feel."

She came to him, hugged him. "Don't worry about me, Theo. I'll come around."

He watched her for a moment and nodded, knowing it would take time, but that she *would*. He returned her hug with good measure.

Less then an hour later they stood in the great hall, and Stephanie gave last orders to the butler and the housekeeper. She finished by saying, "Abbot, Theo told you Lord Huntersham bought the Priory. I want to reassure you that you needn't worry for your positions. His lordship will not throw everyone out and restock when the breed is good—" At the housekeeper's shocked expression, she added, "—so to speak. But you must keep in mind, and you must pass it along, that your loyalty, *all of you,* from now on is to Lord Huntersham."

"And you'd better wait until someone in authority confirms what we have told you," said Theo, far more sternly than was his wont, "before you begin gossiping!"

Stephanie looked around. "I wonder if I've thought of everything. . . . If you've questions, send to Warring Heights. I'll stay there for a time."

After overly emotional goodbyes on the part of the house-keeper, she and Theo left the house for the stables, her usual easy stride restricted by the habit she still wore. "I'd no notion," she said, "how difficult it would be to determine what is mine and what belongs to the estate!" exclaimed Stephanie. "Jane will have to see to her own things in her own good time . . ."

"She'll not feel so lost as you feel, Steph, so will have less difficulty. And I've a much easier time of it," said Theo, "because I've not lived here, really, since I left for Oxford all those years ago."

"Did you remember your pistols?"

"Yes, although why I bothered, I haven't a notion. I'll not use them up at Oxford! The only thing of importance is my library, and any books bought here since I left home belong to the estate library. Mine are all in Oxford in my rooms." His eyes widened and he cast a glance toward his sister. "My rooms. The rent is due in another month or so."

Knowing how much he gave each year for what was, after all, a rather nice apartment, Stephanie grimaced. "You *did* say you'd a goodly sum saved, did you not? What will it bring you if invested?"

"I'm damned if I know . . ." Theo's voice trailed off, his eyes unfocusing.

Stephanie laughed, but there was no humor in it. "You've just realized, have you not, that you'll have no more income?"

A muscle jumped in Theo's jaw. "There is one great differ-ence between us, Steph. Whereas it may be difficult for you to find a position you can live with, I can quite easily become a tutor or a reader or any number of things at one of the colleges. My old tutor will help me find a place, so I'll not suffer any change in my life, except in that I'll have duties that may inter-fere now and again with my work. *You,* however . . ."

"I'll *not* suffer. I'll find a place."

"A place where you'll belong."

"Exactly. A place where I belong."

They arrived at the stables and Theo ordered their horses

tacked up. "Are you certain you are ready?" She nodded. "Then I'll escort you to Warring Heights."

"Won't you join me there, Theo?"

"No. I've decided to spend a day or two with Graham. Mr. Wilkins will put me up as he used to do when we were younger and Graham and I'd been off on adventures. It may be some little time before he and I get together again and he's my friend, Steph."

It was amazing, thought Stephanie, how much it hurt that Theo meant to desert her, although he'd not think of it that way. She worked at keeping any emotion from her voice. "Graham should have time for a little fishing now the oats are in. We were lucky that storm held off until harvest was finished."

"Yes, well, I'm sure that's so," said Theo dismissively. "And it was more pleasant riding to Arundel with the dust settled. However that may be, the fishing's the important thing and with the water up . . . well, I don't know . . ."

Stephanie's lip turned up on one side. "If you were a farmer, Theo, you'd not think that way."

"Hmm?" He seemed to rehear her words. "Oh. Very likely not, but I'm no farmer, am I?"

"Theo, do you think word about the sale of the estate will remain a secret?"

"Of course not. It is spreading already. My guess is that not more than five minutes after Abbot reached the servant's hall, several servants headed for home to pass on the word. How much would you wager against it?"

Stephanie sighed. "Not a groat. But you need not do more than verify it, do you hear?"

"I'm not to do their dirty work for them, is that it? For our father and Huntersham?"

Stephanie nodded grimly.

The butler at Warring Heights was no more surprised than Abbot had been when the twins arrived. "We'd a visit from Lord Lemiston and Lord Huntersham a couple of hours ago.

I'm to send a messenger to Brighton to Sir Francis if you appear here, Lady Stephanie."

"Do you have to, Woods?"

"You know I must."

She sighed. "All right. Do it. But remember, I'm at home to no one but Sir Francis or Jane. Or Theo, of course. I've no wish to see *anyone else*. Is that clear?"

"I understand perfectly." Sir Francis's butler nodded, but his expression declared otherwise, revealing he'd no notion at all what was going on.

"Theo," she said, following her twin back outside, "perhaps you and Graham could come by tomorrow and I'll go fishing with you. If you'll fish on Sir Francis's land, that is!"

"Never going to step on Priory land again, is that it?"

She sighed. "Never is a very long time when there are people I'll wish to see. Grannie Black, for instance, but it will take awhile for me to accept the situation. And so will it for our—*Huntersham's*—tenants. It would be best for everyone if I stay away until Huntersham has made a place for himself."

Theo nodded. "We'll see you tomorrow. Early. The fish, like birds, prefer the early morn for feeding, you know."

Sadly, Stephanie watched her twin ride away and then returned inside where, silently, she allowed herself to be led by Sir Francis's stern-faced housekeeper to a bedroom in a rarely used wing of the old house. Mrs. Woods was another who disapproved of Lady Stephanie Morris and was never one for hiding her feelings. The housekeeper had never been overtly disrespectful, but she had little ways of getting across her censure of her behavior. Obviously, on this occasion, she did not approve of a guest arriving unexpectedly with no luggage, and worse, no notice of the master's approval!

The next morning Stephanie breathed a sigh of relief when she'd once again donned her trousers. She ate with the dawn and was ready when Theo and young Graham arrived. As they were leaving, Francis's butler approached them, clearing his throat.

"You wish something, Woods?" asked Theo.

"Only wished someone to know that that Oakfield fellow has been seen around," muttered the man. "We've been told he's not welcome here and he knows that, but I don't know what we can do about him just strolling around as the gardener says he was . . ." He cast a hopeful eye on Theo who looked at Stephanie.

Stephanie frowned. "Blast! I thought the man was tied to a bed at Arundel . . . Fiddlededeedeedeededee," she added after a moment, an expression she saved for when she was really upset! Another pause and she added, "Perhaps it would hurt nothing if you were to send word he's round and about to his cousin who, I think, wishes words with him."

"But where to send it!"

"Hmm. That is a problem, is it not." She looked at Theo who shrugged. "I see a solution, but such a bother! You could send to the Priory, to Hunters Cove, *and* to Brighton. The message should catch up with him somewhere!"

The butler smothered a sigh. "Very well, Lady Stephanie. I'll do that."

"Do you think it so important?" asked Theo as he and Stephanie strolled to where Graham sat in a gig holding the reins.

Under the seat were fishing gear, a good sized, well-wrapped jug, and a basket that looked large enough to hold food for several more than just the three of them. It appeared to Stephanie as if the men were set for a long day rather than a bit of early morning fishing.

"You won't mind squeezing in, will you?" asked Theo, confident she would not.

Graham was far more likely to want to object, but, having taken orders from Stephanie for years, would hardly do so.

"I've been told," said Theo, "that there is good sport along

Francis's stream up near the fork where it is deeper and a trifle rougher. We'll go there."

"Fine."

Graham cleared his throat. "Lady Stephanie, Theo either can't or won't explain the rumors we're hearing. Is it true Lord Lemiston sold his property to a sailor?"

"The *sailor*," said Stephanie dryly, "is Lord Huntersham who was partner with Lord Lemiston in a shipping concern. Lord Huntersham is Hunter's Cove's lost earl, Graham."

The young farmer was silent for a time. After a pause for thought, he asked, in a slightly belligerent manner, "Just what does he know about the land?"

Theo chuckled, but Stephanie groaned.

"That's what I thought," was Graham's bitter response.

"He's willing to learn," said Stephanie quickly. "Give him a chance, will you?"

"Haven't any choice, do we?"

Theo, in order to change the mood, told Graham a long involved and highly humorous tale of the hunt at Arundel. He had both his sister and Graham laughing long before they reached the fork in the river where they meant to fish that day. The relief he felt that his sister could laugh was so strong it very nearly made him lightheaded, which only increased his whimsical mood.

Three happy fishermen settled to their fishing not so very much later. Not that Stephanie long remained happy. The peaceful, silent, and *inactive* sport had never been a favorite of hers. She'd caught only one fish when she laid aside her pole. Before wandering off, she told Theo she meant to take a closer look at Francis's hedges. As they'd passed them on the way to the stream, some had looked much in need of attention. Theo sent an absent look after her, and very soon he was again sunk in thought. Years previously, he'd discovered that fishing was conducive to deep thinking, helping him concentrate on whatever problem interested him at the moment. Stephanie, on the other hand, found herself thoroughly disgusted with the state of the fences along one side of a Warring Heights farm. She steamed, anger a healing force. Finally, still fuming, she strolled back toward the river.

She'd have words to say to Francis when next she saw him! Not only were the fences and hedges a disgrace, but that particular farmer hadn't heeded instructions concerning the rotation of crops! He would have to go if he were unwilling to adopt new methods, and so Stephanie would inform her old friend. How could Francis have been so unobservant? How could he have let the man get so far out of hand as to have allowed such dilapidated fences and poorly kept hedges?

She was still annoyed when she came into view of her brother. For an instant she couldn't quite comprehend what she was seeing: Not twenty feet from her twin was James Cuthbert Oakfield. One wrist was wrapped. She could see a bandage protruding from his sleeve. It didn't, however, prevent the man from holding, with both hands, a large, old-fashioned horse pistol.

And it was aimed directly at Theo's back.

Grimacing, Oakfield lowered the gun. Cautiously, he moved even nearer, using an exaggeratedly careful style of locomotion, lifting a foot high, pointing the toe, setting it down with great caution . . .

Stephanie, horror struck, stayed frozen for half an instant longer. Then, bending, her eyes never leaving the would-be murderer, she reached for her pistol. She aimed carefully, but her hand trembled slightly. She closed her eyes for an instant, pulling up every bit of concentration she could find.

Oakfield could not be allowed to harm her twin. She must shoot. But even while laying the barrel over her arm and aiming carefully, she remembered the sound of bullet hitting flesh which had appalled her when she'd shot her would-be ravager in what, given all that had happened since, seemed another life.

Once again she pulled back, concentrated, aimed. And this time she had to shoot. Much nearer, Oakfield had stopped and was raising his pistol, pointing toward Theo's unheeding self. Slowly, with care, she pulled the trigger . . .

. . . and almost instantly heard a second shot,

Screaming, Oakfield swung one way,

. . . and a third.

. . . back, stumbled forward, and fell almost on top of Theo.

Theo, carefully laying aside his fishing pole, frowned at the fallen man. He looked around, blinking, trying to shake free from whatever problem of moral philosophy he'd been arguing in his mind.

Stephanie, white of face, stared at him. Anthony, putting his gun away, nodded grimly. Lord Lemiston strode forward and toed the screeching Oakfield's hip.

"Enough of that noise. You'll not die from any of those wounds. Unless you bleed to death. Daughter, I understand you know what to do in such a case." Lemiston stared at Stephanie. "Do it."

Stephanie, at the cold tone, moved to Oakfield's side, knelt. She reached for the trouser leg which seemed to have the most blood. With a knife, she cut it open well up the thigh. Silently she accepted a strip of cloth handed her by Anthony and tied a tourniquet. Then, methodically, she padded and tied tightly a folded cloth over a hole in the man's shoulder. The third shot had hit his right arm above the elbow, and again she put on a tourniquet. "They have to be loosened every so often." She stood up, staring at the man who'd tried to kill her brother. "I won't have a thing more to do with him. I don't even know why I didn't just let him bleed to death."

"You love me," crooned Oakfield who seemed to have gone quite off his head. "You love me. Love me . . . Finally . . . Someone loves . . ."

"Forget it, Cuthbert," said Anthony. "You haven't a notion what you're saying."

"I'll get rid of her brother," muttered the wounded man. "She'll inherit it all . . ." Oakfield finally swooned.

"He didn't know . . ." Lemiston, his Morris brows a tight

vee, compressed his lips for a moment. *"Damn* my forgetfulness. I remember telling Francis they *all* knew Stephanie would get no more than what I'd settle on her at her marriage . . . but I forgot this idiot wasn't in London at that time."

"He's the one who has been shooting at me and pushing me in front of carriages and who tried to kill Steph thinking it was me?"

"Yes. And very likely fell into his own trap which he'd set for you at Arundel."

Theo pushed back his hat. "Well, Steph, my girl, I think you just paid back that debt you owe me."

"Debt?"

"Way back when I returned from Oxford. I agreed to dine with the family, remember?"

"You've the mind of a mantrap, Theo. I'd forgotten all about it."

"Yes, that's all very well, but drat it, Steph, why, when you'd finally a chance to rid me of that murdering sod, just why *did* you save his life?"

"I couldn't watch him bleed to death." Stephanie bit her lip. "I couldn't kill him either. I meant to, but, at the last moment, I changed my aim to his arm. I'm sorry Theo." Remorse filled her. "I just couldn't do it. But I didn't think, did I? He'll recover and come after you all over again!"

"Oh no he won't! You needn't worry about that, Stephanie," said Anthony. "Anyone can see he's quite insane. I'll have him put away where he can do no one any more harm." He frowned. "That bit about finally having someone love him. It never occurred to me . . ."

"That he'd felt rejected by everyone all his life? That he *wanted* someone to love him?" Stephanie glared at Anthony. "No, I don't suppose it would occur to you."

"It should have," Anthony replied calmly, catching and holding her gaze. "Once my mother died, there was no one to love me either. My father had time for no one but my eldest brother, the heir, and my other brothers . . . well, I guess there was too much competition between us, trying to gain the attention he never gave us, for us to love each other."

Stephanie turned away. She remembered one of Grannie Black's teachings: No one and nothing was ever perfectly black or immaculately white. Always, she reminded herself, there were gray areas which shaded truth one direction and then another. Anthony had ruined her life. But, before that, he had suffered what could have been a fatal blow and been his ruination.

He'd survived. She straightened her shoulders. He'd survived and so would she . . .

But it would be hard. So hard.

It would have been so much better if she could have happily gone along just as she had for years—but with Anthony added to her life. Stephanie caught back a sob. She wouldn't cry.

Never again.

But how was she to go on living, never experiencing the loving she and Anthony and enjoyed so much? She sighed, and turned back to discover Oakfield had been laid in the gig. Graham, noting Theo's grim look, offered to drive it.

Lord Lemiston, after a glance at Anthony followed by one toward Stephanie, whistled for his horse. "I'll see a doctor's called," he said. He caught Anthony's eyes and sent a meaningful look to Stephanie. "Ask her to marry you. Now." Anthony grimaced, but nodded agreement.

Stephanie, observing the by-play, felt rising anger. How dare her sire connive with Anthony against her? And then she chuckled at such nonsense: Hadn't Lemiston conspired against her from the very beginning? Which meant that, if he were now favoring Anthony in the wedding stakes, there must be something very wrong with Anthony! Something she'd missed. Something she didn't know.

It occurred to her there was a great deal she didn't know. He'd been gone years. Heaven only knew what he'd been up to, what his adventures had done to harden a character already well set in rakish and extravagant ways! Stephanie turned aside and walked away.

"Stephanie!"

"Go away."

"We must talk."

"We've nothing to say." When he grasped her arm, halting her, she shook him off. "Just leave me alone Anthony black-sheep Ryder!"

"Don't act like a mere female when I know you are no such thing."

"Theo!"

"Yes, Steph?" asked her brother with something which sounded very much like laughter in his voice

"If you love me at all, Theo, make this bastard *leave me alone.*"

"I'm not sure I should," said Theo thoughtfully. "On the other hand, when you're in the sort of mood you're in right now, you are apt to make nonsense of anything he says to you. If you want my advice, Anthony, or even if you don't, you'll leave her alone."

"I can't."

"Why?" asked Theo.

"Because I am in love with the minx!"

"Ah. I thought it might be that. Stephanie, won't you reconsider?"

"Love. He hasn't a notion what it means. He *can't* have any idea of it. He wants to bed me so he thinks he's in love with me."

"See?" asked Theo. "She'll put the worst possible interpretation on whatever you say to her. I'd wait until later when she's herself again."

Anthony stared at nothing at all, and finally sighed. "All right. I've a feeling it's a mistake, but you know your sister better than I do and I think you're on my side."

"I'm on neither *side,*" chided Theo before his sister could jump in with the tirade he could see that notion roused in her. "What I am, is wanting what is best for my sister and, since I think that includes you, I'm trying to make it possible for communications between you to resume sometime in the future. Now, Stephanie, don't you dare!" He caught his sister's hands as she would have hit him. "I'll not let you take that temper out of my hide. If you must hit someone, go hit Oakfield! He deserves it."

"I already *hit* Oakfield," said Stephanie through gritted teeth. She crossed her arms and scowled.

"So you did. Did I thank you for it?"

"You did not."

"Well, I do, you know." She nodded. "You, too, Anthony," he said, turning to the man who, since they'd met, had become a friend. "I hadn't a notion the devil was anywhere near. He'd have killed me for sure this time," he added. Theo looked around, his eyes widening, seemingly seeing the world again, as if for the first time. After a moment he added, "I don't think I'm quite ready for that final adventure." His sister cast herself into his arms. "Now Stephanie, I'm alive! I'm not even hurt! I say . . ."

Theo threw a harassed look at Anthony who grinned and watched with affection as Stephanie hugged her brother and couldn't be made to let go until he'd hugged her back. And then she whistled. Anthony's Sahib looked up from the clover he'd been feeding on. She whistled again and the horse took a tentative step closer, hesitantly, another. Stephanie walked toward the gelding.

"That's theft, Stephanie," said Anthony softly.

"You'll not send the constable for me," she said confidently.

"Will I not? No perhaps not. Stephanie, sweetings, I hereby give you permission to run away on Sahib's back. Please have him sent on to the Priory stables when you've found yourself again."

Stephanie sent Anthony a look half of loathing and half of laughing. She glared, and, refusing to be manipulated by his wry humor, rose into Sahib's saddle. "I'll do that," she said, easily controlling the gelding's startled reaction to a strange rider on his back. They cantered off.

Eighteen

"Francis, you are being very stubborn about this," said Stephanie, pacing from one side of the Warring Heights billiard room to the other and back again. "I tell you I *must* find a position. I'll not hang on your sleeve."

"If you will not allow me to support you, then you may be agent here," said Francis calmly. He laid aside his cue and watched Stephanie pace.

"I'll not if you argue about every thing I know must be done!"

"Manton is going through a bad patch."

"And what excuse have you for allowing Hammish to over-graze his pastures?" She made no attempt to hide the sarcasm.

"Hammish has eleven living children and another on the way. The farm is rather small and he needs every bit of income he can get."

"But don't you see? Over-grazing *now*, he'll have *none at all* in the future."

Francis sighed, tacitly agreeing but not seeing a solution.

"You know why my becoming agent at the Heights is not the answer, Francis. I cannot see good land abused. Please say you'll help me find a place."

"I think you'll find you are still needed at the Priory."

"At the Priory! What in the name of all that's precious do you mean by that?"

"Huntersham wants to do the best he can, but he's ignorant.

You want a position as agent, then that's very likely the only estate in all of England that'll have you!"

"I am to aid and abet the enemy?"

"If you'd stop thinking of Huntersham as an enemy and begin thinking of him as a pawn set in the middle of a situation he'd no notion existed *and* one he tried to amend, you'd not be so unfair," scolded Jane, who sat in the corner with her embroidery.

"Tried to amend? What did he do? Agree to marry me when my father suggested it so his conscience need not bother him?" sneered Stephanie, openly scornful.

"He tried to sell the land back to your father," said Jane, looking up from her embroidery. "He wanted Lord Lemiston to hold it for *you* although it would, of course, in due course, go to Theo."

Stephanie, after a look toward Francis who confirmed Jane's statement with a brief nod, was silenced. She paced again along the side of the baize-covered table, gently flicking a ball from one end of the table to the other and, when she returned, back again. "I didn't know . . ." she said finally. Her lips firmed and she turned abruptly, waving a hand. "But it changes nothing."

"What else is there against him?" asked Francis.

"It appears my unloving sire approves of him in the wedding stakes," she retorted promptly. "That by itself is enough to make me exceedingly wary."

"You are impossible," said Jane. "You've always got an answer for everything!" She turned a mulish expression toward Francis. "Francis, as soon as possible, I'd like notice sent to the paper that I am in need of a position as companion or, if I can do no better, then as governess to young children."

"I'll do no such thing," Francis retorted. "Surely you cannot think marriage to me worse than going into service in a household where you'll be less valued than the butler or housekeeper!"

"But I would. I've never understood how you and Stephanie

can be comfortable rebelling against the strictures laid down to direct our lives in a moral and genteel manner."

"But . . . you . . . I . . . We . . ." Francis cast a look at Stephanie who pretended she wasn't listening. "You became my—"

Jane, flushed, held up a hand. "We won't discuss that. Now Stephanie has decided she no longer needs me, I must go. And I *will* say what I've thought for years: No matter how much I love her I cannot approve the manner in which she behaves— her lack of humility, her inability to accept the authority of those she should respect and honor. It is immoral and ungenteel. Thanks to *you,* Francis, who encouraged her, I have signally failed in *my* duty to her."

"So." Francis's brows crowded together over his nose. "I'm immoral, am I? And I live in an manner less than genteel!"

"You are and you do, Francis. I myself could never accept such ways."

"You who have been my lover for years can say that?"

"No one knew," she said, turning an embarrassed glance on Stephanie. "You've never understood that that makes all the difference. Besides, I was comfortable as things were. I don't like change . . ."

He stared at her. "I see. I think I never knew you. Now I understand why you would never agree to wed me. Why did you not say any of this long ago."

Jane's eyes flickered away from his steady gaze. "I . . . was afraid you'd find a new chaperon for Stephanie. I could not bring myself to leave her."

"I see that you've never understood me, either," he said. "You must think even worse of me than I'd thought if you believe me so unfair that I'd remove you from Stephie's side merely because you think badly of me. Have you never understood that I mean it when I say I believe that people should be allowed to think, to believe, to act as they will so long as it harms no other?"

"But you do harm others! You've harmed Stephanie."

"Have I harmed you Stephie?"

"Of course not. But Jane will never agree. And if your thinking is consistent, you must accept her belief that only by deliberate conformity to the common way can one *not* be harmed." The Morris whimsy rose to the surface, "And accepting that, then you must also see that, on the other hand, any sort of idiosyncrasy is, by definition harmful. You are hoisted on your own petard, Francis."

"So I see." His eyes were sad as they gazed at the woman he'd wanted for years. "I also accept at last that all my hopes are blasted. I will do whatever it is you wish of me and help you however I can, Jane. I'll admit I wish things were different, but . . . I accept, now and forever, that you will never wed me."

Jane's eyes widened. She glanced toward Stephanie, looked down. "Very well," she said on a strangled note and, turning, she rushed from the room.

"Having finally got exactly what she thought she wanted, I suspect she's realizing that may not be what she wants at all," said Stephanie slowly.

"Now don't you start raising hopes just when I've accepted she'll never wed me!" exploded Francis.

"Is that what I was doing?" Stephanie pursed her lips, her eyes narrowing. "But she looked exceedingly startled when you said you'd finally given up all hope."

"Perhaps it is merely," said Francis, sternly, "that although she's never wanted me, it rather flattered her that I'd occasionally ask!"

"Perhaps, but I think it more that she is truly confused about what she wants. She is frightened, perhaps, when we say things that are so far from the general norm. And that bit about not liking change? You've an argument there, you know. She can't help but make a change now, so maybe she'd agree to wed you? Oh, I don't know." Francis cast a thoughtful look toward the door and, quickly, before he went off to try his hand, she added, "However that may be, *I* want your help, Francis!"

A wary look crossed his face. "Stephanie . . ."

"Don't put me off. If I have to, I'll act the man altogether. You may write me a glowing testimonial under the name of Stephen Morris, if you prefer. I'm not going to let a little thing like my gender keep me from the work I love!"

"Huntersham is not your enemy."

"If my sire is promoting Huntersham's suit, the man *has* to have an evil side of which we've yet to learn!"

Francis relaxed once again. "Not if your father has changed *his* mind about you and Theo."

Stephanie paused, thinking about that possibility. "It is unlikely after so many years he would do so. *Very* unlikely. Why do you think he might have done so? What has he said to you?"

Francis shrugged. "He recently admitted that he truly enjoyed the adventuring life but sometimes felt a trifle guilty at avoiding his duty here. I wonder if his feelings toward you and Theo and the Priory weren't somehow used to justify his unacknowledged wish to stay away. However that may be, he no longer confides in me as he once did. But I've seen him look at you. With pride, Stephie."

"Don't lie to me."

"I never lie to you. You know that," he chided.

Stephanie sent him a quick look of apology. "But *pride?* You must have been mistaken."

"You don't sound too certain."

Stephanie took another turn alongside the billiards table. "I will think about it . . ."

"Good. And while you're thinking, give me a game." He picked up his cue. "I could use the distraction," he added, his voice slightly muffled, and his eyes lifting, for a moment, to look in the direction of the room to which Jane would have gone by now.

"It is too bad we are not at the Priory," said Stephanie and, for the first time, managed to say the estate's name without hesitation. "We could fence. I assure you that would do you far more good." As she spoke, she set out the blue and red balls. Her cue, which she'd been using earlier, was set along the other side of the table and she went around to get it. "Will you begin or shall I?"

"Flip you for it," he said.

Both badly in need of distraction, they played late into the night.

Stephanie rode along the coast road, trying very hard not to feel sorry for herself, but it was difficult. She noticed a cloud of dust rising along the road some distance away and wondered who might be riding hell for leather in such unusual heat. The rider was soon near enough to recognize and when she discovered it was Anthony, she turned Aladdin to ride away.

"Don't Steph! It's Grannie Black," he yelled.

"Grannie." Stephanie swung the stallion around.

Anthony was panting when he pulled Sahib to a stop. "She fell. She wants you."

Stephanie put heels to Aladdin's sides. She was already along the road when she heard Anthony call, "She's in your old room!"

Stephanie raised her hand to indicate she'd heard, urging Aladdin on. Grannie . . . nothing must happen to Grannie Black. Too much had changed in her world; she could not bear to lose the woman who had been her rock from her cradle.

Because of Anthony's elation that he'd an excuse to accost Stephanie, Sahib had been run hard. Now, knowing Stephanie would not be able to resist blasting him for frightening her out of her wits, Anthony eased off a bit to cool Sahib during his return to the Priory. He was almost certain his wild love would not run off until she'd blistered him up one side and down the other, so he had time to ease Sahib properly on the way home.

Even knowing they'd soon confront one another, he couldn't help a twinge of guilt. That there were extenuating circumstances, that she'd *not allowed* him to explain—well that was no excuse. Somehow he should have forced her to listen, to understand that Grannie's fall was not all that bad. At the first, she'd been about to run away from him, so he'd shouted the barest of information which would stop her. When she raced off to Grannie's side, he'd had no opportunity to tell her the old woman was not badly hurt. And then she was gone and not to be caught by an already tired Sahib before he could elaborate on the fact he'd only taken Grannie to his home so that she could be cared for while the sprain to her knee healed.

Anthony sighed. He wondered if she'd allow him the opportunity to explain when he *did* catch her up!

Stephanie dismounted before Aladdin was properly stopped and raced in the open doors to the hall. She very nearly collided with Abbot, but steadied him briefly before taking the steps two at a time and racing on down the hall to her old room. She slammed opened the door . . . and stopped short.

" 'Bout time you come to see a hurt old woman," growled Grannie Black. "Well? You got an excuse maybe?"

The old woman looked lost in the big bed, her back supported by a pile of cushions and a table with very short legs set across her lap. On the table sat the tarot deck. Grannie pointed an imperious finger at the cards, her glare indicating Stephanie was to shuffle them.

Stephanie sighed. "I thought you were at death's door."

"I might be for all you care."

"Not true."

"Oh? You'd have come for the funeral meats, maybe?"

"Don't be sarcastic, Grannie. You know why I've not visited since I returned from Brighton."

"Where I hear you stayed all of half a day?"

"Less than that. Not that it makes a farthing's worth of difference. Once I learned Huntersham had bought the Priory I couldn't stay under the roof which sheltered him."

"Couldn't come see your old Grannie, neither, is that it?"

"You live on Priory land. I'd not be here now if I'd spent two seconds learning what was the matter with you. Instead, I heard you'd fallen, that you wanted me, and I set off instantly. Huntersham only had a moment in which to tell me where to find you."

"So you've found me. Come here." Again the old woman pointed at the tarot deck.

"I'd rather not. I think I'd better go. Huntersham can't be far behind me and I'd rather not . . ."

". . . be here when I arrive. Too late, sweetings. I'm here." Stephanie stiffened into immobility.

Grannie looked from one to the other. "Stephanie Morris, come you here and shuffle the cards! At once."

Blindly, Stephanie obeyed, her mind on the man behind her—the man she could sometimes push from her thoughts in the daytime, busy and active and doing anything and everything so that she *not* think of him, but at night he invaded her dreams. She'd wake in a sweat of wanting, of needing, of thwarted love.

There was, after all, one advantage to giving in to Grannie's wishes: Shuffling the cards, she needn't turn and look at him. But her every sense was tuned to the man standing behind her, silent and, or so it seemed, threatening. Stephanie needed every moment to bring her emotions under control before facing him. Even the scent of him seemed to have her trembling . . .

The scent? Thyme! How could he smell of thyme as he had when she'd found him sleeping and covered him with his own coat? As he did in her dreams? Turning, she smoothed the deck into a square, frowning at him.

"Lay them down," said Grannie. Stephanie, half glancing back, did so. "Set them out!" Stephanie sighed and, again half by feel and half by fleeting glance, obeyed.

Then she stared at her nemesis who stared back.

Behind her Stephanie heard Grannie muttering to herself as she turned one card after another. Before her was the man who had come into her life only to turn it topsy turvy, leaving her with a much greater understanding of herself . . . but nothing else.

"I would have told you she wasn't in danger if you'd given me a moment."

"I know," she said.

"I expected you to blame me, to be angry with me for frightening you."

"I am not so illogical, I think."

"Only when it comes to our love for each other. Then you are totally illogical, my sweet."

"Love? For each other?" She raised her gaze, looking over his shoulder. "I don't know . . ."

"I do." He glanced at the old woman who turned another card, the lines on a frowning brow deepening as she laid it down. "We need each other, Stephanie," he said softly, coaxingly. "We are right for each other. We will have a wonderful life together."

"I daren't believe that."

"Why?"

Stephanie bit her lip. Then, realizing how revealing that was, she released it, casting a quick look at Anthony who tipped his head quizzically. "I . . . don't know."

"I understand a bit of it, I think. It must be very difficult when one has thought one's life in a comfortable niche to discover it is going to turn a corner and be entirely different," he suggested.

"Different." Her features settled into stubborn lines. "Yes. *Very* different."

He sighed. "I was afraid of that. You are nagging at Francis to find you a position as land agent, are you not?"

She stiffened, suspicious, wondering who had told him. "How do you know what I'm doing?"

"I was right? You see? I *do* know you. Thoroughly."

"And?"

"And I like what I know, what you are, what you can and will be . . ."

Stephanie blinked. "What I *will* be . . . ?"

"You think you've finished growing? That you'll never

change and become more than you already are?" He smiled. "I've more faith in you, sweetings."

"Bah!"

"This," muttered Grannie, from her bed, "is terrible."

Stephanie, having forgotten the woman behind her while facing the man before, turned. "Terrible?"

"You've only one choice in all the world for a happy life," said Grannie, pointing at the cards laid before her. "See?"

Stephanie sighed. "And that one, I suppose, indicates I must change my ways."

"What?" Grannie Black raised startled eyes to meet her old nurseling's. "Where'd you get a notion that stupid?"

"From a lecture Jane handed out the other night." Stephanie shrugged.

"Your Jane is a good woman," chided Grannie, "but she's far too rigid and far too small-minded to do you any good."

"Then why did she stay for so long?"

"In her way she loves you," said Grannie. "But she doesn't understand you. And she's still more fearful of change than you are!"

"Fearful of change?" Stephanie blinked. "Am I? But if I'm *not* to change my ways, than what is the one solution to my future?"

Grannie stared at her. "You mean you truly don't know?"

"No."

"Look into your heart!"

"My heart tells me I've lost everything."

"No," said the old woman, her mouth a thin line. "Your *head* tells you that. Your *heart* speaks a different language."

Stephanie frowned. "I don't understand."

Arms slid around from the back. Anthony's cheek pressed against the side of hers. "It's obvious where your happiness lies, my sweet. The same place as mine."

"The man speaks sense, child. Listen to him."

"And relax a little," said Anthony, chuckling. "This is very like holding a fence post!"

Stephanie, her eyes staring wildly, almost wailed, "I dare not trust you!"

"That," scolded Grannie, "is what your *head* tells you."

"He's *Lemiston's* friend."

"He is *your father's* friend, yes. Does that make him the enemy?"

"You, too?"

"Do you mean to suggest," whispered Anthony into her ear, "that Sir Francis is saying the same thing? I'll admit to a bit of surprise about that. I thought he found me something of an enigma . . ."

"He is so optimistic as to think Lemiston has changed toward Theo and me," said Stephanie with no attempt to hide her bitterness. "He's insanely willing to see the best in everyone!"

"But your father *has* changed."

"I don't believe that. I can't believe it. I *daren't* believe it! If it were true he'd have bought back the Priory when you offered. Both Theo and I have been left destitute!" Stephanie plucked at Anthony's fingers, trying to make him release her.

Anthony, sighed. "He'll kill me if I tell. He doesn't want it known until he's left for Australia."

"I think you'd better tell or I'll kill you," she said, a nibbling itch of hope setting her heart beating harder.

Anthony hesitated only a moment. "He's set up a trust fund for your brother. A *large* fund which will be more than adequate to Theo's needs both now and in the future."

"Truth?"

He nodded, his cheek rubbing against hers, his morning shave grown just enough to be faintly prickling, distracting, intriguing . . .

Stephanie pushed from her mind the stronger scent of thyme which seemed to come from his clothing as the scent of lavender came from Jane's. She ignored, as well, the sensation of skin against her skin. She forced herself to think about his words. "And me?"

"I'm sorry, my sweet. He still refuses to buy back the Priory."

"Then," she decided, "it must be that he expects Theo to support me. I don't suppose the trustees for that fund would release enough to buy an estate near Oxford, would they?" she finished a trifle wistfully.

"No," said Anthony, trying hard to restrain a chuckle. He almost succeeded. He rocked her from side to side as, laughter lightening his voice, he said, "You, dear heart, are not to be believed. Why will you not accept your fate is with me, right here at the Priory which you love so well?"

Stephanie, feeling as if the ground was being cut from beneath her feet by new revelations, trembled. "Release me."

Anthony spread his arms and stepped back.

Perverse, she thought, her back cold now he no longer held her against his long, lean body. *It's more than perversity that I want him back! It's . . . immoral.*

"You ain't a fool," scolded Grannie. "I didn't raise either one of you twins to be a fool. You know what you want and you know what you must say. Say it."

"I—" Her body began to tremble. "—can't."

Stephanie ducked around Anthony, fearing he'd make a grab for her. Rather disappointed when he did not, she escaped through the door, raced down the stairs, ran across the hall, and out the double doors into the sun.

Once there she blinked rapidly, not knowing if it were the bright day or the threat of tears she fought. Angry with herself, she whistled. Aladdin whickered. He pulled at the reins which a young groom held and, when released, trotted forward. Stephanie, without looking to see if Anthony had followed or not, turned her mount's head toward Warring Heights.

She had changes to make in her thinking, she had to absorb and incorporate the new and discard the old and she had rearranging to do. It would take time . . .

Time.

She was given time. Not that Anthony didn't ride to Warring Heights daily. For four days she refused to see him and for four days the blasted man calmly rode away. It was frustrating.

Why did he not insist? Why did he not force his way to her side? Why did he not *make* her admit what she wanted so desperately to admit?

On the morning of the fifth day Woods informed her that Lord and Lady Lemiston were again in residence at the Priory.

"His blidy lordship," muttered Stephanie.

"Must you?" asked Jane, a tired note in her voice.

For the first time in days Stephanie really looked at her old friend. She discovered deep circles under Jane's eyes and a fragility, which surprised her. "What is it?"

"Your language. You've no need to ape your stepmother's vulgar ways!"

"Ape my . . . Oh. Sorry. But I wasn't asking about what you said. I want to know what's wrong with you?"

"Nothing." Jane's mouth firmed, her eyes falling away from Stephanie's steady gaze. She lifted her fork and played with the buttered eggs on her plate. "Nothing at all."

"There must be. Are you sickening for something?"

"Of course not. When am I ever ill?"

"Well something's the matter." Stephanie studied her friend. "Aha."

"What does that mean?" Jane raised her head, a panicky look on her face.

"You are unhappy you've finally succeeded in convincing Francis you've no respect for him, that you actually dislike him, and that you'll never marry him. It isn't true, of course."

"What isn't true? That I'll never marry him? I can't marry someone who is no longer interested in wedding *me.*"

"It isn't true you dislike him and have no respect for him. And, now you've sent him away, you find you are far more in love with him than you'd ever before admit."

"Men are fickle."

The fleeting thought that she wished Anthony would show more ardor crossed Stephanie's mind and she bit her lip. "Men, you think, are fickle. But if so, then women are perverse."

"Nonsense," said Jane stoutly, but there was a forced note to it.

"Of course we are. Now take my example. I've been sending Anthony away day after day and I'm outraged that he actually *goes*. You, who have tried for years to convince Francis you'll not have him, are angry and hurt he's finally taken you at your word! As I said, perverse!"

Jane set her elbow on the table and rested her forehead against her hand. She refused to agree, but inherently truthful, neither could she disagree.

Stephanie finished her eggs, took a last sip of her coffee, and stood up. "If you've any sense, Jane, you'll take your pride in hand, wring its neck firmly, wrap it up and bury it, and then you'll take yourself directly to Francis and tell him you were wrong, that you love him, that you want to wed him. You might, if you are wise, add that you are afraid and ask would he please help you. And you'll do it now."

"And you?" Jane raised skeptical eyes to meet Stephanie's steady gaze. "You mean to take your own advice?"

Stephanie grinned, her sardonic half-smile very much in evidence. "I've already buried my pride, Jane. I'm on my way to Anthony at this very moment. Wish me luck."

Except that once mounted and on her way, Stephanie slowed more and more until Aladdin strolled along at a walk. Nor could she force herself to urge him to a trot let alone a canter. She reached a path to one of her hidden places along the shore and was thinking of turning into it when she was hailed.

"Steph, my sweet! Stop."

Once again Anthony was racing toward her and once again panic expanded like the air in a cream puff, filling her. This time she controlled it, but her unsteady nerves communicated themselves to Aladdin and he shifted under her. When she ignored him, he twitched. That too brought no response from his rider. Aladdin didn't like it. He made his irritation obvious and for some moments Stephanie was much occupied bringing the horse back under control.

Anthony, his heart in his mouth, stopped some yards from where she fought Aladdin to a stand. "Well done!" he said.

"I don't know what got into him!" she muttered, but she lied and knew she lied.

"I'm glad you didn't run off."

At the expression on Anthony's face Stephanie felt heat rising up her throat. She was glad that, today, she'd tied a kerchief around her neck instead of struggling to tie a proper cravat. "You were riding hell for leather, Anthony. Is something wrong?"

"Very wrong. Stephanie, you can no longer deny me. You must wed me."

"I don't think I trust that look."

"My expression? But what's wrong with it? I'm sure it is as innocent as I can possibly make it!"

"Not quite innocent enough . . . or perhaps too innocent to be believed?"

"Ah well. But you *must,* sweetings. It's imperative. If you do not . . . well I'll not answer for the consequences."

"You are a lunatic, as mad as your cousin," she muttered, still wary.

"Ah! I think your farmer, Wilkins, agrees!"

"What has Wilkins to do with anything?"

"Wilkins has just told me," said Anthony solemnly, "that he'll be damned if he'll take orders from a sea dog who doesn't know a horse chestnut from a mangel-wurzel." A flush crawled up into Anthony cheeks. He caught and held Stephanie's gaze. A trifle ruefully, he added, "I think he meant it, sweetings."

Stephanie's lips tightened but she couldn't repress the sparkle in her eyes. "What in heaven's name did you ask him to do?"

"I didn't! I mean I didn't ask him to *do* anything. All I did was ask how the mangel-wurzels were doing."

"You *must* have done more than that."

"I may have gestured vaguely in the direction of the three-sided field," he said, bending his fingers and looking at his nails.

"Vaguely in the direction of . . . ?"

"There's that long alley of chestnuts in the way, of course."

Stephanie could stand it no longer. She laughed. The laughter felt good and she found she couldn't stop. "Oh, dear," she gasped, looked at Anthony, and was set off again. "Won't take orders from . . ." Her chuckles sputtered on. "Won't take . . . !"

"So," interrupted Anthony, "you see why it is absolutely obligatory that you marry me. Preferably," he added a trifle off-handedly, "before Chris leaves. I'd like him to stand up with me."

"Stand up with *you?*" Stephanie frowned. "He's my father. He'd be expected to give the bride away, would he not?"

"I thought we'd let Francis do that," said Anthony.

Again Stephanie's eyes sparkled. "And wouldn't the local tabbies love that trifling idiosyncrasy!"

"Shall we then?" he asked.

She almost agreed. Then she realized how impossible it was. "How can we? I thought they were to leave any day now. It takes time. Reading the banns and all . . ." she finished on a vague note.

"It seems your father is more perspicacious than even I knew. He has acquired a license so we need not wait for the banns to be called!

For an instant Stephanie felt rebellion that her father had done such a thing. The hesitation was brief, however, since, once she'd decided to do the thing, the thought of waiting wasn't to be borne. She nodded.

With a whoop, Anthony dismounted. Before he could reach her to drag her from her saddle, Stephanie too had alit and was coming toward him as fast as he approached her.

For a very long time they merely held each other, silently making promises about their future, each separately and then, staring into each other's eyes, outloud. When Anthony placed a tender kiss on her lips some time later Stephanie wondered why they must visit the priest. What they'd just promised each other seemed to her to make them just as thoroughly married as saying the traditional vows in a church could do!

However that might be, and for once in her life, Lady Stephanie didn't argue that the unconventional way was better. For once she did the proper thing, celebrating their marriage joyfully and thankfully, and with the belief the future would be as bright as the sun which shone down on their wedding day!

Besides, Grannie had promised, had she not? A lifetime of love, she'd said! Stephanie meant to hold Fate to her promise.

Dear Reader,

I hope you enjoyed this, my first effort at a Regency Historical. I developed an affection for Lady Stephanie and Lord Huntersham . . . but I'll admit that my greatest feeling is reserved for Meg. I hope she teaches Lemiston to love her. I think, now that he's straightened out his head about the past, he just might learn to do so!

My next book, *A Timeless Love* due in February 1997, is a Regency Time Travel. Not perhaps, quite the usual time travel, because I posit an organization in *our* future which rescues art that is about to be destroyed. The organization, Art Rescue Team, or ART for short, must also guard against the purloining of art which is *not* in danger. Because there are villains, ART has ART-Arm, a policing force.

In *A Timeless Love,* our heroine has been sent to the Regency period for just that purpose. Instead of appearing in an empty cabin on ART's agent's ship, she discovers a totally naked stranger has watched her arrival out of empty air. He is, needless to say, shocked. On the other hand, with the miraculous inventions appearing in his time nearly every day, he is able to accept that an invention in the future has allowed her to return to the past.

Still, he's a creature of his time. And she's a woman. He can't allow her to go into danger all by herself. Even after she lays him flat on his back, utilizing unarmed combat training she's learned in the future, he's not willing! However intriguing, however well trained, she is a woman.

Ah! But what a woman!

I hope you will enjoy reading this story as much as I enjoyed writing it.

Letters addressed to P.O.Box 1771, Rochester, MI 48308 will reach me. Please include a self-addressed, stamped envelope for response.

WATCH FOR THESE ZEBRA REGENCIES

BRIGHTON BEAUTY (0-8217-5340-1, $4.50)
by Marilyn Clay
Chelsea Grant, pretty and poor, naively takes school friend Alayna Marchmont's place and spends a month in the country. The devastating man had sailed from Honduras to claim his promised bride, Miss Marchmont. An affair of the heart may lead to disaster . . . unless a resourceful Brighton beauty finds a way to stop a masquerade and keep a lord's love.

LORD DIABLO'S DEMISE (0-8217-5338-X, $4.50)
by Meg-Lynn Roberts
The sinfully handsome Lord Harry Glendower was a gambler and the black sheep of his family. About to be forced into a marriage of convenience, the devilish fellow engineered his own demise, never having dreamed that faking his death would lead him to the heavenly refuge of spirited heiress Gwyn Morgan, the daughter of a physician.

A PERILOUS ATTRACTION (0-8217-5339-8, $4.50)
by Dawn Aldridge Poore
Alissa Morgan is stunned when a frantic passenger thrusts her baby into Alissa's arms and flees, having heard rumors that a notorious highwayman posed a threat to their coach. Handsome stranger Hugh Sebastian secretly possesses the treasured necklace the highwayman seeks and volunteers to pose as Alissa's husband to save her reputation. With a lost baby and missing necklace in their care, the couple embarks on a journey into peril—and passion.

Available wherever paperbacks are sold, or order direct from the Publisher. Send cover price plus 50¢ per copy for mailing and handling to Penguin USA, P.O. Box 999, c/o Dept. 17109, Bergenfield, NJ 07621. Residents of New York and Tennessee must include sales tax. DO NOT SEND CASH.

ZEBRA'S REGENCY ROMANCES
DAZZLE AND DELIGHT

A BEGUILING INTRIGUE   (4441, $3.99)
by Olivia Sumner

Pretty as a picture Justine Riggs cared nothing for propriety. She dressed as a boy, sat on her horse like a jockey, and pondered the stars like a scientist. But when she tried to best the handsome Quenton Fletcher, Marquess of Devon, by proving that she was the better equestrian, he would try to prove Justine's antics were pure folly. The game he had in mind was seduction — never imagining that he might lose his heart in the process!

AN INCONVENIENT ENGAGEMENT   (4442, $3.99)
by Joy Reed

Rebecca Wentworth was furious when she saw her betrothed waltzing with another. So she decides to make him jealous by flirting with the handsomest man at the ball, John Collinwood, Earl of Stanford. The "wicked" nobleman knew exactly what the enticing miss was up to — and he was only too happy to play along. But as Rebecca gazed into his magnificent eyes, her errant fiancé was soon utterly forgotten!

SCANDAL'S LADY   (4472, $3.99)
by Mary Kingsley

Cassandra was shocked to learn that the new Earl of Lynton was her childhood friend, Nicholas St. John. After years at sea and mixed feelings Nicholas had come home to take the family title. And although Cassandra knew her place as a governess, she could not help the thrill that went through her each time he was near. Nicholas was pleased to find that his old friend Cassandra was his new next door neighbor, but after being near her, he wondered if mere friendship would be enough . . .

HIS LORDSHIP'S REWARD   (4473, $3.99)
by Carola Dunn

As the daughter of a seasoned soldier, Fanny Ingram was accustomed to the vagaries of military life and cared not a whit about matters of rank and social standing. So she certainly never foresaw her *tendre* for handsome Viscount Roworth of Kent with whom she was forced to share lodgings, while he carried out his clandestine activities on behalf of the British Army. And though good sense told Roworth to keep his distance, he couldn't stop from taking Fanny in his arms for a kiss that made all hearts equal!

Available wherever paperbacks are sold, or order direct from the Publisher. Send cover price plus 50¢ per copy for mailing and handling to Penguin USA, P.O. Box 999, c/o Dept. 17109, Bergenfield, NJ 07621. Residents of New York and Tennessee must include sales tax. DO NOT SEND CASH.